D0088874

Fort Bragg Library
499 Laurel St.
WITHDRAWN
Fort Bragg, CA 95437

FATES *and* TRAITORS

ALSO BY JENNIFER CHIAVERINI

Christmas Bells
Mrs. Grant and Madame Jule
Mrs. Lincoln's Rival
The Spymistress
Mrs. Lincoln's Dressmaker
The Giving Quilt
Sonoma Rose
The Wedding Quilt
The Union Quilters
The Aloha Quilt
A Quilter's Holiday
The Lost Quilter
The Quilter's Kitchen
The Winding Ways Quilt
The New Year's Quilt
The Quilter's Homecoming
Circle of Quilters
The Christmas Quilt
The Sugar Camp Quilt
The Master Quilter
The Quilter's Legacy
The Runaway Quilt
The Cross-Country Quilters
Round Robin
The Quilter's Apprentice

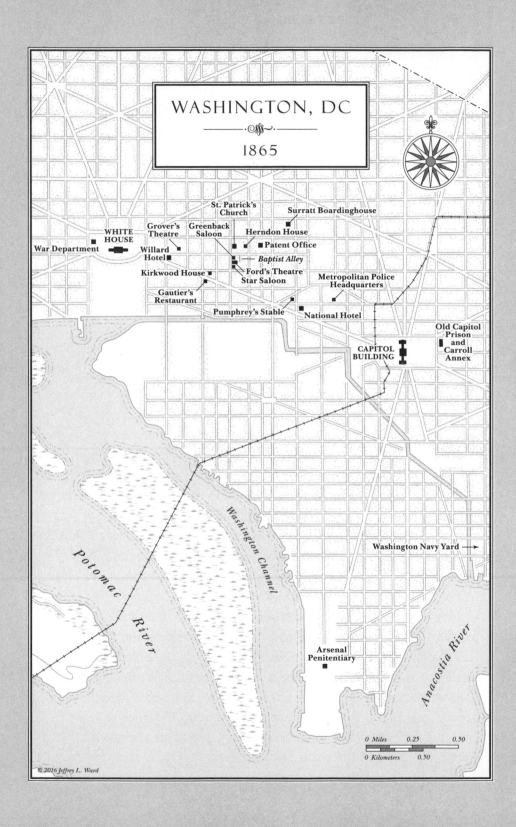

WASHINGTON, DC

1865

War Department
WHITE HOUSE
Grover's Theatre
Willard Hotel
Kirkwood House
Gautier's Restaurant
St. Patrick's Church
Greenback Saloon
Herndon House
Patent Office
Baptist Alley
Ford's Theatre
Star Saloon
Pumphrey's Stable
Surratt Boardinghouse
Metropolitan Police Headquarters
National Hotel
CAPITOL BUILDING
Old Capitol Prison and Carroll Annex

Potomac River
Washington Channel
Washington Navy Yard →
Anacostia River

Arsenal Penitentiary

0 Miles   0.25   0.50
0 Kilometers   0.50

© 2016 Jeffrey L. Ward

FATES *and* TRAITORS

A NOVEL OF JOHN WILKES BOOTH

JENNIFER CHIAVERINI

DUTTON

DUTTON

An imprint of Penguin Random House LLC
375 Hudson Street
New York, New York 10014

Copyright © 2016 by Jennifer Chiaverini
Penguin supports copyright. Copyright fuels creativity, encourages diverse voices, promotes free speech, and creates a vibrant culture. Thank you for buying an authorized edition of this book and for complying with copyright laws by not reproducing, scanning, or distributing any part of it in any form without permission. You are supporting writers and allowing Penguin to continue to publish books for every reader.

DUTTON is a registered trademark and the D colophon is a trademark of
Penguin Random House LLC

LIBRARY OF CONGRESS CATALOGING-IN-PUBLICATION DATA

Names: Chiaverini, Jennifer, author.
Title: Fates and traitors : a novel of John Wilkes Booth / Jennifer Chiaverini.
Description: New York : Dutton, [2016]
Identifiers: LCCN 2016005262 (print) | LCCN 2016009184 (ebook) | ISBN 9780525954309
(hardcover) | ISBN 9780698404137 (ebook)
Subjects: LCSH: Booth, John Wilkes, 1838–1865—Fiction. | Conspiracies—Fiction. | Assassins—
Fiction. | BISAC: FICTION / Historical. | FICTION / Romance / Historical. |
GSAFD: Biographical fiction. | Historical fiction.
Classification: LCC PS3553.H473 F38 2016 (print) | LCC PS3553.H473 (ebook) |
DDC 813/.54—dc23
LC record available at http://lccn.loc.gov/2016005262

Printed in the United States of America
1 3 5 7 9 10 8 6 4 2

Book design by Elke Sigal

This is a work of fiction. Names, characters, places, events, and incidents either are the product of the author's imagination or are used fictitiously. The author's use of names of historical figures, places, or events are not intended to change the entirely fictional character of the work. In all other respects, any resemblance to persons living or dead is entirely coincidental.

To Marty, Nicholas, and Michael, with love and gratitude

"There is but one mind in all these men,
 and it is bent against Caesar. If thou beest not
 immortal, look about you. Security gives way to
 conspiracy. The mighty gods defend thee!
 Thy lover,
 Artemidorus"

Here will I stand till Caesar pass along,
And as a suitor will I give him this.
My heart laments that virtue cannot live
Out of the teeth of emulation.
If thou read this, O Caesar, thou mayst live.
If not, the Fates with traitors do contrive.
—William Shakespeare,
   Julius Caesar, Act 2, Scene 3

FATES *and* TRAITORS

JOHN

1865

If it be aught toward the general good,
Set honor in one eye and death i' th' other,
And I will look on both indifferently,
For let the gods so speed me as I love
The name of honor more than I fear death.
—William Shakespeare,
Julius Caesar, Act 1, Scene 2

A sound in the darkness outside the barn—a furtive whisper, the careless snap of a dry twig underfoot—woke him from a fitful doze. His left leg throbbed painfully, not only the tender, swollen tissue nearest the fracture in the bone but everything from ankle to knee, the muscles sore from too many days in stirrups, the skin chafed raw from the reluctant doctor's hasty splint. Grimacing, every movement a new torment, he propped himself up on his elbows and strained his ears to listen.

There—a low whisper, quick footfalls, and, more distant, the jingle of spurs. And then, incautiously, two men arguing in hushed voices, one commanding, one pleading. A flicker of candlelight illuminated the shallow depression beneath the door of the tobacco barn, and—he jerked his head sharply when a sudden gleam caught the corner of his eye—the glint of a lantern appeared between the slats on the opposite side.

The barn was surrounded.

Blood pounded in his ears as he inched closer to his companion, grimacing in pain as he dragged himself from his makeshift bed on the hay-strewn floor. Covering the younger man's mouth with one hand, with the other he grasped him by the shoulder and shook him awake. "Herold," he murmured, his gaze darting from the door to the four walls. "Wake up."

David Herold woke with a start. "What is it, John?" he whispered hoarsely. "Is Garrett running us off after all?"

Richard Garrett, the lean, grim-faced farmer who had welcomed them into his home earlier that day, had banished them to the barn upon discovering their true identities. Adding to the insult, he had locked them in to ensure that they wouldn't run off with the family's horses in the night. Had Garrett betrayed them to the men now drawing the cordon tight around their refuge? When put to the test, had the Virginia farmer's Southern sympathies given way to craven fear?

Rage flared up within John, hot and searing, only to sputter and die out, extinguished by hard, cold truth. It mattered not how their pursuers had found them, only that they had.

"Our pursuers are upon us," he told Herold, his voice preternaturally calm.

Muttering an oath, Herold scrambled to sit up, his short stature and fine wisps of facial hair making him seem even younger than his almost twenty-three years. "Should we surrender before they open fire?"

"I'll suffer death first." John pulled Herold close and added in a voice scarcely more than a breath, "Don't make a sound. Maybe they'll think we aren't here and go away."

At that moment, the plaintive creak of hinges drew their attention to the door, which was slowly, cautiously opening. A figure stepped into the doorway, thrown into silhouette by a distant lantern. "Gentlemen, the cavalry are after you." It was Jack Garrett, the farmer's eldest son, recently returned from the war. He had been clad in a gray Confederate uniform when they first met—had it really been only the previous afternoon?

"You're the ones they seek." Jack Garrett's voice gathered strength as it probed the darkness. "You'd better give yourselves up."

"John Wilkes Booth," another man proclaimed, emerging in the doorway behind Jack Garrett, a candle in his fist. "I want you to surrender. If you don't, in fifteen minutes I'll burn the barn down around you."

Grasping his injured leg, John drew himself up as tall as he could sit. "And who are you, sir?" he demanded, his voice ringing as it had from the stage of Grover's Theatre, the Arch Street Theatre, the National, the Marshall, Ford's—the scenes of his greatest triumphs. He could triumph here yet. "This is a hard case. It may be that I am to be taken by my friends."

"I'm Lieutenant Luther Byron Baker, detective, United States Department of War, and I order you to turn your weapons over to Garrett and give yourself up."

Herold, trembling and sweating despite the cold, took his head in his hands, moaning softly through clenched teeth. "You don't choose to give yourself up," he told John shakily. "But I do. Let me go out."

"No." John forced his voice to remain steady, his heart thudding in time with the throbbing of his injured leg. "You shall not."

As they argued, their voices low and heated, John's mouth went dry and a fearful tremor seized him. He was aware of Garrett speaking over his shoulder to the other men as he backed away from the doorway, and of Herold slipping from his control. Another ten minutes and the boy's terror would overcome him entirely. Before that moment came, John must sow enough confusion to conceal their escape, or all would be lost.

He seized Herold by the shoulder—to restrain his companion as well as to brace himself against his own rising panic. "Surely we can come to an understanding between gentlemen," he called grandly, projecting his voice through the doorway to the officer lurking outside. "If I had been inclined to shoot my way to freedom, your candle would have made you an easy target."

Silence followed his declaration, and as he watched, the thin light wavered, shadows shifting as Baker carried the candle away and planted it on some hillock in the yard. Boots scraping on hard packed earth alerted him to the officer's return. "Give up your arms or the barn will be set on fire," the lieutenant commanded. A low growl of assent revealed his companions' numbers—a dozen at least, fully armed, no doubt, filled with misguided, righteous anger, panting to avenge their slain leader. John knew nothing would convince them that he had saved them from a tyrant.

In the diminished light, his gaze traveled the length and width of the barn, searching, hoping. There must be an escape, even now. He and young Herold could flee to Mexico, where Emperor Maximilian was offering refuge and substantial bounties to steadfast Confederates. There he would at last be proclaimed a hero, as he had not been in Maryland, Virginia, or anywhere in the ungrateful South. There, Lucy's studies of the Spanish tongue would serve them well.

Lucy, he thought, picturing her as he had last seen her, smiling and beautiful in the dining room of the National Hotel. Sweet Lucy. What did she think of him now? Would her love remain true, or did she too abhor him? Surely he could make her understand that the fractured nation owed all her troubles to Lincoln. The country had groaned beneath his tyranny and had prayed for this end, and God had made John the instrument of His perfect wrath. How bewildering it was, in the aftermath of the deed that should have made him great, to find himself abandoned by the very people he served, in desperate flight with the mark of Cain upon him, but if the world knew his heart, if Lucy knew his heart—

His courage faltering, he forced thoughts of his beloved aside. "My good sir," he called out, stalling for time, thoughts racing, "that's rather rough. I'm nothing but a cripple. I have but one leg, and you ought to give me a chance for a fair fight."

"We're not here to argue," Baker shouted back, anger and impatience whetting the edge of his voice. "You've got five minutes left to consider the matter."

"I don't need five minutes, Booth," said Herold, rising, clenching his hands, pacing, his anxious gaze fixed upon the doorway. "They got us cornered. We got no choice but to give up. Don't you see? We've gone as far as we can."

John would not concede that they had, not while breath remained in his body. Again and again he tried to engage Baker in conversation, but the Yankee lieutenant would neither negotiate nor be distracted, insisting that the fugitives consider their circumstances and make their choices. Increasingly frustrated, John looked to Herold, who paced and gnawed his fingernails to the quick and would clearly be no help at all.

"Well, then," John called to Baker almost cheerfully, "throw open the door, draw up your men in line, and let's have a fair fight."

"Garrett," said another man, whose voice John had not yet heard, "gather some of those pine twigs and pile them up by the sides of the barn."

"What does he mean?" Herold asked, panic infiltrating his voice. "What are they doing?"

"Calm yourself." John strained his ears to detect Garrett's retreat, and soon thereafter, returning footfalls and the sound of an armload of pine boughs falling in a pile near the door. Alarmed, he shouted, "Put no more brush there or someone will get hurt."

"Booth." Herold backed into the center of the barn, gaze darting wildly, hands spread as if to ward off an invisible foe. "Booth—"

"Herold, I told you—" A whiff of smoke in the air silenced him, the crackle of new flame. Quickly he discovered the source—someone had twisted hay into a makeshift wick, set it on fire, and shoved it through a crack between the boards of the barn wall. He watched, thunderstruck, as flames licked greedily at the wooden planks, steadily climbing, cutting through the shadows with garish light.

"I'm going," Herold croaked, pale with terror. "I don't intend to be burnt alive."

As the younger man strode toward the door, John quickly reached out and seized the cuff of his trousers, gasping as stabbing pains shot up his broken leg. "Take another step and I'll kill you."

Herold gaped at him, his mouth open in silent protest, his pouchy cheeks quivering, his face eerily young in the rising light of the blaze. Suddenly John recalled how obediently Herold had served the conspiracy over the past year, how faithfully he had served John throughout their flight from Washington—guiding him through the backwoods and swamps of Maryland and Virginia, finding them safe havens with sympathetic civilians along the way, risking his life in dangerous river crossings, tending John in his infirmity. John remembered, and he regretted his cruel threat.

He must save the boy, if he could not save them both.

"Get away from me, you damned coward," he snarled loudly for the audience outside. As Herold pulled away, John yanked him back again and added in a whisper, "When you get out, don't tell them what arms I carry."

Bewildered, Herold mutely nodded, stumbling backward when John released him.

"Lieutenant Baker," John called out, "there is a man in here who wants to surrender. He is innocent of any crime."

After a moment's pause, Baker called back, "Pass your weapons through the door and come out with your hands in the air."

"He has no weapons." John coughed and waved away a tendril of smoke scented with wood and tobacco and straw. A trickle of sweat ran from his temple to his jaw. "All the arms here are mine."

In a panic, Herold sprinted to the door, only to find it barred against him. "Let me out," he shrieked, pounding on the door. "Let me out!"

The door swung open. A soldier ordered Herold to extend his hands, one at a time, and the moment he obeyed, someone seized his wrists and yanked him out of sight. Before the door swung shut again, John glimpsed rifles and pistols trained upon the entrance, gleaming in the light from the burning barn.

The blaze had scaled the walls and spread to the rafters, roaring and crackling and filling the air with choking smoke. Scooting away from the walls, dragging his injured leg after him, John looked about for something, anything, to put out the fire. Instead through the cracks between the wooden planks he glimpsed the pale faces of Union soldiers outside, angry and curious, emboldened by Herold's surrender. They watched him with hungry avarice, like a vicious pack of dogs studying a cornered stag.

Resolute, he took his Spencer carbine in hand and reached for his crutch. If these were to be his last moments, he would not spend them lying in the dirty straw, helpless and despairing, so his enemies might watch him roast alive. As quickly as he dared, he pushed himself to his feet and steadied himself on the crutch.

He had nowhere to go but into the arms of his vengeful enemies.

Supporting his weight on the crutch, he made his way to the door, wincing as a shower of sparks flew too close before his face. The crutch slipped from beneath his outstretched arm as he reached for the latch, but he let it fall. He would face the soldiers standing, defiant and proud on his own two feet.

He drew himself up as he shuffled into the doorway, and raised his carbine—

And then he was lying on his face in the dirt, his head spinning, his neck trembling electrically as if in the aftermath of a lightning strike, his strong body strangely limp and heavy. He could not open his eyes, or dared not try.

He heard the faint thunder of quick footfalls, felt the strike of the soldiers' boots on the earth transmitted through the ground to his forehead. Something warm and liquid trickled from his neck down his collar past his clavicle, over the old scar he boasted as a war wound, but when he reached up to brush the irritant away, his hand and arm did not respond. Dimly he puzzled over this oddity as the men gathered around him.

"Is he dead?" an unfamiliar voice queried, shrill with excitement. "Did he shoot himself?"

"No," replied Lieutenant Baker. "I don't think so. I don't know what happened."

John wanted nothing more than to riposte with a mocking jest, but the words eluded him, whirling beyond his fingertips like cottonwood seeds caught in a sudden gale. He felt them swirling about him, small and white and soft, thousands upon thousands, felt himself sinking into them as they mounded up around him on all sides. The crackling blaze faded, its light and sound growing faint, but the smell of scorched tobacco and ash lingered in his nostrils, a curious singularity that kept the white softness from engulfing him completely.

There were hands upon him, he realized, inquisitive and none too gentle. He had been shot, he heard someone say. They found the wound on the right side of his neck. Someone had disobeyed orders and had shot the most despised man in America, robbing the Yankees of the trial and execution they surely craved.

John felt himself rising, lifted roughly and carried away from the heat and light that flickered beyond his closed eyelids. He heard the crash of a roof falling in as he was placed on a patch of soft grass, his face turned toward the stars. Slowly at first, and then in a torrent, the blood rushed in his ears, and his head began to pound. He ached all over, his strangely heavy, frozen body sparking with pain.

He had been shot through the neck, he realized, vaguely astonished, as the last of the white softness blew away. He was probably dying.

He tried to speak, but he could manage no more than a wheeze, which was enough to draw the men closer. "Thought he was dead already," one muttered.

"He's on his way to dying," said another. "Hold on, he's trying to talk."

"Tell—" John rasped. "Tell her—"

A slim figure bent over him, lowered an ear close to John's mouth. "Go on."

John took a shuddering breath through the thick fluid collecting in his throat. "Tell my mother . . . I die for my country."

Nearby, a man cursed. Another spat in the dirt. "Tell your mother you die for your country," the slim figure repeated slowly. "Do I have that right?"

John swallowed and tried to nod. The man nodded once and moved away.

He drifted, jolted from time to time into wakeful horror by unexpected surges of pain running the length of limbs that felt nothing else. He could not move. He struggled even to breathe. He closed his eyes to the falling ashes but could not shut his ears against the soldiers' words. One man repeatedly insisted that John had shot himself. John wanted to set the record straight, but he found it too difficult to gather the correct words and put them down again in the proper order.

"I tell you again, that can't be," said Baker. "I was looking right at him when I heard the shot. His carbine wasn't turned upon himself."

The discussion wore on, and John felt himself succumbing to wave after wave of exhaustion. Then two other men approached and settled the matter with a revelation: a Sergeant Corbett had shot the president's assassin. He had the spent cap and an empty chamber in his revolver to prove it.

Corbett, John thought. He knew no one by that name, could not imagine how he might have offended the man aside from killing his president and freeing him from tyranny. Perhaps this Corbett had a pretty little wife who had once waited outside a stage door to greet John with sweet blushes and flowers. He smiled and tried to offer the sergeant a gallant apology, but his lips moved without sound.

"I went to the barn." The new voice rang with zeal. "I looked through a crack, saw Booth coming toward the door, sighted at his body, and fired."

"Against orders," said Baker, without rancor.

"We had no orders either to fire or not to fire," the sergeant protested. "I was afraid he'd either shoot someone or get away."

The lieutenant did not rebuke him.

John drifted in and out of consciousness, succumbing to exhaustion only to be choked awake when blood and fluid pooled in his throat. As the heat from the conflagration rose to a blistering intensity, the soldiers carried him from the lawn to the front porch of the farmhouse, where Mrs. Garrett had placed a mattress for him. Her cool, soft hand on his forehead revived him, and when he struggled to ask for water, she understood his hoarse request, quickly filled a dipper, and brought it to his lips. But it was no use. He could wet his tongue but he could not swallow.

He asked to be turned over, expecting a rebuff, but the soldiers complied, lifting him and placing him on his stomach. Still he could not clear his throat. Hating his helplessness, he asked to be rolled onto his side, and then the other, but that was no better. Panic and despair swept through him at the thought that he would drown in his own sick. Coughing, wrenching his head, he managed to catch the attention of the slim man who had taken his message for his mother. "Kill me," he whispered when the man knelt beside him. "Kill me."

"We don't want to kill you," said the man. "We want you to get well."

So they could stretch his neck, no doubt. But he was already a dead man. And what, he thought wildly, had become of Herold?

The hours passed. His throat swelled, his lips grew numb. He felt himself sinking, only to revive, time and again. He wished the slim officer would sit beside him, to hear and commit to memory his last loving words for his mother. As for last words for his country, as well as for the North, the manifesto he had placed with his sister for safekeeping would have to suffice. Dear Asia, childhood playmate and lifelong confidante, who disagreed with him vehemently on almost every political matter but loved him still—she knew not what he had entrusted to her, but news of his demise would remind her of the thick envelope locked away in her husband's safe. Asia would find his last great written work, his apologia, as well as documents and deeds and a letter for their mother.

Their mother. How grateful he was that she could not see how he suffered.

He realized he had fallen unconscious when he woke to the touch of calloused hands bathing his wounds. He had been pondering something . . . yes, his last words. In Asia's safe, in the home she shared with her husband and children. A sudden worry seized him. Would she burn the papers, fearing they would implicate her, endanger her family? No, not loyal Asia, not the family historian who had begged their mother not to destroy their father's letters as she had fed them into the flames. Asia would spare his writings, and far from implicating her, they would exonerate her. He would have abandoned his mission rather than bring suspicion down upon any member of his family or upon any lady—even one such as Mrs. Surratt, who had lent her tacit support to the plot by harboring many of the conspirators in her boardinghouse, by giving them an inconspicuous place to meet. But none would condemn her for that, a respectable, devout widow unaware of John's true intentions. Of all the women who loved him—and Mrs. Surratt did love him, as one loved a comrade in arms—she alone shared his devotion to the South.

Fluid filled his throat; he choked, gasped, grew dizzy—and rallied, somehow. He wished he had not.

His thoughts turned to Lucy. If only he could retrieve his diary from his coat pocket and gaze upon her portrait before the light faded from his eyes. He could imagine the shock and reproach in hers. She would mourn him, but in silence, lest his notoriety ruin her. He could not blame her for that. Few knew of their secret engagement, so Lucy would grieve, but in time her heart would heal, and with her ties to the assassin forgotten, she would eventually marry someone else. Someone safe, someone her parents could accept. That dull security would be John's last bequest to her.

The sky was softening in the east when a physician came to examine him, a South Carolinian from the sound of it, unsettled by the sight of so many armed Yankees but determined to do his duty. John fought to stay conscious throughout the examination, and was rewarded with one last comedic jest when the doctor announced that he was badly injured but would survive.

If not for the smothering thickness in his chest John would have derided the fool. *Throw physic to the dogs; I'll none of it.*

"But the ball passed clean through the neck," said Baker, incredulous. "How can he live?"

Sighing in consternation, the doctor cleaned his spectacles, replaced them, bent over his patient again, and peered at the holes on either side of John's neck. Then, straightening, he declared that closer scrutiny revealed that the shot had severed the assassin's spinal cord. His organs were failing, one by one, and if he did not drown in his own blood and sputum first, he would slowly suffocate.

"Well," the slim man said, "that's it, then."

John was powerless to resist as the slim man bent over him and briskly searched his pockets, taking from him a candle, his compass, and his diary, in which John had placed Lucy's photograph. Before he could beg the man to let him gaze upon her image one last time, the officer was gone, taking John's belongings with him. But would he carry John's last message for his mother?

Agitated, John coughed and spat blood, gurgling in lieu of speech, desperate.

He thought he would suffocate before anyone responded, but then the lieutenant was at his side, frowning intently down upon him. John jerked his head twice to beckon the officer closer, and though his mouth twisted in revulsion, Baker complied, bending over and placing his ear close to John's lips.

"Tell my mother—" He could scarce draw breath. "Tell my mother that I did it for my country—" He could not fill his lungs; his throat constricted ever tighter. "That I die for my country."

The sun had risen above the distant hills, harsh and unnaturally warm. He clenched his teeth, his eyes tearing against the glare until some pitying soul draped a shirt over a chair to shield his face.

He was John Wilkes Booth. If he had done wrong in ridding the world of the man who would declare himself king of America, let God, not man, judge him.

Out, out, brief candle!

Did he not have a candle in his pocket? No, the lieutenant had taken it, and Lucy's portrait, and his diary, his apologia. But he should need no candle to see by, with the sun so hot upon his face.

Life's but a walking shadow, a poor player that struts and frets his hour upon the stage and then is heard no more.

Yes, and so he should remind the good women who had loved him, to give them some measure of peace. If he could but find pen and paper and ink, and light his candle to see by, for it had grown so dark so suddenly. . . . He strained to pat his pockets but was surprised to discover he could not move, and surprised again that he could have forgotten something so important.

Lieutenant Baker peered curiously down at him. "You want to see your hands?"

He wanted the use of them, but since he could not speak to clarify, he could only lie passively, unresisting, as the lieutenant lifted his hands up and into his line of sight. He glimpsed the tattoo he had given himself as a child, his initials etched upon the back of his left hand between his thumb and forefinger, his defiant, indelible rebuttal to all those who would deny his right to bear the proud name of Booth.

He gazed upon his hands, as limp and insensible as those of a corpse.

"Useless," he croaked. "Useless."

All that lives must die, passing through nature to eternity.

The world would not look upon his like again.

CHAPTER ONE

MARY ANN

1838–1851

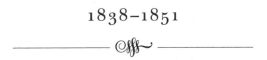

Why wouldst thou be a breeder of sinners? I am myself
indifferent honest, but yet I could accuse me of such
things that it were better my mother had not borne me.
—William Shakespeare, Hamlet, Act 3, Scene 1

On a beautiful spring morning in early May, Mary Ann was safely delivered of a healthy son, and the sight of him swaddled in the soft blue-and-white quilt she had lovingly sewn for him—so perfect, so pure, so full of promise—took her breath away. His hair was dark and silky, his eyes deep blue, his skin blushing roses on porcelain. In the exhilaration and exhaustion that followed her ten-hour labor, it seemed to her that he possessed the best qualities of the precious elder siblings who had passed on before he entered the world. It was almost as if a merciful God had returned them to her in the person of this one perfect child.

As soon as Mary Ann had felt her labor pains come on, she had sent word to Junius, the eager expectant father, at the Holliday Street Theatre in Baltimore twenty-fives miles to the southwest, where he had been thrilling audiences with his masterful portrayals of Othello and Pescara. He had raced home to her at The Farm—their rustic country retreat, one hundred and fifty sublime forested acres in Harford County, Maryland—just in time to witness the birth. The experience filled him with wonder and awe, and as he cradled his newborn in his arms for the first time, Junius suggested that they give his father the honor of naming the baby.

Richard, an Englishman born and bred but a fervent admirer of George Washington nonetheless, proudly selected the name of a distant relative on his mother's side, a courageous and honorable member of the British Parliament who had ardently defended the right of the American colonists to rebel against King George III and to create their own sovereign, democratic nation. Only weeks after the Sons of Liberty had flung British tea into Boston Harbor, John Wilkes had infuriated monarchists by boldly predicting, in a fiery speech to the House of Commons, that the Colonials would rise to independence and power, to greatness and renown, for they would construct their government "on the solid basis of general, public liberty."

"With but a fraction of his namesake's passion, the blessings of American liberty, and the Booth genius as his birthright, there's no reason why this child should not become a great American," his grandfather declared.

"All I ask is that he not become an actor," said Junius.

"He's so small to bear the weight of such grand expectations," Mary Ann gently chided Richard, smiling to soften her words. "Let him be a happy child first."

But six months later, a startling vision came to her, leaving her with the vaguely unsettling certainty that Richard had made a prophetic choice.

She was nursing John by the fireside, his head nestled upon the crook of her elbow, his tiny hand resting on her bosom, the fingers splayed. As she gazed into the fireplace, wondering what the future held in store for her beautiful boy, the flames suddenly leapt upward and seemed to form the word "Country." As she watched, fascinated and frightened, the letters shifted into her son's name before they faded back into dancing flame.

What could it mean? she wondered.

Even as she brooded over the vision, she knew that only time would reveal his destiny. For now, and for many years to come, he would simply be her precious child, whom she loved tenderly and with all her heart.

John Wilkes was Mary Ann's ninth child, the fifth of those who yet lived. The eldest, Junius Brutus Booth Jr., had left The Farm a few months after John Wilkes's birth, much to the chagrin of his parents. For years Richard had tried valiantly to teach his grandson Greek and Latin so that he might be trained as a doctor or lawyer, but despite great efforts to discourage him, June, as they all called him, was determined to become an actor. He had made his debut a few years before while chaperoning his father on tour, playing Tressel to Junius's Richard III in Pittsburgh when the regular player fell ill. His performance had been in every way underwhelming. "June would make a better merchant than an actor," Junius had written to Mary Ann afterward, sounding both relieved and disappointed. June evidently had a better opinion of his own talent, for shortly before his eighteenth birthday, he ran off to join a theatre company in Philadelphia. Handsome, athletic, and bearing the famous Booth name, he won several minor roles and performed them competently, though without brilliance. His swordplay was widely admired and his fellow players liked him, but while they offered him warm friendship, they damned him with faint praise. June was fairly good, mutual friends told Junius diplomatically, slow of speech but competent to the limit of his abilities.

Junius blustered and threatened, but his namesake would not be persuaded to give up his folly and come home. Mary Ann too had misgivings, but what had Junius expected? The children idolized their dramatic, exciting, unpredictable father. They had absorbed Shakespeare at his knee, and they recited verses and soliloquies as other children told riddles. Their home was a treasure vault of scripts, costumes, props, theatre posters, and newspaper clippings of rave reviews. In secret they had watched their father onstage from the wings, awestruck, whenever Mary Ann had been obliged to bring them along to the theatre to collect Junius's salary before he could drink it away. It would have been more astonishing had June not resolved to become an actor, although privately his parents agreed that it seemed unlikely he would ever become a great one.

There was no danger of their second child and eldest daughter,

Rosalie, following her father and brother onto the stage. Quiet and gentle, Rosalie was so reserved that she rarely spoke, and then only in whispers. She was Mary Ann's silent, helpful shadow as she went about her chores on The Farm, tending the garden, watching over the younger children. Though Mary Ann never spoke of it to Junius, she suspected that Rosalie had become profoundly withdrawn as a protective measure after suffering the loss of four younger siblings to terrible illnesses. Mary Ann understood her melancholia all too well.

Yet even after suffering such unspeakable losses, Mary Ann's broken heart had remained strong enough to welcome another child into the family. Junius had been on tour in mid-November 1833 when she had gone into labor on a night the heavens had put on a spectacular display of shooting stars. One had exploded with an earsplitting crack in the sky above Baltimore, lighting up the clouds like dawn and searing the sky with a trailing stream of fire. Bright ribbons of light still illuminated the darkness when Mary Ann's son was born—safely, in perfect health, but with a transparent membrane swathed around his face. Shakespeare had referred to the marvel as "fortune's star," Mary Ann remembered, and Ann Hall and the other servants had declared that it meant that the boy was destined for greatness. Mary Ann had carefully preserved the caul, certain that the heavenly fireworks affirmed that her baby—unusually quiet and alert, his features resembling his father's—was destined for a special fate. From Philadelphia, Junius had chimed in his agreement, adding that he wanted the boy to be named after his two best and most loyal friends, the actors Edwin Forrest and Thomas Flynn, and so the newborn was called Edwin Thomas.

A sister had followed almost exactly two years later, and from New York Junius wrote, "Call the little one Asia in remembrance of that country where God first walked with man." Little Asia Sydney grew into a lovely, dark-eyed, and watchful child, and it seemed to Mary Ann that she marked everything done and every word spoken around her, even before she was capable of speech herself.

Two and a half years later, John Wilkes was born, and two years after that, Mary Ann was delivered of another son, dark-haired, darkeyed, and quiet like his eldest sister, Rosalie. Mary Ann wanted to name him after his grandfather Richard, who had passed away less than two months before, but that name had already gone to another, so she chose Joseph instead.

Junius and Mary Ann agreed that each precious child was a miracle, but Junius struggled to support his many dependents on wages that swiftly vanished into drink and bad investment schemes if Mary Ann could not collect them first. Summoning up the skills she had honed years before peddling flowers in London's Covent Garden, she began selling the produce of The Farm in the markets of Baltimore. Throughout the summer and autumn, she would load a cart with apples, potatoes, peaches, squash, whatever her garden had yielded that week, and drive twenty-five miles to Baltimore, where she would set up a stall in the Lexington Market and sell fruits and vegetables as she had once sold roses and bouquets.

Perhaps because Junius worried about Mary Ann making frequent trips to the city markets alone or with only Joe Hall—the former slave whom Junius had purchased, freed, and hired to run The Farm soon after their arrival in 1822—Junius decided that the family should move to Baltimore.

In summer, when deadly cholera and typhoid swept through the city, they escaped to the cool, healthful wilderness of The Farm, but from autumn through spring, they resided in a modest but charming brick row house on North High Street. Their neighborhood on the east side of Baltimore was populated by butchers, shopkeepers, cabinetmakers, schoolteachers, and the like, with theatres, markets, and the waterfront only a short walk away.

Baltimore had transformed itself in the nearly twenty years since Mary Ann had come to America. The Baltimore & Ohio Railroad carried passengers and freight from the heart of the city to and from the farthest reaches of the Western frontier. The city thrummed with the ceaseless rhythms of steam-powered industry—mechanized looms, brickyards, forges, flour mills, sawmills, factories—and soot and smoke blighted the air. The thudding of the printing press of the *Baltimore Sun* kept the children awake at night until they grew accustomed to it, and then it became the steady heartbeat that lulled them to sleep.

In Baltimore, as in London, as in New York, people of quality admired actors on the stage but disdained to see them socially. Nevertheless, Mary Ann resolved that her children would be accepted in society despite their father's occupation and the wild tales of his drunken escapades that would have ruined the reputation of anyone save a man universally acknowledged as a mad genius. As soon as the children were old enough, she enrolled them in school, in dancing lessons, in elocution and etiquette classes, to make proper young ladies and gentlemen of them. Wielding the skills she had perfected over two decades of sewing elaborate stage costumes for Junius, she sewed fashionable attire for herself and the children so they looked as well dressed and respectable as any inhabitant of the grand marble mansions on Lexington Street and Monument Square.

If any of their neighbors realized that the beautiful English wife of the great tragedian spent several days a week selling fruits and vegetables at street markets to make ends meet, they never mentioned it.

In 1845, five years after the family moved to the city, Junius became so optimistic about his future success that he decided to purchase a home in Baltimore rather than continuing to rent. Although Mary Ann had some misgivings about the expense, she delighted in Junius's good spirits—and in the house he purchased at 62 North Exeter Street, a two-story brick residence with a wide stone porch at the front entrance and a back garden with a charming gazebo. The first floor boasted a dining room, a spacious front parlor, and a kitchen with a sturdy Franklin stove, while the second floor offered several cozy bedrooms, with an attic above and a cellar below. When Junius indulged Mary Ann's request to hang lovely green-and-gold wallpaper in the parlor and to purchase stylish, factory-made furniture, she understood it as his apology for the strain and anxiety his near-constant travels and frequent dissipation inflicted upon her.

She wished her comfortable new surroundings could ease her worries the way Junius intended. A few times she thought she spied a hired carriage parked across the street in front of their home, and she felt a strange prickling on the back of her neck that warned of someone watching her, seething with hostility. She told herself firmly that it was all nonsense, but even on the brightest, sunniest days, she could not rid herself of the sensation that a bleak shadow hung over them all.

Mercifully, the children seemed unaffected by her dark fancies. Rosalie was, as ever, her silent companion around the house and garden, while young Joseph was quiet and content, and studious Edwin and clever Asia excelled at school. One teacher praised Edwin for his intuitive intelligence and quickly receptive mind, while Asia, who was sharply observant and prone to sulks, demonstrated an impressive talent for writing. Mary Ann knew that John Wilkes was as bright as his elder siblings, but he was a dogged scholar who struggled to wrest knowledge out of books and lectures. Though he was far less nimble in the classroom than Edwin and Asia, and though he called himself a dullard, he toiled determinedly, and once he learned something, he never forgot it.

Though school frustrated John Wilkes, he was cheerful, exuberant, and confident everywhere else. Mary Ann's heart softened just to look upon him, so beautiful he was with his dark, silky hair and smooth, fair skin, his ready smile and perfect features. Even for a boy his profile was strong and noble, resembling his father's but refined, perfected, with his mother's beauty. His ardent, impulsive nature was so like his father's that Mary Ann could not help adoring him all the more for it. Like Junius, in a moment of passion or enthusiasm John Wilkes would grant any request or give away anything he possessed to please a friend or comfort a sibling. To Mary Ann's knowledge, he had never once abandoned a friend or slighted an acquaintance, and when confronted with danger, he quickly and coolly assessed the situation, his poise and confidence commanding the other children's respect.

Naturally, the most harrowing of John's escapades occurred well out of his mother's sight, and Mary Ann learned about them only after all was said and done, dismay warring with pride and relief as she absorbed a reluctant confession. One summer evening, John Wilkes and Asia returned home from their play much later than expected, and when their worried mother questioned them, they admitted they had been delayed at the magistrate's office. John Wilkes and his friends had been playing "telegraph" by sending fireworks sailing along a wire strung across the street, and had successfully sent crackling showers of sparks overhead from tree to lamppost several times when an unwitting gentleman had passed beneath the line just as John Wilkes had taken his turn to light the fuse. The careening firework had caught the gentleman's hat, and as he shouted angrily at the boys and bellowed for the police, the other boys had scattered, but John Wilkes, hastily coiling up the wire, had felt a police officer's hand clamp down on his shoulder. "Don't frighten

Mother," he had calmly called to his siblings as he had been led away. Asia, observing the scene from their front porch, had quickly darted after them, pausing only long enough to beg a kindly neighbor to accompany her. At the magistrate's office, John Wilkes had refused to give up the names of his comrades, and Asia had ably mounted a defense, explaining the game and insisting that no harm had been intended. Satisfied, the magistrate had admonished John Wilkes not to obstruct the streets again, and, after imposing a fine, which the generous neighbor had promptly paid, he had smiled at the children and ordered them straight home.

"You could have set that poor gentleman on fire," Mary Ann scolded, "or taken off a horse's head with that wire." Abashed, John Wilkes apologized and promised not to play the game again, but his sweet contrition and Asia's loyalty melted Mary Ann's indignation, and she struggled to keep her expression appropriately stern as she sent them to wash up for supper.

John Wilkes was athletic, popular, and daring, a true and loyal friend and an intimidating adversary, proud of his strength and his fighting prowess. He was often obliged to employ them in defense of his elder brother Edwin, whose withdrawn, bookish nature and affectations—growing his hair long, donning a short Italian cape like a Shakespearean hero—provoked attacks from belligerent classmates.

Junius delighted in reports of John's scrapes and rewarded him with adventurous tales of his old friend Sam Houston, lately renowned as a hero of the Mexican War. He was far less pleased when he learned that Edwin's favorite pastime was to gather his friends together and put on theatricals in a backyard tent. "Don't encourage him," Junius growled by letter to Mary Ann after she had sent him what she had thought was an amusing account of the debut performance of an original drama full of swordplay and double-crosses and bold speeches. "Edwin is to be a cabinetmaker."

It pained Mary Ann to admonish Edwin for his harmless playacting, but Junius was adamant that no more of his offspring should follow him onto the stage. When Edwin absorbed the edict in silence, regarding her sorrowfully with his large, dark, hauntingly expressive eyes, Mary Ann hastened to tell him that he could read Shakespeare as much as he liked, as long as he did not perform.

Not surprisingly, tempering Junius's decree failed to cheer Edwin—but it did provoke a small, triumphant grin from John Wilkes, which he tried unsuccessfully to conceal. Mary Ann wished John did not enjoy his elder brother's disappointment, but she understood the impetus. Edwin always relegated John Wilkes to the least significant roles in his productions, performing bit parts with hardly any lines or clanging a triangle between acts. And yet she could not bring herself to scold John Wilkes for his resentment. She knew she shouldn't have a favorite child, but she could not help herself—John Wilkes was hers. She did her best to make sure his siblings never suspected.

One day while Junius was home on a brief respite from touring, he came down from the attic wearing a black hat, fringed prayer shawl, and a quizzical expression. "Darling," he asked, "is my Shylock robe in your sewing basket?"

"No, I don't have it. Does it need mending?"

"No, but I need it and it wasn't in any of my costume trunks." Junius looked around the room as if hoping to find it misplaced on a book-shelf or armchair. "A few other pieces were missing too. I hope I didn't leave them in Richmond."

"Father?"

Junius and Mary Ann turned to find John Wilkes in the doorway, hands clasped behind his back, eyes wide with innocence. "Yes, son?" Junius replied, his frown softening. John Wilkes was his favorite child too.

"Do you mean the black robe with the shiny spangles in the front?"

"Yes, that's the one. Do you know where it is?"

"I don't want to get anyone in trouble—"

"Speak, boy," Junius thundered.

"Edwin said he needed it for *Richard the Third*." John gestured vaguely over his shoulder. "The Tripple Alley Players are putting it on right now."

"The Tripple Alley Players?" echoed Mary Ann.

"Edwin's theatre troupe. Him, Stuart, George, Sleepy, and some of the other boys perform in the basement of Barnum's City Hotel on Calvert Street." John looked from his mother to his father and back. "Didn't you know?"

Junius seized John by the upper arm. "Lead on."

John gulped and nodded as his father propelled him from the house.

Before long, Junius returned in a fury, yanking a tearful Edwin along by the scruff of his shirt, which Mary Ann quickly recognized as his father's Shylock robe, cut down to resemble King Richard's armor. John trailed along after them, his hands thrust in his pockets, his expression alternately merry and contrite.

Junius had interrupted the play at its climax, he told Mary Ann after he had thrashed Edwin soundly and sent him off to bed without supper. The hotel janitor, hired as the troupe's doorman for a cut of the profits, had challenged Junius for the admission fee, but Junius had shoved past him and had stormed into the makeshift theatre just as Edwin was desperately offering his kingdom for a horse. When his outraged father burst into the room, Edwin bolted for the window, but Junius grabbed his legs when he was only halfway through, rendering the boy ideally situated for a spanking. Edwin's wails attracted a passing policeman, who seized Edwin by the arms, believing he had captured a young burglar. Thus the brief career of the Tripple Alley Players was brought to an abrupt and ignominious end.

The following morning, Edwin remained so humiliated and angry that he waited until his father left and his siblings went out to play before he trudged downstairs and slumped dejectedly at the breakfast table. "John shouldn't have tattled," he groused, digging into the plate of ham and eggs Mary Ann set before him.

"You shouldn't have disobeyed your father," she replied, "nor should you have cut up those lovely costumes I worked so hard to make for him."

Edwin's remorse made her wish she could take the words back. "I'm sorry, Mother," he said, stricken, his eyes welling up with tears. "King Richard needed armor, but I didn't think—I didn't mean—"

She hastened to tell him she forgave him, before his sobs beckoned his curious younger siblings in from the garden and exposed her most sensitive child to more embarrassment. She almost wished John had not tattled, and she certainly wished she could tell Edwin that the Tripple Alley Players could continue, that she would make him his own King Richard costume, and that he need not become a cabinetmaker. But she could not contradict Junius, not with his behavior on tour swinging erratically from acclaimed performances in one city to frightening mad freaks in another.

Junius had an artist's temperament—and she adored him for it—but it required her to be steadfast and strong, to believe in him so fiercely that he would never question his ability to provide for her and their children. The profits she brought home from peddling produce at the Baltimore markets did not trouble him because he had a hand in everything grown at The Farm, and so the earnings were his as much as hers. But if the family came to depend upon Mary Ann's sales too much, he would begin to doubt himself, and all would be lost. In dark moments Mary Ann sometimes felt herself adrift on a sea of willful self-deception, but she would not have traded her tumultuous life with her beloved Junius for anything, certainly not the dullness and dubious comfort of marriage to a lesser man.

And yet worry constantly stalked her hope and happiness. Junius missed performances due to indisposition so frequently that some theatre managers refused to hire him, relenting only after indignant citizens circulated petitions demanding that he be invited to perform. One evening in St. Louis, after his character had died onstage, Junius had suddenly leapt to his feet and bowed deeply to the audience three times and lay down again, only to be resurrected a second time by the audience's thunderous applause—and he likely would have continued to postpone his character's demise had the stage manager not ordered the drop lowered. In New Orleans, wary managers drove him around in a carriage all day to keep him sober, refusing to stop or let him out until minutes before curtain so he could not break away from them and flee to a bar. Sometimes even when sober his villainous characters possessed him so ferociously that his fellow players shrank from him on the stage, the men refusing to engage in any swordplay with him lest he forget the choreography and run them through, the women fearing his Othello would truly strangle them before the scene ended. And yet interspersed between canceled engagements and others interrupted by drunken or erratic behavior were performances of such astonishing brilliance, such incomparable sublimity, that Junius continued to fill theatres, to inspire audiences to spontaneous ovations of thunderous applause. No one knew what the mad tragedian might do next, and that anticipation and uncertainty electrified the theatre the moment he stepped onstage.

Mary Ann was thankful and relieved that Junius could still find work despite his habit of baffling audiences, annoying critics, and infuriating theatre owners. She could not imagine what he might do if he could not sublimate his creative fervor into myriad other lives. One man's life was too small to contain all that Junius possessed, all that possessed him.

The entire family was delighted when Junius booked a two-week engagement at the Baltimore Museum in March 1847, for their home was boisterously merry whenever he was in it. The children eagerly memorized poems to recite and songs to perform for their father, each determined to earn the greatest share of his attention. Mary Ann showed off new stage costumes she had made, prepared his favorite meals, and blissfully fell into his embrace every night.

Mary Ann and the children took great pride in the posters displayed throughout the city announcing Junius's performances, especially the enormous banner hanging atop the theatre that proclaimed MR. BOOTH in letters three feet high. Once Mary Ann caught Edwin, Asia, and John conspiring in whispers to sneak inside and watch from the balcony, but abiding by Junius's decrees that his children must never see him perform lest they be tempted to follow him onto the stage, she quickly put a stop to that.

One afternoon while Junius was supposed to be at rehearsal, Mary Ann glanced out the window and was surprised to see him storming home, shoulders squared and head bowed as if he strode into a gale. She rose and went to meet him at the door, her first thought that the children had disobeyed her, that he had spied them watching him rehearse, that they had fled and he was in hot pursuit.

"Junius?" she greeted him, but the look on his face, flushed with anger and dread, silenced her.

"She's here," he said, short of breath, his usually rich, compelling voice strangled in his throat. "Adelaide. She's come to Baltimore."

Adelaide Delannoy Booth, Junius's wife.

For nearly thirty years, an ocean had separated Junius from his wife and eldest son, an ocean and an even broader chasm of lies and deception and steady financial support meant to keep Adelaide reassured and safely remote. For nearly thirty years, Adelaide had endured her husband's long sojourn abroad, raising their son alone in London and in Brussels, where her mother lived, where she and Junius had met as he toured Europe with a group of traveling players. In all that time, regular, generous payments and utter ignorance of the new family he had created with Mary Ann had kept Adelaide content with their arrangement, but now, now—

Mary Ann's hand flew to her heart, her fingertips brushing the brooch with Byron's portrait that Junius had given her so many years ago, when he had renounced his wife and firstborn son and had begged her to run away with him, when she had agreed to be his forever. "Are you certain Adelaide is in Baltimore?" she asked. Then she remembered the hired carriage she had observed parked across the street from their home, and the strange sensation that hostile, hateful eyes were upon her, and she knew.

"Absolutely certain," said Junius. "She interrupted rehearsal to confront me in front of the entire cast, the crew, staff, everyone. The manager persuaded her to retire to his office, but even with the door closed, they must have heard every word of her denunciation."

Then the story was surely already spreading throughout Baltimore— the story, but not the truth.

Although she was but a girl not yet eighteen and her devout Anglican parents had forbidden her to set foot within a theatre, Mary Ann Holmes knew that the rising young actor Junius Brutus Booth was a genius. All the London papers said so, even those that complained he was driving the city "Lear-mad" with astonishing, revelatory performances that compelled throngs of his exultant admirers into the streets, passionately reciting the mad king's monologues and chanting the star's name. Performances of *King Lear* had been forbidden for nearly a decade—the depiction of a monarch's insanity was uncomfortably familiar as well as impolitic—but with George III's passing in 1820, the Shakespearean tragedy had been revived. Critics agreed that in his brilliant, riveting portrayal of the title role, Junius Brutus Booth had no equal.

Mary Ann knew too that he was handsome, breathtakingly so. This she had seen for herself as she wandered among the farm stalls, food vendors, and fortune-tellers at the Covent Garden market, selling flowers her parents raised in their nursery in Marsh Gate. Often she glimpsed him on his way to or from the theatre, smiling and laughing as he strode along with his fellow actors, his arm slung over a companion's shoulders, or alone, lost in thought, mulling over his lines or cues. He was not a large man, no more than five and a half feet tall, but his piercing blue eyes, intelligent gaze, long dark hair, and striking features gave him such presence that he seemed to tower over other men. Once their eyes met across the teeming marketplace, and for a moment he seemed to pause and hold her gaze, as riveted by her beauty as she was by his. A friend chivied him along, but she remained rooted to the spot until the warmth that had risen within her had dissipated, until he disappeared into the theatre and the spell was broken.

Secretly she saved her pennies until she had scraped together enough to buy a ticket to see him perform King Lear at the Covent Garden Theatre in October 1820. She must have breathed throughout the performance, but later she could not remember doing so, nor could she say whether Junius Brutus Booth had interpreted the character or if the demented monarch's shade had possessed him. Her heart sank with dismay as she watched him succumb to the flattery of Goneril and Regan, and she ached with regret when Cordelia's honest simplicity failed to move him. She suffered to witness his mistreatment by his ungrateful eldest daughters, wept at his descent into madness, and shared his grief when he carried Cordelia's lifeless body from the place of her execution. Afterward, Mary Ann sat motionless in her seat, overwhelmed and spent, as the theatre rang with applause and cheers, as the king, alive once more, bowed to the roaring throng as they showered him in acclaim and flowers.

Eventually she reclaimed her senses and departed, among the last to leave the gallery. Though she knew her parents expected her home, she found herself joining the crush of eager patrons outside the stage door, longing for another glimpse of their idol. She kept to the outermost fringes of the mob, embarrassed to be there at all, but compelled to remain long enough to see Junius Brutus Booth as himself again, the handsome man she watched in the market.

A lady squealed as the stage door opened; a few lesser players emerged and were greeted with a smattering of applause. Then a frisson of excitement passed from the front of the crowd to the back, and she saw that Junius Brutus Booth had stepped into the alley. All around her, ladies and men called out his name, waving hats and handkerchiefs, but she felt powerless to speak, to incline her head or bob a curtsey. Perhaps it was her stillness that drew his attention, for suddenly his gaze locked upon hers. She held her breath as he made his way through the crowd, acknowledging well-wishers in passing.

And then he stood before her. "I've seen you before, miss, in the market," he said, his expression a curious mix of wonder and surprise. "You're the beautiful flower girl, are you not?"

She inclined her head in gracious acknowledgment of the compliment. "I would say that I am, sir, were it not vanity to do so."

His laughter, rich and full, brought new warmth to her cheeks. "It isn't vanity to speak the truth." His marvelously expressive face was both hopeful and apprehensive, but his voice was nonchalant as he asked, "Did you see the play?"

"I did, sir."

"And what did you think of it?"

"I think *King Lear* was created for you, and you for it," she said frankly, for there was no need to embellish what was demonstrable fact. "You were magnificent. Anyone else who attempts the role henceforth can be only a pretender to your greatness."

For a moment he stared at her, curious and silent, but then a great laugh burst from him. "Had Cordelia spoken so eloquently, Lear never would have disinherited her," he said, elbowing the man beside him, another player whom until that moment Mary Ann had not noticed. .

His friend smiled as his appreciative gaze explored Mary Ann from cap to hem and back again. "But then there would be no play, and the stage would be poorer for it."

Those who overheard the exchange applauded their wit, but before the ovation tapered off, the other player made a jest about his desperate need for drink and led Mr. Booth away.

Mary Ann drifted home in a dream, pressing her hands to her cheeks, to her waist, to her heart, the places Mr. Booth's words and gaze had reached her. All evening his enchantment remained upon her, like a soft wool cloak upon her shoulders. Noticing her distraction, her father asked if she felt ill, and when she had no appetite her mother checked her forehead for fever and urged her to drink a cup of beef tea. Obediently Mary Ann drank and forced herself to smile and declared that she felt quite restored, wishing she could tell them how her world had been utterly transformed, knowing that her deeply pious parents would never understand.

The next morning she swiftly filled her basket with the nursery's freshest blossoms and prettiest nosegays and hurried off to Covent Garden scarcely moments after her bemused father opened his Bow Street Market shop for the day. She resolved to linger in front of the theatre for hours if necessary to catch a glimpse of Mr. Booth, but he found her first, startling her by suddenly appearing at her side as she crossed the square. "Do you truly believe my King Lear was magnificent?" he queried, ignoring the perfunctory greetings that custom usually required.

"I do," she replied, somewhat breathlessly. "I believed you were the mad king, although I knew you were not. You seemed to disappear within him." Mr. Booth smiled and seemed to be waiting, so she added, "It was the best performance I've ever seen."

His smile deepened. "Do you mean of all my other roles, or of all other players in this role?"

"Of all the performances I've ever seen." Since there was more truth than honesty in her reply, she added abashedly, "I confess there has been only the one."

"You've been to the theatre only once?"

She nodded.

"That can't be true," he protested. "That would be a tragedy greater than any the Bard ever writ."

She laughed. "Surely not."

"How would you know, having seen only one?"

"I've read them," she countered. He could not know how bold a declaration this was from a girl whose parents forbade any reading material but scripture. Friends lent her novels and books of poetry, which she read secretly at night in her bedchamber by the surreptitious light of a dark lantern.

"That's not the same. Master Shakespeare did not write his great tragedies for the page but for the stage." He regarded her solemnly, his blue eyes shining. "We must remedy this deficit without delay. You must come to the theatre again. Tonight." When she hesitated, he quickly added, "I insist you attend as my guest, although I regret I won't be able to sit with you as I'll be performing. I'll leave two tickets for you up front—but of course, you must tell me your name, so I may say who will collect them."

"I am Miss Holmes," she said, soft and clear, her eyes locked on his. When his lips curved in a smile, she longed to trace their fullness with her fingertips. "Mary Ann Holmes."

"I'll see you tonight, Miss Holmes." With that, he bowed and turned away, disappearing into the crowd.

Before the morning passed, Mary Ann had found a friend to accompany her to the theatre and to provide a convincing tale for her parents. She hated to deceive her mother and father, for they were kind and honest and they loved her dearly, but guilt was a small price to pay to behold the greatest young tragedian perform at his personal invitation.

His performance that night was as enthralling and astonishing as if it were entirely new, and as she and Molly walked home afterward, her friend teased her for being poor company. "You've scarcely said a word all evening," she scolded, linking her arm through Mary Ann's. "You didn't watch the play; you stared. You might have blinked once or twice, but I wouldn't swear to that, although I'm certain your gaze was fixed upon a certain tragedian."

"I don't know what you mean."

"What a handsome couple you would make—both of you dark-haired and blue-eyed, his strong brow, your porcelain skin, his broad shoulders, your slenderness—"

"Such nonsense!"

"What would your mother and father think if they knew you were besotted with the great Junius Brutus Booth?"

"You mustn't tell them. How did you know?"

"One glance at your shining eyes was enough." Molly patted her arm, cheerfully sympathetic. "Of course I won't tell your parents, but they'll guess soon enough if you aren't careful. And so will the object of your admiration."

Mary Ann was uncertain whose discovery she dreaded more.

After that, she saw Mr. Booth nearly every day as she sold flowers on Drury Lane and in Covent Garden. Sometimes he asked her to walk with him, and if she had sold enough flowers to earn a respite, she agreed. If she refused, he usually smiled regretfully and kindly bought flowers from her, bouquets to brighten his dressing room, he explained, or to thank his wardrobe mistress or housekeeper, or to charm a leading lady out of doldrums brought on by poor reviews. Sometimes, though, if he were in a peculiar, choleric mood, his handsome face grew stormy. He would buy every flower in her basket, quickly distribute them to any ladies who happened to be passing, and regard her expectantly as if to say that she had no more reason to refuse. What else could she do then but laugh and take his arm and go walking with him?

As they strolled, they discussed the poetry of William Shakespeare and Lord Byron, the political philosophies of William Godwin, the latest royal scandal—the newly ascended King George IV refused to recognize his estranged wife, Caroline, as queen consort—and amusing theatre gossip, in particular, the latest thrusts and jabs in Mr. Booth's ongoing feud with his distinguished rival, Edmund Kean. Perhaps she exaggerated her role in the conversation to say that they *discussed* such things, for Mary Ann often felt herself overawed by her companion's breadth of knowledge and contributed little more than astonished gasps and breathless questions. To her relief, Mr. Booth seemed not at all annoyed by her innocence but rather charmed, which warmed her heart and stoked her eager curiosity.

Often Mr. Booth offered Mary Ann theatre tickets, which she accepted gratefully but sparingly, thrilling to his sublime performances but wary of raising her parents' suspicions. They would grieve for the state of her soul if they discovered her new passion, but now that she had crossed the threshold of the theatre, she could no longer linger on the streets outside selling flowers, closing her eyes and ears to the wonders within. Sometimes Mr. Booth escorted her to see another company perform, and she thrilled to his touch upon her arm as he sat beside her in a private box.

And yet she preferred the nights when he took the stage. He was a moving, breathing artistic masterpiece, the very ideal of her favorite poets—Blake, Wordsworth, Shelley, Byron—sprung from the page and brought to the fullness of vivid, fiercely passionate life.

She knew she must heed Molly's warning to be careful, at least until Mr. Booth made his intentions clear. And if they were honorable, as they surely must be, how could her parents object? Though Mr. Booth was an actor, he was of a higher class than their own, the son of a successful attorney, a gentleman, educated and prosperous. Over the course of many earnest conversations, she had learned that he was not a dutiful Anglican, as her parents would have preferred, nor was he religious in the conventional sense, but he revered God and sought Him in a multiplicity of sacred texts and denominations. He spoke Latin, Greek, Hebrew, and Spanish, and had studied French, Dutch, Portuguese, and Arabic. He painted and sculpted, and had traveled throughout England and toured the Continent. Before his tremendous gifts had led him to the stage, he had worked as a law clerk, a printer's devil, and an assistant in an architecture firm. Eight years before, when he was but sixteen, he had tried to enlist in the navy, only to have his father intervene; Great Britain was at war with the United States, and Richard Booth, a fervent admirer of George Washington, would not allow his only son to risk his life in a conflict with the nation his hero had founded.

Junius Brutus Booth was handsome and fascinating, and Mary Ann could not resist being drawn to him—and curiously, though she had lived such a small, circumscribed life in comparison, he seemed equally enthralled by her.

One cool November morning as she peddled flowers near Covent Garden, her heart was light with anticipation despite the heavy fog that dampened her wool shawl and set her thick, black hair curling wildly. Her heart leapt when she saw him approaching, her smile broadening in reflection of his.

"Let me see," he said, studying the contents of her basket, his eyes teasing and merry as he pretended to be more interested in her flowers than in her. "I had hoped to find a single perfect English rose." He looked up, caught her eye, and feigned surprise. "And so I have."

"Mr. Booth," she scolded lightly. "You flatter me and insult my flowers. I have many perfect blossoms here, as anyone can see."

Before he could reply, the manager of the Theatre Royal in Drury Lane emerged from the fog. "Why, Booth," he exclaimed, clapping him on the back. "Buying more flowers for the missus? No wife has ever been showered in so many bouquets. Aren't you afraid you'll drown her and the boy in petals and pollen?"

Mary Ann felt the blood drain from her face.

Mr. Booth threw her one stricken glance before replying to his friend, but whether his response was witty or dull, confident or stammering, she could not have said. Her ears rang with the man's revelation, and she was insensible to any other sound.

Mr. Booth was married. He had a wife and a son.

As she absorbed the revelation, he hastily finished his conversation and sent the theatre manager on his way. "Miss Holmes—" he began, but she shook her head fiercely to silence him. She tried to speak, and when she could not find the words, she strode away, instinctively turning toward Bow Street and her father's flower shop. She did not look back.

She expected Mr. Booth to have enough shame never to address her again, but to her astonishment, when she set out with her flower basket the next morning, having slept little and wept much, she discovered him pacing on the street a mere two doors down from her father's shop. "Are you mad?" she demanded before he could speak. "Why would you come here?" She did not wait for an answer but strode off to the market, jostling her basket, heedless of the damage to the bright, fragrant blossoms.

Mr. Booth hurried after her. "I wish to explain myself."

She whirled about to confront him. "Don't you dare plead innocence. Don't deny that you showed me attention beyond mere friendship, that you led me to believe you care more deeply for me."

"Why would I deny it? Of course I care for you. I love you!"

The words she had once longed to hear burned like bitterest gall. "You have a wife and a child."

"Yes, and yet I love you."

He seized her hand to press it to his lips, but she tore it from his grasp, overturning her basket. Instinctively they both stooped to pick up the spilled bouquets, but Mary Ann quickly rose, snatched the flowers from his arms, and dumped them roughly into the basket. "I'm sure you said the same to your wife when you kissed her goodbye this morning."

"Adelaide may be my wife, but you are my beloved, my soul's companion." When she laughed in scorn, he said, "Marriage has nothing to do with love, true and earnest love. It's an iron yoke that crushes all who submit to it. I won't defile what I feel for you by asking you to sub-mit to lifelong enslavement. She has my name—"

"And your child."

"And my child," he conceded, "but you have my heart. If you'll take it."

"Fine words from a husband who seeks a mistress," she retorted. "If marriage would defile me, what would adultery do?"

She turned and stormed away, but she had not gone far when he called after her, "Tell me you despise me. Tell me you don't love me in return. Tell me this, and I'll never trouble you again."

Slowly she halted, knowing that whatever she did next would alter everything that could be, and everything that would. She tried to form the sharp rebuke that would banish him forever, but the words faded from her lips, unspoken.

She gathered up her skirts, tightened her grasp on the basket, and hurried away. But she could not speak the lie that she did not love him.

Their imprudent argument had not gone unnoticed. All day as she sold her flowers, Mary Ann ignored the sidelong glances and curious whispers of the other vendors, fervently hoping that no one would carry tales back to her parents. Mr. Booth must have understood the need for discretion, for in the days that followed, he did not approach her in the market again, not even under the pretense of buying flowers. Instead, a few mornings later, a young boy came upon her, pressed a letter into her hand, and darted off without a word. Having nowhere to dispose of it safely, she slipped the letter into her pocket without breaking the seal. She was certain that the author was watching her, hoping to see her face light up in pleasure as she read his carefully composed lines, but she refused to give him that satisfaction. Yet she lacked the fortitude to throw away the letter unread. Later that evening, by the light of her dark lantern, she read it over and over, her heart warming to his tender apologies.

The next day, the urchin brought another letter as she returned to her father's shop with her empty basket, and the day after that, some-one tucked another missive among her flowers while she was accepting coins from a customer. Every day the letters came, written in beautiful script on fine paper or feverishly scribbled on the backs of theatre handbills. Junius wrote of his sorrow that he had offended her, and of his sincere admiration and respect, and of his enduring hope that she would forgive him. He composed hundreds of lines praising her porcelain skin, ebony hair, ruby lips, and graceful figure. He addressed her as "Mary Ann, my own soul," and signed himself "Your worshipper, Junius."

In more introspective moments, he wrote of his childhood in Queen Street, Bloomsbury, as the scion of Jewish silversmiths and lawyers on his father's side and of strict Anglicans on his mother's. When he felt more lighthearted, he amused her with stories of his early years as an actor, of tromping through the provinces with a company of players in search of an engagement, some coin, and a clean bed; of performing *Macbeth* for the Prince of Orange in Brussels shortly before the Battle of Waterloo; of his professional feud with the acclaimed actor Edmund Kean, who had been so jealous of his young rival's popularity that he had hired mobs of ruffians to disrupt his performances. Though Mary Ann never favored Junius with a reply, with every letter she felt herself drawing closer to him.

Then, a few days before Christmas, an urchin brought her a letter that was almost too painful to read, for when she broke the seal his wife's name leapt off the page. "I will confess my history to you," he had written, "my triumphs, my mistakes. There must be no secrets between us."

Junius was eighteen, he wrote, when he met Adelaide Delannoy while touring in Brussels. She was one of his landlady's three daughters, and although she was more than four years his senior and not pretty, or so his friends had complained, she was well educated and had impressed him with her cleverness and keen business sense. When Junius and his company of players left Brussels to tour elsewhere on the Continent, Adelaide had followed him, taking upon herself the roles of his assistant, adviser, and closest companion. "You will judge me, and well I may deserve it," Junius acknowledged. "Upon our return to England in May 1815, we married at St. George's in Bloomsbury. Our daughter was born in October."

A daughter? Junius and the theatre manager had mentioned only a son. Mary Ann read the passage again, and counted the months, and at once she understood why Junius and Adelaide had been obliged to marry.

The child, Amelia, had died at nine months of age, and grief had driven Junius into fits of melancholy and madness. "Now you know the reason for the mad and bad behavior of those days of years past," he wrote, "although most of the fantastical tales you might have heard were greatly exaggerated."

Mary Ann had heard no such tales, young and sheltered as she had been—a lifetime ago, or so it seemed.

Junius's sorrow had been assuaged, he wrote, though never entirely forgotten, by the birth of his son, Richard, in June a year past. Since then Adelaide had devoted herself entirely to the boy, and to her family in Brussels, whom she often visited.

"Whatever passion I felt for her as a lad of eighteen has since faded," Junius wrote, his regret evident in every dark stroke of the pen. "As has hers for me, or so her nightly indifference proves. For years I believed I would plod through life a proper, dutiful husband, accepting that true love and beauty and the quenching of desire were lost to me forever. But then I discovered you, my darling angel, and having discovered my heart's desire, I must pursue it."

The next day he came to her in the market. He did not speak, but his eyes burned blue fire as he took her hand and folded it around a small piece of stiff paper. Her heart raced at his touch and she trembled, not trusting herself to speak. Only after he bowed and departed did she open her hand and discover a single ticket for that evening's performance at the Adelphi Theatre in the Strand.

It was opening night of a new melodrama in three acts, *Zamoski, or, The Fortress and the Mine*, but Mary Ann saw almost none of the performance. Soon after the curtain rose, Junius slipped into the empty seat on her right, laced his fingers through hers, and when the hero first appeared onstage, he quickly led her away under the cover of the audience's cheers. He took her through a side door and into the backstage labyrinth, past players in various stages of undress, men gargling lemon water as they awaited their cues, ladies peering into looking glasses and carefully applying rouge with rabbit's feet brushes.

Junius pulled her after him into a cramped, windowless dressing room and shut the door behind them. A heartbeat later she was in his arms, his lips warm and hungry upon hers. "I love you," he breathed in her ear, and when he kissed her again, she sighed and felt herself melting into his embrace. "I adore you. I worship you." Again and again his mouth found hers. "Come away with me."

For the briefest of moments she glowed with joy, imagining herself strolling by his side through some distant European capital, attending the theatre on his arm or applauding him from an ideal spot backstage, spending every night in his arms—but somehow she found the will to push him away. "Where would we go? Your life is here, in London, upon the London stage." And remaining in London was out of the question. Even if she thought she could endure the scorn of everyone she knew, theatergoers were a fickle lot. Charges of adultery could ruin Junius's career.

"My life is where I make it, and with whom." He took her gently by the shoulders, his eyes urgent and pleading. "I'm welcome on any stage in the greatest cities of the world. Early in the New Year, my wife plans to take our boy to Brussels to visit her mother. In the meantime I intend to go on tour on the Continent." He seized her hands and pressed them to his lips. "Come with me. I cannot bear the thought of being apart from you for so many long, lonely months."

"And what would we do after your tour? Shall I go home to my mother's house, while you return to your wife's?"

"I don't yet know what we'll do, but a way will be made clear for us. Perhaps we'll go to America."

For a moment Mary Ann felt a thrill of anticipation—but then, with a sudden, sharp pang, she remembered Adelaide and Richard. "Junius, we can't. You're too good a man to abandon your wife and child."

"I would do anything not to hurt them," he said, "anything but abandon true love, anything but suffer the torment of a lifetime without you. I won't forsake my responsibilities. I'll provide for them. They'll never go hungry. They'll never know a day of want."

"They will," she countered. "Even if every material need is satisfied, they'll still suffer the absence of their husband and father."

"I travel so much already, I'm sure their suffering will be very slight indeed."

"I can't believe that's true." Fighting back tears, she clung to him, resting her cheek against the lapel of his fine wool coat. "I couldn't possibly give you my answer now. I need time alone to think. We should both carefully weigh the consequences."

"I've never been more certain," he declared, but he assured her that she could have all the time to reflect that she needed.

If she eloped with him, the repercussions would be vast and far-reaching. Not only would she deprive Adelaide and young Richard of a husband and a father—his presence and affection, if not his income—but she would ruin her own good name and break her parents' hearts. She would be denounced as an adulteress, a whore, and if she bore Junius any children, they would be called bastards. They would be entitled to neither their father's name nor his property. If Junius were to tire of her, to abandon her as he meant to abandon Adelaide—

But no. He never would. His every word, his every glance and gesture, convinced her that she had ignited a fire in his soul as intense and eternal as the one he had kindled in hers. He would never cast her aside.

Junius honored her request for time apart, but he wrote to her more frequently and more passionately than before, sometimes several letters a day, full of tender words about his love, the adventures they would share, the higher obligation they owed to true love than to any other mortal consideration. For Christmas he gave her a beautiful, leather-bound collection of Lord Byron's poems that must have cost a small fortune. It was no simple matter to smuggle the ten volumes up to her bedchamber, but it was worth the risk to keep them nearby rather than leave them with her friend Molly for safekeeping. Byron's provocative verses thrilled her, intoxicated her, and she perceived in each stunning, magnificent line the terrible beauty Junius wielded on the stage. When she dared not risk lighting the lantern she would rise in the middle of the night and read at the window by moonlight, committing entire poems to memory, climbing back into bed and reciting them in whispers until she fell asleep.

On the second day of the New Year, her heart leapt when she spotted Junius watching her from across the Covent Garden square. She nodded to him, then lifted her chin to signal that their time apart had come to an end. It took him five minutes to make his careful, peripatetic way to her side, and as he offered a perfunctory nod and studied the contents of her basket, she said, "I have not yet decided. I only wanted to thank you for the wonderful gift."

He smiled briefly, bending to smell a rose, newly cut, nurtured tenderly from bud to blossom in her father's greenhouse. "You said as much in your letter."

"My letter could not express all I wished to say." She was mindful of her clumsy way with words, her lack of even a small fraction of the genius possessed by Junius, by Byron. "When I read Byron's poetry, when I see you on the stage, I feel—as if I am awake for the first time, and I live in despair of falling asleep again."

"I will tell Lord Byron you said so." He straightened, his smile turning ironic. "Without offering your name, of course, for propriety's sake."

"You're acquainted with Lord Byron?"

"Certainly. He's on the board of directors of Drury Lane. He counts himself among my admirers." Junius spoke without so much as a hint of a boast. "Not long ago, as a token of his esteem, he sent me his portrait, a watercolor miniature on a small oval of ivory."

"Oh, my," Mary Ann gasped. "I should love to see it."

"I should love to show you." His smile faded. "I embark on my tour in a fortnight. Tell me I won't travel alone. Tell me you believe in free love, and that there is no greater sin than suppressing one's passions, that there is no greater good than to pursue truth and beauty and love. This is what I believe; this is what Lord Byron believes. What do you believe?"

"I believe—" Mary Ann's voice faltered. "I believe I cannot so easily steal another woman's husband."

"No, Mary Ann," he said earnestly, shaking his head. "Don't adhere to that old, moribund doctrine that laws are holier than love. I'm not Adelaide's to steal. Possession is not love. If I belong to anyone, it's to you."

"One more week," she implored, "and I'll give you my answer."

She needed only half the time she had requested to make up her mind. She and Junius served the greatest cause of all—true love. She deeply regretted hurting anyone, but she believed—she had to believe—that the grief and outrage her parents and Junius's wife and son would suffer would be the birth pangs of a glorious new creation.

On a cold, windy evening in the middle of January, Mary Ann quietly packed her trunk, wrapping the precious volumes of Byron in dresses and petticoats for protection, concealing her purse with her modest savings in the back, taking cloaks and shawls and stockings suitable for both fair weather and cold. Then she descended the stairs to kiss her mother and father good night, fighting back tears when they told her they loved her and would see her in the morning. She knew that it would break their hearts to find her bedchamber empty the next day, but she prayed that God would forgive her and comfort them.

As she stood before them, struggling to speak, to disguise her torment, her mother rested her knitting on her lap, her brow furrowing in concern. "Mary Ann, my dear child." Her black hair was plaited in a long braid, with only a faint trace of silver threaded through the glossy mass. She had been a great beauty in her youth and could have had any man of the borough she had wanted, and she had married Mary Ann's father for his kindness and piety. "Is everything all right?"

"Of course," she lied, forcing a smile. "I'm merely tired."

"Sleep is the best cure for that," her father said, setting aside his Bible and regarding her fondly. "Remember to say your prayers."

She promised him she would and hurried upstairs before they glimpsed the tears in her eyes.

Alone in her bedchamber, she doused the lamp and lay beneath the coverlet fully clothed, listening to the faint sounds of her parents retiring for the night, starting at every banging shutter and creaking windowpane. Shortly after midnight, Junius's signal came; the scratching of a long branch against her window. She threw back the covers, lighted the lantern, straightened her dress, smoothed her hair—and, lastly, fastened her lovely new brooch to the throat of her dress. The exquisite piece of jewelry was a gift from Junius; when she had pledged him her love, he had taken Byron's miniature on ivory to a jeweler, who backed it in gold and set it for a brooch, a beautiful, unique ornament in lieu of a wedding ring.

She crept down the stairs and opened the door to her beloved Junius. He kissed her before following her inside and up to her bedchamber to retrieve her trunk, which he carried downstairs and outside to the waiting carriage. Her heart thumped at every creak of the floorboards; her ears strained for the sound of her parents sitting up in bed, lighting a candle, her mother sobbing, her father following in pursuit.

The house was silent. She heard a baby cry next door, a dog bark several blocks away, but her parents slumbered peacefully on.

When Junius settled her into the carriage, she gasped, suddenly remembering something precious left behind—Junius's letters, nearly one hundred of them hidden at the bottom of her wardrobe, sorted according to the week and bound with ribbon left over from tying bouquets. "I've forgotten something."

"What is it?" Junius caressed her cheek tenderly. "Wait here. I'll fetch it for you."

"No, it's too great a risk." If her parents woke and caught her in mid-flight, her resolve would crumble. "Let's go."

He nodded, and a moment later, the carriage swiftly carried her away from the only home she had ever known.

Let Junius's words remain behind as a testament to true love. Perhaps after her parents read them, they would understand.

They traveled first to Deal on the southeastern coast of England, giddily celebrating their escape by taking a room at a seaside inn and arranging for supper to be sent up to them, bread and potatoes roasted with leeks and rosemary. Junius cherished all living things, he told her, and he refused to eat the flesh of any beast, fish, or fowl. "Man was not intended to make Earth a slaughterhouse of innocent animals," he said, making her deeply regret suggesting the pheasant.

He had signed the register "J. B. Booth and wife," which sent a frisson of anticipation through her even as a pang of remorse reminded her that it was not and never could be true. It did not matter, she told herself later as they prepared for bed, as he tenderly undressed her, as her skin warmed beneath his touch. She had him. She had his love. She did not need his name or a paper from the church to confirm either.

The next morning, she woke warm and dreamily sated in a tangle of bedcovers to find herself alone. "Junius?" she called, sitting up and drawing the coverlet around herself.

"I'm here."

He sat at a table near the window, pen in hand. Sleet pelted the window and outside the sky was leaden gray, but Junius's face was radiant as he looked up from his writing to admire her.

"Come back to bed," she said, smiling. "We won't be able to sail today."

"I will, as soon as I finish this letter."

Her contentment vanished. "To Adelaide?" He nodded and returned his attention to the page. "What will you tell her?"

"That I hope she's enjoying her visit to Brussels and that her family is in good health. I'll ask her to kiss the boy for me, and I'll send her five pounds."

"You'll say nothing more? Nothing of our elopement?"

"Good God, no. With any luck, she'll never know."

Mary Ann stared at him for a long moment, then lay back upon her pillow and gazed up at the ceiling, unsettled. But by the time Junius came back to bed, she had summoned up the courage to tell him they must return to London. Before she could speak, his kisses silenced her, and soon thereafter his caresses reminded her that she could never go back, nor did she want to.

The next morning dawned clear and calm, and they sailed for France. For a fortnight Junius performed in Boulogne-sur-Mer and Calais, but the reviews were not so glowing that he was tempted to linger. Instead Junius decided that he should tour the West Indies.

Their ship crossed the Channel and stopped at Dover, where, wary of discovery, they went ashore only long enough to stretch their legs and to purchase a little piebald pony they named Peacock. Their ship next stopped at Madeira, an island about three hundred and fifty miles off the coast of Morocco, so enchantingly beautiful that they decided to extend their visit several weeks. But Junius had to earn a living, and as their blissful holiday came to an end, they pondered whether to continue on to the West Indies or to choose some other destination.

They had not yet settled the question when Mary Ann discovered that she was with child.

She feared Junius would be angry or disappointed, for a child would change everything, but to her relief, Junius was delighted. He became even more tender and solicitous toward her, albeit increasingly worried about their amorphous plans. When he wrote to several trusted friends seeking their advice, it was the philosopher William Godwin who urged them to sail for America.

"He warns me that the only way to avoid the scourge of public disapproval is to leave the country," Junius said.

"We've already left our country," Mary Ann reminded him. "Must we go all the way to America?"

"Overseas we can start anew." Junius knelt at her feet and clasped her hands. "In America, no one will know that you aren't my wife—and even if the secret did come out, Americans are individualists, tolerant and free-thinking. They wouldn't care."

Mary Ann doubted that assumption very much, but Junius did his best to reassure her, and eventually he overcame her objections with the plain truth that they had no better recourse.

One bright May morning, Mary Ann woke to find Junius much as she had on their first morning together in Deal, at a table by the window writing letters. First he wrote to his father to ask him to call on Mary Ann's parents and inform them that she was going to America to live with Junius, and that she would be safe, loved, and well looked after.

The second letter, which took much longer to compose, was for Adelaide.

English audiences had grown weary of him, Junius wrote, and his recent tour of the Continent had shown him that fickle European theatergoers too had become indifferent. Across the Atlantic, however, grateful Americans starved for culture would turn out in droves to see him, increasing his fame and his fortune. He might be abroad several years, he warned, but with his letter he would enclose enough money for Adelaide and their son to live on for a year, and he would send her fifty pounds per annum thereafter, more if his fortunes soared as he anticipated.

Junius and Mary Ann booked passage on the next ship to America, a small freighter bound for Virginia with a cargo of wine. The *Two Brothers* was not suited to carry passengers, but after Junius quietly explained Mary Ann's delicate condition, the captain gave them his own quarters in exchange for an ample fee paid in gold.

Passing themselves off as husband and wife, they spent the crossing in relative comfort, keeping mostly to themselves. Junius reviewed his repertoire and planned his tour, while Mary Ann aired, mended, and refurbished his costumes, crushed from many weeks stuffed inside his trunk with his greasepaint, scripts, and old playbills. She had always had a deft hand with a needle, but since their arrival in France when she had assumed the role of Junius's wardrobe mistress, she had perfected her skills. Perhaps she could not advise him on matters of business as Adelaide had done, but she was determined that he would have the finest costumes of any tragedian on the American stage.

Forty-four days after they departed Madeira, the *Two Brothers* landed in Norfolk, Virginia, a humble, rustic settlement of about eight thousand residents on the edge of the Great Dismal Swamp. It was as unlike Mary Ann's beloved London as it was possible for a town to be.

"This is only a trading post," Junius hastened to assure her as the *Two Brothers* approached the wharf and she stoically took in the view of ramshackle buildings, warehouses, and gambling dens along the shore, and the vast, dense wilderness beyond. "We won't remain long."

Mary Ann forced a smile and took his arm as they disembarked. She needed a moment to adjust to the feeling of solid pavement beneath her shoes, but even as she did, a dreadful sight nearly staggered her. "Junius," she gasped, tightening her grip on his arm.

Although some unscrupulous Englishmen still engaged in the slave trade at sea, English common law did not recognize slavery. As soon as an enslaved person set foot on English soil and breathed English air, he was free. Mary Ann had known that slavery still flourished in some regions of America, despite the citizens' exaltation of the ideals of liberty and freedom. And yet until that moment she had never seen Africans in chains, clad in rags, thin and hollow-eyed with hunger. The harrowing sight sickened her.

"I see them," Junius murmured, resting his hand upon hers in a gesture that failed to comfort. "The poor, wretched souls!"

Horrified, Mary Ann could not tear her gaze away. On one bare back she glimpsed interlaced scars, the mark of the lash; on another, welts like intertwined initials burned into the skin.

"Oh, my." Mary Ann covered her mouth with her hand, feeling faint. "Oh, Junius. Some of them have been branded, like—like livestock."

"My dear, I'm grieved to say that, to slave owners, these unfortunate men and women are little more than livestock."

Junius swiftly arranged for a porter to collect their luggage and led her away from the waterfront and its harrowing, heartbreaking sights. They settled in a modest hotel, but thankfully, Junius's prediction that they would not linger in Norfolk proved true. Within a matter of days he had booked a two-week engagement in Richmond, where a grand new theatre, the Marshall, had recently been completed. From the deck of the steamer that carried them up the James River to the state capital,

Mary Ann was much relieved to see grand public buildings and elegant residences rising on the steep hills along the shore. "Civilization at last," she murmured, patting Peacock's flank as they disembarked. It was not London, with its libraries and cathedrals and bustling public squares, but it was a far cry from the wild frontier.

Within days, Junius's successful American debut reassured her that they had not made a dreadful mistake in immigrating to the young nation.

Junius selected *Richard III* for opening night, enthralling the novelty-hungry citizens of Richmond and earning rapturous praise from the local press. As word of the celebrated English tragedian's arrival spread beyond the city, invitations from theatre managers in New York, Baltimore, Philadelphia, Boston, and New Orleans filled the postbox at their hotel, each expressing the most anxious desire to book Junius for lengthy engagements, each offering enticingly generous terms. As he mulled over their proposals, Junius earned more than twelve hundred dollars playing theatres in Richmond and nearby Petersburg.

In early October, Junius and Mary Ann traveled by steamer to New York City, a bold but necessary choice for his next engagement. His longtime rival Edmund Kean had triumphed there only a few months before, packing the stylish new Park Theatre every night and winning rapturous acclaim from the critics. If Junius hoped to establish himself well in America, he would have to surpass Kean in the eyes of the most discerning theatergoers in the most important city in the nation.

"The house will be half empty," Junius growled, stalking in his dressing room on opening night as an icy downpour raged outside. Broadway was flooded, one of the supernumeraries had reported, and traffic was in a wretched snarl throughout the city. "I'll be lucky if it isn't *more* than half empty."

"Junius, calm yourself," Mary Ann cajoled. On tour, Junius could be cheerful and enthusiastic one night and bleakly melancholic the next, swearing that he would not perform, that he despised acting and would never again take the stage. On such occasions it fell to her to quietly reassure panicky managers that the show would go on, and then to soothe and charm Junius until he reluctantly agreed to perform. Sometimes a glass of brandy was necessary to fortify him to face audiences he had inexplicably decided could not possibly comprehend his interpretation of classical works. Junius was always loving and kind at heart, but he could be mercurial, as she supposed most great artists were. Byron's tempests were legendary.

"I was mad to leave London," Junius grated, pausing to glare balefully out the single tiny window. "I'm beloved in London."

"You are also beloved here, by me," she told him, ignoring the sting of his words, "and you will soon be beloved by the people of New York—but only if you take the stage and give them the performance they expect and have paid for."

"I'll return every cent if they'll just go away."

"The management will never agree to that." Mary Ann approached him from behind, wrapped her arms around his waist, and rested her cheek upon his back between his shoulder blades. "Please, my dearest. You know everything depends upon tonight."

He knew it, and eventually he agreed to emerge from his dressing room. The murmur of the crowd struck them as soon as they stepped into the hall, and the usual backstage odors of dust and paint were overpowered by those of damp leather and steaming wool. Junius halted, thunderstruck. "Mary Ann, darling—"

She knew what he wanted. Nodding, she hurried away and stole a peek at the house through a spy hole drilled through the wall in the wings at stage right.

Every seat was filled.

The two thousand hearty souls who had ventured out in the tempest for the New York debut of the celebrated tragedian Junius Brutus Booth were rewarded with the most magnificent, sublime performance they had ever beheld. Watching from the wings as the curtain fell and the applause and cheers rang on and on, Mary Ann beamed and smiled through tears of joy as Junius took one solemn, dignified bow after another. The next morning, the newspapers echoed the accolades he had received onstage, praising him in the most rapturous phrases.

The remaining six performances of his engagement were no less gloriously done, no less wonderfully received. On the last night, overwhelmed with gratitude, Junius broke his custom of refusing curtain calls to bow respectfully to the delighted audience. "I cannot properly express my feelings at the unexpected honor you show me," he called out, his warm, powerful voice thrilling listeners from the footlights to the back row. "I swear I will never forget the great kindness you have shown me, a humble traveling player in a foreign land."

At the end of October they left New York, and on the first day of November, Junius opened to packed houses in Baltimore. Next the tour carried them along to Charleston, where Mary Ann delighted in the picturesque streets, the ocean breezes, and the blessedly mild climate. Since she was nearing the time of her confinement, she and Junius decided that she should remain in their comfortable boardinghouse under the care of their solicitous landlady while he completed his tour of the southern United States alone.

Junius was spellbinding audiences in far-off New Orleans a few days before Christmas when Mary Ann gave birth to a vigorous baby boy, perfect in every way, with ten wonderful little fingers, ten darling little toes, and strong legs that kicked off his swaddling clothes whenever she lay him down in the secondhand cradle she had bought from a neighbor.

Her midwives had been skilled and reassuring, and no doctor had crossed her threshold from the moment her labor pains came upon her until she held her son, Junius Brutus Booth Jr., in her trembling arms. Her milk came quickly and easily, and she was on her feet the next day. On Christmas morning she celebrated her own newborn miracle with her landlady and other residents of the boardinghouse, grateful for the distraction of a celebration, for she missed Junius terribly.

Nor was he the only loved one she longed to see on that holy day.

While the baby slept, Mary Ann took pen in hand, steeled her courage, and wrote to her parents. Tears filled her eyes as she apologized for the way she had left them, for the shock and uncertainty they must have endured. She asked for their forgiveness, assured them she was safe, and described, rather hurriedly, the cities she had visited and the curious American customs she had discovered. She wanted to tell them every detail about Junius's triumphs on the American stage, but she knew any praise for the man they surely considered a villain would be wasted, so she said only that his success was exceeding their expectations.

"I have glad tidings that I hope you will greet with as much joy as I feel in sharing them," she wrote. "On December 22, we welcomed a beautiful son into the world. He is healthy and strong, and I am well recovered. I hope to bring him home to England to meet his grandparents someday."

She felt a pang of guilt for the careful phrasing that suggested Junius had been present for his son's birth, but if she told her parents he was on tour, they would worry needlessly that he had abandoned her. Junius would come to meet his son as soon as word reached him, Mary Ann knew, and she had misled her parents so often and so completely over the past eighteen months that one more half-truth mattered very little in the scheme of things.

Junius had not yet met his namesake when a reply to her letter arrived at the end of January.

January 8, 1822
7 Mount Street, Lambeth, England

My Dearest Daughter,

I fall on my knees and thank God for your letter. My precious child is alive! Perhaps guilt and shame for the manner of your leave-taking and the reasons behind it prevented you from writing sooner, but I am grateful that you did at long last. I pray you will not fall silent again.

It grieves me to tell you that your poor father never read your apology. A few weeks after you left us, he died—of a broken heart, the doctor says. You need not fear that he went to his eternal rest without forgiving you. He was ever a compassionate man, the best of Husbands, the most devoted of Fathers. He is with the Lord now, and I know he looks down upon you from Heaven with love and deep concern.

O my Darling Child, please take your son in your arms, flee your seducer, and come home. Do not let shame keep you away. We will leave Lambeth and live with your aunt in Whitechapel. You have a child to think of now. Do not let lust cloud your reason. How can you hope to build your future happiness upon sin and Mrs. Booth's misery?

I list below the address of my cousin in Boston. Go to him. He and his wife will take you in and pay your passage home. Please write soon to tell me you are on your way. Until I see you again I will remain

Your Frantic and Heartbroken
Mother

With shaking hands, Mary Ann carefully folded the letter and buried it at the bottom of her trunk. She could not bear to throw it away in case it was the last her mother sent. She would never have another from her father.

She curled up on the bed and wrapped her arms around herself, wishing Junius held her instead, muffling her sobs so she would not wake the baby.

Mary Ann's adoration of her newborn son and Junius's affectionate letters brought her much comfort until, at long last, Junius returned to Charleston. He wept with joy when he held his namesake for the first time, kissed him and cuddled him and declared him the most perfect of children.

The child, fondly nicknamed June, would be well provided for, as Mary Ann assured her mother when she summoned up enough courage to reply to her letter, which she had kept secret from Junius. Partway through his first season upon the American stage, Junius was earning more than one hundred dollars a night whenever the theatre sold out, and they almost always did. His fortunes would continue to rise, he promised, but only if he kept the public interested and intrigued. Thus not three weeks after his return to Charleston, Junius set out again, appearing in Savannah, Augusta, Boston, Providence, and Washington City to great public acclaim and financial reward.

When the theatre season concluded at the end of spring, Junius returned to Charleston to collect his little family and announce his plans for their housekeeping. "I earned and saved enough to purchase a comfortable estate for you and me and our darling child," he told her, beaming with pride. "One hundred and fifty sublime forested acres in Harford County, Maryland, about twenty-five miles northeast of Baltimore."

Mary Ann liked Baltimore, but twenty-five miles sounded worrisomely distant. "Did you?"

"Well, I didn't *purchase* it," he acknowledged, misunderstanding her concern. "State law forbids me to own land in Maryland since I'm not an American citizen. Instead I gave the owner a down payment and arranged for a thousand-year lease."

"I suppose that should be long enough," Mary Ann replied, managing a smile. "Tell me, what is our new house like? There *is* a house?"

"Indeed, a charming log cabin." Junius took June from her lap and raised him high above his head, whistling merrily while the baby squealed and laughed. "The soil is fertile and unspoiled, and our property is blessed by natural springs as clear as crystal. We can raise crops, put in an orchard, and create a haven of peace and serenity for ourselves and all living things."

Mary Ann acknowledged that it sounded lovely, and very healthful for the baby, so when Junius suggested they relocate before the heat of the South Carolina summer became oppressive, she agreed.

She hoped for sublime landscapes like those of England's Lake District, which she had never seen but had long admired in engravings and Wordsworth's poetry, but soon after they left the Baltimore city limits in a cart pulled by the faithful Peacock, quaint villages and picturesque farms gave way to rolling terrain and dense, foreboding forest. The poor piebald pony struggled so diligently to haul them and their belongings over the rough, winding road that Junius, moved to sympathy, handed the reins to Mary Ann and walked alongside to ease the burden.

They rumbled past a scant few other farms carved out of the wilderness and came to a tiny hamlet called Bel Air, which Junius assured her had a post office and a general store where she could purchase sugar, flour, coffee, and other necessities. Mary Ann smiled and nodded to conceal her dismay. It was apparent that Bel Air would offer her few entertainments and little opportunity to make friends.

Three miles beyond the village, they at last reached their new home—a sturdy log cabin plastered white with vivid red shutters, set back from the road in a clearing surrounded by towering oaks, walnuts, and beeches. Junius overflowed with boyish enthusiasm as he helped her down from the cart and took her on a tour of the homestead. The house was small but charming, but her apprehensions rose as Junius led her about the clearing, the baby on her hip, a catch in her throat. As he gestured grandly to indicate the fields where he intended to plant barley and potatoes, an ideal place for her kitchen garden, a suitable location to build a dairy, she felt the forest, massive and dense and dark, closing in around her.

"Junius," she ventured as they spread a quilt on a grassy spot near the cabin and sat down to a picnic supper, "what do you know about farming?"

"I've been reading up on it for months, and I'll hire an experienced manager to assist us." He studied her, curious. "You seem worried that we may not be up to the task. Didn't your father grow and sell flowers and seeds?"

"Yes, Junius, but that doesn't make me a farmer's daughter. I don't know anything about running a farmhouse."

"Isn't one kitchen much like any other?" He touched her shoulder and gave her an encouraging smile. "We'll hire a competent woman to help you."

"Junius—" She took a deep breath, hating to spoil his obvious delight. "I think you forget I'm a Londoner. This isolation—yes, it's peaceful and quiet here, and beautiful in its way, but I don't think it will suit me. I crave the bustle and activity of the city—the people, the libraries, the theatres, all of it."

"My darling—" His smile faded. "We can't afford the scrutiny we'd encounter in a city."

"Why? What's happened?"

"Nothing yet, but as my fame grows, it'll become ever more difficult for me to travel without ending up in the 'Arrivals' report in the local papers every time I climb down from a stagecoach or step off a steamer. You remember what the press wrote when you traveled with me last year."

Mary Ann nodded, bouncing June gently on her lap. "Mr. Booth and Lady arrived in the city to-day," was the standard phrase, but other reporters liked to add a line or two describing his lovely traveling companion in the most admiring terms. One had even boldly proclaimed that her dark, lustrous curls, alabaster skin, graceful figure, and rosebud lips made her the handsomest woman he had ever seen.

"Every English actor on tour in America knows me, and they all know Adelaide divides her time between London and Brussels," Junius said. "If they see you, they'll ask questions, and they may carry tales back to her. We can't afford a scandal. No gentleman would escort any lady to see me perform. No manager would hire me. My star would plummet to the earth even more swiftly than it rose. We would be ruined, darling. Surely you see that."

Mary Ann felt tears gathering and forced them back. She had thought that when June was older, they would all travel together, she helping Junius with his wardrobe, little June amusing his father out of his dark moods, mother and child alike admiring Junius from the wings as he enthralled audiences from Maine to Florida.

But she knew he was right. The only way they could protect their secret was for Mary Ann and June and any children who might come after to remain safely out of the public eye.

So she acquiesced, though she had eloped with him to see the world by his side, not to hoe squash and weed a carrot patch in the wilderness.

Junius threw himself into the role of farmer with such intensity and vigor he might have been rehearsing a newly discovered Shakespearean play—*Much Ado About Sowing*, perhaps, or *The Taming of the Weeds*. Mary Ann tended the baby, put the cozy farmhouse in order, scattered feed to the chickens, and gathered eggs while Junius planted potatoes, sweet corn, and okra and hired men to clear the fields for autumn wheat and barley.

As the summer days passed, vigorous toil and the joy of Junius's constant companionship eased Mary Ann's apprehensions. One hot summer afternoon, she stood up from weeding the kitchen garden, arched her back to loosen a knot between her shoulders, gazed out upon a homestead transformed by their labors, and was struck with a sudden swell of pride, admiration, and delight. The Farm was not the home she had expected when she had contemplated their life in America during their long Atlantic crossing, but it was truly wonderful, a sanctuary where life was sacred and love reigned over all.

Every evening at supper Mary Ann and Junius discussed improvements they wished to make to The Farm in the seasons to come, the expense of hiring more help and purchasing equipment, the profits they could reap if the crops thrived, if they grew more than they needed for themselves and could sell the surplus. Junius hoped that one day The Farm would provide for all their needs, except for books and certain tools and supplies they could not make themselves. These renovations would cost a pretty penny, Junius warned, funds that The Farm did not yet earn.

One balmy night after she and Junius had made love and she lay blissful and drowsy in his arms, he kissed her on the forehead and stroked her long, dark hair away from her perspiring brow. "Mary Ann, my dearest," he said, "you know I hate to be apart from you and the boy."

"No more than we hate to be apart from you."

"But I need to earn money." He ran his hand from her elbow to her shoulder and back. "The theatre season will begin soon, and I've accepted several engagements."

"I had assumed you would have to. If you can keep Joe Hall on as foreman and find a capable woman to help me around the house, June and I will manage well enough if you have to travel now and then."

She was surprised when Junius shook his head, for Joe Hall was eminently competent and unquestionably loyal. Months before, Junius had hired him from a prosperous local farmer, but soon the nagging awareness that every cent the diligent man earned went into his owner's pocket so outraged Junius that he had purchased Joe, set him free, and immediately hired him back with the dignity of freedom, choice, and wages.

"Darling," Junius said, and she realized at once she had misunderstood his hesitancy. "Without question I'll have to travel. I'll be on tour for the entire season."

"From autumn through spring? Oh, no, Junius. You can't mean it."

"I promise I'll return home as often as I can."

"Can't you book engagements in Baltimore?"

"Some, yes, but not enough to fill an entire season. This isn't what I want, but it's necessary."

Of course it was. How else could he earn a living if not on the stage? And the audiences would not come to him.

"Junius," she said steadily, "I'm not a timid woman, you know that, but I would be afraid to live here all alone in the wilderness with just me and the baby."

"Joe Hall will be here."

"Not always, unless you forbid him to visit his wife. Her master will never agree to let her stay here."

Junius inhaled deeply. "I'll think of a solution," he told her after a long moment. "I won't have you living in fear."

They lay beside each other, silent, unable to sleep with disappointment hanging heavily above them and loneliness not far off.

"Perhaps you could build a theatre in Bel Air," said Mary Ann.

"Something on the scale of Richmond's Marshall or the Park in New York City."

"That would increase the size of the town by half."

"It would also be necessary to improve the road from Baltimore. Only the hardiest and most determined traveler would attempt that rough washboard of a thoroughfare, even to see the world's greatest tragedian perform."

He laughed softly, and with their unhappiness deferred, they were able to sleep.

A few days later, Junius returned from an errand in Bel Air with supplies—and his solution.

Mary Ann knew someone was approaching the house when she heard the deep, full barking of dogs growing louder, and beneath that, the creaking of wagon wheels and jingling of harnesses. She went outside with June beaming and babbling on her hip, and discovered that the traveler was her own Junius. Three enormous dogs with plush black coats walked about in the wagon bed, tongues hanging out and tails wagging.

"They're Newfoundlands," Junius said, patting the head of one before she raced across the grass to join her companions in chasing one another and sniffing at everything. "Lord Byron reveres the breed."

"Yes, I know." Mary Ann smiled as the largest of the trio bounded over to her, nuzzled her hand with his massive head, and sniffed curiously at June's toes, making him squeal in delight. "He called his own 'in life the firmest friend, The first to welcome, foremost to defend, Whose honest heart is still his Master's own.'"

"'Who labours, fights, lives, breathes for him alone,'" Junius finished. "They'll protect you in my absence."

Mary Ann agreed the dogs would make fine protectors and companions. "I might grow so fond of them that I won't miss you at all," she teased, inspiring Junius to growl madly and nip at her neck until she shrieked with laughter.

She named the largest of the pack Boatswain in memory of Byron's favorite, the bitch Flora, and the smaller male Carlow, and grateful enough she was for their reassuring presence when Junius bade her and June a reluctant farewell in early September and set off on tour. The loyal hounds stayed near the cabin in the daytime, but at night they freely roamed the acreage, their deep barks frightening off any trespassers who might seek to bother the little family.

Joe Hall came to The Farm nearly every day to plow fields, tend livestock, and make repairs to the house and outbuildings as Mary Ann discovered the need. At Joe's recommendation Junius had hired Joe's wife, Ann, a slave from a neighboring farm, to cook, clean, and do laundry. "Hiring another man's slave is not the same as owning one myself," Junius had assured Mary Ann when she expressed misgivings. "We're sparing her from more arduous work and possible ill treatment at the hands of her master."

Mary Ann found it a morally ambiguous distinction, so every week she paid Ann a little extra above the wages she was obliged to carry back to her master. Perhaps one day Ann would save up enough to buy her freedom.

Despite the company of the Halls, the hired hands, and the Newfoundlands, Junius must have worried about leaving his family alone in the wilderness, for a few weeks later, he wrote from Richmond to announce that he had written to his widowed father, Richard, urging him to close his London law practice and join them in Maryland. "My father has longed to see America ever since my grandfather thwarted his plans to join George Washington's forces during the colonial revolt," Junius wrote. "Our need provides him ample reason to make the journey at last."

When Richard Booth arrived in Baltimore in the last week of October, Junius took leave from his tour to meet his father's ship and escort him to The Farm. Mary Ann had spent weeks preparing a bedchamber for the venerable lawyer, with new linens, sturdy bookshelves, a small desk, and a comfortable bed. On the day he was expected to arrive, she and Ann scrubbed every nook of the house, prepared a tasty, wholesome supper, and kept June, dressed in his best little suit, as clean as possible.

In the early afternoon, Boatswain's eager bark announced the gentlemen's arrival. Mary Ann had time to peer into the looking glass, pinch her cheeks, tuck a few loose strands beneath her cap, and ask Ann to wish her luck.

"Are you ready to see Papa and Grandfather?" Mary Ann asked June cheerfully as she carried him outside. He was large for ten months and had already boldly taken a few toddling steps on his strong, stubby legs. As soon as they descended the porch stairs, he wriggled and struggled to free himself from her grasp until she had no choice but to set him down.

As the coach halted in the circle between the barn and the cabin, Mary Ann scarcely had time to pick up June again and call out a greeting before Junius leapt down and swept her up into his arms, baby and all. "Oh, my dearest, my darling," he said, kissing her. "How I've missed you."

He cuddled his namesake a moment before striding back to the coach to assist his father. He was sixty-three, Mary Ann knew, and from his letters to Junius she gathered he was something of a scholarly curmudgeon. When he descended, she beheld a gentleman from a bygone age: a slender, bow-legged fellow in knee breeches, buckled shoes, and a tricorn hat atop a white queue.

"Mrs. Booth," he said, too loudly through a forced smile, hobbling toward her on Junius's arm. "How good it is to meet my son's bride at last."

A wave of relief swept through her. Until that moment, she had not known whether he intended to keep their secret. "Good afternoon, Father Booth," she replied, offering him a respectful curtsey.

The gesture seemed to charm him, and when she introduced him to his grandson, he smiled warmly and chucked the boy under the chin. As June squealed with laughter and seized his finger, Richard's eyebrows rose. "Strong grip, that one," he remarked. "May he have a strong mind as well."

Together Junius and Mary Ann helped Richard settle into his place at The Farm, unpacking his trunks, arranging most of his Latin and Greek books on the shelves in his bedchamber and the rest in the front room beside Mary Ann's collection of Byron's works and Junius's treasured volumes of Coleridge, Keats, Shelley, Dante, Milton, Locke, and Shakespeare. Richard dutifully admired their improvements to The Farm but confessed that the place was so remote and desolate he felt as if he had been marooned on Robinson Crusoe's island.

All too soon Junius returned to his tour. Before he departed, he solicitously sought his father's advice on several matters of husbandry and asked him to undertake a few management tasks in his absence.

Most important, Richard was to be protector, adviser, and companion to Mary Ann, a role he readily accepted.

They had not been long alone together at The Farm when Mary Ann realized that Richard had no interest whatsoever in farming. The minor tasks Junius had conferred on him—more out of a desire to make him feel needed than actual need—he neglected until Joe Hall grew exasperated and took care of them himself. Every day after breakfast, Richard would take a slow, hobbling walk around the clearing accompanied by one or more of the hounds, return to the cabin wanting tea, then settle down with his cup and his books, his favorite shawl draped around his shoulders and spectacles perched on his nose, to work on adapting Virgil's *Aeneid* from a Latin epic poem to an English drama.

Twice a week or more, Richard would become restless, hitch Peacock to the cart, and venture into Bel Air, politely declining Mary Ann's offers to keep him company. She wondered what on earth he could have found in the humble village to entice him back again and again, but he deflected her gentle inquiries. She had almost concluded that he must have befriended a lonely widow when, upon accompanying him on one of his excursions to purchase material to make new clothes for her growing son, she discovered that his inamorata was instead the local beverage of choice, a potent distilled whiskey that sold for nineteen cents a gallon at the general store.

With his secret out, Richard no longer bothered to conceal his indulgences. As he spent more and more time intoxicated, Mary Ann urged him to practice moderation. When that failed, she reported her concerns to Junius, who admonished his father in frequent letters from Baltimore and Richmond. "I have witnessed often with regret the terrible ravages drinking has made both on your Mind and Body," he wrote in late November. "Refrain from that destructive and sense-depriving custom of getting intoxicated. Madness will be the result if you persist."

Unfortunately, his letters evoked derisive chuckles from his white-haired parent but offered little incentive to change. "Tragically, drunkenness is an old family affliction and he has fallen prey to it," Junius confided when Mary Ann gave him the distressing news. "I did not foresee this, nor that dissipation would render my father unfit to oversee the Servants and Laborers, that I may not be cheated and robbed on every side."

Mary Ann assured Junius that she had everything well in hand and that he need not worry. Then she set about making it so. With the help of Joe and Ann Hall and the hired workers, she carried out Junius's plans for improving The Farm—sowing and harvesting crops, planting peach and apple orchards, constructing a large outdoor brick oven for baking bread, building a dairy. Whenever breaks in his tour allowed, and in summer when the theatre season ended, Junius raced home to see his family and threw himself into the work of The Farm with great delight. Richard's dissipation did not improve, but it did not worsen either, which Mary Ann decided to count as a small blessing.

Every year brought new improvements to their homestead, and every year Junius's fame as the greatest tragedian of the age grew—as did their family. Mary Ann knew implicitly that Junius loved her, adored their children, and enjoyed the work of The Farm, but although he professed complete satisfaction with his life, she did not believe he was entirely content. Sometimes she found him brooding over reports of the triumphs of his old rival, Edmund Kean, on the London stage, and she knew it chafed at him that many English critics had never considered him Kean's equal, and now he was too far away to prove them wrong. Sometimes too a shadow of grief would darken his expression as he watched the children play, and she knew he was thinking of his first-born son, whom he had last seen as a toddler and who had become, according to Adelaide's letters, an intelligent, dutiful lad. He longed to see his father, she wrote, a trifle sharply, and both mother and son wondered when Junius might be able to spare time for a visit home to England. Again and again Junius demurred, but Mary Ann worried that eventually he would feel obliged to go.

When Junius was on tour, the burden of separation from his family and the strain of supporting two households weighed heavily upon him—and to her dismay, Mary Ann learned that despite his father's foreboding example, he had taken to drink to alleviate boredom and to brace himself for onerous tasks. Newspapers mentioned performances canceled at the last minute due to the actor's "severe indisposition," midnight walks in the nude, and vehement public declamations in defense of animals. Letters from concerned friends in theatre circles—close enough to know Junius well and to be entrusted with the secret of his second family—urged Mary Ann to join him on his tour, to make sure he stayed sober and showed up for his engagements as she had in their early days in America.

Mary Ann would have gone to him immediately, but with a brood of active young children to mind, she could not simply pack a satchel and set off. Instead she sent Junius tender, affectionate letters urging him to be temperate, and reminding him of the innocent little ones who depended on him. He vowed to heed her wise counsel, but as the months passed, he fell into the familiar pattern of sobriety at home and drunkenness everywhere else.

Mary Ann, ever watchful, ever more distressed, could not mistake the alarming signs of his steady decline. Junius stumbled through one theatre season after another, alarming his fellow players and annoying theatre managers, one of whom complained that Junius had become so unreliable that it was a waste of money to advertise his performances until the curtain rose and he was definitely onstage. His letters home often contained no money, but the shopkeepers of Bel Air willingly extended Mary Ann a generous line of credit, apparently both pleased and proud to assist the family of the world-famous Junius Brutus Booth, Bel Air's own eccentric genius.

When Junius finally returned home in late spring of 1828, Mary Ann wept to see him so exhausted and dissipated. For the first two weeks he scarcely left his bed, eventually moving to a rocking chair on the porch, and soon thereafter to walking the grounds, examining the crops Joe Hall and his workers had put in, and supervising the care of the livestock to be sure they were treated humanely. Every week he regained some of his alertness and vigor, but summer passed all two swiftly and a new theatre season would soon be upon them.

"The life of a traveling player will put me into an early grave," Junius told Mary Ann one evening as they sat outside the little cabin, baby Frederick asleep on his shoulder.

"Don't say such things."

"Mary Ann, I need you with me. The temptation to drink is too overpowering without you near." He drew a soft blanket around Frederick to ward off the evening chill. "I've been offered the post of manager at the Tremont Theatre in Boston. I'm inclined to take it, if you'll come with me."

"What of the children? Surely you don't expect your father to mind them."

"We'll hire the most reliable nurse in Maryland."

"But Frederick's so young—"

"Bring him along, if you'd prefer to have him with you."

Mary Ann would prefer to have all the children with her, but she knew that was impossible. Junius could hardly settle in Boston with a mysterious woman and five young children without causing a scandal.

She demurred, but soon Junius's assurances and her concern for his health overcame her reluctance to be parted from her elder children. And, although she would not admit it aloud, after so many years in the wilderness, she could not resist the allure of Boston's museums, theatres, shops, and libraries.

Guided by Ann Hall's recommendation, Mary Ann hired an excellent nurse to look after the children in her absence, while Junius entrusted the maintenance of The Farm to his father and Joe. In August, Junius and Mary Ann set out for Boston with baby Frederick in her arms and Junius's trunks full of costumes loaded onto the coach. As soon as they were settled at a boardinghouse, Junius began recruiting talent and arranging a slate of performances.

While Junius worked, sweet, curious Frederick offered Mary Ann delightful companionship as she explored Boston. He admired the offerings of farmers' markets and bookstalls with as much wide-eyed awe as he did the museums' art and antiquities, and he offered shy smiles to passersby who paused to admire the handsome mother and son and to compliment her on her child's good behavior.

All the while, Junius resolutely avoided liquor. "If managing a company of vain, temperamental actors does not drive me to drink, nothing shall," he sometimes joked, and Mary Ann would force a smile. She was glad to be with him, to see him sober and working, but it was increasingly apparent to her that at heart he was an actor, not a manager or a businessman. He thrived on enthralling audiences, not counting receipts and paying bills. Running his own theatre, whether in Boston or Baltimore or anywhere else, was not the panacea for the ailments of separation, loneliness, and intemperance they had fervently hoped it would be.

Thus when Junius decided to resign from the Tremont Theatre at the end of October and resume acting, Mary Ann did not object. When he was invited to perform at the Bowery Theatre in New York in early November, Mary Ann encouraged him to accept. "Come with me, you and the boy," Junius urged, but she was suffering from a painful sore throat and fever, so she decided to remain in Boston with Frederick until she recovered enough to return to The Farm.

Not long after Junius departed, Mary Ann's affliction worsened, and within a day, Frederick too fell ill. A week passed in a haze of burning fever and cold sweats, of pain and exhaustion and delirium. She was vaguely aware of her landlady's presence, of gentle hands holding cold compresses to her brow, of a firm voice commanding her to swallow the powders held to her mouth. She heard herself calling out for Junius, begging for Frederick to be brought to her.

Eventually her fever subsided and the fog of illness lifted enough for her to realize that Junius was there, sitting in a chair by the side of her bed, trembling, weeping, his hands clenched around his head as if he wished he could wring misery from the brain within.

It was then that she knew her precious child was dead.

Grief threatened to finish what the disease had begun. By the time Mary Ann had recovered from the relapse enough to beg that her child's remains be prepared for transport to The Farm so that he might slumber peacefully in the beautiful wilderness that had been his first home, his tiny coffin had already been beneath Boston soil a week.

When she was strong enough to travel, Mary Ann returned to The Farm, seeking solace for her unspeakable grief in the hugs and kisses of her four living children. Junius—despairing, grieving, bewildered and shaken to find himself suffering a second time the worst anguish a parent could know—quickly embarked on another tour, hoping to lose himself in work, in a provider's duty, and in the bottle.

Autumn's first frost covered the fields and orchards of The Farm before Mary Ann could bring herself to inform her mother that a grandson she had never met had perished. "I cannot bear to think of the sweetest of my children buried in the cold ground so far from home," she wrote. "I cannot even tend his grave, and I weep to think that it is neglected. Oh, my poor lost babe!"

Mary Ann had not poured out her heart so freely to her mother since girlhood, since the time before she met Junius and deception had irrevocably divided her from her parents. Weeks later, when the post brought her mother's reply, Mary Ann hesitated before reading it, suddenly terrified that her mother would condemn her, that she would blame Mary Ann for Frederick's death, that she would declare it a just punishment for his parents' terrible sin of adultery.

Instead, kindness, compassion, and love filled the pages. "I share your sorrow, my dear daughter," her mother had written. "No one but another parent who has lost a child can truly understand your suffering. Take comfort in knowing that your precious, innocent babe rests peacefully in the arms of our Lord."

Mary Ann wept then, but not only from grief, for in that moment she understood what it was to be forgiven completely, to be loved unconditionally.

Her mother's letter became a well-worn touchstone Mary Ann turned to often throughout the difficult years that followed.

In the aftermath of his son's death, Junius's behavior became increasingly erratic and strange, even frightening. On tour, furious theatre managers had to drag him out of bars where he was entertaining drunken crowds with songs and recitations, and shove him onto stages where it was discovered he was too inebriated to perform. He arrived late for engagements, having missed trains or stagecoaches sleeping off drinking binges. Newspaper reviews praising his sublime genius and declaring him the greatest tragedian of the age were often followed by others denouncing him for canceling performances at the last moment. During a performance of *Richard III* at the Bowery Theatre, Junius's king refused to die as Shakespeare intended but instead fought an astonished Richmond with such fury that he forced him off the stage, up the aisle, and out the front door, swords clashing and gleaming in the gaslights in front of the theatre. A few months later in a performance of *Evadne* in Boston, Junius broke down onstage, forgetting his lines, bursting into laughter and then into tears, and begging to be taken to the lunatic hospital. One winter night, in a state of distraction and derangement, he walked forty miles from Providence to Boston, arriving without his shoes and coat at a boardinghouse for sailors. After word of his arrival spread, a friend, Colonel Josiah Jones, raced over to take charge of him. As the colonel reported to Mary Ann later, Junius had alternated between fits of disorientation and calm lucidity until he was well enough to be escorted to New York, where his most trusted friend, Edwin Forrest, had cared for him until the madness subsided.

"When will Junius be done with these mad freaks?" Richard lamented whenever a new shocking tale appeared in the press or arrived by post.

"He isn't mad," protested Mary Ann. "Among the truly great, genius is often indistinguishable from madness. He's the victim of his art. He assumes his roles so completely that he forgets who he is and where he is for a time, but he always returns to himself. He never suffers these 'mad freaks,' as you call them, when he's at home."

Richard was obliged to concede that point. Junius lived for the stage, but The Farm was the only place he was truly himself. And that was where Mary Ann knew him best. She loved him fiercely—madness, genius, industry, intemperance, everything he was, everything that made him what he was. He was her Byron, and she his devoted muse. Come what may, nothing would ever change that.

Dazed and sick at heart, Mary Ann returned to the parlor and sank down upon the sofa. For more than twenty-five years, a vast ocean and a thick tangle of lies had separated her from her husband's wife, but now Adelaide had come to Baltimore. Lightheaded, Mary Ann felt heat rising in her cheeks even as her hands grew icy cold. She clasped them together in her lap, but that did not cease their trembling.

She was unaware Junius had followed her until he sat beside her on the sofa. "My son Richard has come to America too, and has been here more than a year," he said.

"Why did he come?"

"Perhaps because he hadn't seen his father in ten years, not since my last visit to England."

"Of course. Forgive me—a foolish question." How old would Richard be now—twenty-seven? Twenty-eight? A man grown, surely curious about his long-absent, famous father, and determined to forge the neglected bond that should have been his birthright.

"He may have come because—" Junius hesitated. "The truth is, I haven't sent Adelaide any money in quite some time. I suspect she sent Richard here to confirm that I'm still working, still earning."

"Oh, Junius—" Mary Ann left it there. It would accomplish nothing to scold him for neglecting Adelaide's payments. The damage was done.

When Richard arrived in America, Junius told her, he had been stunned by a new acquaintance's accusation that he could not possibly be the legitimate son of the great tragedian Junius Brutus Booth, for everyone knew that the celebrated tragedian had a beautiful wife and a thriving brood of children in Maryland. Aghast, Richard had settled in Baltimore, where he had quickly discovered his father's secret and had written to his mother urging her to come to America and prove his legitimacy. Adelaide had been in the city five months, watching the house on Exeter Street, gathering evidence, doing nothing to distract Junius from earning money until she could confront him.

"With the manager looking on and the entire cast and crew listening at the keyhole, I could not deny her charges," Junius said. "Nevertheless, I ordered her to return to London. She refused, and she declared that she would not leave America until it was proven in court that she is my true wife and Richard my legitimate son, entitled to all the rights thereof. I could not suffer her another moment, and as I stormed off, she shrilled after me that I should expect to hear from her attorney."

"We'll have to tell the children." Mary Ann rose, wringing her hands, dreading what must come next. "They must hear it from us, not on the streets."

June was away on tour, but Rosalie was in her bedchamber and the four youngest were playing outside. Mary Ann knew she would never forget the children's stunned, pained, bewildered expressions when she and Junius gathered them together and told them, as gently as they could, that their parents were not married, that another woman was their father's wife, and that she had come to demand what she felt he owed her.

Asia's eyes narrowed as she absorbed the news, and Mary Ann could see her shrewd mind at work. "You married that other lady and had a son," she queried her father, "and then five years later you eloped with Mother?"

"It was closer to six years," said Junius, as if each word were an effort, "but yes, daughter, that is so."

Asia frowned. "So *her* six years mean everything, and Mother's twenty-six years with you mean nothing?"

"According to the law, yes."

Asia tossed her head to show exactly what she thought of the law.

Soon thereafter, Adelaide's lawyer presented her terms. In exchange for the enormous sum of two thousand dollars and assurances of the continued payment of her annual stipend, she would forego a lawsuit.

Junius had no choice but to submit. A lawsuit would ruin the family, which was already strained by the shocking revelations. With the decision made and the need to earn money greater than ever, Junius packed his costume trunks and resumed his tour, apologizing profusely for leaving Mary Ann and the children alone in the center of the storm. "We'll pay her off, and that will be the end of it," he said, kissing Mary Ann on his way out the door. "Once she's satisfied, she and Richard will return to Brussels."

"I'm sure they will," Mary Ann said, because she knew he needed to hear it, but a new chill pervading the neighborhood told her that the damage had already been done, and it was irreparable. The previous day, Asia had returned from dance lessons fuming about snide remarks from other students who had overheard their mothers gossiping. Joseph had fled home in tears after his longtime friends said they were not allowed to play with him anymore. Every day Edwin shrank from the bullies who jeered and called him a bastard, but John Wilkes made them pay with his fists, often coming home with a bloodied nose, fresh bruises, and torn clothing.

Hiding her distress, Mary Ann told the children to ignore the taunts and say nothing if anyone asked about their parentage. "Least said, soonest mended," she reminded them, fighting to keep her voice steady, her features smooth. They nodded, Edwin in resignation, Asia mutinously as if to say she would not be cowed into holding her tongue, and John Wilkes with a stubborn frown and fists balled at his sides. Eventually, Mary Ann hoped, Adelaide would take her ransom and go away, and perhaps eventually the unpleasantness would be forgotten.

One afternoon, she was in the parlor sewing a summer pinafore for

Asia when she was startled by a harsh shout in front of the house. Suddenly apprehensive, she rested her hands in her lap and listened, expecting to hear one of the children cry out for her to come tend some injury.

"This is the house of Junius Brutus Booth, whoremaster, his slut Mary Ann Holmes, and their bastard children!"

For a moment it seemed to Mary Ann that her heart stopped.

"This is where the whore lives," the voice shrilled again. "Mary Ann Booth, prostitute and mother of bastards!"

Her ears ringing, Mary Ann forced herself to stand, to cross the room, to conceal herself beside the window and cautiously draw back the curtain. A woman paced back and forth on the sidewalk in front of the house, tall and stout, her gray-and-black hair worn in a loose bun beneath an overlarge hat, her cheeks florid, her face twisted in an ugly scowl. "This is where the tragedian lies with his trollop!" she shouted, glaring this way and that to draw the eye of every passerby, of every startled neighbor peering out a window. "This is where the Holmes bastards wrongly claim the name of Booth!"

Dizzy, Mary Ann let the curtain fall and stumbled into the other room, where she was violently sick in the washbasin.

Adelaide—for the woman could be no one else—abandoned her cruel pageant when her voice grew hoarse and faint, but two days later she reappeared, parading back and forth in front of the house, shouting cruel taunts, accosting neighbors with questions about whether they knew what sordid business went on within the deceptively modest house. A few days later she returned, and then two days of blissful silence, followed by three days of torment.

Onc day John Wilkes came home, his face a blotched mess of tears, blood, and mucus. "The boys at school call you a whore," he sobbed angrily as she tended his wounds. "They say I'm not a Booth, but I am, I know I am."

"You are," she soothed, fighting back tears. "Of course you are, my darling boy."

Mary Ann's letters carried the outrageous news to Junius, who fumed to Adelaide's lawyer through the post that their financial agreement was contingent on her silence. Adelaide countered that she had agreed to forgo a lawsuit, not to refrain from pleading her case in the court of public opinion. If Mary Ann did not care to have her sins aired before her neighbors, she should not have stolen another woman's husband.

As Adelaide's tirades along North Exeter Street persisted, Mary Ann and the children counted the days until Junius finished his tour and the family could withdraw to the countryside for the summer.

Once there, Mary Ann felt herself restored by The Farm's isolation, which had never seemed more wonderful. The headaches and insomnia that had plagued her since Adelaide first confronted Junius disappeared; the children laughed and shouted at play again; the haunted, haggard look faded from Junius's visage. Even the earth and sky seemed to bless their homecoming, with warm sunshine and gentle rains falling upon rich soil that yielded abundant crops. When Mary Ann took her first cartload of vegetables to the Baltimore market, her harvest sold quickly and at favorable prices, and so by late morning she had made a tidy profit. The next two weeks brought similar results, but on the third, she was enjoying a noontime of especially brisk sales when a familiar angry voice shrilled, "Here is the whore Mary Ann Booth, selling vegetables instead of her body for a change!"

Scarcely able to breathe, blood pounding in her ears, Mary Ann began packing up her stall.

"Where are her bastard children?" Adelaide demanded, so painfully loud that she must have been only a few stalls away, though Mary Ann refused to look. "Where is the whoremaster who sired them, the great Junius Brutus Booth, who abandoned his lawful wife and legitimate son to run off with this Covent Garden strumpet?"

Mary Ann's cheeks burned in the heat of what felt like hundreds of curious, demanding stares. With as much dignity as she could muster, she drove the cart away from the market at a measured pace, and eventually Adelaide's voice faded behind her.

She wanted nothing more than to hurry home to her children, her dear sons and daughters who never spoke an unkind or resentful word against her, despite the tribulations inflicted upon them by the choices she had made more than a quarter century before. She wanted to hurry home, but she knew she could not, not with a load of fresh vegetables in her cart and money yet to earn. Instead she took a deep breath to steady her nerves, drove to a market on the east side of the city, and set up her stall in the first vacant spot she could find. The best locations had been claimed hours before, but she did fairly well nonetheless, selling enough of her produce by late afternoon to call it a good day's work.

The next week, she had scarcely set up her market stall when Adelaide again found her. Hiding her distress as best she could, Mary Ann packed up her cart and retreated to the east-side market. The following week she asked Joe Hall to accompany her, and they avoided the more lucrative west-side market altogether and set up the stall in a choice spot on the east-side venue. That day was blessedly free of hostile demonstrations, but Adelaide tracked her down a fortnight later. Mary Ann kept her expression carefully stoic as she packed up and decamped to the west market.

On and on it went, all summer long and into the fall. Angrily Junius offered to go to the market in her place, but he was needed on The Farm, and his presence at the markets would allow Adelaide to create an even more scandalous scene, which was surely exactly what she craved. Mary Ann did not doubt that Adelaide took malicious delight in the visible wounds she inflicted upon her rival—the new gray hairs, the shadows beneath her eyes, the hollows in her cheeks that appeared after sleep and appetite fled.

But humiliating Mary Ann was not all that Adelaide wanted. Soon word came through the lawyers that she intended to sue Junius for divorce on the indisputable charges of abandonment and adultery. Maryland law required a two-year residency in the state before she could file suit, and Mary Ann knew that Adelaide would take great pleasure in making all of their lives miserable in the interim.

Junius could avoid his vengeful wife by embarking on a tour, but he could not go alone. Someone must accompany him to keep him sober, to persuade him to take the stage when melancholy threatened to keep him away, and to collect his pay before he could squander it.

Twenty-five-year-old June was married now, with a life of his own, one he could not abandon to chaperone his father. John Wilkes eagerly volunteered, entranced by the thought of traveling the country and having adventures with his magnificent father rather than staying home and struggling doggedly with his books and lessons. Cheerful, outgoing, strong, and filled with a zest for life, John Wilkes would have been the ideal companion for his father, but he was only nine years old.

At nearly fourteen, Edwin—somber, studious, frail, withdrawn—was chosen instead. He was too dutiful to protest, but his large, expressive eyes fixed on Mary Ann in a silent plea to keep him home and at his studies.

It seemed wrong to take their most intellectual, erudite son out of school and keep their most reluctant scholar in it, and if John Wilkes were only a few years older, perhaps they could have given each boy the role he preferred. But there was nothing to be done, so Edwin resignedly packed a satchel, silently hugged Mary Ann goodbye, and followed along in the shadow of his eccentric, impulsive father to serve as his dresser, aide, and guardian.

John Wilkes and Asia were consumed with jealousy, and nothing Mary Ann said—nothing she was willing to reveal about traveling with the mad genius Junius Brutus Booth—would dispel their notion that Edwin was embarking on a golden holiday. They could not possibly understand the miseries of travel—carriages rattling over rough roads; frigid railroad cars; squalid, vermin-infested hotel rooms; questionable meals; exposure to all manner of disease, filth, and vice. Nor could they fathom how arduous, fraught, and exhausting Edwin's duties were. They knew only that he helped their father don his costumes and rehearse his lines, day and night his constant companion, entertained and enthralled by the sights and sounds of new cities and scenery and the long-forbidden world of the theatre. They could not imagine their slender, withdrawn elder brother blocking the doorway so their father could not leave their hotel room in search of a drink, or trailing after him as he strode through an unfamiliar city all night working off the frenetic energy of a performance, or cajoling him out of a black funk of melancholy and onto the stage. John Wilkes and Asia were too young to understand what they themselves had not experienced, but Mary Ann knew, and worry and regret for her sensitive son often kept her awake late into the night.

As the months passed, the younger children's envy grew. Asia knew that as a girl she could not possibly serve as her father's chaperone, and so she had never expected the honor, but John Wilkes felt greatly wronged to have been left behind to endure the dullness of school and the shame of illegitimacy. Too often he returned home furious and bloodied after defending his mother's honor with his fists. Any boy who dared call Mary Ann a whore and him a bastard never made that mistake in John Wilkes's hearing a second time.

"Am I a Booth, Mother?" he would ask her as she tended his wounds, and she would assure him he was—but with Adelaide and the rest of the Baltimore adamantly insisting that he was not, his uncertainty persisted.

Eventually, although Mary Ann grieved to be parted from her favorite child, she and Junius decided that eleven-year-old John Wilkes must be removed from the neighborhood that had become for him a battlefield. They enrolled him in Milton Academy, a Quaker boarding school in Cockeysville, Maryland, twelve miles from The Farm and yet a world away. It was a very fine place, a three-story stone building with an excellent library and charming views of the countryside. The headmaster, Mr. John Lamb, was a Quaker, so although John Wilkes would receive a rigorous course of study, Mary Ann trusted that he would be treated with kindness, gentleness, and simplicity in all things. They could scarcely afford the tuition—seventy dollars per term, plus an additional ten dollars for Greek and Latin classes—but Mary Ann took comfort in knowing that her darling boy would be safe.

Upon her return from escorting John Wilkes to Cockeysville, Mary Ann managed a tremulous smile as she described for Rosalie, Asia, and Joseph the forested grounds of his new school, the students' plain dress, and the Quakers' quaint custom of addressing one another as "thee" and "thou." Rosalie nodded thoughtfully, Joseph looked faint with relief that his parents had not forced him to enroll with his brother, and Asia bravely declared that she hoped John Wilkes would enjoy himself and learn a lot, but her bleak expression betrayed her misery. Mary Ann's heart went out to her clever, moody daughter. Rosalie was reliable if silent company, and Asia had a few good friends at school, but with John Wilkes gone, life at 62 North Exeter Street and The Farm was certain to be lonelier than she had ever known it.

On the first day of the autumn term, Mary Ann's heart sank as Asia dressed and packed her satchel, her movements slow and deliberate, as if her limbs were weighed down by woe. In years past, John Wilkes had walked Asia to school every morning, unfailingly cheerful, ready with a joke or a funny tale or an adventure to plan. Even if he ran ahead to greet a friend along the way, he always returned to his sister's side before they reached the schoolyard gate. Now Asia would walk alone, forced to endure the whispers and stares and taunts of the other children, suffering for her parents' sins. At least Adelaide would not be among the tormentors, for she had ceased her spiteful vigils outside their home, perhaps tiring of them, perhaps saving up her malice for the inevitable lawsuit.

"Would you like me to walk with you?" Mary Ann offered.

"No," Asia said, too quickly. Mary Ann nodded, understanding that her presence would only make matters worse.

Her expression a study in fierce determination, Asia kissed her mother, bade Rosalie goodbye, and set out for school. As soon as she closed the door behind her, Mary Ann hastened to the front window only to discover that Asia had halted on the porch at the sight of a young man in a thick tweed coat and cap sitting on the bottom step. He turned at the sound of the door closing, and at once Mary Ann recognized the round face, wide brow, and downturned mouth of Edwin's friend John Sleeper.

"Sleepy?" Asia greeted him, bewildered.

He scrambled to his feet. "Hello, Asia."

"Hello." She studied him. "Edwin isn't here."

"I know that."

"John Wilkes isn't here either."

"I know. That's why I thought maybe I should walk you to school instead."

Bristling, Asia glared at him—but suddenly her expression shifted from indignation to pity. Perhaps she detected, as Mary Ann had, something in the set of the young man's jaw that hinted at barely concealed loneliness. With Edwin off on another merry theatrical jaunt with Father, Sleepy too had lost his best friend and closest confidant.

"Thank you," Asia said. "That would be nice."

So Sleepy walked her to school that morning, and he met her outside on the sidewalk almost every day after that. "I can't bring myself to turn him away," Asia admitted to Mary Ann a month later. "I know he's doing it out of friendship for Edwin, but I'm not even sure that I like him."

Mary Ann was fairly certain Sleepy liked Asia, but she kept her observations to herself.

By wintertime, Asia's relentless, determined escort had asked her not to call him Sleepy anymore but to use his given name. "I objected," Asia told Mary Ann afterward. "John's name is too dear to me to squander it on just anyone."

"You call your brother Wilkes."

"Not always. But it doesn't matter, because we agreed that I would call him by his middle name, Clarke." Asia shrugged dismissively. "It's his name, after all, and I hardly care. And yet I don't understand why he insists that *I* call him Clarke, while everyone else still calls him Sleepy."

"Who knows?" said Mary Ann, though she was quite sure that she did. Asia was only fourteen, but Sleepy, a year older than Edwin, was seventeen, no longer a child. Sleepy often played the clown, but he would have to be a fool indeed not to see that Asia was not only his best friend's sister but also a blossoming young beauty.

Milton Academy's curriculum was so rigorous that John Wilkes could visit his family only rarely, and privately Mary Ann lamented that she saw little more of him than of Edwin, whose somber, haunted gaze revealed that his travels with his father had aged him beyond his years. Whenever Junius brought him home for brief visits, Edwin's exhaustion and relief and unmistakable yearning to stay pained Mary Ann deeply, but what choice did the family have? Junius must tour and he must perform or they would all starve, and there was no certainty that he would do either without a guardian—much to Mary Ann's consternation. He was a man grown, and a man ought to be able to control his vices and conduct his own affairs. Sometimes she thought she might burst from the strain of repressing her anger and disappointment and fear, but she dared not rail at him. She would not become a shrew, complaining and criticizing, tearing him down when he needed so desperately for her to build him up, to hold him together. Their home must remain his safe haven, free of judgment and recriminations, or he might grow despondent and decide not to return to it.

Then Edwin wrote from Boston to inform her of his stage debut, when he had been obliged to fill in at the last moment as Tressel to his father's Richard III. A fortnight later he portrayed Cassio in *Othello* at the Providence Museum, and two days later he played the virtuous secretary Wilford opposite his father's villainous Sir Edward Mortimer in *The Iron Chest*. It seemed impossible that her sensitive, reserved, intelligent son could have taken the stage against his father's wishes, forcing Mary Ann to wonder and worry that perhaps Junius, flinging away his earlier decree that his children would not be actors, had instead bullied Edwin into the company for the sake of his wages.

John Wilkes lacked the empathy to worry as his mother did, and saw only treachery in his elder brother's accomplishments. "None of us were to be actors like Father," he protested when he returned home in February for a brief holiday between terms. "First June, now Edwin. Why not me? Why do I have to go to school?"

"Education is a privilege," Mary Ann reminded him. "Edwin longs to attend Milton Academy as you do."

"I'd gladly change places with him." John Wilkes's handsome features, usually as sunny as spring, had darkened into a scowl. "Acting is the family trade."

"It isn't, but even if it were, it's not the trade your father wants for you."

What John Wilkes could not comprehend was that Edwin's additional obligations as a player had only doubled his toil. In April, tearful and exhausted, he begged his parents to allow him a fortnight at home, and Mary Ann resolved that he should have all the rest he needed. She wished June could take his younger brother's place, but not quite a year before, he had abandoned his wife and child for the allure of the gold fields of California and the company of a pretty young actress. Privately Mary Ann and Junius lamented, but they realized it would be the height of hypocrisy if they condemned June for what they themselves had done, so they did not rebuke him in their letters, but only urged him to be careful, to write to them often, and to remember his financial responsibilities to his young daughter.

With June unavailable, Junius was obliged to set out for Richmond without the steadying presence of a sober companion. He departed cheerfully enough, with fond embraces for Mary Ann and the children and promises to visit as soon and as often as he could. "I swear to you, darling," he vowed as he departed, holding her by the shoulders and kissing her firmly, "I shall indulge in nothing stronger than coffee and tea while I'm away."

Mary Ann was glad to hear it, but soon thereafter she received word via a telegram from the outraged manager of the Marshall Theatre that Junius had never arrived. Frantic, Mary Ann sent off a flurry of telegrams to theatre acquaintances, but no one knew where Junius had gone. He had simply disappeared.

"I'm sorry, Edwin, darling," Mary Ann said, her voice shaking as she packed his suitcase. "Someone must be sent, and there is no one else."

"I understand," he said dully, but he could barely meet her gaze when she saw him off at the train station.

Several anxious days passed before Edwin sent word that he had found his father wandering drunk and disoriented in the countryside north of Richmond. Junius's pocketbook was empty, forcing Edwin to borrow fifty dollars from local theatre friends to pay for their fare to Baltimore. When at last the weary travelers reached home, Mary Ann's heart broke to see the resignation and misery in Edwin's eyes. He knew he could never again expect to be granted leave from his duties as his father's keeper.

At long last summer approached, promising freedom from schoolwork for the children and a welcome escape to The Farm for Mary Ann. Since Junius and Edwin were away fulfilling his last obligations of the theatre season, when Mary Ann was asked to attend a picnic at Milton Academy to celebrate the end of John Wilkes's school year, she invited Asia to accompany her.

They set out early in the morning, Mary Ann attired in a lovely pale gray gown and a hat adorned with lilacs, Asia wearing her best white dress and a bonnet adorned with daisies. The train carried them to Cockeysville, where they and several other parents and visitors continued on by wagon to Milton Academy. The wagon rumbled along over rocks and tree roots through a dense woodland of tall trees and thick underbrush until they reached a broad, uneven clearing. Several neat, sturdy buildings of stone and oak stood on the far edge, and as they approached the largest, Mary Ann saw that long tables were arranged in rows before it, and three hundred or so students and guests mingled nearby.

As two young Quaker men helped the ladies down from the wagon, Mary Ann glimpsed her son among the crowd of boys who had sauntered over to welcome the newcomers. "Wilkes," Asia cried, laughing from joy at the sight of his warm, familiar smile. He looked well, so happy and strong that Mary Ann's heart nearly burst from gladness.

Soon thereafter, faculty, students, and guests seated themselves at the long tables, making no distinction of rank or place, and enjoyed generous portions of delicious, wholesome, simple fare. After the meal, the headmaster led them to a sunny clearing around the north end of the main building, where a stage had been erected for student recitations. The audience was nearly put to sleep by a young boy stammering out a Wordsworth poem, only to be spellbound moments later by a lad of about twelve years of age who delivered a remarkably stirring soliloquy from *Othello*.

"He's quite good," Mary Ann whispered to John Wilkes, seated beside her, her gaze fixed on the performer. "He has an excellent voice and a commanding stage presence, don't you agree?"

When John Wilkes did not reply, Mary Ann glanced his way to find him nodding nervously, his face pale. Before she could ask him if he was ill, he bolted to his feet and strode to the foot of the stairs leading up to the stage, awaiting his cue.

Asia muffled a gasp and seized her mother's hand. John Wilkes had not told them he intended to perform. They both forgot to applaud as the young Othello bowed deeply several times before ceding the stage to John Wilkes.

He flew up the stairs and burst upon the stage in a fury. "I say my daughter is my flesh and blood," he declared, trembling with Shylock's anger and despondency. Nearby, a tutor read out the lines of Salarino, Tubal, and the servant, but John Wilkes alone commanded the stage, bringing to life the old Jewish merchant's storm of passion, his ebb of despair, his wild rejoicing.

Mary Ann watched him, enthralled. A stunned, awestruck silence followed his exit, but a thunderous crash of applause quickly shattered it. John Wilkes was called back upon the stage, smiling and blushing, to bow again and again.

"Who is this young player?" queried an elderly Quakeress seated on Asia's other side as John Wilkes took one last bow and quit the stage. "Does thee know his name? He is a comely youth."

"He's my brother," Asia replied proudly as the applause faded and another pupil took the stage, his expression frightened and wary. He would be a difficult act to follow, as Junius might have said had he been there. He would not have objected to his son's taking the stage for a simple school recitation, Mary Ann told herself, hoping it was true. He had lifted the prohibition for June and Edwin, after all, and John Wilkes had acquitted himself well.

Suddenly a motion in the corner of her eye drew her attention, and she glanced over to discover John Wilkes crouched low behind his sister, tugging on her sleeve. "Slip away from 'thee' and 'thou' and meet me over there in the hollow," he murmured, grinning mischievously. "I've something to tell."

He darted off, and with an apologetic, imploring look for their mother, Asia swiftly followed.

"John, Asia," Mary Ann whispered sharply, drawing disapproving stares from those seated nearby. When her children neither halted nor replied, she muffled a sigh and went after them, murmuring apologies to the spectators whose view she obstructed in passing.

She walked quickly, but John Wilkes and Asia easily outpaced her, and the sounds of the ongoing performance faded behind her as she hastened after them through a stand of trees. It broke open upon a shady hollow, where she discovered John Wilkes sprawled out upon the soft, thick grass, gazing up at the sky through the branches high overhead. "Sis," he exclaimed when Asia reached him, and as she caught her breath, he took her hand and tugged playfully, pulling her to a seat beside him. "I have a curious tale to share."

A strange note in his voice compelled Mary Ann to halt rather than join her children in the clearing. Instead she concealed herself in the shadows of the trees, straining her ears to listen.

"Tell me all," she heard Asia demand, with mock seriousness. "Leave out no detail."

Grinning, John Wilkes leaned his head back against her knees and dug into his pocket for a folded piece of paper. "A band of gypsies has been prowling hereabouts, and one of them told me my fortune."

"What did she say?" Asia teased, trying in vain to snatch the paper from his grasp. "That you'll find your heart's desire? That fame and fortune will be yours? Or perhaps she gave you the answers to your history exam?"

"Nothing so good as that." Still grinning, John Wilkes unfolded the paper. "I wrote it down, but there was no need, because it was so bad I won't soon forget it."

"What do you mean?"

He shrugged, nonchalant, or making a good pretense of it. "She studied my palm and saw only ill fortune." Glancing at the paper, he cleared his throat and spoke in the voice of an old crone. "'Ah, you've a bad hand; the lines all crisscross. It's full enough of sorrow. Full of trouble. Trouble in plenty, everywhere I look. You'll break hearts; they'll be nothing to you. You'll die young, and leave many to mourn you, many to love you too, but you'll be rich, generous, and free with your money. You're born under an unlucky star. You've got in your hand a thundering crowd of enemies—not one friend—you'll make a bad end, and have plenty to love you afterwards. You'll have a fast life—short, but a grand one. No, young sir, I've never seen a worse hand, and I wish I hadn't seen it, but every word I've told is true by the signs. You'd best turn a missionary or a priest and try to escape it.'"

"Why, that's nonsense, Wilkes," Asia protested, shuddering. "The proof is in her own words. You have many friends, and no enemies except for those silly boys back home, and they can't count for much."

"I guess that's so," John Wilkes admitted, slowly refolding the paper. "I asked her, if it's in the stars or in my hand, how could I escape my fate, even if I did join the clergy?"

"You can't mean you'd really do *that*, all because of one old woman's wild ramblings."

"Of course not. Me, a minister?" John shook his head. "Afterward I said to her, 'Do you expect me to pay you for this evil dose?' Well, she did. She took my money all right, and said she was glad she wasn't a younger woman, or she'd follow me through the world for my handsome face."

He laughed merrily, but Asia could barely manage a smile.

Deeply troubled, Mary Ann silently withdrew and returned to her seat in the audience, where she sat through the remaining recitations, brooding over the gypsy's dark tidings and her own vision of John Wilkes's future that she had glimpsed in the fire when he was but a babe in her arms.

She imagined the Fates contemplating the tapestry of her son's destiny—Clotho spinning the thread of his life from distaff to spindle, Lachesis measuring its length, Atropos dispassionately cutting it, determining the manner and hour of his death. "Be kind," she implored in a whisper, though she knew the mythical Fates were creatures of imagination and superstition, impervious to her pleas.

She pushed the unsettling image aside, and another swiftly took its place—Junius, declaiming from the stage in the role of Julius Caesar. " 'Men at some time are masters of their fates,' " she murmured, remembering. " 'The fault, dear Brutus, is not in our stars, but in ourselves, that we are underlings.' "

Whether Shakespeare had intended to encourage or to warn, she could not say.

At long last, Adelaide's required period of residency was completed. She promptly sued Junius for divorce, whipping up a new frenzy in the press. Junius did not contest her suit, and before long the matter was settled, and the decades-long sham of a marriage was over.

Soon thereafter, Junius asked Mary Ann to marry him.

She was startled by how intensely his proposal pleased her, and yet, despite her certainty that he loved her dearly, something held her back. "After thirty years, you would ask me to submit to—what did you call it back in London? The iron yoke of marriage?"

He took her hands. "We will submit to it together, for the children's sake."

With great effort, she refrained from noting that the yoke lay lighter upon his shoulders than hers. She had given him a peaceful home, adoring children, the work of her hands, her beauty, her life. He had given her love and passion and fidelity, but also innumerable hours of worry and immeasurable anxiety. For his sake she had broken with her parents, betrayed her faith, ruined her good name—and yet without Junius, her world would have been constrained to a few city blocks of London, circumscribed by her home, her church, the flower shop, the Covent Garden market. She might never have known what it was like to be truly, completely, ardently loved, to live the sort of passion other people only read about in Byron's poetry. Her darling children would not have existed, and she could not imagine life without them. Nor could she imagine living without Junius—but it seemed impossible that they could continue on as they had done, now that no impediment stood between them and lawful marriage. The public had a long memory for scandal, and with each passing year, the burden of the choices she and Junius had made would grow heavier upon their children's shoulders, more bewildering, more unfair.

And so Mary Ann accepted Junius's proposal.

They married on the tenth day of May 1851, John Wilkes's thirteenth birthday. "At last we are respectable," Mary Ann told her husband wryly as they walked home from the courthouse, her gloved hand on his arm. Earlier that morning he had declared that she was as beautiful as on the day they first met, and she had laughed, well aware that love altered his perception. Though hard toil and care had kept her from growing stout, she had lost her girlish grace and her once glossy black hair had faded. Worry and contemplation had marked her brow with a pair of indelible lines, with finer ones etched in the corners of her eyes and mouth. For his part Junius had grown a trifle stockier, and drink and dissipation had marred his noble face with fine red veins and bags beneath his eyes, but his gaze was as piercing and expressive as before, and she found him no less handsome. If anything, she found him more beautiful and loved him all the more for knowing his faults and how valiantly he fought to overcome them.

Later that evening, John Wilkes found her alone in the garden, lost in thought, her gaze fixed on the wedding band Junius had slipped onto her finger only a few hours before. His arms were rigid by his sides, his hands balled into fists, his jaw set, his eyes flaring with anger and triumph.

"Now I am a Booth," he said emphatically, but she was his mother, and she heard the lingering question in his voice.

"Yes, darling boy, you are," she said, holding out her arms to him, drawing him into her embrace. "You are John Wilkes Booth, and let no one deny it."

CHAPTER TWO

ASIA

1851–1864

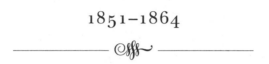

Time shall unfold what plighted cunning hides,
Who covers faults at last with shame derides.
—William Shakespeare,
King Lear, Act 1, Scene 1

Although her parents had insisted that nothing would change after they were legally wed, it seemed to Asia that a heavy burden had been lifted from her mother's shoulders, and Father became exultant, even triumphant. Declaring that the Booth family had entered a joyous new era, he resolved to build them a beautiful new residence in the Gothic style on The Farm, and he immediately hired James Johnson Gifford, the architect of the Holliday Street Theatre, to supervise the construction. Asia and her siblings marveled at the artist's renderings of the elegant two-story, eight-room cottage in the shape of a cross, which boasted a massive central chimney, a broad front portico, steeply pitched gables, and diamond-pane windows.

"That's the room I want for myself," Wilkes announced one afternoon as he and Asia spread out the plans on the dining-room floor and studied them while Mother and Rosalie set the table for supper. He pointed to a bedchamber on the second floor, and with his arm extended, the cuff of his sleeve shifted to reveal fine black markings like spindly veins on the back of his left hand.

"Wilkes, what did you do?" Asia whispered, seizing his hand. Half-heartedly he tried to pull away, but she held fast, muffling a gasp when she discovered the initials JWB surrounded by a wreath of stars crudely pricked into his fine, smooth skin with India ink. "Wilkes, a tattoo? What were you thinking?"

Wilkes extricated himself from her grasp just as Mother glanced questioningly their way. In unison the brother and sister lowered their gazes to the plans, but as soon as Mother resumed her work, Wilkes whispered, "I'm a true son of Junius Brutus Booth, and I want everyone to know it. I'm no bastard. I'm as good as anyone. That's what I was thinking."

Often thereafter, Asia spotted him rubbing his right thumb absently over his homemade tattoo, as if reassuring himself that the initials were indeed his by right.

Whenever Mother murmured about the rising construction expenses, Father quieted her with kisses and declared, "My dear wife must have a home befitting our great love." That never failed to bring a soft brightness to her eyes and roses to her cheeks, and she confided to Asia that she would be glad to move up from the old log cabin that had come with the property, for the family had outgrown it long ago. Father invited Joe and Ann Hall, their faithful longtime employees, to make the cabin their home, a gift that was gratefully accepted.

Construction on Tudor Hall, as Father had christened the new residence in honor of Henry Tudor, the earl of Richmond and slayer of King Richard III, continued after Wilkes returned to Milton Academy and all through the winter and into the spring. It was not yet complete when June unexpectedly returned to Baltimore.

Mother wept from joy to embrace her eldest child again after three long years, but Asia was so astonished to see her eldest brother that at first she could only stare and wonder. It was unmistakably him—a bit thinner and weathered, and more careful in his speech, but otherwise seeming little changed for his three years in San Francisco. Strikingly handsome at thirty years of age, June had inherited their father's noble features and Roman profile but none of his dramatic genius, or so Asia had overheard her parents lament. He was an excellent athlete, a powerful boxer, and an impressively skilled swordsman. Those talents had kept him steadily employed as a reliable actor in supporting roles, but it was in management and directing that he excelled.

Mother immediately sent Joseph running to the Holliday Street Theatre to tell Father of his namesake's return. "My boy! My boy," Father exclaimed as he burst into the house with Edwin and Joseph on his heels, and tears filled his eyes as he embraced June. "It's glorious to see you. Why didn't you send word that you were coming? Have you come home to stay?"

"Why didn't Miss Harriet Mace accompany you?" Asia inquired, for that was surely the most interesting question; no one else would be bold enough to ask about the woman for whom June had abandoned his wife and daughter.

"Asia," Mother admonished gently.

But June smiled affably, not offended. "I sent you a long letter before I set sail from San Francisco. Didn't you receive it? I don't expect to stay more than a fortnight, and that, dear Asia, is why Harriet remained in San Francisco."

If only Wilkes were there to make the family circle complete, Asia thought wistfully as they gathered around the supper table and June enthralled them with tales of his adventures in far-off California. In the three years he and Harriet had lived in San Francisco, it had transformed from a frontier settlement of a few hundred haphazard shacks in the mud to a thriving city of fifty thousand residents, the population swelled by gold miners, aspiring prospectors, and a great many entrepreneurs eager to part them from their earnings.

"Unless you've seen it, you can't imagine the wealth pouring into San Francisco," said June. "Fortunes are plucked from streams every day, or earned by merchants peddling picks and shovels and sieves. I've seen men buy houses with gold nuggets as big as my thumb."

Except for gold, June told them, above all things Californians craved entertainment. Many of the first public buildings constructed in San Francisco were theatres, but so few truly talented players performed in the West that those who were willing to leave their comfortable situations in the East for the rustic frontier were appreciated all the more. "Prospectors often throw purses of gold on the stage to reward a player that has particularly pleased them," June said. "After performances, the cast and crew sweep the stage and divide up the gold dust they gather."

"Really?" asked Joseph, awestruck.

"Yes, really." Grinning, June reached across the table to tousle his younger brother's hair, but then he sat back and fixed an expectant gaze upon Father. "The people of San Francisco and Sacramento yearn for entertainment of the highest quality. They would pay generously to see the great tragedian Junius Brutus Booth."

June explained that he had been hired as the stage manager for the new Jenny Lind Theatre in Portsmouth Square, a magnificent, beautifully appointed playhouse with seating for two thousand. For months, his partners—and every theatergoer who learned who his father was—had begged him to persuade the celebrated thespian to tour California. "You could earn a fortune, Father, more than enough to justify the long journey."

"The long, very difficult, and very dangerous journey, I think you mean," said Mother.

"You flatter me, son," said Father, his expressive brow furrowing, "but lately I've contemplated retirement, not undertaking the most arduous tour of my career."

"All the more reason to seize this opportunity to reap great profits before you pack away your costumes for good," said June. "Just think how eagerly audiences will fill the theatres—and how handsomely they'll reward you—if they believe this may be their last chance to see you perform." He turned to Edwin. "You'll earn a fortune too. You'll have your pick of roles, as many and as varied as you could possibly want."

"What if I don't want any roles?" Edwin's dark eyes revealed a deep unhappiness, the set of his jaw a mutinous determination. "What if I don't want to go?"

"Yes, Junius, what of that?" said Mother. "Edwin is eighteen. He's served you faithfully for six years. Shouldn't he be permitted to resume his education, if he wishes?"

"If Edwin doesn't want to join the tour, he needn't," said June. "I'm happy to serve as Father's escort, valet, dresser—whatever he needs."

"In that case," said Father, avoiding his wife's eye, "I'd be a fool not to consider it."

In the days that followed, Asia often came upon her parents conferring in strained whispers, her father enumerating their many financial concerns, her mother anxiously reminding him of the hardships and dangers of travel. Whether her father wore down her mother or simply overruled her, Asia did not know, but before long Father announced his decision: He would seek fortune and acclaim in California, June would escort him, and Edwin would remain behind to resume his long-neglected education.

In late June, Junius Brutus Booth Senior and Junior departed for New York, stopping along the way at Milton Academy to bid farewell to Wilkes. In their absence, Edwin seemed to brighten by the hour. He and Mother animatedly discussed enrolling him in school in the fall, and perhaps engaging a tutor in the meantime to fill the gaps in his education and spare him embarrassment. Edwin had such a quick, shrewd mind that Asia had no doubt he would soon make up for the years of neglect.

Thus it was a shock to them all a few days later when her father's telegram threw Edwin's fledgling plans into disarray. Immediately upon arriving in New York, Father's courage had fled, replaced by overwhelming loneliness and apprehension. June was loyal and amiable, but Edwin knew their father's quirks and routines, his preferences and fears, and had proven himself adept at anticipating and sorting out problems before the great thespian knew anything was amiss. Father begged Edwin to join him before their steamer left for Panama, or he could not possibly go to California.

Asia felt a pang of sympathy as all hope drained from her brother's expression. "You don't have to go," she told him as he read the telegram a second time. Mother, her eyes filling with tears, wordlessly nodded.

"If I don't," he replied dully, "the tour will be canceled."

"Then let it be canceled," Asia said.

"We can't afford that. We all know it."

"Oh, Edwin," Mother lamented, sinking into a chair. "I had hoped to spare you this."

"Never mind." Woodenly, Edwin bent to kiss her forehead. "I'm not my father's favorite, but at least I know he needs me."

After telegraphing his assent to Father and June, Edwin quickly packed for the journey with help from his mother and sisters. Mother assembled a wardrobe suitable for the tropical climate—two straw hats to protect him from the intense sun and heavy rains, several linen shirts and trousers, and sturdy boots for the hike over the isthmus. "I've packed a few of your costumes too," she told him on the morning of his departure, her voice trembling. "You'll surely be asked to perform your usual roles in *Richard III* and *Othello.*"

He thanked her sincerely but without enthusiasm, and Asia grieved to see that the old look of haunted misery had already returned to his eyes.

Edwin reached New York in time to board the steamer and set out for Panama with his father and elder brother. And then there was nothing for those left behind to do but wait, anxious and apprehensive, for word that the men had reached their destination safely. News came sparsely and sporadically, so they learned well after the fact that the travelers had reached the warm azure waters of the Florida Keys, that their ship had put in at Jamaica and Cuba to take on more coal, that the vessel had arrived at the Isthmus of Panama. It seemed to Asia that she and her mother and Rosalie held their breaths during the interminable, anxious days while the men traveled by canoe up the Chagres River, winding through the lush, perilous rain forest to Gorgona, where they would journey on through rocky, mountainous terrain on foot and by pack mule. Even when word came that the travelers had reached Panama City, the family back at home could not breathe a sigh of relief, for cholera was epidemic in the city, and the men were obliged to isolate themselves in a hotel room to avoid contagion until the steamship *California* arrived to transport them a fortnight's journey north up the coast of Mexico and California.

Only after Asia, Mother, and Rosalie learned that the *California* had arrived safely at San Francisco on July 28, and that their loved ones were in good health and high spirits, did the unrelenting tension ease. Two days later, Father opened his tour at the Jenny Lind Theatre in the role of Sir Edward Mortimer in *The Iron Chest* to admiring reviews. After a fortnight in San Francisco, they moved on to the American Theatre in Sacramento, where Father would have a brief engagement before venturing farther inland to towns and settlements closer to the gold fields.

In the meantime, life in Baltimore went on as ever, infinitely less exciting than Asia imagined the California tour to be. Wilkes came home from school for the summer recess, which was wonderful, but with Tudor Hall still under construction and the old cabin occupied by Joe and Ann Hall and their children, the Booths could not withdraw to the comfort and peaceful solitude of their country estate for the summer. The only scandal worth writing to California about was that Edwin's friend John Clarke Sleeper, who had been studying law at his mother's insistence, had abandoned his books to become an actor, commencing his new career with a regular engagement at the Chestnut Street Theatre in Philadelphia. He wrote Asia an odd, abrupt letter in which he told her he had changed his name to John Clarke, because no actor wanted to be considered a sleeper on the stage, but Asia should continue to call him Clarke, as she had since she was fourteen.

"I suppose he wants me to tell Edwin," Asia said dubiously after reading his letter aloud to Mother and Rosalie, and felt heat rise in her cheeks when they exchanged a knowing look. Clarke was *not* courting her—and if he thought he was, he had better stop it.

A t the end of the summer, fourteen-year-old Wilkes and twelve-year-old Joseph too left home, enrolling as cadets at St. Timothy's Hall in Catonsville, a military academy established during the Mexican War to educate future generations of officers and soldiers. St. Timothy's counted the sons of some of Maryland's finest families among its pupils, with the expectation that they would become the next leaders of business and government. Mother's cheeks had flushed with pride when the acceptance letters had come, and before he set off on tour, Father had embraced them both and told them he was certain they would bring honor to the Booth name.

Wilkes was proud of his steel-gray cadet's uniform, but although Asia admitted he looked dashing in it, she found the academy's twenty-four-page rule book, with its emphasis on order, discipline, and obedience to authority, severe and intimidating. "I'll enjoy the challenge, a taste of the soldier's life," Wilkes assured her. "Maybe I'll become a general, like George Washington. Wouldn't that have made Grandfather proud?"

In mid-September Wilkes and Joseph set out from Baltimore on a thirteen-mile train ride to Catonsville, but soon, Wilkes's letters home hinted at deep displeasure with the strict military regimen he had been so eager to experience. A clanging bell jolted the cadets awake every morning at half past five o'clock, spurring them to leap from bed, form an orderly line, and march off to the washroom, where they scrubbed their hands and faces in a common trough of frigid water. Dried and dressed, they then marched to the classroom for exercises in penmanship and mental arithmetic, and only afterward were they permitted to assemble in the dining hall and quell their growling stomachs with breakfast. Military drills in accordance to the United States Army's infantry manual and classes in religious studies rounded out the day, until the cadets dropped into their beds at twilight, too exhausted for mischief. Before dawn the next morning, the wearing routine began anew, with only Wednesday and Sunday afternoons off to give them a much-needed respite.

"Something is rotten in the state of Denmark," Wilkes wrote cryptically, as if he believed his letters were opened and read before being posted.

With rising dread, Asia feared that it was only a matter of time until Wilkes either escaped his prison or rebelled against his jailers. Joseph would fare well enough—in fact, the academy might be the making of him—but Wilkes's expansive, joyous nature was not meant to be constricted to military regimen and rule. If not for his new friends, with whom he formed bonds of affinity forged in hardship, she doubted that Wilkes could endure the term. Asia was not surprised to learn that the same charisma that inspired affection and admiration at home would draw his fellow cadets to him, especially in such a harsh and unloving environment. His cheerfulness, affability, generosity, and zest for life must have offered the other lonely, homesick boys a light of hope in a very dark place.

Trusting that his new friends would sustain Wilkes when she could not, Asia fervently hoped that her brother's strict taskmasters would not bludgeon all the fine qualities she loved best out of him and fill him up with military pomp and nonsense.

As autumn passed, letters home from California became even more worrisome than those from St. Timothy's. Despite positive reviews and appreciative audiences, the tour was not succeeding as June had promised and Father had expected. In Sacramento, torrential rains had forced gold prospecting to a halt, the swollen river had flooded the city, and the muddy streets had become impassable mires. Theatres closed, supplies dwindled, expenses soared, and even the plainest food became scarce. Miserable and weary, Father resolved to return to Baltimore immediately, and since he had not yet earned the fortune June had promised, he demanded that his son pay the difference from his own purse—two thousand dollars, or nearly every penny June had to his name.

Soon thereafter, June wrote that they had returned to San Francisco as soon as the road had become passable. June had gone home to Miss Harriet Mace and his job as stage manager of the Jenny Lind. Edwin, adamantly refusing to serve as his father's attendant any longer, had joined a group of traveling players in a wild scheme to perform for the laborers in the distant mining camps in the Sierras. Before parting company, the brothers had put their father aboard a steamer to Panama City with his trunks packed full of costumes, a collection of seashells he had gathered on a Mexican beach, and a great many bags of gold dust, his earnings from the tour as well as the payment he had extracted from June.

"They sent Father alone?" Asia exclaimed, taking the letter from her mother to read it for herself.

"They couldn't have." Mother shook her head in disbelief and sank into a chair. "They shouldn't have."

"But why didn't Edwin seize the opportunity to come home? He never wanted to go on this tour. Why join a group of traveling players in the wilderness when he could have seen Father safely home and then given up the stage once and for all?"

"Perhaps because Edwin knows no other trade, and believes it's too late to pursue his education." Mother shook her head, her expression clouded with regret and worry. "Perhaps because, although he took to the stage reluctantly, he's discovered that he's an extraordinarily gifted actor, and he has accepted his fate willingly."

"He could have brought Father home and accepted his fate in Baltimore," said Asia sharply, but in reply, her mother only sighed.

So commenced another torturous period of anxious waiting, broken by an alarming letter from a stranger, a wealthy Texan who had encountered Father at the port of Chagres on the Caribbean coast of the Isthmus of Panama. Somewhere between San Francisco and Chagres, Father had been robbed of every last sack of gold and had been stranded, penniless and distressed, with no means to continue his journey. The kindhearted Texan explained that upon recognizing the famous tragedian, he had been moved by Father's plight, had paid his fare, and had seen him safely aboard a steamer to New Orleans.

At this Mother broke down in tears, but she quickly composed herself and sent off a flurry of letters to theatre friends in the Southern port city, imploring them to watch for her husband's ship and look after him upon his arrival. And then, days later, good news at last—Father wrote from New Orleans to say that he had been engaged at the St. Charles Theatre. He expected to receive more than one thousand dollars for a week of performances, after which he would take a steamer to Cincinnati, and from there he would board a train home to Baltimore.

Mother paced and wrung her hands. "Perhaps I should travel to New Orleans and escort him safely home."

"It would do no good," said Asia. "Even if you left today, by the time you'd arrive, Father would have already left. You'd pass somewhere on the Mississippi and never know it."

On the last day of November, Mother received a telegram from another stranger, the captain of the Mississippi riverboat *J. S. Chenoweth*. Her husband was gravely ill, the captain had tersely reported from Louisville, and she must meet the ship at its next destination.

Swiftly, Asia and Rosalie helped their mother pack a satchel with enough clothing for a few days as well as cordials and medicines. Alone, Mother set out on the next train for Cincinnati, leaving her daughters at home to await word as patiently as they could. "Mother will nurse Father back to health in due time," Asia assured Rosalie, who replied with a bleak, silent look, full of doubt.

Asia hastened to prepare a sickroom, but her activity was cut short by a telegram from Mother in Cincinnati.

Father had died of dysentery on the riverboat before the captain had wired Mother to meet him, before the steamer had even put in at Louisville. In truth, Mother had been summoned to retrieve her husband's remains.

· · ·

For three days Father lay in state in the parlor, the walls draped with mourning white, the portraits and mirrors covered, all adornments removed except a marble bust of Shakespeare, which seemed to gaze down upon the late tragedian through the thick glass plate in the coffin lid with sorrow and regret, willing him to rise. Truly, he looked to Asia as if he might heed the Bard's silent plea, for when the iron coffin had been brought into the house, her father's noble visage had appeared so lifelike, so uncorrupted, that she dared hope he yet lived.

"Darling, I'm so sorry," her mother had choked through her heavy black veil, her voice broken and shaking, "but it is useless. He is lost to us."

Mother had reached for her, but Asia had eluded her grasp and, half-blinded by tears, had gone running for the doctor to rouse her father from what she hoped was merely a state of deep unconsciousness. But of course the doctor could do nothing for them, nothing but confirm that the great, beloved man was truly gone.

Wilkes and Joseph had been summoned home from school, and they joined their mother and their sisters in keeping vigil by their father's catafalque as hundreds of citizens from every rank and station in life called to pay their respects—white and colored, theatre folk and theatre patrons, longtime friends and admiring strangers who had never exchanged a word with Father but revered him as the genius tragedian who had enthralled them from the stage.

June and Edwin were not among the family numbly thanking the callers for their prayers and good wishes. As soon as she returned home from Cincinnati, Mother had written to both absent sons in care of June, having no idea how to reach Edwin in the Sierra Nevada. She urged them not to come home for her sake but to remain in California to work and, with any luck, to earn their fortunes. "They will hear of their father's death by other means before this sad letter reaches them," she told Asia as she sealed it, her voice an aching, broken lament.

The thought of her distant brothers' shock when they read of their father's death in the papers pained Asia, but there was nothing to be done. The dreadful tidings spread with the lightning speed of the telegraph, drawing a shower of letters and telegrams of condolence upon the home at 62 Exeter Street. Newspapers in cities across the nation eulogized her father in the most somber, respectful phrases, declaring him without equal on the stage in life and immortal in death. Theatre folk from Boston to New Orleans vowed to wear black crepe on their left arms for thirty days in his honor. Poets composed memorial odes to his artistic brilliance, now lost to bereft audiences on both sides of the Atlantic. But knowledge of these and other tributes scarcely registered on hearts numb from sorrow and disbelief. Even as Asia gazed upon her father lying in repose, she could not believe that he was dead, that a mere disease could have quenched the inexhaustible fire of his genius.

On the frigid afternoon of Saturday, December 11, Reverend Atkinson of Christ Church presided over Father's funeral services in the parlor, with the family, the Baltimore Dramatic Association, members of several Baltimore orchestras, and many friends in attendance. After the last benediction, the minister led the mourners in a slow procession upon a crunching blanket of icy snow while thick flakes whirled overhead, two miles through the city streets to Baltimore Cemetery. A band played a dirge composed in Father's honor as his coffin was ceremoniously interred in a mausoleum, awaiting burial when the ground thawed in the spring.

When the door clanged shut, Asia recoiled as if she had been struck, pressing her lips together to hold back a sob. All around her the crowd of mourners began to disperse, but she stood frozen in place, her gaze fixed upon the mausoleum.

"June and Edwin never should have let Father travel alone," Wilkes muttered close to her ear. "They dumped him aboard that steamer as if he were a parcel and walked away. June I can almost forgive. His life, his home, his lady—they're all in California. But Edwin—" He shook his head, his eyes red-rimmed, his handsome face pale with outrage. "Edwin never should have left Father's side."

"You can't blame our brothers. They couldn't have known Father would fall ill."

"I never would have abandoned Father as they did," Wilkes countered. "Would *you* have sent him on his way alone?"

Choking back sobs, Asia shook her head. They all knew their father, knew his weaknesses. Sending him on such a long journey unaccompanied was negligence and utter madness. But she could not condemn her absent brothers, knowing how bitterly they would condemn themselves when they learned of their fatal mistake.

"I can and do blame them." Hands thrust into his coat pockets, Wilkes turned and strode away, but not before she heard him add, "Edwin most of all."

Soon thereafter, Wilkes and Joseph returned to St. Timothy's Hall, and to Asia it felt as if they had taken the last air and light and warmth of home with them.

In the days that followed, Asia helped her mother piece together the tragic story of Father's last days. From the testimony of his fellow passengers on the *J. S. Chenoweth*, they learned that on the steamer's first day on the river, the great tragedian Junius Brutus Booth had been observed pacing in the salon, his hands clasped behind his back, his head bowed in deep thought. The next day, however, he was nowhere to be found. Inquiring after him, a gentleman named James Simpson had been informed by porters that he had retired to his berth, complaining of fever and lethargy. As the days passed and the celebrated actor did not emerge from his stateroom, Mr. Simpson grew ever more concerned, so he knocked on Father's door to offer assistance. To his dismay, Simpson discovered him alone and neglected, suffering terribly from dysentery, augmented by his inexplicable decision to quench his thirst by drinking deeply from the impure waters of the Mississippi when his symptoms had first appeared.

The good Mr. Simpson had immediately ordered the room cleaned and fresh linens put on the bed. After seeing to it that the ailing tragedian was washed, wrapped in a clean dressing gown, and fed a nourishing gruel, he kept vigil at his sickbed, trying to make sense of his confusing tales of his travels in California. Regrettably, Mr. Simpson wrote, "I could understand nothing but that he had suffered a great deal and had been exposed very much."

There was no doctor on board. Mr. Simpson nursed Father as best he could, but he steadily declined, his speech barely intelligible, though he seemed to listen intensely when Mr. Simpson read aloud from the New Testament. His eyes grew dim with tears, his expression distraught, and once he tried to express his gratitude by weakly embracing Mr. Simpson as the kind man smoothed his pillow.

On the fifth day, at about one o'clock in the afternoon, Mr. Simpson asked Father what else he could do to ease his suffering. "Pray!

Pray! Pray!" he had replied, giving his benefactor one last beseeching look before he closed his eyes forever.

"Yes, yes—that was just what your father would have thought right to do when he knew, at last, that death would overtake him," said Mother after Asia read Mr. Simpson's letter. "To endure patiently, to suffer without a complaint, and to trouble no one."

Asia nodded silently, blinking back tears, but in the weeks to come, she would reflect upon her mother's words and bitterly mark that their troubles had only just begun.

The tolling of funeral bells had scarcely faded when the first creditors descended upon the household—first coming delicately, murmuring apologetic phrases, and then in a furious rush like a pack of greedy curs on a narrow bone. Father had died intestate, and his entire fortune amounted to less than five thousand dollars. Of that, only a few hundred were in cash.

"This is what genius and decades of toil have amounted to," said Mother in disbelief as her daughters went over the figures in vain hope that she had made a mistake. "My darlings, my poor girls—I fear we have not been provided for."

"We have property," Asia said, though she could not prevent a note of fear from creeping into her voice. "We are not destitute."

But the next day, spurred on by his vengeful mother, Richard Booth sued Mother for the entirety of Father's meager estate.

Mary Ann Booth had concealed some of his late father's assets from the assessors, Richard alleged, including his elaborate and costly professional wardrobe, a piano, and substantial reserves of cash. Every penny in cash was accounted for, she countered. Adelaide's settlement and the expense of supporting so many dependents had drained her late husband's accounts, and fellow travelers had confirmed that he had been robbed of all the gold he had acquired in California. As for the tragedian's extensive collection of stage costumes, Mother had sewn them with her own hands, and the appraisers had concluded that they rightfully belonged to her.

As the lawsuit dragged on, Asia marveled at her mother's public show of serene strength, knowing that the unexpected blow had come just as the shock of her husband's death was receding, and the raw anguish of nascent widowhood emerging. Even after the state of Maryland ruled that the beautiful garments Mother had lovingly crafted for her husband were "personal apparel not to be accounted for in the estate of the deceased," obliging Richard Booth to abandon his senseless lawsuit, Mother remained badly shaken, reeling from the double loss of beloved husband and provider. In a matter of weeks, her raven-black hair went ash-gray, her cheeks lost their rosy bloom, her voice grew distant, and her gaze seemed to fix on something longed for swiftly receding, like a ship disappearing over the horizon.

And even though Mother had not had to relinquish a single cent more to Richard or Adelaide, legitimate creditors relentlessly drained their portions from the little Father had left behind until, in the end, if his widow and children were not destitute, they were not far from it.

By the time the first buds of spring unfurled into pale green leaves on the trees lining Exeter Street, Mother had decided to rent out their Baltimore residence and move to The Farm. Into a drayman's cart went all their furniture, clothing, glassware, china, quilts, books, art, mirrors, and the marble bust of Shakespeare, but all of her husband's other personal effects—diaries, letters, memorabilia from his long and illustrious career—were banished to the cellar.

"Shouldn't we take this with us?" Asia asked, wrinkling her nose against the musty damp as she studied the carefully stacked, padlocked trunks in the flickering light of her mother's lamp. "We have plenty of room to store everything at Tudor Hall."

"They'll be safe enough here." Mother gathered her skirts in one hand, raised the lamp high, and began climbing the stairs without giving the precious collection a second glance. "It grieves me too much to look upon them now. Come, Asia."

Wordlessly Asia obeyed, although she could not rid her imagination of vivid scenes of destruction—fire, flood, vermin, mold—that could consume the priceless artifacts before her mother could bring herself to retrieve them.

At The Farm, Joe and Ann had arranged the furniture and unpacked the family's belongings before their arrival, but even amid the trappings of familiarity, Tudor Hall felt strangely foreign and empty, so new it still smelled of raw oak and fresh paint. Asia and Rosalie followed their mother as she wandered from room to room, adjusting a lampshade, moving a portrait from one wall to another.

Suddenly Asia was struck by an overwhelming sense that the elegant home would never truly be theirs, for the family it had been created for no longer existed.

When Wilkes and Joseph joined them after school closed for the summer—closed forever for the two brothers, as Mother could no longer afford their tuition—that strange sense of wrongness diminished somewhat, but Asia still felt it, like an unexpected draft in a room when all the windows were shut.

The Farm was their only source of income, as the payments on Tudor Hall, taxes, and legal fees would almost entirely consume the thirty-five dollars Mother earned in monthly rent from their Baltimore residence. Their only recourse, she concluded, was for Wilkes to become a farmer, with Joe Hall to advise him and manage the hired hands. Asia thought it was an enormous responsibility to place upon a fifteen-year-old's shoulders, but with June and Edwin away, Wilkes had become the man of the house.

Wilkes embraced his new responsibilities with his usual enthusiasm and good cheer, exultant to have escaped St. Timothy's forever. Earnest and attentive, he worked alongside Joe, tilling the fields, sowing wheat, corn, and rye. All summer long, warm sunshine and gentle rains nourished the crops, which flourished and grew, promising an abundant harvest. Asia was glad to see her brother thriving in his new role, not only for the sake of the family's finances but also because his happiness comforted their mother.

But their early hopes were spoiled in late autumn, when the crops were brought in, measured, and sold for a bewilderingly small profit. It marked a bitter end to a troubling season, for when Wilkes and Joe had hired hands to help with the harvest, Asia had discovered something new and distressing in her brother, a curious fixation on rank and place—instilled in him, no doubt, by the military regimen at St. Timothy's. Father had always been egalitarian, sometimes to a fault, a man of the people who would invite poor strangers off the streets of Baltimore to join the family at the dinner table, who could converse as easily with a ditch-digger as a governor. But in Wilkes's heart, his pride had ever been at war with his love of equality and brotherhood, and somewhere along the way he had adopted the Southern notion that employers should not freely associate with their laborers.

On an ordinary day in Baltimore, his hauteur might have passed unnoticed, but not so in Bel Air at harvest time. There it was the custom for the colored freemen to eat lunch and dinner in the fields, while the Irish immigrants with their sunburnt faces and soiled clothes joined their employer and his family at the table in the big house. Wilkes was deeply uncomfortable with that arrangement, and on the first day of the harvest, he asked his mother, Rosalie, and Asia to remain upstairs while he dined alone with the Irishmen—a compromise, he called it, between his conscience and local tradition.

Mother looked taken aback. "Won't the men feel slighted?"

"How will you explain our absence?" asked Asia.

"Leave that to me," said Wilkes, smiling reassuringly, so charming and confident that they acquiesced, bemused but trusting. Their father would not have hesitated to break bread with the workers in his employ, Asia reflected, nor would Grandfather Booth, with his deep admiration of the first American patriots, have given the matter a second thought. It was curious to see Wilkes departing from the example of the two men he most admired.

Shortly before noon, Asia, her mother, and her sister withdrew to their rooms upstairs, where they read or sewed as they listened to the sounds of chairs scraping, cutlery tinkling, and low voices rumbling in Irish brogues below. Eavesdropping from the top of the stairs, Asia heard a younger man inquire after the ladies of the house, and Wilkes reply with a light remark about indisposition.

As the days passed, the workers' inquiries increased in frequency and skepticism. "We need the hands for the harvest," Asia warned her mother. "It would not do to offend them."

"Let Wilkes manage them," her mother replied, gazing out the window.

Asia realized that her mother was too deep in the throes of mourning to challenge Wilkes's newfound authority. Counting the days until the harvest would end, she resigned herself to the pretense that the ladies of the household were in the grasp of some dire chronic illness. It was only later, when she went into Bel Air on errands, that she heard spiteful whispers and observed sidelong glances. When she mused about it to friends, they reluctantly admitted that the Booths were no longer well liked among the county's white laboring class, who muttered that the whole high-and-mighty family had dirty British blood mixed up with Southern notions, a foul brew indeed.

Asia hoped to shield her grieving mother from the ugly gossip, but some well-meaning neighbor must have warned her. The following year, in hopes of avoiding a reprise of the unpleasant drama, Mother rented the fields to a white tenant farmer rather than make Wilkes responsible for raising crops and managing laborers. He did not seem insulted that his mother had relieved him of his duties, but rather spent the spring and summer indulging in a gentleman's leisurely pastimes— riding, hunting, attending picnics, and cutting a dash with the pretty young ladies of Bel Air. Somehow Mother contrived to provide him with a swift new horse he named Cola di Renzi, a fine leather saddle, and money to spend at his favorite tavern in the village. When village life grew too constrained for him, Wilkes rode off to Baltimore instead, grinning merrily and promising to behave himself even as his eyes danced with eagerness to see friends and to pay court to whatever silly, pretty young belle had most recently caught his eye.

To Asia's great joy, despite his many other amusements, her beloved brother never neglected her. They spent hours strolling together through the forest where they had played as children, Wilkes marveling at the wonders of nature, Asia admiring and envying his unfailingly cheerful disposition, so unlike her own. They recited poetry and read books together, histories of the United States and other nations, *The Life of Algernon Sydney*, Plutarch's *Lives* and *Morals*, and the works of Nathaniel Hawthorne. They both adored music; Wilkes played the flute, or they sang duets, accompanying each other on piano or guitar. A fearless, skillful rider, Wilkes declared himself determined to conquer Asia's fear of horses and teach her to ride, and in time she became quite a wild and daring horsewoman, able to keep up with him on swift rides through the dangerous and isolated countryside.

Throughout those joyful midsummer days, the wheat fields waved in the breezes, growing tall and golden as they ripened, but that year's harvest bewilderingly proved even worse than the one before. After setting aside enough for the family and livestock for the winter, they discovered that they had nothing left to sell or trade for necessities they could not produce themselves. By late 1854, as frost settled upon the fields and snow began to fly, both food and money had become scarce.

"We've never had to subsist entirely off the bounty of The Farm," Asia reminded Wilkes one evening as they walked their horses after a short, brisk ride. "I'm not so sure it can be done."

"Oh, don't let us be sad," Wilkes exclaimed, his hazel eyes shining with fond earnestness. "Life is so short, and the world is so beautiful. Just to breathe is delicious." He inhaled deeply, throwing back his head and closing his eyes. "Go on. Try it."

To humor him, and smiling in spite of herself, Asia obeyed, inhaling deeply of the cold, crisp air. When he teased her for an answer, she admitted that she did feel somewhat better.

Mother's genius with the needle kept them fashionably attired in their genteel poverty, concealing worn hems and threadbare elbows with a costumer's deft tricks, but keeping up appearances became an ever more difficult ordeal. Wilkes gallantly skipped meals so that his mother and sisters could eat their fill, and when they protested and tried to fill his plate from their own, he laughed, held it out of their reach, and declared that a friend had treated him to a hearty lunch at the tavern, or that he had stuffed himself with apples missed in the harvest while riding past an orchard earlier that day.

"I don't believe you," Asia once retorted, hunger sharpening her temper. "How can you be so cheerful when you're surely as famished as the rest of us?"

"Heaven and earth," he exclaimed, laughing. "How could I be otherwise? How glorious it is to live! How divine to breathe this breath of life with a clear mind and healthy lungs." Before she could pull away, he clasped her hand, drew her to him with his palm on the small of her back, and waltzed her around the dining room. "Be happy, sister. Tell me that you are!"

She could not help laughing through her protests that he was mad and ought to let her go, yet later that evening when she was alone, with her merriment fading, her stomach muttering its hollow complaints, her worries for their future seized her in an even stronger, colder grip than before.

· · ·

One gray midwinter afternoon, a letter arrived at The Farm bearing belated New Year's wishes from a longtime friend and great admirer of Father's, a professor of literature at Columbia College. After extolling her husband's genius and legacy, the professor urged Mother to publish his biography. No one understood the man behind the thespian as well as she, and if the family did not publish an official memoir, they could be sure that unscrupulous, opportunistic hacks would foist their own scandalous versions upon the public.

Asia had loved to write from the time she was old enough to hold a pencil, and a thrill of anticipation raced through her as she contemplated the professor's suggestion. "Let us honor Father by writing his biography," she implored, kneeling beside her mother's chair and taking her hand. "Father's personal papers document the events of a great man's life. Let us—Wilkes and I—intertwine them with family reminiscences and show the world the man we all knew and loved so dearly."

With Wilkes's help, she overcame her mother's reluctance and obtained her blessing to retrieve Father's trunks from the cellar of their Baltimore residence the next time they collected the rent. They could not bear to wait until the end of the month, so the next morning, Asia and Wilkes set out for the city, bundled up warmly to stave off the cold, chatting excitedly about their project and the potential profits it might bestow upon a household that badly needed them.

Asia was delighted with her brother's enthusiasm, not only because she would be glad for his companionship and assistance as she labored over the manuscript but also because the project would be a productive outlet for his restless energy. Politics had become his favorite diversion, but Asia worried about the company he kept, and about his new, unsettling habit of making offhand remarks in defense of slavery. Stranger still, he seemed utterly indifferent to how his words shocked his mother and siblings and offended Joe and Ann Hall, whom he very well knew had suffered terribly under slavery. Asia suspected that Wilkes had acquired these disturbing new ideas from the same young men, a few years older than he, who had invited Wilkes to join the local chapter of the Order of the Star-Spangled Banner, or as it was more colloquially known, the Know-Nothing Party. The fledgling political group was enjoying astonishing success in Maryland and most of the North, sending hundreds of new representatives to Congress and winning the governor's chair in eight states. The Know-Nothings vowed to control the wild, unprecedented flood of Irish immigration threatening the jobs and voting power of the native-born, and they pledged to end regional conflicts between the slave states and territories and the free, especially the horrific, bloody violence erupting in Kansas and Nebraska.

In November, Wilkes had been chosen as a steward when congressional candidate Henry Winter Davis had visited Bel Air for a campaign rally. Wilkes had worn the party badge and had carried a banner, and Mother had sewn him a splendid costume for the event, a wine-red coat trimmed in velvet, a fawn-colored vest, and gray trousers. Asia heartily endorsed the party's opposition to unchecked immigration and to the expansion of slavery into new territories, but their hostility to Catholics displeased her. Although she remained an Episcopalian like her parents, she had discovered beauty, peace, and comfort in the Catholic faith as a student at the Carmelite Convent school on Aisquith Street in Baltimore. She hoped that the Know-Nothings would renounce their prejudice before they infected Wilkes with it.

Their father's biography was the perfect undertaking to divert Wilkes's attention from politics. At 62 North Exeter Street, Asia and Wilkes chatted with their tenants and warmed themselves by the fire in the familiar green-and-gold parlor before loading their father's trunks of memorabilia into the wagon and heading back to Tudor Hall. The sun had broken through the clouds, and though the stiff wind blew no warmer, the bleak midwinter seemed suddenly bright with promise.

In the days that followed, every morning after breakfast and chores Asia and Wilkes convened in the parlor and delved into their father's trunks. They discovered a treasure trove of information about his life in the theatre—countless old letters, journals, books, playbills, and posters from 1817 through 1852, from his London debut through his many successful decades in America. They discovered the particulars of theatre engagements arranged nearly half a century before, and detailed accounts of his bitter rivalry with the celebrated thespian Edmund Kean. His correspondence—which he had left in perfect order, dated, indexed, sorted into proper categories, and bound with ribbons—was by turns fascinating, startling, and illuminating. As they studied his journals and read his letters aloud, the cadence of his speech inspirited their voices, so vivid and familiar that it was almost as if the words had resurrected the man. Memories of the grimmer aspects of his life fell away as they immersed themselves in a rising tide of love and admiration and pride for the great thespian and his achievements.

One afternoon as Asia read aloud a letter written to her father by the philosopher William Godwin, she glanced up to discover her mother standing frozen in the doorway, her face pale and stricken, her eyes brimming with tears.

"Is something wrong, Mother?" asked Wilkes.

"Surely you don't intend to include private letters in your book," she said, her voice strangely hoarse and distant.

"Not all of them, or the biography would run twenty volumes," said Asia. "But letters of particular historical value and interest, yes."

"No." Mother swept into the room, snatched the letter from Asia's hand, flung open the door of the stove, and threw the paper into the fire. "No, you will not."

"Mother," Asia exclaimed, horrified, as her mother seized a bundle of letters from the nearest trunk and fumbled to untie the ribbon. "What are you doing?"

Without a word, Mother opened a letter, ran her gaze over it, and threw it upon the flames. Another letter followed it, and another. Asia and Wilkes begged her to stop, but a morbid grief had possessed her, rendering her insensible to their distress. Nor could they physically restrain her—the trunks and everything in them were her property, and their respect and deference for their mother ran too deep. They were powerless to do anything more than plead with her to stop, stung by loss and bitter indignation each time the flames leapt upward to consume another precious memento.

"Leave us something for remembrance," Asia begged as another bundle of letters turned to ash.

Mother hesitated, and for a moment Asia's hopes flared up as greedily as the flames. "Here," she said, tearing a piece from the bottom of one letter and holding it out. "Tom Flynn's signature."

Numbly Asia took it as the rest of the letter was dispatched into the stove. Soon she held Edmund Kean's autograph too, and Thomas Apthorpe Cooper's, but the celebrated actors' signatures were poor compensation for all that her mother was destroying.

Blinking away tears, Asia glimpsed Wilkes nudge a slender book out of sight beneath the divan with his foot. Pretending to search for her handkerchief, Asia furtively tucked the nearest bundle of letters beneath her skirts. Whenever her mother's gaze was averted, she concealed another priceless relic, while Wilkes, with heavy sighs to cover the sound of rustling paper, shoved stray mementos beneath furniture and behind curtains whenever Mother was not watching.

But despite their best efforts, she destroyed nearly everything, sparing only a few mementos of their parents' courtship and artifacts from their father's association with Lord Byron and other men she revered.

That evening, alone in her bedchamber, Asia examined the letters and documents she had concealed within her petticoats and wept to discover how little of value remained. A few days later, in a clandestine meeting in the barn, she and Wilkes shared what they had salvaged from the flames. Asia burst into tears, flung her arms around Wilkes, and kissed his cheek in thankfulness when she discovered that he had saved three of their father's precious journals, assuring that his voice would not be silenced utterly.

The biography would suffer grievously for the loss of so many irreplaceable personal papers, but Asia was determined to write it nonetheless. Mother had not rescinded her blessing for the project, though she had made the work immeasurably more difficult.

Unbeknownst to their mother, Wilkes devoured their father's salvaged journals, reading and rereading them, his mouth drawn into that familiar schoolboy frown, his long, graceful fingers turning the pages with careful reverence. Once he beckoned Asia from the parlor where she sat sewing with Mother and Rosalie and led her to the kitchen, where they would not be overheard. "Listen to this," he murmured, retrieving a book from his coat pocket and opening it to a page marked with a strip of parchment. "Father wrote, 'Mind happily belongs to no age, clime, sex or condition. Instances can be quoted when even from the most despised classes, Genius has developed itself and towered above all the circle of the human race.'"

"Indeed?" Asia peered over her brother's shoulder and read the list of names that followed, men of humble birth and mixed heritage who had vanquished expectation and convention to ascend to the pinnacle of accomplishment in their chosen fields: Galileo Galilei, Napoleon

Bonaparte, Hannibal of Carthage, Christopher Columbus, and Junius Brutus Booth.

"Father believed—and I have become convinced—that fame and glory are marvelous prizes." Wilkes's eyes shone with the light of epiphany. "Any man with talent and perseverance may claim them, regardless of his parentage."

"Fame and glory are *earthly* prizes," said Asia. "They carry a high price, and they tarnish. Father's life is proof enough of that."

"But to be remembered through the ages," persisted Wilkes. "That is a kind of immortality. Few men enjoy it. Few men dare to aspire to it."

"Most men have better sense," retorted Asia irritably.

Inspired by their father and Byron and other tragic, romantic heroes of days gone by, Wilkes built himself fantastic temples of fame, which he described for her often, in the most glowing phrases. No visions or dreams of the future were too extravagant, too great—and yet, even as his obsession with acquiring the immortality of fame troubled Asia, she could not say that he was entirely wrong.

John Wilkes Booth would make his mark upon the world, upon history. Everyone in the family had always known that an extraordinary fate awaited him. Mother's fireside vision and the gypsy crone's fortune had foretold it. The only question was how.

While Wilkes absorbed lessons from their father's journals and dreamed of fame, Asia brooded over his future. Their father was dead. Their mother was lost in a deep cavern of grief from which she seemed unable to emerge. Their elder brothers were hundreds of miles away. Rosalie was withdrawn and cared little for the world beyond The Farm, and Joseph was yet a boy. There was no one but Asia to guide Wilkes—aside from his legions of friends, who might lead him astray rather than toward the golden future he longed for and deserved.

Asia mulled over the possibilities. At almost seventeen years of age, Wilkes was neither scholar nor farmer, as time and toil had shown. He had once fervently aspired to become a soldier, an ambition sparked at St. Timothy's and nurtured ever since by heroic tales of martial glory, but Mother had always firmly discouraged any such plans. Before long Asia concluded that the most obvious and immediate answer was for Wilkes to take up the family trade and become an actor. He was handsome, charming, and athletic, and the revered Booth name would grant him access to the most respected circles of the theatre world. By his mother's decree he had inherited his father's vast and marvelous collection of splendid costumes, jewelry, makeup, and stage weapons. Edwin was making his fortune and acquiring great acclaim on stages as far away as Honolulu and Sydney, while June enjoyed modest success in California. Why should Wilkes, the most graceful, charismatic, and exuberant of the three brothers, not expect to fare at least as well as they?

"I've contemplated following Father onto the stage ever since I portrayed Shylock at the Milton Academy as a schoolboy," Wilkes confessed when she proposed her plan for his future career. "No, my ambition has an even earlier origin. I've longed to prove myself ever since Edwin assigned the best roles in his Tripple Alley Players productions to his friends and stuck me with banging a triangle between acts."

Since Wilkes had not been able to learn acting from the great tragedian himself as Edwin had, Asia suggested that he embark on a program of theatrical study. With Asia assuming the role of tutor, they pored over their father's volumes of Shakespeare, memorizing speeches, studying illustrations, and imitating the characters' poses.

Wilkes was, as he had ever been, a slow and dogged student, struggling to comprehend the texts, perspiring from exertion as he forced the lines into his brain as if he were shoving boulders through a keyhole. Asia admired his persistence even when his slow and tedious pace made her grit her teeth with impatience. He was determined to learn the plays by heart, without a single word omitted or extra syllable appended.

In time he committed to memory the parts of Caesar, Marcus Antonius, and Brutus from *Julius Caesar,* although Asia wondered if he ever truly understood the play, for he delivered his lines as if Brutus were the hero of the drama. "Brutus is an honorable man," Wilkes argued whenever she tried to convince him otherwise. "Even Marcus Antonius says so."

"He is speaking ironically," said Asia. "He doesn't really mean it."

"His words are true regardless," said Wilkes. "Brutus is the only character in the entire tragedy who puts the good of Rome before himself. He sacrificed his life and his fortune to bring down a tyrant. He was the George Washington of his day."

"I don't think so, and neither did Shakespeare." Asia paged through the script until she came to the proper scene in the second act. "Think of what Artemidorus said when he tried to warn Caesar about the plot against him. 'If thou read this, O Caesar, thou mayst live. If not, the Fates with traitors do contrive.' Traitors, Wilkes, not patriots."

"But those are the words of a man loyal to Caesar. You can't take that on faith. I'm sure King George the Third and all his Tories denounced Washington as a traitor too."

Vexed, Asia cited other excerpts from the text, but when her brother refused to be persuaded, she wearily suggested they move on to *Richard III*, where there could be no mistaking the true villain of the piece.

Next they turned to *The Merchant of Venice*, a remarkable portion of which Wilkes remembered from his school days, but when Asia encouraged him to take on *Romeo and Juliet*, he shook his head, dubious. "I could never be a nimble skip-about like Romeo. I'm too square and solid."

"Study Mercutio, then," Asia proposed, although she profoundly disagreed with her brother's assessment. Wilkes was limber and graceful, and he seemed to acquire more admirers among the fairer sex with each passing month. She could well imagine ladies filling theatres to watch him portray the tragic hero of a star-crossed romance.

But her enthusiasm for her scheme faltered when she came upon him practicing alone in the forest when he thought himself unobserved, shouting Shakespeare's masterfully crafted speeches, his phrasing all wrong, his emphases draining all sense and meaning from the lines. Whereas Edwin possessed an instinctive, intuitive grasp of Shakespeare's language, Wilkes seemed to understand it no better than he had as a schoolboy.

Wilkes required a master teacher to guide him if he ever hoped to become half the thespian their father had been. Asia's hubris shamed her. She possessed no more than a schoolgirl's comprehension of Shakespeare and an infrequent observer's understanding of the stage. How had she ever imagined herself capable of preparing Wilkes to take up their father's mantle?

Although she hid her increasing dismay, forcing smiles and offering constant encouragement, Wilkes gradually became aware of his deficiencies. "What hope do I have of achieving success on the stage?" he lamented as they abandoned their books one afternoon in early spring to go riding through the pale green, rain-soaked forest. "Buried here, torturing the grain out of the ground for daily bread, what chance have I of ever studying elocution or declamation?"

"We'll find a way," she assured him. "Your voice is a beautiful instrument, with perfect music in it. You need only a master teacher to prune, cultivate, subdue, and encourage."

"Oh, only that?" he retorted, disappointment and embarrassment giving that perfect instrument an edge. Earlier that day, a bundle of letters from Edwin had arrived all the way from the South Pacific, where he had gone on tour with the renowned British actress Laura Keene. He had performed to great acclaim for British colonists in Sydney, Australia, and for King Kamehameha IV in the lovely island village of Honolulu. Theatre critics around the world hailed him in glowing reviews as a worthy successor to the great tragedian Junius Brutus Booth, dismissing June with faint praise and disregarding his other children entirely.

It was not in Wilkes's nature to endure being overshadowed by any man, even a beloved brother. Mother had been unable to hire a tenant farmer in the spring, and all summer, while Joe Hall and the hired hands attempted to raise crops in their increasingly unproductive fields, Wilkes kept to his studies, redoubling his efforts to master Shakespeare's soliloquies, the art of costumes and makeup, stage fighting, and dancing.

One afternoon in the middle of August, Asia was gathering mayapples and dewberries in a shady grove when she heard horse hooves upon the road, announcing Wilkes's return from a brief visit to Baltimore. Wilkes's smile gladdened her heart as he approached, brought the gleaming black stallion to a halt, and swiftly dismounted. "Well, Mother Bunch, guess what I've done," he crowed. "I made my first appearance on the stage yesterday evening, one night only, but with my name in great capitals on the playbill."

For a moment Asia could only blink at him. "What do you mean?"

His laughter at her astonishment rang with merriment and pride. "Last night I played Richmond in *Richard III* at the Charles Street Theatre in Baltimore."

His jubilant demeanor told her that he had passed the test of his debut, somehow. Relief made her lightheaded. "John Sleeper Clarke's theatre?"

"Indeed, and as you might have expected, Sleepy asked me to give you his best regards." Wilkes threw her a mischievous smile and took her hand. "Come. Let's tell Mother and Rosalie together."

Rosalie greeted the announcement of Wilkes's debut with raised eyebrows and a soft murmur of surprise, but their mother was greatly displeased. "Your first appearance on the stage is—premature," she said, wringing her hands. "It grieves me to say this, darling, but you've been manipulated by unscrupulous people seeking notoriety and money by the use of your name."

"That's not true," Wilkes said, but Asia detected uncertainty in his voice.

"In the world of the theatre, the name Booth is synonymous with genius," said Mother. "You're young and untrained—talented, yes, but unformed, unpolished. You cannot sacrifice your father's legacy to your own haste."

"It's not Wilkes's fault that he's had no opportunity to learn from Father as June and Edwin did," said Asia. "How else will he prepare if not by performing small parts in good theatres close to home?"

Mother fixed Asia with a gaze so piercing that Asia almost regretted speaking up in her brother's defense. "You're not wrong, but I doubt very much that news of this impetuous debut will please Edwin any more than it pleased me."

The next morning, and without a word of complaint, Wilkes cheerfully resumed his theatrical studies, apparently undaunted by the indefinite postponement of his next appearance on the stage. Weeks passed before the post could deliver Edwin's reaction to Wilkes's debut to Tudor Hall. He admonished Wilkes for misrepresenting his performance as a triumph when Clarke and other trusted friends had described it as nothing short of a grave embarrassment. The proud Booth name upon the playbills had guaranteed a packed house, and before those hundreds of witnesses Wilkes had performed so badly that the audience had hissed him. "I have worked too hard to allow my raw, untrained brother to tarnish our father's legacy," Edwin scolded in his familiar, elegant script. "If and when John Wilkes takes to the stage again, he must do so under an alias so that he does not ruin the name of BOOTH."

That was all their mother needed to know. "You may return to the stage when Edwin decides you are ready, and not one hour before," she declared, and Wilkes had little choice but to obey.

In subsequent letters, Edwin promised that he would return home soon, perhaps as early as the following summer. He had become concerned that another actor would claim the title of the greatest living tragedian—his own rightful inheritance—if he did not return to the eastern United States "while Father's memory remained dear to the American heart." In advance of his return, he hired a business manager, the theatrical agent Benjamin Baker, to promote his career back east by securing engagements for him in playhouses all along the Atlantic coast.

As the year flared with the brightness of autumn and faded into winter, Mother anticipated Edwin's return with anxious desperation. She had been unable to hire a tenant farmer the previous spring, and Joe Hall and the hired hands had failed to raise enough food to sustain the household through the winter. At her behest Wilkes drove their small herd of cattle to the livestock market and sold them for more than sixty dollars, but although they spent nearly all of it on provisions for the long, cold months ahead, the larder and cellar remained disconcertingly bare compared to years past.

Asia could not remember a season of such intense cold and heavy snows. Sometimes the drifts were so deep and the winds so frigid that the family could scarcely venture beyond the house and outbuildings. As their provisions failed, they upheld their strict vegetarian father's decree that no animals would be harmed on The Farm by poaching off their neighbors' acres instead. Wilkes trapped a wild-eyed possum, and caught a flurry of partridges, and once he shot a neighbor's turkey. "Every spring Woolsey's flock feeds off the grain scattered in our best field," he said by way of an excuse. "And let's not forget his habit of moving our boundary marker by night. He's taken over such a large portion of our meadow that I probably took this turkey from land that is rightfully ours."

By February everyone at Tudor Hall had fallen ill at least once for the lack of nourishing food. From the last of her savings, Mother scraped together enough money to send Wilkes off to a distant farm to purchase a milch cow, but a treacherous storm struck soon after he departed. When he failed to return that evening as expected, Asia, Mother, and Rosalie waited up all night for him, too anxious to give voice to their deepest fears, which were relieved only after he arrived the next morning leading a stout black cow. He laughed and teased them for their worry, and only later did he admit that he had arrived at the Parker Lea farm nearly frozen, and had been taken into the house speechless and stumbling, half-asleep, then rubbed briskly and slapped awake, and restored by brandy and a warm bed.

Asia shivered with horror as Wilkes spun his harrowing tale, his smile and nonchalance belying how close he had come to freezing to death.

Eventually spring came, supplementing their meager diet with wild greens and the first early harvest of the garden—rhubarb, spinach, and ramps. The family watched for Edwin's letters and awaited his arrival with increasing desperation, but summer waxed and waned with no sign of him save occasional telegrams announcing that he was on his way.

"Mother waits for Edwin like Penelope for Odysseus," grumbled Wilkes, a sting of jealousy in his voice, "as if he were a conquering hero, retuning home to save us from starvation and suffering."

Asia refrained from confessing that she awaited Edwin in precisely the same way. The Booths at Tudor Hall needed rescue as badly as any heroine from Greek tragedy ever had.

It was mid-September when at last Edwin arrived. A crowd of awestruck country lads trailed after his stagecoach as it rattled along the road from Bel Air to The Farm, eager for a glimpse of the world traveler, the local boy who had set out for California four years before and had returned home a famous, and presumably wealthy, man.

When the coach halted in front of Tudor Hall and Edwin descended, Wilkes ran forward to embrace him, but Asia found herself rooted in place on the piazza, flanked by her mother and her sister. Edwin's long, black curls hung to his shoulders just as Asia remembered, and his dark eyes gleamed with the same bright intensity, but he strode up the path with a new poise and assurance. His clothes were finely tailored from expensive wools and silks, his rich velvet cloak cut in the Spanish style, and his cravat adorned with a dazzling pin, a diamond set within an enormous gold nugget.

As Edwin approached the house, arm in arm with Wilkes, the country lads scrambled to take down his heavy trunks and haul them up to the house on their shoulders, marveling at their weight.

"Edwin, my boy," Mother cried, holding out her arms to welcome him home.

Edwin beamed and hurried to embrace her, but as he did, his smile faded, his expression clouded with shock and bewilderment. Asia felt a sudden flush of shame as he took in their gaunt faces, their threadbare clothes. Mother had described their dire circumstances in letter after letter. Had Edwin assumed she exaggerated the depths of their misery?

"Mother," Edwin murmured as he took her in her arms. "Dearest Mother. There are no words for how much I've missed you."

Whatever illusions their reunion had dispelled, Edwin recovered his composure by the time he crossed the threshold of Tudor Hall. The trunks were carried in after him, the eager porters compensated for their labors and sent on their way. After the embraces and greetings and questions were done, scarce refreshments offered and graciously declined, the family learned that Edwin's trunks were filled with evidence of his triumphs in the West and the South Pacific—rapturous reviews clipped from San Francisco newspapers, playbills announcing engagements in Sydney, a proclamation passed by the California state legislature declaring Edwin Booth a treasure, a priceless gift the citizens of California would graciously share with the rest of the United States.

Mother glowed with pride as she beheld this vast array of evidence of his tremendous success, but she wept with joy when Edwin revealed one last treasure, securely fastened to his belt and concealed beneath his cloak—a purse heavy with gold.

In the aftermath of Edwin's homecoming, everything changed. For the first time since Father's death, their bellies were comfortably full, their sleep untroubled by anxious dreams of a bleak and uncertain future. Edwin paid his mother's debts at the shops in Bel Air and settled Wilkes's tabs at the Traveler's Home tavern and Murphy's

Billiard Hall. He purchased new wardrobes for his mother and sisters and treated them to luxuries they had long done without—writing paper and ink, books and sheet music, plenty of coal, new lamps and an ample supply of oil to fill them. Mother smiled again, and when she delighted in Edwin's amusing stories of his adventures in the West and in the South Pacific, for he was careful to share only cheerful tales, ten years seemed to fall from her age.

Though only twenty-three, experience had bestowed maturity upon him, and he immediately assumed his rightful place as head of the household. Entrusting The Farm to the care of the ever reliable Joe and Ann, Edwin closed Tudor Hall and moved his mother and younger siblings to Baltimore, renting a comfortable townhouse at 7 North High Street in their old neighborhood. But even as his family rejoiced in his return and in the restoration of all their old comforts and necessities, a frisson of resentment ran through every smile. They could not forget Edwin's prolonged neglect, nor, though they never spoke of it, could they entirely forgive him for abandoning Father on the pier in San Francisco.

Mother showered Edwin in affection and expressed sincere and abundant gratitude for his many gifts, but her condemnation of his singular, fatally disloyal act was made manifest when Edwin asked for his father's magnificent collection of costumes and theatrical props as his inheritance. He gaped, astonished, when she refused. "Why not?" he asked, a trifle sharply. "I think it's fair to say I earned them."

"Perhaps that's true, but you've asked me too late." Mother smiled regretfully, but Asia detected a glimmer of steel in her gaze. "I've already given them to John Wilkes."

"But I would make far better use of them," Edwin protested.

"Perhaps, perhaps not. Only time will tell." She waved a hand in a gesture of graceful dismissal. "As I say, you're too late. Such a decision, once made, cannot be undone, even if time and hindsight grant us the wisdom to regret it."

Edwin inclined his head respectfully, but if his mother's rebuke wounded him, he gave little sign of it. And yet, somehow, an undefinable quality in his demeanor told Asia that he accepted his family's judgment and knew he must make amends.

Soon thereafter, Edwin embarked on tour, filling theatres and earning rave reviews and rapturous comparisons to the great Junius Brutus Booth everywhere he went. He deliberately followed the Southern routes their father had trod, dazzling audiences at Grover's Theatre in Washington City before moving on to Richmond, Charleston, Savannah, Montgomery, and New Orleans. Asia thought it was an inspired plan to reclaim the territory where their father had enjoyed such success, and where Edwin could renew ties with theatre owners and managers he had met as his father's young valet and apprentice player.

Only after whetting the public's anticipation with his rising fame and ever more rapturous reports in the press that the celebrated Booth genius was alive and well in the heir apparent did Edwin set his sights on New York, a thespian's true testing ground, where riches and acclaim were bestowed upon the best and the brightest. "Hope for the Living Drama!" declared the playbills for his opening at the Bond Theatre on Broadway. From what Asia read in the papers, theatre critics and audiences alike agreed that Edwin deserved all the applause he could bear.

Nearly a year after Edwin's return, he at last decided that Wilkes might begin his apprenticeship. Wilkes promptly joined William Wheatley's company at the Arch Street Theatre in Philadelphia as a supernumerary, calling himself J. B. Wilkes to avoid tarnishing the celebrated family name with his neophyte efforts. As a humble supe, nineteen-year-old Wilkes remained in the background, attired as a soldier, servant, peasant, or nobleman as the play required, his costumed presence helping to set the scene, though he had no lines to speak. He earned a mere eight dollars a week, insufficient to pay for his room at a boardinghouse near the theatre, much less the new clothes, tavern meals, brandy, and occasional train fares to Baltimore he also required. Mother paid his expenses out of the funds Edwin provided for the household, although Asia doubted her elder brother knew.

Asia realized that Wilkes had John Sleeper Clarke as well as Edwin to thank for the opportunity, unprofitable though it was. Clarke's fame as a talented comedian was growing all along the East Coast, and he had decided to further advance his career by taking on a management role at the Arch Street Theatre. It was Clarke who had convinced Wheatley to hire Wilkes—and although Asia adamantly denied it, her mother and Rosalie teased that he had acted not out of friendship to

Edwin or Wilkes, but to prove his devotion to Asia. Over the course of the year Clarke had called at the Booth residence whenever he was in Baltimore, even if Edwin was away on tour, but he could not possibly persist in the delusion that he was courting Asia, for she had not given him a single word of encouragement. She was grateful that he had found a place in his company of players for Wilkes, but gratitude was not affection. Surely Clarke was not too besotted to understand that.

For months Wilkes toiled away in bit parts in the background while Edwin filled theatres in great cities portraying the characters their father had made his own—Shylock, Pescara, Iago, Richard III—as well as Hamlet and Romeo, roles Edwin's ethereal, compelling grace enabled him to inhabit better than the legendary tragedian ever had, if the enraptured theatre critics did not exaggerate.

"I'm not jealous of our dear brother nor discouraged for myself," Wilkes wrote home to Asia in the first week of January 1858, with his usual good cheer. "In fact, I have high hopes that this will be the year 'J. B. Wilkes' makes audiences sit up and take notice. And the moment I make my reputation as an actor, I will take back the name our father made great."

Soon thereafter, Wilkes wrote again with delightful news: He had been cast in speaking roles in both of the Arch Street Theatre's newest upcoming productions. They were small parts, to be sure, far beneath actors of Edwin's stature, but if Wilkes could distinguish himself with a flash of brilliance onstage—winning over the audience, earning a spontaneous burst of applause—it could speed his ascension through the ranks.

In late February, the Booth ladies traveled to Philadelphia for the opening night of *Lucretia Borgia*, for not even the reclusive Rosalie would dream of missing Wilkes's official debut. They knew Wilkes would be too busy preparing for the show to meet them at the train station in Philadelphia, but Asia was astonished to find Clarke waiting on the platform in his place, his cheeks red from cold.

"Shouldn't you be at the theatre, preparing for curtain rise?" Asia asked after he had greeted them with a stiff formality that struck her as rather ridiculous considering his long acquaintance with their family.

"I'm not in the cast," he said, offering Asia his arm. "Our *Lucretia Borgia* is adapted from Victor Hugo's play, a melodrama set in Renaissance Venice. There's no good part in it for a comedian."

"Surely you're wanted backstage, then." Glancing at his crooked elbow from beneath arched eyebrows, Asia stepped gracefully aside so that it would appear that Clarke had offered to escort her mother instead, as was proper. His smile faltered slightly as he stepped closer to Mother, but he otherwise did not acknowledge his gaffe. Taking his arm, Mother fixed Asia with a look of reprimand over her shoulder as Clarke led her away.

"I don't understand how Clarke can be so amusing on the stage and so stilted off it," Asia murmured to Rosalie as he helped their mother into a hired carriage.

"You make him nervous," Rosalie whispered back. "Only before you is he afraid to look a fool."

"Well, that's foolishness itself. I've known him since—" But she could say no more, because Clarke had turned to her, hand outstretched, to assist her into the carriage beside her mother.

"How is Wilkes?" Mother asked as they rode to the theatre. "I do wish we could see him before curtain rise."

"He's doing well, Mrs. Booth." Clarke looked quite well himself, attired in a fine black wool suit and topcoat, expertly tailored, and a black felt hat, evidently new. Edwin, who never squandered an opportunity to sing his friend's praises, had told Asia that Clarke's onstage pratfalls and comic escapades had made him a wealthy man, and his ventures in management proved that he was prudent too. Asia had merely nodded, unwilling to offend her brother but reluctant to appear to admire his friend. She was well aware that Edwin and her mother conspired as matchmakers, but to her Clarke would always remain mischievous, round-faced Sleepy from the neighborhood, a good enough fellow but hardly her heart's desire.

They arrived at the Arch Street Theatre at half past six, just as the doors were opening. Clarke escorted them past the ladies and gentlemen lined up at the box office, shivering in their cloaks and furs and chattering with anticipation while they waited to purchase their tickets: fifty cents for a seat on the main floor, fifteen for the balcony. After seeing the Booth ladies to their places on the main floor, Clarke bowed and hurried off backstage with promises to carry their good wishes to Wilkes.

The gas footlights shone, the audience took their seats, and the quiet murmur of voices fell to an expectant hush as the orchestra struck up the melancholy strains of an old Italian melody. The curtain rose upon a festive twilight scene, a celebration of Carnival in Venice. False moonlight shone on the marble façade of a palace, its arched columns rising above the street, and upon the Grand Canal beyond it, where gondolas passed, silent and graceful. Downstage, men and women strolled by in rich clothes and painted masks, their lecherous mouths, crooked noses, and staring, empty eye sockets ominous and unsettling.

Suddenly six young cavaliers burst onto the stage—and Asia seized her mother's hand as she spotted Wilkes among them. She recognized elements of his grand costume from their father's magnificent wardrobe—the fine silk hose and velvet shoes, the snug black tunic he had worn as Hamlet.

"There never was a tale more full of horror," one of the cavaliers declared ominously. "There never was a deed more black and damning!"

Then Wilkes stepped forward. "Aye, a dark and bloody deed," he intoned, "perpetrated by some malicious demon, who revels in blood and crime!"

Unaware that she had been holding her breath, Asia exhaled softly and settled back into her seat. Her brother had delivered his first line well, with strength and clarity. Though he had always found learning a part an arduous labor, once he memorized something, he knew it forever—and to her enormous relief, he apparently knew this one.

Finally able to relax, Asia lost herself in the story as it unfolded amid the vibrant spectacle of Carnival. Strolling among the revelers was the duchess of Ferrara, the beautiful, powerful, and ruthless Lucretia Borgia. Clad in a low-cut gown lavishly embellished with jewels, her identity concealed behind a mask, she had come to Venice seeking her long-lost son, Gennaro, whom she had sent away as an infant twenty years before to protect him from her enemies. Wilkes portrayed Ascanio Petrucca, Gennaro's best friend and comrade in arms.

At a fatal moment, in her distraction and anguish, Lucretia allowed her mask to slip—and the cavaliers immediately recognized her. A thrill of shock and apprehension ran through the audience as the angry young soldiers surrounded her, swords drawn. She fell to her knees, weeping, tearing her hair, and begging for mercy.

"Madam," the first cavalier snarled, leaning toward her, "I am Maffio Orsini, brother to the duke of Gravinia, whom you caused to be stabbed in his dungeon!"

"Madam," a second declared, drawing closer, "I am Jeppo Liveretto, brother of Liveretto Vittelli, whom your ruffians strangled while he slept!"

Then Ascanio Petrucca stepped forward. "Madam, I—" Wilkes's voice shook. "I am Pondolfo Pet— Pedolfio Pat— Pantuchio Ped— Dammit, what am I?"

The audience burst into laughter—except for the Booth ladies, who gasped in dismay.

The actress playing Lucretia knelt in supplication before the vengeful cavaliers, her climactic moment spoiled. The players carried on as if unaware of the roar of laughter washing over them—all the actors, save one. Wilkes turned to face the audience, grinned ruefully in acknowledgment of his mistake and their merriment, and joined in the laughter.

"No, John," Asia heard her mother murmur. "Carry on, carry on."

He could not have heard her, but he promptly fell back into character and joined the other actors as they struggled to restore the play to its proper course. But the suspenseful mood had been shattered. Through once-riveting scenes that now seemed ridiculous, the play limped toward its tragic climax and the mercifully swift drop of the curtain.

While tepid applause and laughter and impolite imitations of Wilkes's stammer rang out all around them, Asia clapped with such fierce determination that her palms smarted. The rest of the audience rose and made to depart, but Asia, her mother, and Rosalie remained in their seats as if they had every reason to expect a curtain call.

But of course none was forthcoming. "Poor John," said Mother, rising from her seat.

"If not for that one mistake," said Asia spiritedly, "it would have been an excellent performance."

Rosalie too stood. "I wonder what Edwin will say."

Asia felt a catch in her throat imagining Edwin's reaction to news of his brother's disastrous performance. Oh, poor John indeed. The gleeful viciousness of the newspaper reviews would seem a gentle rebuke compared to Edwin's wrath.

Clarke kindly said nothing of Wilkes's appalling blunder when he arrived to escort the Booth ladies to their hotel, but his expression of consternation spoke volumes. "John Wilkes looked well on the stage," he told Asia as they parted company. "He showed moments of true talent, and he'll improve with experience. Every player has a performance like this in his past. Before you know it, this night will be no more than a memory, a comic story he'll bring out every once in a while to amuse friends and to encourage the new supes."

Tears of gratitude sprang to Asia's eyes as she thanked him.

Later, when Wilkes finally joined them at the hotel for a late supper, his manner was chagrined, yet astonishingly sanguine. "Tomorrow night when I play Dawson in *The Gamester*, all will be forgiven," he said. "It's a choice part, one of the villains. I've no doubt I'll win over the audience with my splendid costume."

"Perhaps you should endeavor to win them over with your splendid performance," said Asia, but Wilkes merely laughed and told her not to worry.

But the following evening, the moment Dawson appeared upon the stage, the audience erupted in hoots of laughter, hisses, and mock applause. As the derisive whistles and taunts drowned out the dialogue, Asia watched with rising alarm as her brother stood rooted in place, dumbstruck and dismayed. As the uproar swelled, Wilkes came to his senses and hurried offstage. Only then did the audience settle down and allow the play to continue.

And continue it did—without Dawson, the villain who was supposed to lead the title character into ruin. Wilkes never again emerged from backstage—whether by his own volition or at the manager's command, Asia could only guess—obliging the other actors to improvise around his absence.

Afterward, when Wilkes met his mother and sisters at the hotel, he was subdued, embarrassed, and sparking with anger. The company had pulled him from the play, he complained. If it had been up to him, he would have persisted, and eventually the audience would have allowed him to perform. Compounding his humiliation, he had been so certain of his triumph that he had invited a particularly charming young lady to the performance. "Though after tonight," he grumbled, "I don't expect she'll allow me to call on her again."

Asia thought he should be more concerned with his career than his prospects with the young lady, but she said nothing rather than contribute to his misery.

The following morning, the Booth ladies returned to Baltimore on the first train, leaving Wilkes to carry on, somehow, for the rest of the season. To Asia's relief, Clarke's reports confirmed Wilkes's cheerful claims in letters home that although his pride suffered and his fellow players were greatly annoyed with him, the manager continued to cast him in small but necessary roles, and the disasters of February were not repeated.

Mother was not reassured. "I think he wishes he had chosen another profession," she confided to her daughters in early April, "but he won't acknowledge it."

As for Edwin, whatever admonishments or encouragement he might have sent to Wilkes through the post, neither brother ever told.

As the theatre season drew to a close, Wilkes announced that he was leaving the Arch Street Theatre Company. Clarke tried to talk him out of it, but after the final performance in June, Wilkes packed his trunks and returned to Baltimore. "Next season I'll seek my fortune in the South, in Richmond or here in Baltimore," he told Asia, smiling, brimming with confidence.

She remembered then that once he had confided to her his wish to become a Southern actor, beloved of the Southern people whom he so admired, yet some undercurrent of restless dissatisfaction in his manner compelled her to take Clarke aside the next time he called and ply him with questions.

"I can't speak ill of your brother," said Clarke, "not to you."

"If we are to remain friends," she said, resting her hand on his forearm, "and I do hope we are friends, you must always speak the truth to me, whether it be good or ill."

Reluctantly, Clarke admitted that the Arch Street Theatre Company had accepted Wilkes's resignation with relief and great satisfaction. "The players expected a son of Junius Brutus Booth to take the profession more seriously," he said. "John Wilkes often seemed lazy, disrespectful, unwilling to put in the work required. He was careless rather than earnest, with none of the humility a director expects from his supes. Some of the players—not I—say he has an overblown sense of his own talent and feels entitled to plum roles he hasn't really earned. He resists criticism and carries himself as if confident that his good looks and last name are enough to guarantee success, with no real effort required on his part."

Heartsick, Asia inhaled deeply to steady herself. "Thank you for telling me this, however much it pains us both. Wilkes never would have said a word."

"I wish I had happier news to share." Clarke hesitated. "There is one thing more, but it's sordid, and maybe I shouldn't—"

"Tell me. I need to know everything."

"There was some talk that he had another reason to leave Philadelphia in haste. A girl living at his boardinghouse revealed that she . . . that she is in a delicate condition. Rumor has it that Wilkes is responsible, and that he was obliged to pay a considerable sum of money to the family to compensate her for her shame and ruin."

"Oh my." Asia pressed a hand to her heart, lightheaded with dismay. Wilkes had always admired the ladies and enjoyed their admiration in turn, but this . . . Oh, would that he had been more careful, more discreet. "Tell me, does the offended party know my brother as J. B. Wilkes, or as the son of Junius Brutus Booth?"

Immediately her cheeks burned with shame that her first question had been about the status of the Booth family name rather than the health of the mother and child, but to her relief, she saw no rebuke in Clarke's eyes, only sympathy. "I don't think anyone was ever deceived by your brother's alias," he said.

She nodded. If the sordid tale was true, the money for the ruined girl must have come from Edwin. Wilkes did not have it, and he would never diminish himself in their mother's eyes by appealing to her in such circumstances.

"Asia—" Suddenly Clarke took her other hand. "Forgive me. I would not have hurt you for the world."

"You would have hurt me far more had you concealed the truth from me," she assured him frankly. "If there is ever anything about my brother I ought to know, you must promise to tell me, however delicate the subject may be."

As he vowed to do so, she thought that she would seem ungrateful if she snatched her hand away, so she let him hold it awhile longer.

. . .

Wilkes spent most of the summer of 1858 playing billiards in pool halls in downtown Baltimore, wielding the cue with such natural grace and athleticism that he soon earned a reputation as a master. He won nearly every game, earning enough so that he did not have to go hat in hand to Edwin, begging for loans to cover his expenses—fine clothes, meals at taverns with friends, brandy, cigars. Mother confessed to her daughters that she was torn between pride and chagrin, impressed by his skill, glad for his small measure of financial independence, but dismayed that he had not found a more prestigious outlet for his talents.

Late August found Wilkes in Richmond, Virginia, where Edwin had secured him a position with the Dramatic Star Company, the resident troupe of the renowned Marshall Theatre. As a supernumerary he stood to take in $440 for the season, substantially more than he had earned in Philadelphia, but still less than what Edwin earned in a single week. As the season opened, Wilkes was cast in minor speaking roles in the first two productions—a test of his abilities, he surmised, and after the mishaps in Philadelphia he could hardly blame the managers for insisting upon that.

In his letters home, he confided to Asia that despite a few early stumbles, the theatergoers of Richmond had embraced him warmly. "They love me for our father's sake," he wrote. "My physical resemblance to our beloved Parent fills them with affection and nostalgia. No one is fooled by the billing 'J. B. Wilkes' on posters and programs. I heard my name—Booth—called out, one or two nights, and my likeness to Father was mentioned in the papers."

Wilkes was pleasantly surprised to discover that the citizens of Richmond were equally hospitable and congenial outside the theatre. "Whereas the people of the North place actors outside of society and shun their company," he marveled, "Southerners take us into affable friendship." He was welcome everywhere, he wrote proudly, and was often invited to dine with gentlemen and to call on admiring ladies.

Asia was happy that he had found friends, and she was very relieved indeed that experience and hard work had at last brought to fruition the talent he had shown as a schoolboy, but she was dismayed by how readily he had adopted the manners and prejudices of the South. In

startling contradiction of their father's egalitarian and abolitionist beliefs, Wilkes often noted approvingly Richmond's strictly regimented
distinctions between the white race and the colored. "Here in Richmond, I see every day proof that slavery affords the greatest happiness
of master & man," he wrote on one occasion. "The North, and even
Maryland, has much to learn from this City but of course they are too
proud to study."

Wilkes's ebullience diminished somewhat in September, when Edwin swept into Richmond for a month-long engagement at the Marshall,
a greatly revered star to his younger brother's lowly supernumerary. Edwin stayed in the city's finest hotel, employed a valet to tend to his costumes and serve his meals, and was given the theatre's best private
dressing room. As the visiting featured actor, Edwin selected the plays
that would be performed, assigned the parts, and arranged the grueling
rehearsal schedule, with the company eagerly leaping to obey his every
command.

One glorious performance followed another. Even Wilkes grudg-
ingly acknowledged that the supporting actors marveled at Edwin's
brilliance and pushed themselves to equal his passion and subtlety. As
enthralled audiences filled the theatre again and again, the managers
reveled in astonishing profits and the critics fairly swooned with admiration. "Edwin Booth's engagement is one of the most successful we
have ever known here," the *Daily Richmond Examiner* glowed. "The audiences are large and highly intelligent—the plays performed there are
of the most elevated character—and the best order is maintained
throughout the house. Mr. Booth's playing commands the highest
mark of admiration: silence. His exhibition of that terrible passion—
Remorse—so difficult to counterfeit—produced almost breathless silence: a silence which was not broken at the close of the scene."

After Edwin moved on to Boston in mid-October, Wilkes's letters
took on a decidedly disgruntled tone. It vexed him to struggle inces-
santly in Edwin's shadow, which fell over him no matter how many
miles separated them. It was profoundly unfair that he had no teacher
to help him learn his craft as Father had instructed Edwin throughout
their many years as traveling companions, or a mentor to guide him
and cast him in strong roles as June had done for Edwin in San Francisco. Always, always, everything was done for Edwin and denied

Wilkes. "I am anxious to get on faster," Wilkes complained in a letter home to his mother, who promptly beseeched Edwin to be more helpful to him.

Asia was not sure if Edwin complied, but time and again, Clarke endeavored to help Wilkes advance in his profession. Asia had not forgotten how he endeared himself to her with his frank, forthright confidences regarding Wilkes's departure from the Arch Street Theatre, and so when Edwin urged her to consider Clarke an acceptable suitor, she found her longstanding resistance wavering. She had known Clarke since childhood, and as Edwin and her mother often reminded her, he had become successful and wealthy. Asia had no independent fortune of her own, whereas sober, steadfast Clarke would be a good provider. And so the next time Edwin happened to mention his friend in conversation, Asia acknowledged that she had become quite fond of him. Within a week Clarke asked for her hand in marriage, and after weighing his proposal overnight, she consented.

Mother rejoiced, Edwin fairly burst with happiness, and June telegraphed his congratulations from California. Joseph, melancholic and pensive at eighteen, smiled fondly and wished her well, and Rosalie confessed that she would miss her desperately but understood that women had to marry if they could.

Only Wilkes condemned the match, protesting in sharply worded, hastily scrawled letters from Richmond that Asia should not, must not allow Edwin to dispose of her as he pleased. "You must not bestow your Person upon someone who has not won your heart," he declared. "This is no marriage of true minds. He is not equal to your intelligence, your brilliance, your wit. And what's more you do not love him. This is plain to me and surely also to him."

Wilkes was not entirely mistaken. She did not love Clarke. She liked him well enough, but she knew she felt for him only a small fraction of the affection her mother had felt for her father and none of the passion. But hardship and heartbreak had taught Asia never to mistake passion for happiness. For most of her life, her fate had depended upon the fortunes of a mad genius—brilliant, impetuous, and utterly unreliable. She had adored her father, but the fact that Clarke was nothing like him added to his appeal. If she were to be perfectly honest, she had accepted his proposal to please Edwin and to assure her future security. With no other suitor contending for her hand, was that not reason enough?

Wilkes adamantly insisted that it was not, and he implored her to reconsider even up to the very day of her wedding. Despite his profound disappointment, on April 28, 1859, he nonetheless traveled from Richmond to witness the ceremony at St. Paul's Episcopal Church in Baltimore. After she and Clarke spoke their vows and exchanged rings and sealed their bond with a kiss, an enormous wave of relief swept over her, for the deed was done and could not be undone, and surely Wilkes would make his peace with her decision and belatedly give her his blessing.

Her hopes were short-lived. At the wedding supper, Wilkes caught her in a brief moment alone and murmured in her ear. "Always bear in mind that you are a professional stepping-stone. Our father's name rings with power in the theatrical world. It is dower enough for any struggling actor."

Heartsick, Asia tore herself away from her beloved brother and cleaved to her husband's side until Wilkes departed for Richmond. She said nothing to Clarke about the venomous warning—not that day, nor in all the weeks that followed. It would only poison the men's already tenuous friendship, which had never recovered from Wilkes's ill-fated season at the Arch Street Theatre.

She could only hope and pray that Wilkes would have a change of heart.

Her own heart changed—grew, blossomed—as she settled into the comfortable home Clarke had rented at 430 Franklin Street, about a mile south of the Arch Street Theatre. In those early weeks of their fledgling marriage, he proved to be more attentive and loving than she had imagined, generous with compliments and affection, often leaving books and other small gifts for her to find as she went about her day.

She was grateful to discover that she had every reason to anticipate a long and happy marriage with a kind man who loved and adored her.

In August, Wilkes returned to the Marshall Theatre in Richmond, Joseph enrolled in medical school, and Mother, Rosalie, and Edwin moved into the Clarke residence in Philadelphia, although Edwin was often traveling on tour. It would have been more romantic, perhaps, if the newlyweds had the house to themselves, but Asia was thankful her mother and sister were near. Although her petticoats and skirts still concealed her secret from strangers, she was already with child.

As summer turned to autumn, Asia contentedly prepared the nursery and the layette, sewing gowns, knitting soft booties and caps, and piecing small quilts in abundance, for she expected her baby to arrive in midwinter. "Give the babe that old Job's Tears quilt you made for me at Tudor Hall," Wilkes joked in a letter from Richmond. "Cut it down to size, make three or four cradle quilts from it, I don't mind. I never could bear that sorrowful canopy. It always made me fear I'd see old Job at the foot of my bed, naked and bent, with long white locks, and beard hanging to his knees, and shedding tears as big as the quilt's patches."

"What a thing to say about a quilt made with a sister's love," Asia added indignantly after she finished reading the letter aloud to her mother and sister, but she smiled, for she knew Wilkes looked forward with great delight to the arrival of his little niece or nephew.

The family's anticipation of a precious new addition brought a welcome note of happiness to a season of increasing discord throughout the land, for the rising enmity between slave state and free was reflected in their own household. Joseph and Rosalie were indifferent to politics, but Edwin, Mother, Clarke, and Asia staunchly advocated the liberty and freedom of the North, as Asia was certain her father and grandfather would have done. Wilkes alone took the part of the South, especially his beloved adopted home of Virginia, where he had always been treated with kindness and respect by theatergoers, far more so than in the North. It was only natural that he should return the affection the South had offered him in such abundance, Asia supposed, but sometimes she suspected Wilkes exaggerated his ardor to vex Edwin.

Then, in November, an astonishing turn of events forced her to reconsider. The militant abolitionist John Brown, who had been convicted and sentenced to die for his failed attempt to instigate a slave uprising in Harpers Ferry, Virginia, was awaiting execution in a Charles Town prison. As the date approached, rumors flew about that abolitionist partisans were plotting an assault on the village, intending either to break Mr. Brown out of prison or to storm the scaffold and rescue him from the hangman's noose. President Buchanan had ordered four infantry companies under the command of Colonel Robert

E. Lee to Charles Town to meet the threat, but Virginia governor Henry Wise, fearing that this would not suffice, called out the state militias to reinforce the federal troops.

Asia, her mother, and Clarke, avid newspaper readers all, followed the story in the press with alarmed fascination. Only later did they learn that Wilkes had been caught up in the tumultuous events.

Wilkes's letter home spun a thrilling tale, rendered only slightly less harrowing by the knowledge that he had written it after he had already returned safely to Richmond. On the evening of November 19, he was preparing for his bit part in the comedy *The Toodles* when the alarm began to peal in the bell tower on Capitol Square. When Wilkes rushed outside, he discovered that a special train had just pulled into the station at Broad and Seventh, directly across the street from the Marshall Theatre, halting only long enough for the city's militia companies to climb aboard before speeding them off to the defense of Virginia. As he watched the celebrated Richmond Grays, the Richmond Blues, the Howitzer Company, the Virginia Riflemen, the Old Guards, and the Young Guards scramble onto the train, smartly attired in splendid uniforms, impressively outfitted with knapsacks, bedrolls, and muskets, Wilkes was seized by the irresistible compulsion to join them.

He sprinted to the train and asked two of the Richmond Grays for permission to board. When they refused, citing orders that no one was allowed on the train but men in uniform, Wilkes employed his boundless charm to persuade them to sell him enough pieces of their own costumes to allow him to pass. By the time the train reached its destination, he had befriended enough soldiers and had spent enough coin to acquire a nearly complete uniform—snug gray trousers and shirt, white sashes crossed over his chest, a greatcoat adorned with a shoulder cape, a gray hat cocked at a debonair tilt and secured with a chin strap.

In Charles Town, Wilkes served as a scout and a guard, and he was present on that bright, cold, blustery morning of December 2 when Mr. Brown was escorted from the prison to the scaffold, seated atop his own dark-walnut coffin in the bed of a wagon pulled by two white horses. "I felt a throb of anguish as he climbed to the gallows, his old eyes straining their anxious sight for the multitude he vainly had thought would rise to rescue him," Wilkes wrote. "He was a brave old man. His heart must have broken when he felt himself deserted."

Although Wilkes vehemently disagreed with Mr. Brown's cause, the convicted man had faced death so bravely that he had earned Wilkes's respect. "This experience has changed me utterly," he confided to Asia, and when she beheld the carte de visite he had enclosed of himself attired in the uniform of the Richmond Grays, she remembered how ardently as a boy he had wished to be a soldier, a longing that—incongruously, she thought—had been inflamed rather than extinguished by his grueling experience as a cadet at St. Timothy's Hall.

But he was not officially a soldier, and after the train carried the militia to Richmond late in the afternoon of December 4, their duties fulfilled, Wilkes had every intention of returning to civilian life and resuming his chosen profession. But the managers of the Marshall Theatre resisted. Wilkes had vanished without warning less than an hour before curtain. He had been absent two weeks, obliging the rest of the company to scramble to cover his roles. His sudden, inexplicable disappearance was unsettlingly reminiscent of his father's erratic behavior, but Junius Brutus Booth's genius had compensated for his faults. John Wilkes Booth was not so richly blessed, and thus he was fired.

His term of unemployment was so brief, Wilkes reported cheerfully, that he had not enough time to write home about it. When the Richmond Grays learned that he had been sacked, a large contingent of the First Virginia Regiment marched upon the Marshall and demanded that the managers reinstate him. Cowering before the wrath of the soldiers, reluctant to offend the sons of the city's elite who formed its ranks, the managers promptly restored Wilkes to the company.

Then and thereafter, Asia enjoyed Wilkes's stories of his military adventure, but Edwin rebuked him for breaking his contract with the Marshall and jeopardizing his career all for a "mad lark" that proved entirely unnecessary, for neither rescue attempt nor attack on Charles Town had ever come. "The Richmond Grays are no better than a band of privileged boys playing at war," Edwin groused via the post from Louisville. In a stinging flurry of letters, he rebuked Wilkes for deserting the company and for squandering the opportunities Edwin managed to secure for him despite his growing reputation as an arrogant, indolent minor player.

Asia knew that Wilkes chafed beneath Edwin's rule, even as he marveled at his brother's talent and benefitted from his success. The vast difference in their rank was as evident at home as it was in the theatre world, for whenever Wilkes visited the Clarke residence, he could not avoid seeing the grand portrait of Edwin their mother had hung upon the drawing-room wall, or taking note of the laurel wreath she had arranged around the frame, or glancing at the scrapbook on the marble table nearby, in which she had carefully preserved the laudatory letters Edwin received from the leading members of society in the great cities where he had performed—New York, Boston, Washington City, New Orleans, and Philadelphia. It seemed to Asia, as it surely did to Wilkes, that he now shared the title of favorite son with Edwin, if he had not lost it entirely.

But although Edwin was astonishingly gifted, he was far from perfect. He was prone to deep descents into melancholy, and he suffered from what he called the family curse—an overwhelming compulsion to drink. Asia could not fathom how Edwin had ever been tempted to indulge after seeing what liquor had done to their father, but after weeks, sometimes even months, of sobriety, he would suddenly disappear on a drinking binge several days in duration. His manager kept Edwin sober when he could and tended the trembling, hungover actor when he failed. In time the manager was replaced by a devoted new friend, the theatre critic Adam Badeau, who became Edwin's traveling companion, acting coach, literature tutor, and guide to the customs and manners of the elite circles of society to which Badeau had been born. Badeau succeeded better in the role of caretaker than the manager he had displaced, but even he was surpassed by another—a lovely, charming young actress named Mary Devlin.

Edwin and Mary had first met in Richmond in 1856, when Mary played Juliet to Edwin's Romeo at the Marshall Theatre. Edwin had been immediately captivated by her exquisite, dark-haired beauty, her lively and intelligent mind, and her ineffable, warmhearted charm, but she was only sixteen, and the ten years that separated them included a sordid history of heavy drinking and—or so Asia suspected from bits of conversation between her brothers she chanced to overhear—shocking promiscuity on Edwin's part. "I have lost my heart," he had written home to Mother shortly after they met. "It has found a resting place." His love for Mary was so true that he believed he could never deserve her, and as soon as his term at the Marshall ended, he broke off all contact with her. But two years later they met again in Boston, again in the roles of Romeo and Juliet. Mary was eighteen, Edwin was successful and sober, and his determination to protect her from himself melted away beneath the warmth of her affection. In time, Edwin asked her to become his wife.

In February 1860, Asia was safely delivered of a beautiful baby girl, whom a besotted, overjoyed Clarke insisted upon naming after her mother. Asia contributed the middle names of Anne Dorothy, and they soon took to calling her Dottie. Although their little daughter was blessedly healthy and strong, Asia and Clarke agreed that they should not hazard the trip to New York City to attend Edwin's wedding in July. Soon thereafter, when Edwin and Mary invited Mother, Rosalie, and Joseph to live with them in Manhattan, Clarke confessed to Asia that he was glad to see them go. The rising discord between the Booth brothers had strained the household, with Clarke invariably taking the part of his best friend and Asia loyally defending her favorite brother.

"Maybe distance will help John Wilkes master his jealousy," Clarke said on the first night they and little Dottie had the house all to themselves.

"Perhaps," Asia retorted spiritedly, "if Edwin did not insist that they divide the country's theatres between them, keeping the more lucrative North for himself while restricting Wilkes to the South, Wilkes would not feel slighted and constrained."

"Oh, come now. Wilkes has often said that he wants to be first and foremost a Southern actor, beloved of the Southern people." Clarke scowled and shook his head. "And it's plain to see that if secession comes, as many in the South vow it will, he'll cast his lot with rebellion and slavery."

"Wilkes loves his country," Asia protested. "Yes, he's sympathetic to the plight of the Southern people, far more so than you or I, but he's no firebrand secessionist."

But Asia found little evidence to prove her brother's loyalty in the months that followed, when Wilkes declared that the election of Abraham Lincoln as president augured doom for the United States, or when he raised a New Year Eve's toast to South Carolina for courageously seceding from the Union, or when he similarly celebrated each state that followed into rebellion. In April 1861, he sent Asia a rapturous letter after Mr. Lincoln's attempt to send a ship to resupply the Union troops held under siege at Fort Sumter in Charleston Harbor ended in failure when South Carolina militia repelled the steamer and Union Major Anderson was forced to surrender. As she read her brother's letter, Asia, heartsick and afraid, could no longer ignore what had been evident to her husband all along: Wilkes was in wartime what he had been in his youth, an ardent lover of the South and her customs, a staunch defender of Southern principles. Though his native state of Maryland remained in the Union, in his heart Wilkes was as zealous a Confederate as any gentleman of the plantation aristocracy.

As the war erupted and spread, Wilkes continued to ply his trade, crossing borders to tour both in the Union and the Confederacy. He made no secret of his Southern sympathies, only reluctantly conceding to Asia's pleas not to express his passionate, unpopular opinions in public. He could not refrain from praising the Confederacy within the family, however, which only widened the gulf of enmity that separated him from Edwin, who refused to listen to Wilkes's heated denunciations of President Lincoln and Northern policies, and from Clarke, who flatly told Wilkes he was a fool, and that he had cast his lot with criminal rebels who would inevitably be crushed beneath the might of Northern righteousness.

"Oh, Sleepy in his rage and thunder," said Wilkes dismissively when Asia begged him to hold his tongue when he visited. "I care not one bent penny for his opinion. I wouldn't cross the threshold of this fine house except to see you."

It truly was a fine home Clarke had recently purchased for their growing family, for a son, Edwin Booth Clarke, had joined the family in 1861, and another daughter, Adrienne, two years later. Their elegant mansion at 229 North Eighteenth Street reflected Clarke's success and prosperity, but Asia was sure she would never know another happy day if Wilkes made himself unwelcome there. Thankfully, Clarke avoided her brother rather than banning him outright, and Wilkes continued to visit her frequently. With the windows shut tight against eavesdroppers, he would sit in her parlor and sip coffee and speak the harshest invective against the Union, against President Lincoln, against the entire cabinet and all the generals of all the armies of the North until her head swam and she begged him to desist.

On one occasion, Wilkes arrived in a fury, scarcely pausing to remove his coat and hat before he began pacing the room, denouncing the mass enlistment of Irish immigrants, who were as eager to prove their loyalty to their new homeland as they were to earn a soldier's pay. "It is the unwisest move this country has yet made," he thundered. "The pressing of hordes of ignorant foreigners into regiments, buying up citizens before they land, to swell their armies. It is a thing Americans will blush to remember one day when Patrick coolly tells them that *he* won their battles for them, that *he* fought and bled and freed the darkies. The time will come, whether conquered or conqueror, when the braggart North will groan at not being able to swear they fought the South man for man. If the North conquers us it will be by numbers only, not by native grit, not pluck, and not by devotion."

"If the North conquers *us*," Asia echoed, aghast. "Wilkes, *we* are of the North."

"Not I," he exclaimed. "So help me Holy God, not I. My soul, life, and possessions are for the South."

"Why not go fight for her, then?" snapped Asia. "Every Marylander worthy of the name is fighting her battles."

He sank heavily into a chair, running a hand over his beautifully sculpted chin, his handsome brow, a fairer version of their father's. "I have only an arm to give," he said. "My brains are worth twenty men, my money a hundred. I have a free pass to go anywhere. My name and my profession are my passport. My knowledge of drugs, my money, they provide the means—one of the means—by which I serve the South."

Asia studied him, dawning awareness sending a shiver up her spine. Even the child within her womb stirred and kicked as if afraid. "Wilkes," she said in a low voice, suddenly conscious of Clarke toiling over his ledger in his study not far away. "A man came here the other day inquiring for Doctor Booth. I thought perhaps he sought Joseph, but—"

"I am he," Wilkes admitted, "if by doctor one means a dealer in quinine, which some say is more valuable than food in the South these days."

"You deliver medicines to the rebels?"

"Yes."

"How?"

"Hidden in horse collars and such."

"You run the blockade?"

His smile broadening, he crossed the room and took her hands in his, and for the first time she noticed his calloused palms. "I have spent many nights rowing."

"Wilkes, you must desist," she implored, shocked. "Think of the danger. Think of the penalties if you were caught."

But although she argued herself hoarse, she knew that her warnings and admonitions were in vain. The brother she adored was a spy, a smuggler, a rebel, and each terrible word meant death. She knew with chilling horror that if her brother had twenty lives, he would sacrifice each one for the Southern cause. He was and ever had been a man so single-minded in his devotion, so unswerving in his principles, that he would yield everything, everything, for the convictions that had become his consuming passion.

CHAPTER THREE

LUCY

1864–1865

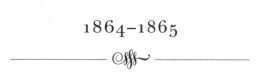

Things base and vile, holding no quantity,
Love can transpose to form and dignity.
Love looks not with the eyes but with the mind.
And therefore is winged Cupid painted blind.
—William Shakespeare,
A Midsummer Night's Dream, Act 1, Scene 1

On Election Day, Washington City was hushed and still, cold and gray. By midmorning the thick, ominous clouds hanging low over the capital broke open in a downpour, so although Lucy had hoped to go riding, she, her mother, and her elder sister instead retired to the ladies' parlor of the National Hotel, resigning themselves to a long wait, anxious for news and for Papa's return from New Hampshire, the state he represented so proudly and so well in the Senate.

Senator John Parker Hale had left the previous day for Dover amid a general exodus of men from the capital, all determined to cast their ballots in what Papa said was the most important election the nation had ever faced. Secretary of War Stanton had secured permission for thousands of soldiers from the crucial states of Maryland, New York, and Pennsylvania to go home to vote, confident that the loyal Union soldiers would overwhelmingly support the Republican ticket as they had in the off-year elections. Hundreds of elected officials and civilian government employees had joined them, emptying the hotels and boardinghouses, packing train cars, and speeding off to determine the fate not only of Mr. Lincoln but of the divided nation and all its inhabitants, Union and Confederate, white and colored, soldier and civilian, free and enslaved.

To Lucy the city's apprehension was as tangible as the falling rain, and she yearned to go out, to call on knowledgeable friends, to gather facts as if they were precious jewels with which she could bribe the capricious Fates. She wished even more fervently that she could vote, that women had some voice in selecting the leaders whose decisions shaped the course of their lives as much as any man's. She would have cast her ballot for Mr. Lincoln, not out of blind loyalty to the Republican Party, but because she was certain that Mr. Lincoln must remain at the helm of the ship of state if it were ever to reach the calm waters of peace.

She had good reason to hope that the voters would choose wisely. After a dismal summer full of stalemate, discouragement, and defeat on the battlefield, General Sherman's capture of Atlanta in early September had suddenly transformed Mr. Lincoln from an embattled administrator into a triumphant commander in chief. As hope for an imminent victory had spread throughout the Union, Radical Democracy Party candidate General Frémont had withdrawn from the presidential race, and as Election Day approached, Democrat general George B. McClellan, the popular but hesitant military commander who did not advocate his own party's platform of peace through concessions, had increasingly seemed a dangerously imprudent choice.

"If Abraham Lincoln is reelected, the war will continue and many thousands more will suffer and die," Papa had conceded the previous day as she helped him pack his bag for the overnight journey. "However, his reelection would mean that eventually the war will be won, the nation reunited, and the poor souls now held in bondage forever free. Abraham Lincoln is not only the wisest choice. He is the only choice."

Lucy wholeheartedly agreed, and when she kissed her father's cheek as he set out for the train station, she prayed that when he returned to Washington, he would find the entire city resounding with the glorious pealing of bells announcing Mr. Lincoln's victory.

To while away the hours, Lucy, her mother, and her sister sewed, read, knit socks and scarves for the soldiers, and wrote letters to friends. Shortly after noon, a telegram arrived from Papa announcing that he had voted and he expected to be back in Washington in time for supper.

"That's all?" asked Lucy, dismayed. "Not a word of the elections?"

Lizzie, her elder by six years, smiled as she held up the narrow paper by two corners. "It's only a telegram, dearest sister, not a lengthy dispatch from the field, and it cannot predict the future."

"Yes, of course, but even so I had hoped Papa could tell us something of voter turnout or the mood of the people."

"There probably isn't much to tell yet," said their mother, smiling fondly. At fifty, she was wise and loving, and very much adored by their father, who consulted her in all matters domestic and political, even if he did not always take her advice. She had been a great beauty in her day, and although Lucy, not yet twenty-four, would never wish to be thought vain, she was secretly thankful that she had inherited her mother's lustrous black hair, enchanting blue-gray eyes, and porcelain complexion. She knew that twenty-nine-year-old Lizzie, similarly blessed, was thankful also.

"I suppose it *is* too early for any news," Lucy admitted, sighing as she settled into a chair by the window. The downpour had turned the streets of Washington City into rivers of mud, and she spotted only two gentlemen making their careful way through it, and one slow carriage pulled by two diligent horses turning the corner from Sixth Street onto Pennsylvania Avenue. In such foul conditions, only the most passionate voters would make it to the polls.

"Perhaps one of your White House beaus will call with early returns," teased Lizzie, taking up her knitting again.

Lucy turned away from the window, all innocence. "I don't know whom you could possibly mean."

"Mr. Robert Lincoln, for one."

"He is not my beau." Robert did not like to contend with rivals for any woman's affections, so he had abandoned his pursuit of Lucy early in their acquaintance. Rumor had it he had recently begun courting Miss Harlan, daughter of the senator from Iowa. "Regardless, he's off at Harvard and probably knows no more about the election than we do."

"Mr. John Hay, then."

"He too is no more than a very dear friend, as you well know." Lucy put her head to one side, considering. "Although as the president's secretary, he'll surely know how the election is going as soon as anyone in the White House does. Perhaps we should invite him to join us for tea."

"Yes, let's," said Lizzie, brightening.

"Girls, I'm surprised at you," their mother said with mock sternness. "We cannot invite such a busy young man to tea on such short notice on such an important day merely to pump him for information."

"Why not?" asked Lucy.

"Because we're already expecting other guests, or have you forgotten?"

In her concern for the election, Lucy entirely had, but she gladly welcomed the distraction of visiting friends—even if they were not handsome beaus with news from the polls.

The downpour had slowed to a steady drizzle by midafternoon, when a few ladies of their acquaintance, politicians' wives and daughters like themselves, arrived to discuss plans for an upcoming fair to raise funds for the United States Sanitary Commission, which provided medicines, bandages, food, and other essential goods to the Union soldiers. Although General Grant's advances upon the Confederate capital of Richmond and General Sherman's victories in Georgia made victory and peace seem tantalizingly near, the Union Army's need for supplies was as urgent as ever, and it fell to the women at home to provide.

Lucy, Lizzie, and their friends staunchly believed that their service was essential to the Union cause, that they too had enlisted for the duration of the war, though they wore no uniforms and held no rank. Earlier in the war, Lucy had wanted very much to answer the call for women to train as nurses for military hospitals, but her ambitions were quashed when the superintendent of army nurses, Miss Dorothea Dix, decreed that she would hire only matronly women of at least thirty years, plain in appearance and in dress. To be included among their ranks Lucy would readily don a simple brown dress without hoops and assume an expression of unsmiling seriousness, but she could do nothing about her age or her beauty.

Thus vastly unqualified to be a nurse according to Superintendent Dix, Lucy had thrown herself into the work of fund-raising, sewing, knitting, and visiting bedridden soldiers in the vast number of military hospitals scattered throughout Washington City. She cheered up the wounded men with pleasant conversation, wrote letters home for those who could not write their own, held trembling hands, soothed troubled minds with gentle songs, bathed feverish brows with cool cloths. She felt necessary and needed and useful, and although she prayed for a swift end to the death and destruction of war, she dreaded to think that victory and peace would mean the constriction of her life to a small circle of domesticity in her father's house, or some future husband's.

Her mother's example encouraged her not only to hope for more but to aspire to it. "I wasted my youth, but I was saved by an excellent wife," Lucy had overheard her father confess to friends on more than one occasion. While her mother was by every measure the very ideal of womanly devotion to family, hearth, and home, she was also shrewd and intelligent, the first reader of her husband's most important speeches, an attentive editor of his drafts of legislation. Whenever significant measures came to the floor of the Senate, she would spend hours observing the contentious debates from the visitors' gallery. "Your mother's queries force me to sharpen my arguments," Papa had told his young daughters on the eve of what became his famous 1856 address to the Senate indicting President Franklin Pierce's Kansas policies and defending the Republican response to the crisis. Though she had been but a girl of fifteen at the time, Lucy had never forgotten how her father's voice had rung with pride, how deeply he appreciated his wife's insight and wisdom. At that moment she resolved that when she was a woman grown, she too would endeavor to be so valued a partner to so great a man.

Through the years, Lucy had given much thought to her future husband, to the mysterious someone she was fated to meet and marry. He would almost certainly have to be a man of politics or the law, so that she might serve her country as her mother did. He would have to be an abolitionist like herself, of course, and he would have to support woman's suffrage. Most important, he would have to be a man of great moral courage, like her father, willing to defy party leadership if they cared more about accumulating wealth and power than serving the needs of the country, unafraid to voice unpopular opinions in the cause of justice. If a gentleman possessed these excellent qualities of mind and character, and if he were devoted and kind, she would marry him even if he were plain and poor—although she would not object if he were handsome and wealthy too.

The Sanitary Fair meeting made an hour pass swiftly by, but eventually the animated discussion ended, their guests departed, and the interminable waiting resumed. Lucy imagined John Hay conferring with Mr. Lincoln at the War Department as they awaited the telegrams that would announce the fate of the president and the destiny of the nation. If only she could contrive some excuse to join them there—but of course, no well-bred young lady could do such a thing without risking scandal, or at least disapproval. Papa's position was too uncertain for her to satisfy her curiosity at such a price.

At six o'clock the Hale ladies withdrew to their suite to dress for dinner. Lucy finished first, and as she waited for Lizzie and their mother, she studied the scene outside her window. In the light of the gas lamps lining the street below, she observed many gentlemen with umbrellas and rolled-up trousers braving the mud and rain on Pennsylvania Avenue and Sixth Street, undoubtedly searching out news of the election, although the early returns were not expected until eight o'clock. Shortly before seven, Papa at last arrived, the faint odor of tobacco smoke lingering about him, his coat and hat damp from rain though he had carefully brushed them before entering. "What have you heard, Papa?" Lucy asked, kissing his cheek in welcome.

Travel weary though he was, her father smiled, his relief and joy evident. "The soldiers are turning out in droves throughout the North, and they have ever been loyal to Mr. Lincoln. We have every reason to hope that he will win the day."

Delighted, Lucy laughed and flung her arms around him. "Thank goodness," her mother said fervently, hand to her heart, and Lizzie swiftly chimed in with her agreement.

"I won't be able to sleep tonight until I receive official word," said Papa, raising a hand to dissuade them from celebrating too soon, "but for now, I am very much encouraged."

Their hearts immeasurably lighter, the family went down to the hotel's dining room, careful to modulate their speech and expressions, well aware of the many pairs of eyes and ears turned their way. Twice messengers interrupted their supper with notes for Papa, which he accepted graciously and read slowly and carefully, his expression betraying nothing. Each time he gave his wife the barest of nods as he tucked the telegrams into his breast pocket, and Lucy inwardly rejoiced. Although her father and Secretary of the Navy Gideon Welles did not get along, her father had many friends in that department, having toiled for seven long years to pass legislation abolishing flogging and, more recently, serving as chairman of the Senate Naval Affairs Committee. Surely, Lucy surmised, the messages came from well-placed officials within those ranks, and just as surely, they brought good news that her father would reveal as soon as the family retired to the privacy of their own rooms.

It was all Lucy could do to finish her meal with grace and decorum, biding her time until her father at last suggested they retire. Concealing her excitement behind a demure smile, she rose and followed her parents from the dining room and upstairs, her arm linked through her sister's. Only after the family was alone in their suite with the door to the hallway firmly closed did her father take the messages from his pocket and hand them to her mother. "Reports from Baltimore, Boston, and Philadelphia are optimistic," he said. "The news from Indiana and even Pennsylvania is equally promising." Then he smiled and shook his head, almost disbelieving. "It seems too that Mr. Lincoln may claim an overwhelming victory in New York."

"Oh, how wonderful," exclaimed Lucy.

"It's not over yet," her father cautioned. "Mr. Lincoln may very well have won, and I pray that he has, but the outcome of many an election has turned on the results of a few key districts." His smile grew rueful, with a hint of sadness it pained Lucy to see. "I daresay we four know that as well as anyone, do we not, my dears?"

The Hale ladies knew all too well. Although they anticipated that they would soon celebrate Mr. Lincoln's reelection, their own dear father and husband had not retained his high office. Despite his many years of exemplary service, despite his status as the incumbent, at a contentious meeting at Rumford Hall in Dover the previous June, the Republican party of New Hampshire had not nominated him as their candidate for the senatorial election. Papa would serve out the remaining four months of his term, but in March, his long, distinguished career in the United States Senate would come to an end.

Although Lucy intended to stay up and keep her father company until a messenger brought the final election results, shortly after midnight, long after her mother and sister had retired, she confessed that she could no longer keep her eyes open. "Go on to bed, darling," her father urged, taking her by the shoulders and kissing her on both cheeks. "When Mr. Lincoln's victory is certain, I'm sure you'll hear it."

Many years in Washington City had honed Papa's prescience. At two o'clock, Lucy groggily awoke to the sounds of men raucously singing "Rally Round the Flag, Boys" on the sidewalk outside the hotel, and somewhere in the distance she heard the faint strains of a brass band playing a spirited march. She drifted back to sleep, only to be jolted awake sometime before dawn by the booming of cannons. Cannon salutes to mark important victories had become so commonplace that she did not fear, as she would have only a year ago, that the capital was under attack. Instead she settled back to her slumbers, relieved and thankful that the wise people of the loyal North had decided to keep Mr. Lincoln at the helm of the ship of state.

In the morning, after a celebratory breakfast in the hotel dining room, where a good many Southern sympathizers revealed themselves by staring glumly into their coffee cups and pushing away their plates of eggs and sausage and toast barely tasted, the Hales settled in the drawing room with the morning papers, reading aloud reports of particular interest, marveling at the fullness of Mr. Lincoln's victory. Lucy learned that at about half past two o'clock in the morning, a crowd of Pennsylvanians led by a Captain Thomas had gathered outside the White House to serenade the president. Loudly and joyfully they had entreated Mr. Lincoln to address them, erupting in cheers when he had at last appeared in an upstairs window. "I earnestly believe that the consequences of this day's work will be to the lasting advantage, if not to the very salvation, of the country," he had told his admirers, or so the *Daily National Republican* reported. "I am thankful to God for this approval of the people; but, while deeply grateful for this mark of their confidence in me, if I know my heart, my gratitude is free from any taint of personal triumph. I do not impugn the motives of anyone opposed to me. It is no pleasure to me to triumph over anyone. But I give thanks to the Almighty for this evidence of the people's resolution to stand by free government and the rights of humanity."

"President Lincoln is as humble in victory as any other man would be in defeat," Mama said after Papa finished reading his remarks aloud.

"Indeed," said Papa, setting the paper aside. "But all loyal citizens of our democracy have reason to be proud today. The fact that we held a presidential election in the midst of a terrible civil war proves that a nation of free people can endure the gravest of divisions, the most dire of national calamities. If the rebellion had forced us to forgo or even to postpone this national election—well, then it would not have been exaggeration to say that the rebels had defeated us."

"But they have not," said Mama as she took her husband's hand. "They have not, and they shall not."

It was a decisive victory, the only outcome that allowed for the preservation of the Union, but in the days that followed, the Hales' rejoicing was restrained, not only because of Papa's circumstances, but because they were well aware that peace and the restoration of the Union would not come until the war was won.

After supper one evening, the family retired to their suite on the second floor, but just as her father fit the key in the lock, Lucy realized that she had left her reticule in the dining room. "Would you like me to come with you?" her mother asked.

"There's no need," Lucy said as she turned to go. "I won't be but a moment."

Gathering up her skirts, she hurried downstairs as quickly as decorum permitted. When she inquired at the dining room, the maître d'hôtel told her he had found the small beaded bag beneath her chair and had left it with the front desk clerk. Lucy thanked him and went to claim it, but she halted abruptly a few paces from her destination, transfixed by the sight of a handsome gentleman signing the guest book. She recognized him at once, as any devotee of the theatre surely would—the dark, silky locks tumbling rakishly over a strong brow; the perfectly sculpted chin, the broad chest and strong shoulders; the alabaster skin; the full, expressive mouth. Even his slightly bowed legs were endearing, emphasizing a slender waist, a strong arm. Elegantly attired in trousers of dark gray, a close-fitting black coat, a wine-colored waistcoat, and a gray silk cravat, John Wilkes Booth was the perfect embodiment of masculine beauty, precisely as she remembered from the last time she had seen him perform.

She had stood transfixed and gazing at the actor too long; the clerk glanced up and smiled inquiringly. "May I be of some assistance, Miss Hale?"

Steadying herself with a quick breath, Lucy nodded and returned his smile as she approached the desk. "Yes, please. My reticule wandered off, but the maître d'hôtel assures me you have corralled it here."

At the sound of her voice, Mr. Booth had turned to smile politely her way, but she did not meet his eye. Her heart was pounding too fast, and she found herself terrified of his searching gaze, certain it would detect the sudden, overwhelming intensity of her emotion.

"Certainly, Miss Hale," the clerk replied. "It's locked in the safe. I'll retrieve it for you at once."

With that the clerk deserted her, disappearing into a back room and leaving her alone with the famous thespian. She sensed Mr. Booth studying her and she felt heat rise in her cheeks. Should she nod politely? Give him her hand? Seize his hand in both of hers and babble profusely about how much she admired his work? She fervently wished her mother were with her, and yet she was equally glad she had come downstairs alone.

"Forgive me for presuming upon so slender a thread of our acquaintance," said Mr. Booth unexpectedly, his voice rich, full, and thrilling. "But you are Miss *Lucy* Hale, are you not?"

She inclined her head but still could not look directly at him. "I am, sir."

"I thought so. I confess, Miss Hale, you have caught me in a moment of utter consternation, and I know not how to proceed."

Surprise compelled her, at last, to meet his gaze. "How so, Mr. Booth?"

"Ah! Then you do recognize me. That makes everything so much easier."

Charmed, intrigued, she felt herself smiling. "What makes what easier? Pray enlighten me."

"I meant only this—when I heard the clerk speak your name, and I recognized you, I found myself torn between politeness and propriety.

Surely I ought to thank the young lady who has fortuitously appeared at my side for the lovely bouquet of flowers she sent me a year ago, but custom demands that I not address her until we are properly introduced, and yet there is no one here to perform that duty. I was at war with myself, thinking that I ought to speak, knowing that I must not." He shook his head, his brow furrowing in amusement and feigned helplessness. "What is a well-meaning gentleman to do when confronted with such a thorny thicket of tangled obligations?"

"Apparently you found your way through it."

"Indeed, yes, and without tearing my coat or losing my hat." He peered at her, his smile broadening. "You *are* the Miss Lucy Hale who sent flowers to my dressing room at the Washington Theatre in May of last year?"

"I am she," Lucy admitted, very much embarrassed. How she wished, too late, that she had heeded Lizzie's warnings to constrain the expression of her appreciation to applause! "Please forgive me my girlish impetuosity. I was—overcome with admiration for your portrayal of Charles de Moor. I had seen *The Robbers* before, but never had the villain seemed so startling and terrible and yet wonderful—strong and passionate, and yet tender and penitent. You were astonishing, absolutely brilliant—" She caught herself. "If I may say so, Mr. Booth."

"You may indeed say so, as often as you like. It may surprise you, but I encourage such talk."

She laughed, still embarrassed, but feeling a bit relieved as well. "A note would have sufficed, I suppose."

"Perhaps, but ink on a page is too dull and plain to properly represent the loveliness of the sender. Flowers suit her much better."

Lucy rarely found herself at a loss for a witty reply, but Mr. Booth's ineffable charm rendered her lightheaded and tongue-tied. "Will the people of Washington City be so fortunate as to enjoy another one of your performances soon?"

"Alas, they will not, unless they're clever enough to find themselves in New York City at the end of the month."

As Mr. Booth resumed signing the register and set down the pen, Lucy's heart inexplicably plummeted. "Then you will not be staying long enough to perform in Washington?"

"Not this time. I'm traveling on other business. My only upcoming engagement is at the Winter Garden in Manhattan, a performance of *Julius Caesar* with my elder brothers for the benefit of the Shakespeare monument to be erected in Central Park. Junius will portray Cassius, Edwin Brutus, and I Mark Antony. This will be the first time the three of us have appeared onstage together."

"How wonderful." Lucy did not know Junius, but she had seen Edwin Booth perform several times. She agreed with the general consensus that he was the greatest tragedian of the day, but John Wilkes was by far the more handsome of the two. "Such a momentous occasion. I'm sure you'll have a sell-out crowd. Dare we hope for a repeat performance here in the capital?"

Mr. Booth shook his head. "Unfortunately, I think not. It was no small feat to arrange our conflicting schedules to allow even this single night's engagement."

"What a shame," she lamented. "I should love to see the three sons of the great Junius Brutus Booth perform Shakespeare onstage together."

"Perhaps you shall," he said, as if struck by sudden inspiration. "If you wouldn't find the train ride to New York objectionable, I could arrange for tickets to be held at the box office for you."

For a moment she could only blink at him, astounded. "That is very generous of you, Mr. Booth," she managed to say, "however, I couldn't possibly—"

"Do forgive me, Miss Hale," he said, his dark eyes endearingly concerned. "You must think me terribly forward. By tickets, I meant four— for you, and your parents, and your sister."

"Of course," Lucy murmured, both relieved and disappointed. Of course Mr. Booth had not intended to invite her to New York City alone to watch him perform. For a fleeting moment she imagined sitting in the audience with her family at the Winter Garden, delighting in the performance of the three celebrated Booth brothers, applauding as John Wilkes took his bows, warming to a smile that was meant for her alone—but then she imagined her mother's eyebrows raising as she learned of the invitation; her parents exchanging a long, knowing, skeptical look; Lizzie regarding her with astonishment and shaking her head in dismay.

Her parents would consider the invitation entirely improper. Their families did not know each other, and they hailed from vastly different worlds. Senators did not see actors socially, and neither did their daughters.

"Thank you very much, Mr. Booth," Lucy told him with feeling. "I would very much like to accept, but my family is obliged to remain in the capital for the foreseeable future. I cannot tell you how sorry I am that I won't be able to witness what I'm sure will be a magnificent production."

"I'm sorry too," he replied affably, but something in his expression told her that he knew the real reason she had declined. "But perhaps our paths will cross again someday, and I can give you my own, utterly biased review."

In spite of her distress, she smiled. "I do hope so."

"Perhaps we could read the play together, and I could attempt to re-create the performance for you." Somewhat ruefully, he added, "If you would like that, and if the absence of my brothers doesn't make the idea less appealing."

"I would like that very much, with or without your brothers."

At that moment, the clerk emerged from the back room with her reticule, which she accepted with her thanks. She offered Mr. Booth her hand in parting, he made an elegant bow over it, and she hurried off, heart pounding, wishing—or nearly so—that for just one day, she could be the sort of bold young woman who would have accepted his invitation.

Something—embarrassment, perhaps, or a girlish desire to keep the memory all to herself, to savor in private—kept her from telling anyone about her encounter with the famous actor. For several days thereafter, she looked for Mr. Booth surreptitiously whenever she strolled through the hotel's public rooms, but to her disappointment, she did not see him again.

She assumed he had concluded his business in the capital and had moved on to New York to meet his brothers, so when her father almost bumped into Mr. Booth one evening as he was entering the dining room and they were going out, surprise struck her with almost physical force, an electric thrill running from head to heart and to all her extremities like a frantic signal on a telegraph wire.

"I beg your pardon," Mr. Booth said to her father, bowing and step-ping aside to allow them to pass.

"Not at all," Papa replied as he bowed in return and led his wife and daughters from the dining room. Lucy inclined her head slightly to Mr. Booth as she passed by, and to her astonishment, he winked back.

"Excuse me, sir," Mr. Booth called after them as they proceeded to-ward the staircase, as if he had only then recognized Papa. "Are you not Senator Hale of New Hampshire?"

Papa paused and acknowledged that he was. After the two gentle-men introduced themselves, and Mr. Booth had commended Papa for his vote on a particularly obscure piece of mining rights legislation, Papa introduced his ladies to Mr. Booth. When Lucy gave him her hand—his palm was more calloused and rough than she expected of an actor—she tried to regard him sternly, silently reproaching him for deceiving her father. Mr. Booth's eyes twinkled with such mischievous merriment that she could not keep up the pretense, and she smiled in return.

Now they had been formally introduced, and by her father, no less. If they met in public again, there was no point of etiquette forbidding Mr. Booth from striking up a conversation with her, if he wanted to.

Lucy and her family saw Mr. Booth again the following morning at breakfast, but her father was eager for his coffee so they did not pause to chat but only exchanged a few pleasantries in passing. And then, just as suddenly as before, Mr. Booth vanished. Lucy could not imagine what business kept him traveling to and from Washington City if he were not performing, but since his absence denied her any more chance meetings in the hotel, she had no opportunity to ask.

She searched for him in the papers instead. On November 24, the *New York Herald* rewarded her diligence with an announcement of the Booth brothers' upcoming production of *Julius Caesar*, which, the re-porter proclaimed, "ought to be chronicled as a great event in the his-tory of drama in this city." Junius and John Wilkes Booth were less familiar to New York playgoers than their brother, but "they are spoken of as worthy associates of Mr. Edwin Booth, so well and so favorably known here." The piece concluded with a glowing declaration that read as both praise and challenge: "If there is any real taste for a great and pure dramatic entertainment in this city, the house will be one of the most densely crowded ever seen."

It surely would be, Lucy thought, muffling a sigh of regret, and she could have been there, an admiring and keenly interested witness to theatre history.

The day after the historic performance, the Hales settled down to share the morning papers after breakfast, their usual practice when the Senate was in recess. Lucy hoped to find a brief mention of Mr. Booth, but she had barely begun to scan the headlines when Lizzie gasped in alarm. "Last night the rebels tried to burn New York City," she exclaimed.

Papa had been reading letters in an armchair by the window, but he quickly set them aside as Lizzie and Lucy took turns reading aloud the shocking reports. At about nine o'clock the previous night, blazes had broken out almost simultaneously at the St. James Hotel, Barnum's Museum, and the St. Nicholas Hotel. Then, over the next three hours, flames had erupted and had burst through upper windows of the Metropolitan Hotel, Lovejoy's Hotel, and the Lafarge House—which shared a building with the Winter Garden Theatre. At midnight five more hotels as well as several other buildings suddenly caught fire. Thankfully, the blazes had been extinguished before the structures could be badly damaged, and no lives had been lost. Afterward, investigators concluded that dozens of Confederate agents, many of them "importations from Richmond, Petersburg, and Canada," had stolen into the city Friday morning carrying in their luggage jars of phosphorous and turpentine. They had checked into rooms at the various hotels, had soaked the beds and blankets with combustible liquids, and had ignited them with Lucifers matches.

"How frightened the people of New York must be to discover that rebel spies have infiltrated their city," said Lizzie shakily.

"My dear, it's entirely possible that some of the arsonists have lived among them all the while, as their neighbors and friends, and continue to do so," said Papa carefully, as if not wishing to frighten them. "Confederate sympathizers lurk in every Northern city, and only the most brazen announce themselves."

"I find their choice of targets even more disturbing than their secrecy," said Mama, a deep crease of worry appearing between her brows. "Why attempt to burn hotels and theatres rather than factories and warehouses, unless the purpose is to take civilian lives rather than to destroy military resources?"

Lucy shuddered, imagining women and children shrieking in pain as they fled the tall buildings of New York City, their clothing engulfed in flames. No lives had been lost, she reminded herself as she searched the columns for any other mention of the Winter Garden. Then, at last, a small notice caught her eye: The performance of *Julius Caesar* had been briefly interrupted when a gentleman seated in the dress circle had observed firemen arriving to extinguish the flames at the Lafarge House. He had told the ladies in his company that the theatre was on fire, his remark had been overheard, and as the alarm spread, nearly everyone in the audience rose at once to flee. At that moment an inspector with the Metropolitan Police, who happened to be present for the show, had called out, "It is only a drunken man. Keep your seats." His deception had quelled the rising panic and had no doubt saved many lives by preventing a general stampede for the exits, and the play had continued without further disruption.

Lucy was greatly relieved to know that Mr. Booth and his brothers had not been harmed, but it was not until the following Wednesday that she learned that their historic performance had been a resounding success despite the alarming interruption. "The audience was fairly carried by storm from the first entrance of the three brothers side by side in their respective parts," the *New York Herald* reported. "Brutus was individualized with great force and distinctness—Cassius was brought out equally well—and if there was a lack of real personality given to Mark Antony, the fault was rather in the part than in the actor."

Indignant, Lucy winced at the slight to Mr. John Wilkes Booth, but she decided that she could hardly trust the opinion of a reporter who could not spell the character's name correctly.

She was glad to see that the *National Intelligencer* appreciated the talents of all three of the Booth brothers equally. Asserting that the production was "unprecedented in the records of the drama," the writer praised each of the brothers Booth by name, declaring, "Never, even on the British stage, to our knowledge, have artists of such merit, as on this occasion, been associated in any one tragedy of the Great Dramatist." The reporter went on to lament that a production of such elevated artistic merit had not taken place in "this large, refined, and intelligent city of Washington, the capital of a great nation, combining as it does a class of people as critical as any in America." Lucy wholeheartedly shared in his disappointment.

But that very evening, she discovered that the quality of Washington theatricals might affect her very little in the months ahead. After considering his options, her father had decided to muster support among his Republican friends in the Senate to petition President Lincoln to appoint him Minister to France.

Lucy absorbed her father's announcement with a curious mixture of excitement and regret. Although Papa's appointment was by no means certain, Lucy and Lizzie promptly began studying French, a language they had learned at boarding school but had used only rarely in the years since. The idea of living in Paris as the daughter of a high-ranking diplomat—the parties they would enjoy, the fascinating people they would meet, the fashions, the museums—delighted Lucy beyond measure, and yet Washington had recently acquired a fascination all its own, thanks to a certain actor who occasionally made it his home.

Mr. Booth checked in to the National Hotel again on the first day of December, retrieving his key from the clerk just as Lucy returned to the hotel from a concert, escorted by her cousin John Parker Hale Wentworth.

"Lucy," Parker said in a strained voice as they crossed the foyer. "Why do you squeeze my arm so tightly?"

She murmured an apology and loosened her grip, pretending she did not see Mr. Booth standing there, willing her heart to stop racing. Then he turned, and he saw her, and his face lit up and he smiled so warmly that she felt herself melting. Then she noticed something else— a thick white bandage jutting out from the top of his collar. "Mr. Booth," she exclaimed, worry making her forget discretion. "What happened? Are you injured?"

Mr. Booth frowned and gingerly touched his neck and collarbone. "I thought I had hidden that bandage better."

Lucy felt heat rising in her cheeks. "Forgive me for crying out. I should have pretended not to notice it."

"It's difficult to ignore," he acknowledged, sparing Parker a polite nod and what might have been an appraising glance. "I'm glad you didn't pretend. Your concern for my well-being is touching." He extended a hand to Parker. "John Wilkes Booth."

"Yes, of course. Lucy mentioned that she had made your acquaintance." Smiling, Parker shook Mr. Booth's hand. "Parker Wentworth. And I can verify that Miss Hale's concern is sincere. She greatly admires your work on the stage."

Mr. Booth's eyebrows rose as he turned an amused glance upon Lucy. "Is that so?"

"Indeed. She has quoted reviews praising your portrayal of Mark Antony in New York last month so often, and has added such fulsome praise of her own, that one might think she had seen it herself. She has already made me promise to escort her to the opening night of your next performance in Washington City, whenever that should be."

Thoroughly embarrassed, Lucy nonetheless could not help laughing. "My cousin exaggerates," she said with mock outrage, giving Parker a little push. "I insist you pay no attention to anything he says. His favorite sport is tormenting me."

"Only because I excel at it," Parker replied, smiling.

"Cousins," echoed Mr. Booth, looking from one to the other. "I should have guessed."

"Please don't say there's a family resemblance," said Lucy, feigning a shudder. "I would feel obliged to wear a heavy veil whenever I go out."

Mr. Booth's smile deepened. "Now one would suppose you to be brother and sister."

"My sweet cousin adores me, no matter how much she teases," said Parker, tucking Lucy's hand in the crook of his elbow again.

"But tell us, Mr. Booth, how did you come by this injury?" she inquired, her mirth swiftly fading. "Was it a stage battle gone awry? Your reputation as an excellent swordsman precedes you, but perhaps you shared a scene with a far less agile actor."

"There was nothing staged about the battle that gave me this." Mr. Booth's fingertips brushed his collar again. "It's an old wound, recently reopened after vigorous exercise that I now heartily repent."

"You fought for the Union?" asked Lucy, surprised.

"No, not I." He shook his head and uttered a small, involuntary laugh. "Except in the sense that I acquired this wound while we were still one nation, undivided. I was an officer with the Richmond Grays when John Brown attacked Harpers Ferry, and I served as a scout in one of the regiments sent to capture him. In the furor surrounding his capture, I was shot in the neck by one of his compatriots."

"Good heavens!"

"Not to worry, Miss Hale. I recovered sufficiently in time to serve as a guard at Brown's execution." Mr. Booth shook his head. "Whatever one might think of his beliefs or the crime for which he was convicted, he died bravely for a cause he believed in. He earned my respect for that."

"You were with the Richmond Grays?" asked Parker. "I thought that the Booth family hailed from Maryland."

"Certainly we do, but I was a featured player at the Marshall Theatre for several seasons, and in that time the people of Richmond embraced me with such affection that Virginia became my adopted home. The sons of the best families of Richmond were members of the Grays, so when they implored me to join their ranks, how could I refuse?"

"You could have been killed," said Lucy faintly, sickened by the thought.

"But I was not killed. I survived with a single scar." He winced and adjusted his collar to conceal more of the bandage. "But it never properly healed, and remains prone to injury, which is why I was discouraged from enlisting for this war."

"Goodness, Mr. Booth," said Lucy. "I never imagined you had such adventures in your past."

"He's a battle-scarred hero as well as an artist," said Parker. "I'm heartily glad to have met you, sir."

Mr. Booth thanked him, assured Parker that the pleasure was mutual, and then bowed and bade them good evening. They wished him the same, and then, as they all turned and made their way to the staircase, they laughed to discover that they were all going to the second floor. They parted at the top of the stairs, Mr. Booth kissing Lucy's hand before he strolled off down the corridor.

"I can't remember ever seeing my sweet cousin blush so often and so deeply," Parker teased as he escorted her to her family's suite. "I believe you fancy Mr. Booth. What will my aunt and uncle think when they learn that their youngest daughter—"

"You mustn't tell them," Lucy implored, halting abruptly, making him stop short of the door too. "I hardly know him. I admire his work, but I don't fancy him. I couldn't. If you say anything, they'll misunderstand, and you'll upset my mother—"

"Hush, cousin." Parker patted her hand where it rested on his arm. "I was only teasing you. Mr. Booth is an actor. Of course he wouldn't think himself worthy to court you, and even if he did, you'd never encourage him."

"Of course not." More firmly, she added, "Certainly not."

"From what I hear," said Parker, lowering his voice conspiratorially as he led her on down the hall, "John Wilkes Booth enjoys the company of many ladies of a certain class—actresses, and others."

Lucy suspected he meant prostitutes, and she bristled with indignation on Mr. Booth's behalf. "I'm sure that's merely idle gossip."

"I certainly hope so." Parker paused outside the Hales' door and rapped twice. "In any case, dear cousin, I think you needn't fear that Mr. Booth will develop a romantic attachment to such an excellent young woman as you."

"I don't fear it," Lucy replied as the door opened and her mother greeted them warmly. No, that was not what she feared at all.

Mr. Booth remained at the National Hotel almost a week, and Lucy saw him every day, but usually only briefly—as they passed on the stairs, as they sat down to breakfast with several tables and dozens of other guests between them, as she perused the library in the drawing room and suddenly found him beside her, reaching past her to take down a book of poetry from a high shelf, brushing her sleeve with his own, smiling down on her mischievously as she gazed up at him, transfixed by his ineffable beauty, his dangerous proximity.

He was always so perfectly courteous, so engaging and amiable, that she almost could not believe her eyes when she passed by the gentlemen's lounge one evening, glanced through the doorway, and discovered him alone and apparently despondent. He was lost in a brood, slumped dejectedly in an armchair in a corner away from the windows and the fire, one hand tangled in his dark, silky locks, the other clasping a brandy. Startled, she almost called out to him, but propriety restrained her. She averted her gaze and was about to continue on her way when she sensed movement and glanced back over her shoulder in time to see that he had risen from his chair and was following after.

She slowed her pace, and a moment later he was by her side, bowing and wishing her a good evening. "Mr. Booth," she said, "I don't mean to intrude, but you look so unhappy, so unlike yourself. Is something wrong? Is your injury troubling you?"

"No, not at all. I'm happy to say I'm on the mend."

She studied him. "You don't look very happy."

"Miss Hale, I assure you that—" He hesitated. "Indeed, I confess that I am not. May I confide in you?"

"I sincerely wish you would."

He offered her his arm, and with a thrill of delight and apprehension, she took it. He escorted her to the lobby, to a chair by the window where everyone could see them and yet none could overhear, so that both propriety and intimacy were satisfied.

"Miss Hale," he said, breathing a sigh that made her long to hear him say her name again. "I confess you have caught me in a low moment. I have just received word that the schooner transporting my stage wardrobe has wrecked at Bic—" He covered his mouth with a fist and cleared his throat. "It has been lost at sea, and all my trunks of costumes, playbills, and scripts with my notes representing years of study have been lost with her."

"Oh, Mr. Booth, how dreadful. Can they be replaced?"

He shook his head. "The playbills, I have collected throughout my entire career as an actor. I can find other copies of the scripts, but I cannot hope to reproduce all of my notes. The costumes and makeup and jewelry and other toggeries of my profession, however—" He paused to clear his throat again, and she noticed that his eyes were red-rimmed. "They belonged to my late father, and were exquisitely made by my own dear mother—silks, satins, ermines rendered into works of art over the course of many years. They were priceless, and are irreplaceable, and represented the entirety of my inheritance from his estate."

Lucy's heart ached for him, and without thinking, she leaned forward to place her hand upon his. "I'm so sorry. Such a terrible loss."

Grimacing, he nodded, and with a deft, graceful gesture he was suddenly holding her hand. "It is only a player's wardrobe. I've no doubt men lost their lives in the wreck of the *Marie Victoria*, so you can imagine how ashamed I feel, sitting here in comfort mourning my lost possessions. And yet, in losing them, I feel as if I have lost my father all over again."

"Of course you do," she said, her heart going out to him. "They were cherished family heirlooms, as well as the necessities of your profession. Is there any chance that the cargo of the schooner might be salvaged?"

"If it could be, it would belong to whomever brought it up from the depths. But it's just as well that I'll never see my costumes again. The salt water will ruin them utterly, and I don't think I could bear to see them in such a state."

"I wish I could find the words to comfort you."

He managed a smile and gently squeezed her hand. "You are, at this moment, providing all the comfort I could hope for."

She felt her heart glowing, and she held his gaze as he held her hand, and she did not care who might observe them or what they might make of it. Mr. Booth was nothing like the other young gentlemen of her acquaintance, the sons of politicians and lawyers and men of business. She knew so little about him, and the mystery of the hidden depths beneath his outward charm, the passion and fire she had glimpsed behind the characters he had portrayed on the stage, intrigued and beguiled her. She understood that it would be a fallacy to confuse the actor with the virtuous men he played, and yet surely he must possess their noble qualities himself in order to perform them so convincingly.

She longed to know him better.

That night after retiring to her family's suite, she pondered Mr. Booth's loss, wondering if he was mistaken, if in fact there was some way his father's wardrobe could be salvaged and restored to him. She did not pretend to be well versed in maritime laws and customs, but her father was an expert on nautical matters and had many friends in the highest ranks of the United States Navy. If anyone could help Mr. Booth reclaim his inheritance, it was her father.

"Papa," she said, setting aside the novel she had only been pretending to read, "if a ship is wrecked, but another vessel is able to salvage the cargo, to whom does it belong? The original owner or the man who brings it to shore?"

Her father peered at her over the top of his glasses. "It depends on the circumstances. Are you speaking of a hypothetical vessel and cargo, or did you have a specific shipwreck in mind?"

"A real and very recent shipwreck, the *Marie Victoria*. She was lost only a few days ago near a place called—Bic, I believe it was."

"Good heavens." Her father sat back in his chair and regarded her with mild surprise. "I had not heard she was wrecked."

"I know very little about the accident, only what I overheard in the lobby earlier today."

"Lucy," her mother chided mildly. "It does not become a lady to eavesdrop."

Lucy threw her a mischievous smile. "I know, which is why I did not linger to hear the entire story. Besides, I thought our own expert would be better informed." She turned back to her father. "So, Papa, in this case, would a man who had lost cargo in the wreck have any reason to hope it might be restored to him?"

"If a man were transporting cargo on this particular ship, he should rather hope the United States Navy never hears of it, or him." Father stroked his chin, brow furrowing as he studied her. "Lucy, darling, would you recognize the gentlemen you overheard if you saw them again?"

"I—I think I might. I'm not sure. Why?"

"The *Marie Victoria* is a British schooner, and a notorious blockade runner. Her captain is infamous for smuggling coal oil and other goods to Wilmington and Richmond by way of Nassau in the Bahamas. Le Bic, where you heard she was wrecked, is a village on the Saint Lawrence River in Quebec. One can easily guess the ship's cargo, and its destination."

"Do you suppose Lucy overheard spies discussing a run of the blockade?" asked Lizzie.

Lucy quickly waved a hand to dispel any such notion. "They would be very poor spies indeed to discuss such things in the lobby of one of Washington's busiest hotels."

"It's more likely Lucy overheard insurance men calculating the payout the ship's owner might demand," their mother remarked, "and counting themselves very fortunate that their companies had not in-sured the *Maria Victoria.*"

Papa smiled, but his expression quickly turned grave. "We can't know for certain whether the captain of the *Marie Victoria* intended to run the blockade on this voyage. Even if he did, surely not every man who arranged to transport cargo in her hold meant to send it into the heart of the Confederacy, but rather to one of the schooner's many ports of call along the way. Even so, Lucy dear, if you see those gentle-men again, point them out to me. The Department of the Navy would do well to keep an eye on them, just in case."

Lucy nodded, unwilling to promise, not trusting herself to speak.

"Goodness, John," said her mother. "You're frightening her. Look at her wide eyes. She's gone quite pale."

"No, I'm fine." Lucy managed a smile. "I'm merely furious at myself for not having paid better attention. To think I might have uncovered a spy ring." She sighed, comically sorrowful. "I would make a terrible Pinkerton agent."

As her parents and sister laughed, Lucy inhaled deeply to settle the nervous fluttering in her stomach. She knew Mr. Booth had once con-sidered Richmond his adopted home, but surely the war had severed his ties to the Confederate capital, and he could not have intended to send his trunks of costumes there. But even as she convinced herself of that, she could not help wondering what business had taken him to Canada, and how his affairs had become entangled with those of an infamous blockade-runner.

Sleep did not bring her any reasonable answers, and the next morning when she saw Mr. Booth at breakfast, anxiety and bewilder-ment rendered her unable to glance in his direction lest she betray her emotions, no matter how often he tried to catch her eye. But then she remembered his pain and grief when he had told her of the loss of his father's bequest, and her heart went out to him. It was unfair to condemn him on evidence so circumstantial it was not really evidence at all.

She offered him a nod across the dining room, and when he smiled back, seeming both relieved and gladdened, she was struck by the as-tonishing thought that perhaps his affections were growing at a pace with hers.

After breakfast, as her family rose from the table, Lucy watched from the corner of her eye as Mr. Booth quickly finished his coffee, dabbed at his mouth with his napkin, and pushed back his chair. Glancing over her shoulder, she saw the encouraging smile and the small gesture that meant he wanted her to linger, so when her family reached the foot of the stairs, she announced that she had forgotten her handkerchief and would meet them upstairs after fetching it.

"Lucy has become so forgetful lately," she overheard her mother remark to her father and sister as they went upstairs. Silently berating herself, she resolved to be more discreet.

She found Mr. Booth in the lobby seated in one of the chairs by the window where they had spoken the previous day. He stood at her approach, and smiled, and she found herself impossibly glad. How could she ever have suspected him of any wrongdoing?

He kissed her hand in greeting, and as they seated themselves, he said, "I have thought of how you can console me for the loss of my wardrobe."

Her heart leapt, but she kept her voice light. "You seem quite happy this morning, hardly in need of any consolation at all."

"I am happy, because I'm here with you, and because you smile at me so sweetly, but I assure you I'm thoroughly grief-stricken. Only you can rescue me from plunging into melancholy."

"Only I? Then I certainly must try to help you if I can."

"An evening of excellent music is precisely what I need," he declared. "On Monday evening, the Grand German Opera Company is performing Charles Gounod's *Faust* at Grover's Theatre. I'm confident that the distraction of the play and your excellent company will cure me of heartache."

She was both thrilled and dismayed, longing to accept, certain that her parents would want her to refuse. "Your prescription is a difficult one for me to fill," she replied. "Perhaps your physician could suggest another remedy?"

"No, only this will do." His dark eyes conveyed both amusement and understanding. "But even the best apothecaries require assistance for their most difficult cases. Shall we invite your sister to join us?"

Lucy thought quickly. "No, not my sister." Lizzie was dutiful and cautious, and she would insist upon informing their parents, who would in turn insist that their daughters decline the invitation. "But someone else—yes, that would do."

"You shall join me tomorrow evening, then?"

She heard the nervous flutter in her laugh and hoped that he did not. "Since you insist that this is the only cure for your unhappiness, I don't see that I have any choice."

"You could decline, and allow me to suffer."

"No, I could not."

They both fell silent, and she basked in the warmth of his gaze—curious, hopeful, happy—and she felt her suspicions melting away. Everyone knew the Hales were abolitionists and firmly for the Union. Surely Mr. Booth would not regard her so fondly if he did not share her beliefs, and his gaze was very fond indeed. . . .

She felt her cheeks growing warm, so quickly she stood, gave him her hand in parting, and hurried off to send a message to the only suitable chaperone whom she could trust to keep her confidence.

Parker readily accepted her invitation to take her to tea at the Willard Hotel, but he eyed her with wary amusement when she ordered a second plate of his favorite cakes. "To what do I owe this exceptional generosity?" he inquired, helping himself to a cherry tart sprinkled with almonds and sugar.

"I would like you to escort me to the theatre tomorrow night."

"Gladly, and no bribery required." He sipped his tea and peered at her, curious. "Is the celebrated thespian John Wilkes Booth performing?"

"No, but he shall meet us there."

Parker set down his cup, wincing uncomfortably. "I take it my aunt and uncle are unaware of this." When she said nothing, he sighed. "Lucy, I don't like to deceive them. If Mr. Booth is courting you, they should know. If you've accepted him as a suitor—which, I might add, I find both unwise and untenable—you should do so openly, or you make it seem sordid and improper."

"I don't know if he wishes to be my suitor."

Parker laughed shortly and sat back in his chair. "Trust me, dear cousin, he does. He wants something from you, at any rate."

"Parker!"

"I meant political connections, advancement, something of that kind. We can't discount the other, though." Parker frowned, thinking. "Do you care for him enough to defy your family?"

"I'm not sure how I feel."

"The truth, sweet cousin."

"I'm not certain if I care enough for him to disappoint my parents by choosing someone so . . . unsuitable." How she wished Mr. Booth were not an actor! "Why distress them when I don't know my own heart yet, or his? I must know him better, and he must know me, before it's reasonable to judge whether we are meant for more than friendship. To that end, I must spend more time in his company."

"And that's where I come in."

"Yes." She reached across the table and laid her hand on his. "I will not see him alone, without a chaperone, but I require someone who understands the need for discretion."

"You must realize that if you go about the city in his company, people will observe you, and word will make its way back to your parents."

"People will not observe me in *his* company, but in my cousin's, and my cousin's friend's. You do like Mr. Booth, do you not, and would like to consider him a friend?"

"Yes, I suppose I would." Parker took up his fork and broke off a bit of crust from his tart, but he did not taste it. "Duplicity can lead to bad ends. Will you promise me that I won't call at your hotel one morning and discover that you've eloped with him in the dead of night?"

"You have my solemn vow that I shall not."

Parker frowned and set down his fork. "Very well, then, but understand that I consent under protest, and only because I fear you'd see him without a chaperone if I didn't agree."

She thanked him profusely, promising him platters of cakes in gratitude for his kindness. He smiled wanly and told her that all he asked was for her to be wise, careful, and discreet, and not to make him regret his decision.

The following evening, Lucy dressed with care and waited apprehensively for her mother or father to suggest that Lizzie accompany her and Parker to the theatre, but to her relief, Lizzie had made plans of her own to attend a levee with a longtime friend visiting from New Hampshire.

"You look radiant," Parker told her as he helped her into a carriage. Too nervous to speak, Lucy thanked him with a tremulous smile that grew steadier, happier, when they arrived at Grover's Theatre and she glimpsed Mr. Booth through the carriage window, chatting with a small crowd of admirers near the entrance. When he saw Parker emerge from the carriage, he hurried over to help Lucy down, and his warm smile and admiring look rendered her dizzy with joy.

The opera was excellently done—that much she remembered, although if she had been obliged to describe any particular scene, she would have been at a loss for words. As sublime as the music was, as impressive the sets, as suspenseful the plot, it was Mr. Booth who held her in thrall, his presence by her side, his ineffable grace, his masculine beauty utterly intoxicating. She wished the evening would never end, and although she applauded the performers as they took their bows, she silently berated them for not improvising a sixth act so that she might enjoy Mr. Booth's company awhile longer.

But eventually the cast disappeared backstage, the audience rose, and Lucy was obliged to depart with them. Parker kindly allowed Mr. Booth to offer her his arm first, and so it was he who escorted her up the aisle and outside, where the crowd milled about on the sidewalk, chatting about the performance as they awaited their carriages.

Suddenly Parker touched Lucy's shoulder. "Look there," he said, nodding off to her right. "We were in even more distinguished company tonight than we knew."

She followed his line of sight and immediately recognized the towering, narrow frame of President Lincoln. He stood on the steps with Secretary of State William Seward and one of his personal secretaries, John Nicolay, on his left, his head inclined to better hear their conversation. On his right arm was Mrs. Lincoln, attired in a lovely gown of blue wool trimmed in white ribbon, chatting with none other than Mr. Lincoln's other secretary, Lucy's friend John Hay.

"Oh, dear," she murmured, turning her head, but not soon enough. Mr. Hay looked her way and smiled in recognition, but then his gaze traveled to Mr. Booth and settled upon her hand resting on his arm. Mr. Hay again fixed his gaze upon Lucy's, his eyebrows raising in wary astonishment.

Suddenly Mr. Booth stepped toward the president and his party, and Lucy was compelled to go along. Alarmed, she tried to slow their progress. She was very fond of Mr. Lincoln and his wife, but she had no desire to speak with Mr. Hay at that moment, to introduce him to Mr. Booth, to explain their presence together. "Shouldn't we wait for the carriage here, where it's less crowded?" she pleaded.

Mr. Booth seemed not to hear her. His gaze fixed intently on the president, he worked his way through the throng almost as if he had forgotten Lucy was on his arm.

"I say, Booth," called Parker, struggling to keep up with them. "If you wish to meet Mr. Lincoln, I'm sure my uncle could arrange an introduction another time."

The crowd had grown so thick that Mr. Booth could not move any closer to the Lincolns and their companions unless he knocked others aside. He halted, staring at the president with inscrutable intensity. Lucy gave his arm a gentle pull. "Shall we find our carriage, Mr. Booth?" she asked. "My parents will expect my cousin to bring me directly home."

His gaze riveted on Mr. Lincoln, he nodded but otherwise did not move. Lucy threw a beseeching glance to Parker, who shrugged and shook his head, as bewildered as she.

"Come on," Mr. Booth said suddenly, turning and guiding Lucy back the way they had come. He said nothing as he hailed a carriage and assisted her into it, then waited for Parker to seat himself before closing the door.

"Aren't you riding with us?" asked Lucy, appalled to hear a piteous tremor in her voice.

"I think it would provoke too many questions if we all arrived at the hotel together, don't you?"

Lucy nodded, and she felt Parker's hand close around hers. "Never mind, Booth," he said easily. "I'll see my cousin safely home. Thank you again for the tickets."

They bade one another good night through the carriage window as the driver pulled away.

"Well, Lucy?" Parker inquired as the carriage halted in front of the National Hotel. "Was the evening all you had hoped for?"

"Not all," she admitted, "but I wouldn't have missed it for the world, and I owe you at least one plate of cakes for your trouble."

In balance, it had been a lovely evening. She and Mr. Booth had parted awkwardly, but even so, she longed to see him again.

The next morning, Mr. Booth appeared at the top of the staircase just as her family was going down to breakfast—or perhaps it was not happenstance at all. He addressed them all cordially, his strange mood of the previous night entirely lifted. Lucy's parents chatted with him so pleasantly that Lucy dared hope that they might grow fond enough of him to set aside their objections to his profession and allow him to court her openly, if that was what he wanted. If she could overcome her own objections. She was reluctant to become an actor's wife—but there she was, putting the cart before the horse, exactly as she had told Parker she must not do. It was utter nonsense to think of marriage when she and Mr. Booth had only just met, and when he had not declared his intentions.

And yet she could not help herself.

She was despondent when he left for New York at the end of that lovely week, and she thought she might burst from the effort of concealing her unhappiness from her family. If they noticed her downcast spirits, they probably blamed the same dispiriting news that troubled them all. On December 8, the day of Mr. Booth's departure, the Senate had removed Papa as chairman of the Naval Affairs Committee, adding insult to injury by appointing a longtime rival as his replacement. Greatly desiring to keep the post through the end of his term, Lucy's father appealed to a trusted colleague and friend, Senator Charles Sumner of Massachusetts, to help reinstate him. Although Senator Sumner advocated on his behalf, when the Republicans caucused, only seven senators voted to retain Papa as chairman. Instead he was offered leadership of the Committee on the District of Columbia, a far lesser post he promptly declined.

"Never mind," Lucy told him, kissing his cheek. "We shall soon be en route to France in any case."

Her father smiled, though his eyes were sad, and he told her no man could ever wish for a kinder or more loyal daughter. She felt a stab of guilt as she smiled her thanks, for a truly kind and loyal daughter would not hide the secrets of her heart from so devoted a father.

After an interminable four days, her spirits soared to see Mr. Booth picking up his key from the front desk once more. The smile he gave her across the foyer was so joyful and admiring that Lucy was certain that absence had made his heart grow fonder, as it had hers.

Ever bolder, they found reasons to cross paths at the hotel as often as they could and conversed as long as they dared, discussing poetry, Shakespeare, the news of the war. Lucy listened, spellbound, as Mr. Booth told her about his family, who lived in New York City and Philadelphia. He tried to visit them at least every two months if he could manage it, and he exchanged letters with them almost weekly, more often with his mother and sisters than with his brothers. Wistfully, he told her about the tragic loss of his revered father, and about his childhood in Maryland. "Did your family own slaves?" Lucy asked him tentatively, afraid for the answer.

To her relief, he shook his head. "My father, like his father before him, abhorred slavery. They were true Englishmen and could never reconcile themselves to our peculiar institution."

"Oh, I'm so glad," Lucy exclaimed. Mr. Booth hesitated a moment before going on to describe how, when he was first establishing his rural Maryland homestead, his father had purchased a slave from a neighboring farmer, had immediately freed him, and then had hired him back as his foreman. Lucy listened, entranced, her heart warming to every word, immeasurably pleased to know that Mr. Booth too came from a staunchly abolitionist family. Somehow that singular, important similarity diminished the vast differences between their backgrounds, at least a little.

Mr. Booth also told her of his conflicted feelings for his brother Edwin, envy intermingled with admiration so intense it was almost worship. His elder brother was the more gifted actor, he admitted, but the friendly rivalry that had emerged years before while they were both performing at the Marshall Theatre in Richmond—he as a lowly supernumerary and Edwin as a visiting star—had inspired him to commit himself wholeheartedly to mastering his craft. "I would not be half the actor I am today if not for my brother," he said. "He pushed me to strive for greatness, as I had never pushed myself."

Lucy's heart ached when Mr. Booth confided to her how a recent tragic loss had made him bitterly regret every jealous moment of their youth: In February of the previous year, Edwin's beloved wife had died of pneumonia.

"Mary was at their home in Boston with their young daughter, Edwina," Mr. Booth told her, his voice low and sad, but steady. "Edwin was performing in New York, but he was held in the tight grip of the old family curse—a relentless craving for drink—and he was in no fit state to read the telegrams sent to him at the theatre, urging him to come home at once. Finally Mary's doctor thought to telegraph the theatre manager, who urged my brother to read his telegrams. He did so, and he immediately raced for home, but he arrived too late. His beloved wife had already passed." Lucy had never thought Mr. Booth more beautiful than when he gazed off into the distance then, lost in memory, his exquisite features shadowed with sorrow and regret. "Edwin was utterly devastated, and he cursed himself for being too drunk to understand that his wife was dying. He has not touched a drop of liquor since that dreadful night, and he has been a perfect father to my poor motherless niece."

Lucy was deeply moved that Mr. Booth had chosen to share such confidences with her, and she wished she had profound, revelatory secrets of her own to share, to strengthen their burgeoning friendship. When she confessed this wish to him one day as they sat alone in the drawing room, he smiled. "I'm glad that you've been so cherished and protected and provided for, that you don't have any sad secrets to reveal," he said, stroking her cheek with his fingers, leaving her trembling and faint beneath his touch. "You are perfect exactly as you are—good, kind, innocent, affectionate. Be thankful, as I am, that you have not been made hard-hearted and mistrustful by a cruel world."

And she was thankful, since it pleased him so much.

She teased him about his frequent travels, and lightly queried him about when he might take the stage again so she might enjoy a performance. To her exasperation, which she was careful to conceal from him, he replied with equally light answers. He had gone to New York, he might tell her, or Philadelphia or Maryland, but not why, or whom he saw there. She told herself that he was traveling on business, though she knew not what kind, or that he was visiting his family, which was entirely plausible. She knew it was possible that he traveled in order to visit illicit lovers, but she dared not ask, so fearful was she of the answer. He had taken to informing her when he would depart the National Hotel and when he expected to return, a subtle change in their friendship that filled her with hope and delight. He seemed now to think, as he had not before, that she ought to know his whereabouts, that she had a particular claim on his time.

Surely that meant they were courting, albeit in secret. She was thankful and relieved that he understood the necessity without her needing to explain or apologize for it.

One frigid afternoon as sleet scoured the windows of the National Hotel, Mr. Booth made good on his suggestion that they read *Julius Caesar* together. Mr. Booth's voice, rich and resonant, drew a small crowd to the library as they sat by the fireplace, she reading out the bit parts, he reciting the most significant lines and speeches from memory. So vividly did he re-create Shakespeare's drama that Lucy forgot about the onlookers until the final scene concluded and they burst into applause.

"You performed all the roles brilliantly," said Lucy warmly after the crowd at last dispersed and left them alone. "I wonder, which is your favorite? Mark Antony, the part you performed with your brothers in New York?"

He smiled, clearly pleased by her praise. "I prefer Brutus."

"Ah, yes. It must be a thrilling challenge for an actor to take on the villain."

"Villain?" He sat back in his chair and clutched at his heart, feigning a deep wound. "Did I perform so badly that I misled you? My dear lady, Brutus is the hero of the piece."

Lucy laughed. "Nonsense! He was a murderer."

"He was a patriot."

Her mirth faded, overtaken by curiosity. "I believe you are in earnest."

"Never more so. Brutus loved Rome. He loved his country more than any other man in the play—more than Caesar, more than Cassius, and certainly more than Antony. He could not allow his beloved country to be ruled by a tyrant. 'As Caesar loved me, I weep for him. As he was fortunate, I rejoice at it. As he was valiant, I honor him. But, as he was ambitious, I slew him.'"

"Mr. Booth, I confess you have me at a disadvantage, as you know the play much better than I," said Lucy, smiling and shaking her head, "but Brutus and his conspirators were traitors, and murderers, and I cannot consider them heroes. I don't believe that was Shakespeare's intention."

"Brutus took one dictator's life to save all of Rome," said Mr. Booth, all traces of amusement fading from his expression, his voice rising. "Thus I call him hero. In the words of the motto of my beloved Virginia, '*Sic semper tyrannis.*'"

For a moment Lucy could only stare at him, rendered speechless by his sudden, indiscreet passion. "Mr. Booth, I daresay you should not shout the motto of a rebellious state so publicly," she murmured. "Someone might misunderstand you."

An instant later, his angry frown had disappeared, transforming into a mischievous smile. "It seems to me someone already has."

Then she understood. "Shame on you, Mr. Booth," she scolded, as relieved as she was delighted. "You've been teasing me."

"I meant every word," he said, but although he sounded utterly sincere, she would not be fooled a second time.

O n the evening of December 16, Lucy dressed for supper early and told her family that she would wait for them downstairs, darting out the door before anyone could raise objections. As he had promised, Mr. Booth met her in their usual place by the window in the lobby, but as soon as they sat down, he told her that he would be leaving very early the next day for Maryland. "To visit family?" she inquired, though she knew his family no longer resided there.

"Sadly, no, not this time," he replied.

Though reluctant to spoil their leave-taking with annoying questions, she could not resist one more. "What weighty matter beckons you away from Washington, then?"

He smiled, looking rather satisfied with himself. "You mean away from *you.*"

"Perhaps I do," she retorted airily. "Perhaps I don't really care where you go or what you do but feign interest only to be polite."

His laugh rang out rich and full. An older couple passing through the lobby glanced their way and smiled indulgently.

"If your curiosity must be satisfied," he said, "I'm going to look at a plot of land in Charles County. I've been thinking about purchasing a farm."

She regarded him in astonishment for a moment. "You wish to become a gentleman farmer?"

"Would that not be more suitable for a senator's daughter than an actor?"

Mortified, she looked away. "I would never wish to hurt you, Mr. Booth, but I beg you to understand that my parents have certain expectations for me."

"They are absolutely correct to do so."

"And I have certain expectations for myself."

He gazed at her, longing and hope and worry intermingled in his compelling dark eyes. "Miss Hale, I think I understand what you're too demure to say. Forgive me if I'm being forward, but I must know. Is it only my profession that you find objectionable?"

"It is not objectionable," she murmured, conscious of other guests passing through the lobby. "You're exceptionally talented. You're the son of the great tragedian Junius Brutus Booth, born to the stage—"

"Miss Hale." He took her hand, his touch gentle, his gaze firm. "Let us be frank. Is my profession the only impediment, or is there something else? Do you have an understanding with another gentleman? Have I misinterpreted your kindness as affection, and am I speaking entirely out of turn?"

"No, no, certainly not." Heat rising in her cheeks, she withdrew her hand from his and clasped hers together in her lap. "There is no other gentleman, not for me."

"And your feelings for me?"

"Have you not guessed?"

"Then dare I hope that if I give up the stage, you might encourage me to court you?"

"I—I confess I thought we were courting already."

"To court you openly, then, with your parents' blessing?"

The crux of the matter could no longer be avoided. "I would never ask you to give up a profession to which you have devoted your life and for which you are so well suited. However—" She hesitated. "Please don't despise me for this, but my parents would never approve, and I love them too dearly to break their hearts."

"I could never despise you, my dear, dear Miss Hale."

His voice was so warm and tender that she felt a thrill of hope and expectation surge through her with all the force and height of a spring tide—as powerful, as natural, and as dangerous. Emboldened, she asked, "Then what do you feel for me?"

"How can I speak the truth of how confounded I am?" He ran a hand through his silky black hair, suddenly agitated. "If not for you, how clear the future would be to me! How easily I could grasp the ambition closest to my heart! What exquisite timing, that just as I am about to set foot upon the path I have chosen, that I should find myself in love!"

"I don't understand." Shocked, stung, Lucy fought to keep her voice even. "Did you think this declaration would please me? You don't sound like a man happy to find himself in love. I certainly wouldn't wish to interfere with any unrealized ambition you hold so dear."

"Lucy, darling, you mistake me."

"I certainly hope I do."

"I've set a course for my life, leading me toward a solemn duty I must fulfill."

She felt a pang of apprehension. "Are you planning to enlist, despite your old injury?"

"No, not that." He gave her a strangely lopsided smile and reached for her hand, but she kept them clasped in her lap. "But it is a service to my country."

"Tell me what it is, and I may be able to help you achieve it."

He shook his head. "I could not ask you to share my fate."

"Is that not what marriage is?" she countered. "The intertwining of fates? The sharing of love and life and all that it brings, for better or for worse?"

He regarded her in silence for a long moment. "Yes, of course it is." Again he reached for her hand, and this time, she let him take it. "I love you, my darling Lucy. I will prove myself worthy of you."

"I don't doubt that you are, Mr. Booth."

"Please, call me John."

Lucy felt close to tears, but she struggled to keep her composure, mindful of the guests and staff passing through the lobby. What should have been a glorious, romantic moment had turned deeply painful, bewildering. Did he want to marry her or not? Did they have an understanding or were they agreeing to part company?

"Lucy, dear," her mother called.

Startled, Lucy looked up to discover her parents and Lizzie waiting for her at the foot of the grand staircase. Heart sinking, she wondered how long they had been standing there, watching. They could not have overheard a word, but so much could be inferred from what they must have seen.

She and John rose and went to meet them, and as they all exchanged greetings, Lucy marveled at how immediately John appeared to be his usual genial self again, lighthearted and courteous. He was an actor, she reminded herself, wondering what her own expression betrayed.

To her surprise, her father invited John to join them for supper, and to her relief, John declined. "I'm leaving Washington early in the morning," he said, regretful, "and I have much to do before I go."

"Another time, perhaps," her mother said.

John thanked her, wished them all a good evening, and departed with a bow.

"What on earth were you two discussing so earnestly?" asked Lizzie, linking her arm through Lucy's as they followed their parents to the dining hall.

"The future of our country," Lucy said, the barest tremor in her voice. "Duty and ambition."

"Indeed?" Lizzie's eyebrows rose. "I would not have guessed that Mr. Booth cared for such weighty subjects. Apparently I've misjudged him."

Lucy managed a smile and, employing all her strength of will, she refrained from glancing over her shoulder to see if John had lingered at the top of the stairs to watch her go.

John had told her that he intended to depart early the next morning, but he had not mentioned when he intended to return. As winter deepened and Christmas approached, the Hale family made arrangements to return to New Hampshire for the holidays, and Lucy resigned herself to the possibility that she might not see John again until the New Year.

Three days before Christmas, Lucy, Lizzie, and their mother were packing their trunks when they heard the door to the suite open and close. "I'm home, darlings," her father called out wearily.

His ladies had time to exchange glances of surprise and worry before they went to greet him. They had not expected him for hours, especially since it was the last day before the Senate adjourned for the holidays. He had intended to present a bill to incorporate the association of the Sisters of Mercy in the District of Columbia, and he surely would not have left before seeing that through.

They kissed him and helped him out of his coat and hat, trying not to fuss, though his expression of disappointment and resolve troubled them more than his early homecoming. "Did you present your bill, darling?" asked Lucy's mother as he removed his shoes and settled into his favorite armchair with a sigh.

"I did."

"Was it tabled, Papa?" asked Lizzie.

"On the contrary," he said. "I obtained unanimous consent to present it. It was read first and second times, again by unanimous consent, and was referred to the Committee on the District of Columbia."

"But that's good news," said Lucy, bewildered. "Why are you so downcast?"

"I don't want you to worry," he said, which all but ensured that they would. "When I arrived at the Capitol this morning, I found Senator King of New York—former senator, I should say—waiting for me in the rotunda. He had come to inform me privately, as a courtesy, that he had written a letter to the president recommending John Bigelow to be appointed Minister to France."

"But Senator King said he supported you," said Mama.

"Apparently he changed his mind." Papa sighed again, took out his handkerchief, and ran it over his brow. "He gave his letter to Secretary Seward, who promised to deliver it personally to Mr. Lincoln today."

Mama frowned, pensive. "Is there a chance that Mr. Lincoln will discount Mr. King's letter and choose you instead?"

"Highly doubtful, my dear, since the secretary of state has endorsed it. Secretary Seward is not only one of the president's closest advisers, but also a personal friend. Mr. Lincoln trusts his opinion implicitly."

"Who on earth is John Bigelow anyway?" queried Lucy, indignant. "He couldn't possibly be more qualified for the post than you."

Her father smiled wanly. "The president might disagree. Mr. Bigelow is the current United States Consul General in Paris."

That gave Lucy pause, but only for a moment. "Perhaps you could take over as Consul General."

"Perhaps." He rose and held out his arms, and they quickly embraced him. "Oh, my dear girls. Such steadfast confidence you have in me, more than I could possibly deserve."

"Nonsense," said Mama briskly. "President Lincoln will remember your many qualifications and find an excellent post for you, if not in France, then somewhere even more delightful."

He managed a rueful smile. "Maybe Santa will leave a cabinet position in my stocking."

They laughed, relieved to see his characteristic resilience come to the fore.

Later that same evening, Lucy was banishing Thackeray's tedious *The History of Henry Esmond* to its shelf in the drawing room when she heard footsteps behind her and, glancing over her shoulder, she discovered John crossing the threshold. "Good evening, Miss Hale," he said courteously, bowing.

She felt a pang of regret that he had resorted to the old formalities. "Good evening, Mr. Booth. How was your journey?"

"Longer than I had expected, and as uncomfortable as I had feared."

She nodded, turned back to the shelves, and pretended to search for a book. "At least it's over, and you arrived safely. Did you buy a farm?"

"No, just a horse," he replied. "Miss Hale, have you dined yet this evening, and if you have not, would you care to join me in the dining room?"

Her heart leapt, and for a moment she considered attempting a second repast, but honesty, prudence, and an aversion to gluttony won out. "Thank you, but I dined earlier with my family."

"Then I shall give you your Christmas present now." He reached into his breast pocket, withdrew a slender box wrapped in red paper, and held it out to her. "Merry Christmas, Lucy."

She hesitated before accepting it. "Mr. Booth, I—"

"John, please."

"John—" Then words failed her. She carefully unwrapped the box, lifted the lid, and discovered inside an elegant silver locket nestled in a bed of white paper. With trembling hands, she opened the locket and found his portrait within, a fair likeness that nonetheless failed to capture how handsome he truly was.

"Please accept this as a symbol of my esteem and affection," he said. "I hope you will always wear it close to your heart, where I hope always to be."

She pressed a hand to her lips, lightheaded, and inhaled deeply to steady herself. "It's beautiful," she said when she could speak. "Thank you."

"Shall I put it on you?"

She nodded, handed him the box, and turned around, lifting her hair out of the way, wondering how she would explain this new adornment to her family. An electric thrill passed through her when she stood within the circle of his arms, when his hands brushed the back of her neck.

"There," he said after fastening the clasp and setting the box aside. "Turn around and let me see you."

She did as he asked, scarcely able to meet his gaze for the way it made her feel—unbearably, exquisitely wonderful.

"You are extraordinarily lovely, Lucy Hale."

"You are too kind, John Wilkes Booth," she said, trying for a light tone, and from the look on his face, not quite achieving it. "I regret that I have no gift for you."

"I want only this," he said, taking her hands in his. "The honor of your promise to wait for me, and not to enter into an understanding with any other gentleman, until I can prove myself worthy and win your parents' blessing."

She felt tears gathering. "That, I am only too happy to give."

He kissed her then, his lips soft and searching on her own. For a moment she melted into bliss, but then a thrill of alarm compelled her to pull away. "John, darling, no. No one can discover us like this. It would ruin any chance we have of winning over my parents."

"Of course," he said huskily, taking a step back. "But know that I shall cherish my Christmas gift, even if I can't tell a soul about it. I won't forget that you gave it to me, and you mustn't either."

"Of course I won't forget. How could I? I give you my promise with my whole heart."

"And I will keep it safe in mine." He bowed, bade her good evening, and departed just as two gentlemen entered and seated themselves by the fire, too engrossed in their own conversation to notice them.

Lucy turned back to the bookshelves, trembling, exhilarated. She pretended to read the embossed titles, but her heart was pounding, her thoughts racing, so she snatched down a well-worn volume of *A Tale of Two Cities* and hastened away, breathless and guiltily glad that her father would not be moving the family to France after all.

Before she entered the suite, she tucked the beautiful locket beneath her bodice, and when she undressed for bed later that night, she took care to keep it out of Lizzie's sight. In the morning she went through the same secretive contortions as she put on a gown of rich blue wool, choosing it not for its color though friends assured her it set off her dark hair and gray-blue eyes beautifully, but because of its high neckline, which concealed the locket's silver chain. She enjoyed the feeling of the cool, smooth metal against her skin, and she decided that when she next saw John, she would lay her hand upon her bosom so he would know the locket, and her promise, were kept safely close to her heart.

But she did not see him at breakfast, nor did she encounter him elsewhere in the hotel all day. It was not until that evening, after her father had settled into his armchair by the window and she had brought him his slippers and the evening papers, that she glanced out the window and was for a brief moment rendered motionless by the sight of John about a block away, striding toward the National Hotel in the company of three men she did not recognize.

"I believe I'll follow your example and read for a while," she told her father.

He glanced to the pile of papers on the end table. "Would you like the *Herald* or the *Evening Star*?"

"No, thank you, Papa," she said, hastening to the door. "I'm more in the mood for Dickens."

"Have you finished *A Tale of Two Cities* already?" he asked absently, returning his gaze to the paper. "You brought it upstairs only yesterday."

"No, I haven't, but I've read it before, and *A Christmas Carol* is better suited for the season."

When he nodded, she quickly slipped into the hallway and shut the door behind her, breathing a sigh of relief. Deception did not come naturally to her and she prayed she would soon be done with it.

Flinging aside caution and propriety, Lucy raced down the stairs and seated herself in her favorite chair by the window just as John entered with the three men. So absorbed were they in their conversation that they did not glance her way as they crossed the lobby on their way to the front desk.

Studying them, Lucy knew she had not seen them at the hotel before, and she was fairly certain they were not registered guests. All three of the strangers were well dressed, if not as handsomely as John. The eldest was a gentleman of about thirty, neatly attired in a dark suit and coat, nearly bald except for a heavy fringe of brown hair half encircling his crown. A thick vandyke hid his mouth, but not his expression of displeasure. The youngest man could not have been more than twenty, with a boy's smooth, pale skin and fine, light-brown hair. He was tall and quite elegantly dressed, and his deep-set eyes, long nose, and prominent brow gave him a scholarly air. The last of John's companions seemed only a few years older than the youngest, and he seemed to be the most cheerful, with a round face and rosy cheeks, carefully combed hair, and a small, neatly trimmed mustache. His attire distinguished him from the other men in that his trousers were blue with stripes up the side. Lucy immediately recognized the uniform of the War Department Rifles, signifying that he was a member of the Union regiment composed of the clerks and messengers of the department and its bureaus.

Mystified, Lucy watched as John spoke with the front desk clerk briefly, then left his companions and strolled down the hall toward the dining room. He soon returned, and from across the lobby his eyes met Lucy's and he smiled. She raised her eyebrows in a silent question, hoping he would join her, but he gestured surreptitiously to the three strangers and shrugged helplessly to say that he was regrettably engaged. She offered him a small, understanding smile in return, then turned her gaze to the window as if she had come downstairs only to enjoy the view of passersby merrily going about their Christmas shopping. When she looked back, John was leading the three men upstairs to the second floor, and soon thereafter, a waiter hurried along in their wake carrying various bottles of liquor, glasses, and a bucket of ice.

Lucy lingered by the window for a suitable interval before rising and following after, but as soon as she placed her hand on the banister she remembered *A Christmas Carol*, and so she went to the drawing room to retrieve it before returning upstairs. At the landing, she hesitated, glanced to her left toward her family's suite, then looked down the hall in the opposite direction, where John's room lay around the corner. It was strange that he had not spared the few moments necessary to introduce his guests to her, and not only as a point of etiquette. If the three gentlemen were his friends, would he not want to show her off proudly as his particular friend, as she was, if she did say so herself, a pretty, graceful, and charming young lady? And if the men were business associates, should he not want to impress upon them that he was well acquainted with the daughter of a respected senator?

Likely John had not meant to slight her, she told herself, and whoever the gentlemen were and whatever had prompted their visit, it surely had nothing to do with her. She ought to return to her family before they began to wonder why she had been detained.

She considered a moment longer before heading quietly down the hall back toward her family's suite.

Lucy lay awake beneath the soft comforter beside her sister long after the rest of the family had fallen asleep, her thoughts wildly tangled and taut. She puzzled over John's companions, about his trip to Canada, his unsettling involvement with an infamous Confederate smuggler, his frequent travels on vague matters of business, and the strange, undefined duty to his country that he insisted ruled his fate. She weighed everything she knew of him from her own experience against all that she had heard through rumor and gossip, wishing she could ignore the details that troubled her and embrace only those that affirmed that John was indeed the good, noble, loving gentleman with whom she had fallen in love, whom she hoped to marry.

And then, all at once, the tangled threads unknotted, and the truth—or the closest she could reasonably hope to come to the truth, without verification from John—stretched before her, a single, unbroken ribbon binding all the disparate elements together.

She knew what John was, and she realized why he had not told her.

Understanding quieted her restless mind. Eventually fatigue overcame her and she sank into restless sleep.

It seemed only minutes later that gentle shaking woke her. "Lucy, it's time to get up," said Lizzie, her hand on Lucy's shoulder. "You overslept. You'll have to hurry if you want breakfast before we leave for the train station."

Lucy scrambled out of bed, momentarily disoriented. She had no appetite, but she did have other important business to conduct before she boarded the train to New Hampshire.

She made a quick toilette, interrupting her preparations once to assure her parents that they should go down without her and she would join them in the dining room soon. After they departed, she counted to one hundred to give them time to descend the grand staircase before she left the suite, hurried down the hallway, and knocked upon John's door.

When he answered, he took a step back, astounded to see her. "Miss Hale," he said, glancing past her into the corridor. He had washed and was freshly shaved, except for his mustache, and was clad only in his trousers and shirt. "To what do I owe this unexpected and rather indiscreet—"

"We must talk." She put a hand to his chest, pushed him back into the room, and followed him inside, quickly closing the door behind her.

"Lucy," he exclaimed. "Are you mad? You can't be here. What if you're seen?"

She knew the risk to her reputation and felt faintly ill from worry, but she had no choice. "John, I'm going to ask you a question, and I want you to answer with complete honesty, even if you think you should not."

He smiled, perplexed. "This all sounds quite serious."

"It is."

Brow furrowing, he folded his arms over his chest. "Very well. Ask, and I shall answer."

"Are you a spy?"

He stared at her, dumbfounded. "What?"

"Are you a spy for the War Department, or are you a Pinkerton agent?"

He blinked, coughed, and then, to her astonishment, he began to laugh. "You believe," he managed to say, "that I am a spy for the Union?"

"It makes perfect sense. Your travels, your unexplained business affairs, your strange meeting last night with a soldier from the War Department Rifles, this undefined but enormously important duty of yours—" She studied him, confused, his mirth making her feel ignorant and foolish. "You said your old wound prevented you from enlisting for the war, but this service to your country you could perform without the risk of reopening your wound."

"Oh, I don't know about that, darling. Spies risk injury every day."

"Don't laugh at me. I'm in earnest. Tell me the truth. Are you a secret agent?"

"Lucy, my love." He smothered his laughter, took her hands, and held her gaze steadily. "I swear to you on my life that I am not a Union spy."

"Or a Pinkerton?"

"I am also definitely not a Pinkerton."

A dizzying wave of relief, confusion, and indignation swept through her. "What are you, then?" she demanded, snatching her hands from his grasp. "If I'm to marry you, I must know. What business calls you away from Washington so frequently? Why were you in Canada? Who were those strange men last night?"

"That's unkind," he protested, smiling. "They weren't strange. They're actually quite ordinary."

"You know what I mean. Don't make a joke of this."

"Lucy, dearest." His voice softened, becoming tender, reassuring. "I am not in the spy business. I'm in the oil business."

She stared at him, uncomprehending. "What?"

"The oil business. For many months now, I've been speculating in oil." He smiled, amused and affectionate. "I am one of three founding partners of the Dramatic Oil Company. We own several rather profitable wells in Pennsylvania, and we're looking to expand. I traveled to Canada to consult with coal-oil experts."

"But one of the men who visited you last night is with the War Department Rifles. I recognized the uniform."

"Soldiers can speculate in business like any other man. Their pay is so poor, I'm surprised more of them don't."

"But why would you take your costumes to Canada if you went there to consult with oil experts, especially since, as you've said, you haven't performed since that night in New York with your brothers?"

He shrugged. "Last summer I exchanged some letters with a theatre manager in Quebec about a possible engagement, so I thought it would be best to be prepared. Unfortunately, nothing could be arranged, and I have only the loss of my wardrobe to show for it."

She studied him, uncertain. "Why have you said nothing of this? If you're in the oil business, why haven't you told me?"

"You never asked."

"It wouldn't have been polite," she protested. "To think that I've been unbearably anxious because of my parents' objections to your occupation and all the while—"

"Ah, but the source of your parents' grievance remains," he pointed out. "I am not an oilman, wholly and exclusively. I am an actor who has become involved in oil speculation. I do hope to eventually relinquish the first for the second, but until then, your parents will still have reason to withhold their blessing."

"But now we have hope. We have a plan."

"We always did, Lucy darling. I never would have pledged myself to you if I had not been certain that someday I would resolve the matter and be able to marry you."

"You knew this," she said, a trifle sharply, "but I did not."

He had the decency to look chagrined. "Indeed, and I see now I behaved very badly in not telling you. I'm truly sorry."

"Yes, you did behave badly," she scolded, joy softening the sharpness of her rebuke, "but this is wonderful news. Wonderful!"

"I'm glad you think so," he said, amused. "I quite agree. I only wish I'd shared it earlier."

"You should have, and from now on, you mustn't keep such secrets from me. I confess that sometimes I feel as if I hardly know you. Don't you trust me?"

"Of course I trust you." A pained, searching expression clouded his handsome face. "And you know me better than anyone does."

She was not sure if she believed him, but pride and gratitude rose as a wave of warmth from her chest into her cheeks. She wanted very much to be the one person in the entire world to whom he entrusted his secrets.

He held out his arms to her, and she gladly fell into his embrace, resting her cheek and her right hand against his chest, inhaling deeply of his scent—tobacco smoke, cedar, and something else uniquely his. But her family was waiting and she could not linger, so they parted with a kiss and promises for a happy reunion on the last day of the year. John checked to make sure the corridor was clear before she slipped from the room and hurried downstairs to join her family at breakfast. She felt all aglow, more hopeful than she had been since she and John first met. This could be her last Christmas as Miss Lucy Hale. By the end of the year soon to come, she could be Mrs. John Wilkes Booth.

It was only later, as she sat beside Lizzie on the train to Dover speeding past the picturesque snow-covered hills and fields and villages of New England that she wondered why John considered his speculation in oil to be a solemn duty to his country, so important that love might interfere. The Union needed fuel to run its factories and light its war rooms, she concluded. John was not wrong to call it service to the cause.

Christmas was gloriously merry back home in New Hampshire, with parties and dinners with friends and loved ones, enchanting music and delicious feasts, solemn prayers and delightful stories read aloud by the fireside, sleigh rides and Yule logs, a festive tree with gifts hidden among the branches for the children and fond reunions spiced with amusing gossip for the adults.

Several of Lucy's friends and cousins complimented her on her radiant appearance and lively spirits, and more than a few teased that she must have some secret new beau, or perhaps a former beau in whom she had taken a keen new interest. Robert Lincoln was mentioned in the speculation, of course, and John Hay, and Oliver Wendell Holmes Jr., whom she had met while on vacation in Maine in 1858 and with whom she had enjoyed a delightful correspondence and several pleasant outings well into the early years of the war. One particularly cheeky friend suggested that Lucy had heard again from William Chandler, who had become infatuated with her upon their first meeting years before and had written her several love letters and poems before her parents had asked him to desist, since Lucy had been but twelve years old at the time.

"I have not heard from Mr. Chandler, nor will I, as he is married now," Lucy protested, laughing. "He wed the former Miss Caroline Gilmore, the governor's daughter."

Amid the teasing and laughter, no one seemed to notice that she did not deny being in love.

As delightful as it was to enjoy the comforts of home and the company of beloved family and longtime friends, Lucy was eager to return to the capital and to John. A few days after Christmas, the Hales boarded the train for Washington, staying over in New York, Boston, and Philadelphia to celebrate the festive season with friends along the way. They finally returned to the National Hotel late in the evening on December 31, but although Lucy had eagerly anticipated the promised reunion, and hoped to share a discreet kiss with John at the stroke of midnight, he was nowhere to be found.

Since New Year's Day fell on a Sunday that year, the traditional receptions and entertainments would be delayed until January 2, but the mood at the National Hotel remained festive and glad, and it seemed the entire war-weary city welcomed the New Year with reinvigorated hopes. Mr. Lincoln—who had risen in Lucy's esteem year after year, until she had come to revere him almost as much as her father did—had won reelection, alleviating fears that a change in leadership would lead to disastrous consequences for the North and the poor souls held in slavery in the South. On Christmas Day, General William T. Sherman, having reached the end of his march across Georgia at the Atlantic shore, had sent the president a telegram bearing a unique holiday greeting: "I beg to present to you, as a Christmas gift, the city of Savannah, with 150 heavy guns and plenty of ammunition, and also about 25,000 bales of cotton."

Lucy hardly dared hope that at long last the war and all its bloodshed, sorrow, and deprivation was entering its final days, but her father and mother agreed that victory and peace had never seemed nearer. Eighteen sixty-five would be the year the war was won, peace was restored, and the shattered nation reunited, the people predicted, with an optimism they had not known since the early days of the war. It would also be the year Lucy would marry the man she loved, or so she dared secretly to hope.

Her heart leapt with joy when John entered the dining room at breakfast, and if she had not been seated with her parents and surrounded by dozens of strangers, she might have bounded from her seat and embraced him. He paused by their table to wish them a happy New Year and to inquire about their Christmas, but to Lucy the entire conversation was exquisitely painful, a mere taste of John when she desired so much more.

It was hours later before she saw him in the drawing room alone— or nearly so, for an elderly couple sat in the best chairs by the fireplace, glancing up from their books now and then to complain about the frosty weather. "My New Year is off to a most auspicious start," John murmured as he offered her his arm and led her to the farthest bookcase, where they pretended to search for a particular elusive title. "All that this glorious day needs to be complete is your kiss."

"I wish I could kiss you, here and now." Lucy withdrew a small box from her reticule. "Since I cannot, I give you instead your Christmas gift—belatedly, but no less fondly offered for that, I promise you."

"Lucy, darling." He accepted the box and bowed, and when he lifted the lid and saw the small silver ring inside, his surprise gave way to delight. "How exquisite."

"The engraving is nearly identical to the scrollwork on my locket," she pointed out as he slipped the ring onto the pinky of his right hand. "They complement each other so well, one can imagine that they were created by the same silversmith as part of a set."

"They were made for each other, though that was not revealed until they were brought together in this place. How like the two of us they are." He closed his eyes and kissed the ring, then smiled at her with such warmth and intensity that she felt faint with desire. "I will cherish this gift always. Thank you, my darling Lucy."

Before she could reply, she heard the soft clearing of a throat. "Lucy, dear."

Lucy whirled around to discover her mother standing just inside the doorway, her expression stony. "Yes, Mama?"

"Have you found the book you wanted?"

"No, no, not yet. Mr. Booth—he kindly offered to help me."

"How kind indeed. Your book will have to wait. Your father must pay a condolence call on Chief Justice Chase, and he would like us to accompany him."

"Dear me." Shocked, Lucy thought at once of her friend Kate

Sprague, his lovely daughter, who was expecting her first child. "Who has died?"

"Mrs. Helen Chase Walbridge, Mr. Chase's youngest sister, of a sudden illness. She was buried today in Ohio." Her mother fixed John with a steady look. "You will excuse us, please, Mr. Booth."

"Of course. My condolences," he replied, bowing.

"Poor Kate," said Lucy as her mother linked her arm through hers and led her away. "To lose a beloved aunt at the start of a fresh, bright new year seems especially heartbreaking."

"The heart always breaks a little with every love lost," her mother said. "Please don't break mine sooner than you must, dearest Lucy."

Aghast, Lucy quickly assured her that she hoped never to do so, but her mother offered only a wistful smile in return.

The Hales' visit to the home of their grieving friends left them contemplative, almost melancholy, but later, when they retired for the night, Papa told his family that they must not let sympathy for their friends depress their own spirits, or kindle superstitious fears that the year ahead would bring more and worse losses because the first day had been blighted by mourning. "We must put our faith in God and our trust in one another, and all will be well, whatever comes," he said, kissing first Lizzie and then Lucy on the brow.

Upon waking before dawn the next morning, Lucy felt solemn and still, forgetting why until her father's words returned to her. "Whatever comes," she murmured, falling silent when Lizzie stirred beside her. She felt a pang of worry recalling her mother's expression as she had stood in the doorway of the drawing room, regarding John coolly before beckoning Lucy away. Something in her manner had signified aversion, and Lucy feared that it had nothing to do with John's profession. She hoped she was mistaken. Her parents had conversed with John in perfect cordiality earlier that same day. Perhaps sympathy for her friend Kate had made Lucy superstitious despite her father's admonitions.

She could not entirely banish her sense of unease as she chatted pleasantly with her family over breakfast, but her trepidation diminished later as she, Lizzie, and their mother dressed in their finest gowns and had their tresses beautifully arranged for the traditional New Year's Day reception at the White House. The annual reception was the highlight of every Washington social season, and was by custom a three-hour affair in which Mr. Lincoln stood in one of the beautifully appointed public rooms of the Executive Mansion shaking hands and welcoming visitors—his cabinet secretaries first, then the foreign ministers, followed by the justices of the Supreme Court, distinguished officers of the army and navy, and certain eminent government officials. At one o'clock, the doors to the White House would be opened again to admit the public, two or three hundred at a time—anyone who wished to meet the president and his wife badly enough to endure the long wait and the crush of the throng.

Papa's high office entitled the Hale family to enter early with the honored guests when the gates of the Executive Mansion were ceremoniously thrown open at noon. Swept along by the crowd, they made their way to the Red Room, which soon was filled with a glad and glittering coterie of ladies in elegant gowns and sparkling jewels and gentlemen in handsome suits or dashing military uniforms, with most of the foreign delegation attired in the splendid costumes of their native lands. As she and Lizzie followed their parents through the chamber to join the receiving line in the Blue Room, Lucy overheard the brilliant cacophony of many tongues—Russian, German, French, Spanish, and English in a variety of charming accents.

As soon as they entered the Blue Room, Lucy glimpsed Mr. Lincoln on the other side, shaking hands and offering a cordial welcome to all who passed before him. He seemed to be in unusually excellent health and spirits as he received his illustrious guests, his eyes clear and shining with good humor, his handshake firm and vigorous. Over the course of the war, Lucy—and indeed, all of Washington—had observed how the president had become gaunt and aged beyond his years, but on that day Lucy was glad to see that he seemed much restored.

The president, who was not usually known for his impeccable taste in dress, looked very smart that day in a plain black suit and white kid gloves, understated and elegant. At his right hand stood his secretary John Nicolay, making introductions, and to his left was Ward Lamon—tall, strong, and imposing, the president's good friend, former law partner, and self-appointed bodyguard.

"Did you hear," Lizzie said close to her ear, in the tone she adopted for gossip, "that last month Mr. Lamon submitted his resignation?"

"I did not," Lucy replied, astonished. "Are you sure? He's famously loyal to the president. Why would he wish to vacate his post?"

"I have it on very good authority that he's become increasingly frustrated with the president's refusal to take precautions against assassination," said Lizzie. "One evening in early December Mr. Lincoln attended the theatre with Senator Sumner without taking a guard as escort, and that, apparently, was too much for Mr. Lamon. He turned in his letter of resignation the next day."

"It would appear that Mr. Lincoln refused to accept it."

"Indeed, although whether he's changed his habits to Mr. Lamon's satisfaction is another question."

Lucy nodded as they moved up the queue a pace closer to the presidential party, where she could see a trifle better. Just beyond Mr. Lincoln and his two aides stood Mrs. Lincoln, shaking hands and chatting pleasantly with everyone who passed in the line, smiling graciously at those who were too bashful to approach her. She carried herself with queenly grace and dignity and was, as ever, elegantly attired, although she still wore the dark, somber colors of half mourning in memory of her poor lost young son, Willie, who had succumbed to typhoid fever nearly three years before. Her gown was fashioned of a heavy purple brocade silk, richly trimmed with black velvet, with an exquisitely fine black lace shawl upon her bare shoulders, and delicate gloves, a floral headdress, and luminous pearl jewelry to complete her costume.

To Mrs. Lincoln's immediate right stood John Hay, whom Lucy had not seen since the evening he had spotted her on John's arm outside Grover's Theatre, and whom she fervently hoped would have the good sense and discretion not to mention that occasion in front of her family. Beside him stood Benjamin Brown French, the commissioner of public buildings. Lucy was surprised to see him given such pride of place, for it was well known that he and the president's wife, once good friends, had fallen out due to her controversial overspending.

Lucy liked Mrs. Lincoln and sympathized with her for the tremendous burdens she endured as the wife of a wartime president, with her concerns for her husband's health, her fears for his safety surely foremost among them. Lucy thought it unfair and ungallant that the press treated Mrs. Lincoln with such gleeful cruelty, and she shuddered at the thought of suffering such malicious scrutiny herself. As much as she admired her father and respected his accomplishments in the Senate, she sometimes wondered whether she might be more content to marry a man whose profession did not expose him, and therefore her, to constant public examination.

And so, she thought ruefully, she fell in love with an actor.

When the Hales reached the top of the queue, Mr. Lincoln greeted Lucy's parents first, shaking their hands and wishing them a happy New Year with his customary warmth and familiarity. Then he welcomed Lizzie and Lucy, so amiable, kind, and courteous in his manner that Lucy felt somehow that he regarded her as both a distinguished guest and the dear daughter of close friends. Mrs. Lincoln was equally gracious, complimenting the sisters on their gowns and offering regrets on her eldest son's behalf that he was not present to receive them. "His law studies keep him terribly busy," she lamented, "but Harvard will have a school holiday later this month. Would you both like to come to tea with me and Robert when he comes home? I know he would be delighted to see the lovely Hale sisters again."

"We would like that very much," said Lucy, and Lizzie chimed in her agreement. Mrs. Lincoln promised to send them word as soon her secretary could arrange a date, and then the queue proceeded and Lucy and Lizzie were obliged to move on.

Next in the presidential party, John Hay behaved nearly as courteously as his employer as he shook their hands and wished them a happy New Year, but after Lizzie followed their mother and father out of the queue, he held Lucy's hand a moment longer. "Was that indeed you on the arm of John Wilkes Booth outside Grover's Theatre that night," he inquired, smiling ironically, "or was that vision a hallucination brought on by the bitter cold?"

"It was not that cold," she said, lowering her voice, "and you know very well it was I."

He shook his head, bewildered, exasperated. "Does that mediocre actor actually think to court you?"

"That is unkind and unjust," she protested in a murmur, glancing after her parents and Lizzie, who were quickly disappearing into the crowd. "Have you ever seen him perform? He's quite gifted."

"I think his appeal on the stage resides rather in his romantic beauty of person than in any talent or industry he possesses."

Despite her indignation, she could not help smiling. "Why, Mr. Hay, if I didn't know better, I might think you were jealous of Mr. Booth."

"Not so. Not I."

"All appearances to the contrary notwithstanding."

"Miss Hale, in all seriousness—" He hesitated. "Mr. Booth has . . . a reputation. I sincerely hope he is not courting you."

"Why? Because he is an actor?"

"Because he is no gentleman." He clasped his other hand over hers that he already held, his expression one of deep concern. "The matter is too delicate to discuss here—and to a lady, anywhere, ever—but as your friend, I urge you to be cautious."

She felt apprehension stir, and yet loyalty and love compelled her to say, "I cannot relinquish one friend based upon such vague accusations from another."

And then the queue, held up too long, pushed forward, and Mr. Hay was obliged to release her hand. "We should speak again," he said, raising his voice to be heard as she was carried along.

She nodded and turned away, quickly making her way through the crowd until she caught up with her family and fell in step beside her sister.

For Lucy, the brilliance had faded from the reception, and she was all too willing to go when her mother suggested that they depart before the gates were opened to the public at one o'clock and a crush of thousands of eager citizens filled the reception rooms. Mr. Hay's warnings haunted her as she accompanied her family on a round of calls to the homes of her mother's friends and her father's colleagues, greeting acquaintances with smiles and embraces, listening to excellent music at one reception and savoring tasty delicacies at another, all the while mulling over the unsettling exchange. Despite her teasing words to Mr. Hay, he had not truly seemed to speak out of jealousy but out of concern.

And yet—she loved John. When she had doubted him, he had explained himself, and she had found her worries unwarranted. She could not condemn him based upon rumors and idle speculation. That was not love. If she could not find it within herself to trust him, she did not deserve him.

But for his part, Mr. Hay had proven himself a good and trustworthy friend, and he had nothing to gain by spreading false tales. He had barely been able to bring himself to reveal the little that he had said. Perhaps it was not romantic to be cautious, but she would rather be cautious and unromantic now than sorry later.

She was not some giddy, reckless girl, Lucy told herself as her family completed their merry rounds and headed back to the National Hotel. She was a sensible, prudent young woman, and if she married John—when she married him—it would be with clear eyes and an open heart. John would make of his past an open book, and satisfy her every question, or she could not marry him.

She held fast to her resolution as she followed her parents into the lobby and upstairs to their suite, assuring herself that John would pass every test.

Having eaten their fill at the series of receptions, the Hales had no appetite for supper, but their New Year's revelries were not yet finished. After a brief respite in the relative quiet of their suite, Lucy and her family proceeded downstairs to the lobby for a dance hosted by the hotel's proprietors. The tables had been cleared away to create space for a dance floor, the chairs arranged along the walls and black marble pillars for those who preferred to sit and watch rather than whirl about. From an alcove near the foot of the grand staircase, a chamber orchestra played waltzes and reels to the delight of the entire assembly.

Among them, soon none was happier than Lucy, for after she had danced with a congressman's son from Kentucky and a bespectacled young doctor visiting from Pennsylvania, John appeared by her side, smiling warmly, one hand behind his back, the other extended to her. "Miss Hale," he said tenderly, "would you honor me with a dance?"

She nodded, gave him her hand, and let him lead her on.

"How was your day of New Year's revelry?" he inquired as they took their places. "Did you enjoy the president's reception?"

"Very much so, thank you."

"And did the president look well?"

"Remarkably so, I'm pleased to say, better than he has since the early months of the war."

Mr. Booth nodded thoughtfully. "I would have liked an introduction. Perhaps the next time you visit the Executive Mansion, I may accompany you."

"You could have met the president today," she teased. "All you had to do was join the many thousands who were admitted at one o'clock."

"Not I," he declared as the orchestra struck up a sweet melody. "I would not enter with the rabble. I would be among the dignitaries admitted at noon or not attend at all."

She laughed and assured him she would do what she could to arrange a more agreeable introduction.

They danced one dance after another together, heedless of long-held custom that decreed they were obliged to mingle and not devote themselves to any one particular partner. When they were breathless from dancing, they sat or strolled the length of the room instead, conversing beneath the music, as privately as if they were alone.

Once, at the end of a set, Lizzie led a captain on leave from the First Massachusetts Cavalry to the two chairs by the window where Lucy and John were engrossed in conversation. Lizzie made introductions and quickly accepted a request to take the floor with another gentleman, leaving Lucy to choose between dancing with the captain or incurring scandal by rejecting a brave Union officer to remain with John, which was really no choice at all. So Lucy danced with the captain, and was as pleasant, graceful, and charming as she could be, for etiquette demanded no less and his faithful service to the nation made him deserving of her respectful attention. But as soon as the dance ended and the courteous captain escorted her from the dance floor, John was at her side, bowing, gracefully extending a hand, beckoning her once more into his arms. She found herself powerless to demur, as if all the doubts and worries of the day required a counterargument of equal force, compressed into the all-too-brief duration of the ball.

At the end of the night, John escorted her to her parents, whom he addressed respectfully, only to receive civil but coolly abrupt replies in return. Lucy felt herself flush with embarrassment and regret, understanding too late that she had made herself the subject of gossip, deceived by the splendor of the music and the firelight and the graceful, vigorous movements of the dancers that she and John had been alone in a world of their own, unencumbered by responsibility, duty, and custom.

"What were you thinking?" Lizzie whispered as they followed their unsmiling, silent parents upstairs to their suite.

"I was a fool," Lucy murmured, sick at heart.

"I'm the elder sister. I should have interceded."

"You tried," said Lucy, remembering her sister's warning looks and discreet gestures, which in the heady intoxication of the hour she had convinced herself meant nothing. "It's not your fault—"

"Girls," their mother broke in as they reached the landing. "If you must say it in a whisper, perhaps you shouldn't say it at all."

Lucy slept restlessly that night, and woke to a strange, sinking pressure in her chest and a roaring in her skull, as if thunder rumbled ominously overhead. The storm that soon broke, not unexpectedly, was her mother.

"Lucy, dear, would you stay a moment?" she asked as the family prepared to go down to breakfast. Obediently, Lucy nodded, dreading the reprimand that was sure to come, that she knew she deserved.

As soon as her father and Lizzie left, her mother regarded her sternly. "Lucy, you must realize that you made yourself the subject of gossip last night with your extravagant attentions to Mr. Booth."

"I know, Mama, and I'm sincerely sorry."

"I'm pleased to hear it, but do you understand what you did wrong?"

"Yes, Mama, and I promise I'll never again be so indiscreet. I shouldn't have danced so often with the same partner to the exclusion of all other gentlemen."

Her mother's eyebrows rose. "Nor should you have walked off alone with that same partner, nor sat so long with your heads bent together as if you were conspiring in whispers."

"That too," said Lucy, abashed.

"Darling—" Her mother sighed and took Lucy's hands in her own. "You seem much infatuated with Mr. Booth, and I confess it worries me."

Lucy stung to hear her love dismissed as infatuation. "Mr. Booth has become a very dear friend, and I'm quite fond of him."

"I know, child. I daresay everyone present at the dance last night knows. However, you mustn't let this friendship go too far."

"What do you mean?"

"You cannot think of allowing Mr. Booth to court you. He is entirely unsuitable for you, and your father and I could not give you our blessing."

Tears filled Lucy's eyes, and she slipped her hands from her mother's grasp. "You've made that decision already, and yet you hardly know him."

"Lucy, darling, *you* hardly know him."

"I know him well enough to be certain he's a good man, worthy of me in every sense. If you object because he's an actor, rest assured he won't be one for much longer. He has gone into the oil business, and is a full partner in a company he founded."

"It is not only his profession that gives us pause. Trusted friends have warned your father and me that Mr. Booth has publicly expressed sympathy for the South."

"For the Southern people, perhaps, for he considers himself a Southerner by birth, but certainly not for the Confederacy."

"I'm afraid that's not so. He has also been overheard denouncing the president as a tyrant."

Lucy was taken aback, but she could not bear to leave John undefended. "Many Northern newspapers have done the same. It seems that you and Papa have formed your opinions about Mr. Booth based upon rumors rather than your own experience."

"We cannot disregard the counsel of wise friends where our daughter's well-being is at stake." Suddenly her mother's shoulders slumped and she sank into a chair, her expression profoundly sad. "My dear daughter, I remember the first blush of young love—the wonder, the exhilaration—and I know, as perhaps you do not, how it can cloud one's judgment."

"I know it can." She thought she did. "But there is judgment and there is prejudice. I'm sure if you and Papa knew Mr. Booth better, and judged him on his own merits, you would esteem him as I do." She knelt beside her mother's chair and took one of her hands in both of hers. "Could you not give him the chance to prove himself? Think of the dreadful gossip we've heard about Mr. Lincoln, about my own dear Papa. Only a small fraction has any truth to it, and that's usually twisted beyond all recognition."

"I cannot deny that." Her mother frowned, pensive, and for an agonizing moment Lucy held her breath. "I suppose, if you promise to be more discreet, I could persuade your father to allow Mr. Booth to court you, so that we—and you—could better evaluate his character and suitability. Anyone can feign the manners of a perfect gentleman for a little while, an actor better than most, but I trust that time will bring his faults to the surface."

Lucy flung her arms around her mother. "Oh, Mama, thank you."

Gently, her mother took Lucy by the shoulders and held her at arm's length, the better to look steadily into her eyes. "There will be conditions," she warned. "You must never see Mr. Booth without a chaperone, not even in the National. You must be more mindful of your reputation, and put on no more shameful displays as you did last night."

Lucy flushed and lowered her gaze. "Of course. You have my word."

Her mother cupped Lucy's chin with her hand and raised it so their eyes met. "Finally, when all is said and done, you must accept our decision regarding Mr. Booth. You must promise not to marry him without our blessing."

"I would never marry anyone without your consent," said Lucy, shocked that her mother thought she might. "I'll abide by your decision, yours and Papa's. That's how confident I am that Mr. Booth will prove himself worthy."

"We'll see," her mother replied, simply and sadly.

Blinking away tears, Lucy smiled, rose, and held out her hands to help her mother to her feet. But her smile swiftly faded. She had expected to be forbidden to see John again, and yet somehow she had emerged with her mother's permission, albeit reluctantly given, to allow him to court her. Why, then, did she feel bereft, as if something precious had been irretrievably lost?

Her mother's certainty that time would bring John's faults to light proved prescient, perhaps intentionally so. It was hardly surprising that when Lucy was compelled to keep a wary eye out for reasons to doubt John, to mistrust him, she found them.

The first week of the New Year continued promisingly enough. Lucy's mother convinced her father to let John court Lucy, to discourage clandestine meetings and to give him a fair chance to rise in their esteem. He occasionally dined or breakfasted with the family, and he and Lucy sometimes met in the drawing room to read together, though always with one of her parents, Lizzie, or cousin Parker seated nearby, ostensibly absorbed in a book, but frequently glancing up from the page to study the couple.

John's tolerance of the new, unwanted scrutiny wore thin after a fortnight. He never complained—he couldn't, as their chaperone would surely overhear—but Lucy perceived his umbrage in a new tension in his neck and shoulders, in an unfamiliar strain in his voice. Neither did he become more forthcoming about the nature of his work. He passed in and out of the National at unpredictable hours and rarely explained where he had been and with whom he had met. He traveled to Baltimore on January 10 and returned two days later with little to share about the trip beyond a few lackluster remarks about the weather. "I did nothing but meet with dull men about investing in oil wells," he said when she prompted and prodded him for more. "It's a tedious business and I won't bore you with a lengthy description."

"Let me decide if I find it boring," she implored, but he merely laughed indulgently and kissed her—Lizzie, their chaperone of the moment, had averted her eyes—and told her that he would rather hear about her tea with Mrs. Lincoln and Robert Lincoln at the Executive Mansion.

He remained so stubbornly resistant to her entreaties that she had to consider that, although he might not be a spy, he was perhaps engaged in some other clandestine work for the War Department, a task where his knowledge of the oil business and his skills as an actor came into play. She hoped that someday soon he would trust her enough to reveal his secrets to her, if she could not figure them out on her own first.

On a Friday evening soon thereafter, John returned to the stage for a single night to play Romeo to Miss Avonia Jones's Juliet in her farewell benefit at Grover's Theatre. As he had promised long ago, Parker escorted Lucy to the performance, and she watched, enthralled and awestruck, as John transformed himself entirely into the tragic young lover. The stage was his to command, his voice veritable music, his movements the most graceful dance. She fell in love with him anew with his every expression of love for Juliet, and she wept when he took his own life rather than survive his lost beloved.

The next day, she could not resist reading aloud to her family the glowing reviews he received in the papers. "What glorious praise from the *National Intelligencer*," she declared. "Just listen: 'As earned by his Romeo, we hasten to add our laurel to the wreath which the young actor deservedly wears; to offer him our congratulations, and to say to him that he is of the blood royal—a very prince of the blood—a lineal descendant of the true monarch, his sire, who ranks with the Napoleons of the stage.' Oh, and this: 'His death scene was the most remarkable and fearfully natural that we have seen for years upon the stage.'"

"Yes, I seem to recall hearing that Mr. Booth has often died upon the stage," her father remarked, his gaze fixed on his own newspaper.

Lizzie laughed, but Lucy ignored the barb. "'His elocution was faultless, his step as light as vanity.'"

"What does that mean?" asked Lizzie, wrinkling her nose. "'As light as vanity'? I'm not so certain it's a compliment."

"'He is full of genius,'" Lucy read on determinedly, "'and almost as perfect an artist as his brother Edwin. One could be forgiven for believing that his love for Miss Jones was real.'"

"I'm not at all surprised to learn that the younger Mr. Booth is skilled at feigning love," said Mama, taking a sip of coffee and regarding Lucy over the rim of her delicate china cup.

Cheeks burning, Lucy read the remaining reviews in silence.

Her family was civil to John when he was present, but in private it was as if they had linked arms and braced themselves against him. If John was aware of this, he did not complain, nor did he express any concern about their resistance to his celebrated charm. And yet he was occasionally ill tempered and abrupt, only to be smiling, affectionate, and as courteous as ever the next time Lucy saw him. His mood seemed to shift with the wind, turning Lucy this way and that like a weathervane, powerless to hold fast against bewilderment and hurt.

A week after his triumph at Grover's Theatre, John left for Baltimore, and from thence he went to New York, and on to Philadelphia, and then back to New York, until Lucy could scarcely keep track of his travels and began to wonder if his letters were crossing in the mail. At Lizzie's urging, she fended off loneliness and worry by redoubling her labors for the Union cause, visiting the wounded in the city's many military hospitals, organizing fund-raisers for the Sanitary Commission, and knitting innumerable pairs of thick, warm socks for soldiers in the field. She also took time for the more lighthearted distractions of levees, dinner parties, and dances, though she missed her favorite partner too much to entirely enjoy them.

One grand event she would have loved to attend was the magnificent state dinner Mr. and Mrs. Lincoln hosted at the White House on February 13 for sixteen senators and their wives, including Lucy's parents. Lucy and Lizzie were so eager to hear every detail that they waited up for their parents to return home, even though it was half past eleven o'clock before they finally returned to the suite, tired but smiling.

"The table took up the entire length of the state dining room," their father told them as he removed his coat and shoes and glanced about for his slippers. "Mrs. Lincoln was seated at the center of the table, with the president immediately opposite her. Your mother had the honor of occupying the place to Mr. Lincoln's left."

"I think the exalted place they gave *me* was meant to honor *you*," their mother said, regarding their father fondly as she nodded to his slippers, halfway hidden beneath the ottoman. "The table was beautifully decorated with vases of flowers arranged by the president's head gardener, and the French caterer Jacobs prepared the meal, so I won't torment you with descriptions of how absolutely delicious every bite of every course was."

"What did Mrs. Lincoln wear?" Lizzie asked as she went to fetch her father's slippers.

"An exquisite gown of white crepe, with delicate puffs and trimmings of lilac," their mother said. "On her head she wore a wreath of lilac and white flowers—you know how she adores flowers—and her ears, throat, and wrists were adorned with lovely pearl jewelry."

"And what was her mood?" Lucy prompted. She knew her friend Robert often worried about his mother's strained nerves, an unfortunate consequence of her eminent position.

"Quite good. She presided over the gathering with elegance and grace." Her mother hesitated and, with a small, fond, sympathetic smile for Lucy, she added, "There was one matter that seemed to trouble her. You're aware, I'm sure, that Robert has long desired to join the army."

"Yes, so he has told me, but his mother absolutely refuses to give him her blessing." On one occasion, not long after he graduated from Harvard, Robert had angrily declared that if he could not live as he wanted, he would at least escape the "glass house" of Washington. The next Lucy heard, he had returned to Massachusetts and had enrolled in Harvard Law School.

"Be that as it may, his father apparently decided to grant his wish," her father said. "Your friend is now Captain Robert Lincoln, and in a few days he will begin serving as an assistant adjutant general on General Grant's own staff."

"Oh, my goodness." Lucy placed a hand over her heart, stunned. Another brave friend, sent into danger. "How is Mrs. Lincoln bearing it?"

"I imagine she had choice words for her husband in private," said her father dryly.

"She assured everyone at the table that she was very proud of her son and wholeheartedly supported his decision to serve," said her mother. "Later, though, she confided to me that she feels nervous and afraid, even though her son will be so well placed at military headquarters that he'll probably never see a single battle."

"I hope that's true," said Lucy fervently. "Robert won't like that, of course, but for his sake and his parents', I hope he remains miles away from the front lines."

Nodding his agreement, her father stifled a yawn.

"There was one other curious thing." Her mother put her head to one side, frowning slightly as she pondered a memory. "Just before the sweets were served, Mr. Lincoln turned to me, smiled kindly, and inquired, 'How good is your Spanish, Mrs. Hale?'"

The sisters exchanged bewildered glances. "Were you talking about Spain at the time?" asked Lizzie.

"No, nor was the subject Mexico or Panama or any other Spanish-speaking nation."

"What did you say?" asked Lucy.

"I told him my Spanish is worse than my French but far better than my Portuguese."

"What an odd question," said Lizzie.

"Yes, very odd," said their father, making no effort to disguise a second yawn, so they quickly agreed when he suggested that the rest of their report could wait until breakfast.

The next day was Saint Valentine's Day, and when the post arrived shortly before noon, Lucy received a lovely acrostic poem John had composed in her honor, a sweet, romantic gesture that reminded her anew how much she adored him. A week later, on February 21, Parker told her that he had received a telegram from John, and that he intended to return to Washington late the following evening. Overjoyed, Lucy kissed her cousin to thank him for the welcome news. John had been gone almost four weeks, traveling here and there and back again visiting family and conducting business, so frantically busy, he lamented in his letters, that he could not spare even half a day in the capital. Now, at long last, he was coming back to her.

Their reunion on the morning of February 23 was as joyful as she could have hoped. When they met in their favorite chairs in the lobby, he kissed her hand, and she kissed him in return on the cheek—swiftly, modestly—while Lizzie pretended to be fascinated by a family with three young children passing by the window.

"Thank you for the lovely poem." Smiling mischievously, perhaps to punish him a little for being so long away, Lucy added, "It is not the first love poem a gentleman has written for me, but it is certainly my favorite."

"As long as *I* am your favorite," he growled, feigning jealousy, a pretense his shining eyes immediately betrayed, "I don't care if a beau you spurned years before was a better poet."

For his valentine gift, she gave him a photograph of herself and a book of Byron's poems, because he had once confided that his parents had enjoyed reading them together. She apologized for the belated nature of the gift, unable to resist adding that she would have been able to give them to him earlier if he had not been away so long.

"For a gift as lovely as this," he declared, admiring her portrait, "I would be willing to wait another fortnight, months if I had to."

It was a tender sentiment, Lucy thought, but he had missed her point entirely.

As if to make up for lost time, John was more affectionate and attentive than ever, until Lucy was blissfully willing to forgive his long absence and his exasperating reticence. She even dared hope that her parents, who had thus far not discovered any evidence to support their doubts, would surrender their fiercely entrenched defenses and cede the battle to John.

But just as she thought an armistice might be at hand, John revealed an aspect of his character she had not previously suspected, and for the first time, she found herself at a loss to defend him.

In the first week of January, Ohio congressman James M. Ashley had reintroduced into the House the Thirteenth Amendment abolishing slavery throughout the United States. Thanks in no small part to the tireless efforts of Lucy's father, the amendment had already passed the Senate, and on January 31, the House had held the final debates before their voting commenced. Dozens of senators, including Lucy's father, had attended to witness the historic moment, as had the justices of the Supreme Court, several members of President Lincoln's cabinet, and many foreign ministers. Lucy, Lizzie, and their mother had arrived early to claim good seats in the gallery, which for the first time had also admitted people of color. The Negro men and women had watched the final speeches and heard the vote taken in solemn, breathless quiet, breaking into cheers and joyful weeping when the measure passed. Although three-fourths of the states would have to ratify the amendment before it would become the law of the land, people of color and abolitionists nonetheless rejoiced, certain that slavery had been dealt a fatal blow. As they had walked home, exultant and proud, Lucy, Lizzie, and their mother had agreed that the successful passage of the amendment would someday be recognized as the greatest achievement in Papa's long, tireless, and storied career as an abolitionist and lawmaker.

A few days after John returned from his lengthy travels, Lucy and John met in the drawing room to catch up on the news from their time apart. Still glowing from her father's triumph, Lucy described the fiery debates in the House and the momentous final vote, but she had not quite reached the end when John's handsome features twisted into a bitter scowl. "Lincoln is intent upon making himself a king," he said.

For a moment Lucy could only stare at him. "What on earth do you mean?"

"He does not seek to govern but rule," John declared. "He wants to crush out slavery by any means—robbery, rapine, slaughter, and bought armies. He presumes to walk in the footprints of old John Brown, but he is no more fit to stand with that rugged old hero—great God, no! John Brown was a man inspired, the grandest character of this century. Lincoln would be another Bonaparte, overturning this blind Republic and crowning himself king!"

Parker had looked up from his novel as the harsh invective increased in volume, and he fixed John with a level gaze. "I say, Booth, you might want to calm down. People might mistake you for a copperhead."

"Has freedom of speech been abolished along with the writ of habeas corpus?" John snapped, but he lowered his voice, shifted in his chair, and suddenly bolted from it. "I need some air. Good evening Lucy, Parker." He bowed and strode from the room.

"John is no copperhead," Lucy told her cousin, though his outburst had left her shaken and confused. "He doesn't sympathize with the Confederacy, but with the Southern people, who have suffered much throughout this dreadful war. It's only natural that he should be concerned about their fate. He's a Marylander, and he considers Virginia an adopted home."

Parker regarded her speculatively for a long moment. "If you say so, dear cousin," he finally said, sighing in resignation and settling back down to his book.

Lucy had looked forward to John's return to Washington so eagerly that it was disturbing to find herself unexpectedly relieved when he told her that he would be traveling to Baltimore for a few days. Upon his return on the first day of March, when they crossed paths in the lobby, she acknowledged his cheerful greeting by inclining her head, unsmiling, and she did not offer him her hand.

"I had expected a better welcome than this," he protested, smiling.

Her heart stirred, but she could not rid her memory of his outburst in the drawing room, his harsh words, his angry glares. "Several weeks ago you asked me to acquire this for you," she said curtly, taking an envelope from her reticule, "but I'm not sure whether you want it anymore."

His smile turned quizzical as he accepted the envelope. "You're in a fine mood today." Opening it, he withdrew a ticket granting admission to the Capitol rotunda for President Lincoln's second inauguration, one of only a precious few her father had been allotted for family and friends. "Thank you very much, darling. Of course I still want this. Why would you think I might not?"

"After your angry denunciation of Mr. Lincoln in the drawing room the other day, I made the reasonable assumption that perhaps you might not wish to see him renew his oath of office."

He stared at her for a moment before bursting into laughter. "You're not still upset about my little speech, are you?"

" 'Little speech'?" She folded her arms. "Yes, of course I'm still upset. I admire President Lincoln. He's a great man, and I would've voted for him if I could have."

He shrugged and tucked the invitation into the inside pocket of his coat. "I would say that it's fortunate you couldn't vote, then, except it would've made no difference to the outcome."

She shook her head, incredulous. "Is that truly how you feel?"

"Don't be angry, dear girl." He took her hands and drew her closer, though she resisted, still annoyed. "I regret upsetting you, and I'm grateful for the ticket. We can't expect our opinions to match perfectly on every single political issue. Very well, so I'm not as enamored with Mr. Lincoln as you are. It breaks my heart to think you might love me less for that."

"You don't look particularly heartbroken."

"Oh, my darling, you forget I am a very good actor." Grinning impishly, he tapped her nose with his forefinger. "Inside I weep and tear my hair."

"Nonsense," she retorted, but her anger was subsiding.

"Inside I have donned sackcloth and ashes." He kissed the backs of her hands. "Now, be a good girl and tell me you love me."

She was not quite ready to do that. "You'll have a very good view of the ceremony, but it's just as well that you won't be seated on the platform with me and my family. Those exalted places should be reserved for people who actually *want* Mr. Lincoln to be president."

He feigned misery. "You mean to say you won't condescend to stand amid the rabble with me?"

"And risk enduring another of your disloyal diatribes? Never."

"I am loyal to my country," he protested, and when she tossed her head, he teased and cajoled until he managed to coax a smile from her, but not her agreement to relinquish her excellent seat to stand with him instead.

She could not stay angry with him long, for as the capital prepared for Mr. Lincoln's second inauguration, the jubilant, optimistic mood of its citizens and visitors became infectious. The people of the North had every reason to be hopeful, Lucy thought. In mid-January, the Union navy had captured Fort Fisher, which closed the port of Wilmington, North Carolina, and severed supply lines to the Confederacy from abroad. After capturing Savannah, General Sherman's armies had seized Columbia, the capital of South Carolina, and the next day, the rebels had surrendered Fort Sumter and evacuated Charleston. In the meantime, General Grant had drawn a noose of Union forces around Petersburg and was steadily pulling it closed, tightening his stranglehold and threatening the Confederate capital of Richmond twenty-five miles to the north. On the eve of the commencement of Mr. Lincoln's second term as president and commander in chief, a Union victory seemed more certain than ever before.

In those first days of March, thousands of visitors flooded Washington City, filling the hotels and boardinghouses until Lucy half expected to see streams of guests spilling out from the doorways and windows into the streets. At the National Hotel, she and John could find no quiet place to sit and talk privately, for hapless gentlemen and even a good many ladies who had been unable to secure rooms sat up through the night in the crowded parlors instead.

On the night before the inauguration, a fierce and terrible storm struck the capital, jolting Lucy awake with a crash of thunder and a scour of hail upon the roof. "Lizzie?" she murmured as she propped herself up on her elbows, disoriented, heart pounding. "Are we under attack?"

"No, silly girl," Lizzie replied, sounding barely awake. "It's just a storm. Go back to sleep."

Lucy lay down and snuggled closer to her sister, hoping the tempest would soon subside. Eventually she drifted back to sleep, and woke hours later to a gray and rain-soaked dawn. One glance out the window revealed that the night's torrential downpour had turned Sixth Street and Pennsylvania Avenue into thick rivers of mud.

"Will they cancel the parade if the streets cannot dry in time?" Lucy asked her sister as they made their toilette and dressed. A magnificent procession was planned, with soldiers, cavalry, and bands, as well as representatives from fire departments, civic organizations, and fraternal lodges from all across the North, all to march with banners aflutter and flags unfurled.

"I can't imagine that they would cancel," said Lizzie. "The newspapers say that fifty thousand will gather at the Capitol to watch and thousands more will line the parade route. They won't disappoint all those people because of a little mud."

"I wouldn't say a *little* mud," said Lucy dubiously, but she decided to trust her elder sister's optimistic prediction.

The Hale ladies would not be among the crowds enjoying the parade anyway, nor would they accompany Papa to the Senate to claim seats in the gallery while he assumed his usual place in the chamber, so that they might observe the traditional valedictory address of the outgoing vice president and the speech and swearing in of incoming vice president Andrew Johnson. Her father's usual seat in the chamber was his no longer, and they all felt the bittersweetness of the occasion. Before they could celebrate Mr. Lincoln's oath taking and address, Papa would have to relinquish his Senate seat to his successor.

He had decided against observing the Senate proceeding from the gallery, like any ordinary spectator, and when he had wearily asked his ladies if they might dispense with that part of it, they readily assured him that they would indeed prefer to avoid the crowds. "I was rather hoping you'd suggest we simply take our seats on the East Portico early," Mama said, and Papa smiled wistfully and thanked them all.

Rumbling over narrow, pitted side roads to avoid the parade route, Lucy's father directed their carriage as close as they could get to the Capitol and they walked the rest of the way. The guards recognized the former Senator Hale and allowed the family through, so they proceeded to the east front of the Capitol and the platform reserved for honored guests, seating themselves just as the doors opened and the crowd of observers and dignitaries that had packed the Senate chamber spilled out onto the portico. Lucy took in the scene, awestruck and wistful, wishing her father had kept the Senate seat he had filled so honorably. No longer a senator, he did not yet know what he would become. The position of Minister to France had gone to another gentleman, and no one, not the president nor any of his secretaries or aides, had mentioned any other possibilities to her father. For the future of the country, Lucy was optimistic and hopeful, but for her father, for their family, she was stricken with doubt.

An eager audience thousands strong had packed the muddy Capitol grounds beneath overcast skies, and when Mr. Lincoln emerged onto the East Portico with Chief Justice Chase at his side, a piece of paper in his hand, the newly completed Capitol dome rising in magnificent splendor high above, the people let out a thunderous roar of welcome and jubilation. As the president came forward to deliver his speech, the clouds suddenly parted, the sun broke through, and golden light shone down upon him like a benediction from heaven.

"How glorious," Lizzie murmured. Lucy nodded, too overwhelmed by the profundity of the moment to speak. Just as her father had said, in the midst of its most terrible crisis, the country had held national elections, and even those who had not cast their ballots for Mr. Lincoln had accepted the result. Their democracy had endured, and its faithful citizens had every reason to believe that they had been tested and had triumphed, and could surely survive any other challenge the future might bring.

The president's address was brief, simple, and profoundly beautiful—clear and poignant and warm, full of forgiveness and reconciliation. The president spoke of the war, and how slavery was the undeniable cause of it, and how four years earlier everyone, North and South alike, had wanted to avoid war, but one side would make war rather than let the nation survive, and the other would accept war rather than let it perish. He suggested that the Lord had allowed them to fall into war as punishment for the offense of slavery, and that the war could be a mighty scourge to rid them of it. All people, North and South alike, hoped and fervently prayed that the war would soon end, but if God willed that it should continue "until all the wealth piled by the bondman's two hundred and fifty years of unrequited toil shall be sunk, and until every drop of blood drawn with the lash, shall be paid by another drawn with the sword," they must accept that the Lord's judgment was true and righteous.

Tears filled Lucy's eyes as Mr. Lincoln closed with an extraordinary expression of forgiveness and magnanimity. "With malice toward none," he urged his listeners, "with charity for all, with firmness in the right, as God gives us to see the right, let us strive on to finish the work we are in; to bind up the nation's wounds; to care for him who shall have borne the battle, and for his widow, and his orphan, to do all which may achieve and cherish a just, and a lasting peace, among ourselves, and with all nations."

Lucy reached for Lizzie's hand and squeezed it tightly as Mr. Lincoln turned to Chief Justice Chase, who came forward to set an open

Bible on a wooden stand. Mr. Lincoln placed his right hand upon it, the chief justice solemnly administered the oath of office, and when the last words were spoken, President Abraham Lincoln bent and kissed the holy book.

The crowd, thousands strong, roared their approval, the Marine Band broke into a stirring tune, and an artillery salute boomed. After bowing courteously to the throng to acknowledge their ardent cheers and thunderous applause, Mr. Lincoln left the portico for the lower entrance, where a carriage waited to carry him back to the White House.

Like most of the Washington elite, the Hale family did not plan to attend the public reception at the Executive Mansion that evening, which would have obliged them to stand in line for hours with six thousand citizens, all eager to shake the president's hand and offer him congratulations. Instead they would defer paying their respects until they could do so much more pleasantly at the Inaugural Ball two evenings hence.

Contemplative, hopeful, and yet inevitably downcast, the Hales retired to their suite and tried to settle down to writing letters, reading, or sewing, but Lucy sensed that they all felt somewhat adrift. Suddenly she remembered John and the ticket she had given him. She had not glimpsed him among the vast multitude, but she was certain he had attended, and she hoped that Mr. Lincoln's powerful oration had moved him. John was a sensitive soul, and she did not see how he could fail to respond in kind to the president's message of hope and reconciliation.

Suddenly a knock on the door shattered the pensive quiet. Lucy's father rose to answer, and from her chair by the window Lucy glanced up from her book to see a messenger with a letter. Papa took it, offered the lad a few coins, closed the door, and stared at the folded paper, one hand lingering on the doorknob, as if he dreaded to discover whatever news it contained.

Eventually he inhaled deeply, squared his shoulders, and opened the note. Lucy studied him, shifting quietly in her chair so she could see his expression better, but he neither brightened nor blanched. Instead he read the letter over again as if he could not quite believe it.

"Lucy, dear," he said, meaning his wife, "how *is* your Spanish?"

"As I told President Lincoln," she replied, eyes widening, "it is worse than my French, but far better than my Portuguese."

"Well, you'll have to make a quick study of it, you and the girls." He smiled, slowly and incredulously, until he fairly glowed with relief and happiness. "President Lincoln wants to know if I would consider accepting the post of Minister to Spain."

They all ran to embrace him, offering kisses and congratulations and laughingly brushing aside his cautions that the president had not made him an official offer quite yet. "It will be forthcoming," Mama assured him, and she urged him to sit down with paper and pen and immediately respond that he would accept the prestigious position if it were offered. Papa happily agreed that he should, and they gathered around his desk as he swiftly wrote a gracious reply to the president, breaking into applause when he sealed the letter. As her father took it downstairs to entrust it to a messenger, Lucy was overwhelmed with a dizzying mixture of elation, pride, and dismay. She would be going abroad after all, crossing the ocean to enjoy an exciting adventure in a strange, marvelous, foreign land, far from home, far from John.

After such a momentous day, they all found it difficult to sleep, but they woke the next morning cheerful and refreshed—even Lucy, despite the pangs of grief she felt whenever she imagined bidding John farewell. They were pleased that President Lincoln had honored Papa with such a prestigious post, thankful that their family would be provided for, thrilled to imagine the wonders that awaited them in Madrid, and somewhat daunted by the many tasks they must complete before they sailed for Spain.

As they went down to breakfast, Lucy's father reminded them that President Lincoln had not publicly announced the appointment yet, so they must not discuss it in the dining room or speak of it to anyone. As her mother and sister nodded, Lucy asked, "May I tell John?"

Her father paused on the staircase. "Yes, in fact, I think you should inform him right away."

Lucy nodded, and when she saw the glance that passed between her parents as they continued down the stairs, she knew they were very glad that hundreds of miles would soon separate their daughter from her suitor.

John was not at breakfast, and the drawing room and lobby remained so packed with visitors who had come for the inauguration that she had no hope of taking him aside for a private chat anytime soon. Thus when Parker called later that morning, and after her father entrusted him with the secret of his pending appointment, Lucy took him aside and quietly asked him to accompany her to John's room. His eyebrows rose, but he agreed.

Lucy's hand trembled when she knocked upon John's door, but she steeled herself with a deep breath, smoothed her skirts, and silently rehearsed what she intended to say. A minute, perhaps more, passed in silence, so she knocked again, louder, and this time she heard stirring within. Suddenly the door swung open, and John stood before her, bleary eyed and unshaven, his trousers and shirt unkempt and wrinkled as if he had slept in them. "Lucy," he said, startled, quickly running a hand through his hair and tucking in his shirt.

"Good morning, John." She recoiled slightly at the faint, stale odor of liquor on his breath. "I'm sorry we caught you still abed."

"Late night?" asked Parker archly. "Did we celebrate the inauguration with a little too much enthusiasm?"

John shrugged and managed a wan smile.

With an effort, Lucy kept her expression smooth to conceal her displeasure at his shameful dissipation. "May we come in?"

After a moment's hesitation, John nodded and stepped back to allow them to enter. Parker gestured to the only chair, which Lucy took, while John glanced around for a moment before sitting down heavily on the edge of the bed. Parker closed the door and remained standing near it, hands in his pockets.

"To what do I owe the honor of this visit?" John asked, his voice hoarse, his eyes bloodshot.

"I have news. Exciting and yet distressing news."

Lucy clasped her hands in her lap and told him of Mr. Lincoln's offer, her voice trembling. John's brow furrowed in confusion as he listened, but when she finished he ran a hand over his jaw and stared at her as if she were already hundreds of miles away. "You're leaving," he said, his voice curiously flat.

"I am."

"Is there anything I could do to persuade you to stay?"

At his post near the door, Parker stirred, but Lucy did not glance back at him. "I couldn't live here at the hotel alone. It would be improper."

"Don't you have a maiden aunt you could live with?" John's voice carried an edge. "Someone on this side of the Atlantic?"

"I must go to Spain with my family. It has been decided, and I would never be able to convince my parents to let me stay behind." Nor did she wish to, for although it would be unkind to tell John so, she was thrilled to be setting off on a grand adventure. Although she would miss him terribly, she trusted that she would see him again upon her return. How foolish she had been to think that he might be happy for her.

His shoulders slumped, but his gaze remained fixed on hers. "So it may be years before I see you again."

"Not so long as that, I hope," she said, but his dispirited glower silenced her. Until that moment, it had not occurred to her that he might not wait for her.

She could bear no more. Abruptly she stood, but John too rose and took her hands. "Will you still dance with me at the inaugural ball tomorrow night?"

"Of course. John, I won't be leaving the country for weeks, and my feelings for you are unchanged."

"And yet everything else has changed."

He raised her hands to his lips, disconsolate, and she found herself powerless to contradict him. Resigned, she glanced about, wishing she could find the words to comfort him, and her gaze fell upon an envelope on the dresser, a pen, and ink. Gently she withdrew her hands from his grasp, and as the words of John Greenleaf Whittier came to mind, she wrote,

> *For of all sad words from tongue or pen*
> *The saddest are these—it might have been.*
> *March 5th, 1865*
> *In John's room.*

Tears in her eyes, she set down the pen and handed the envelope to John, who read them, let out a soft moan of anguish, seized the pen, and added a few lines above hers. Wild-eyed, he thrust the envelope at her, and she read the verse in silence.

Now in this hour that we part,
I will ask to be forgotten never.
But in thy pure and guileless heart,
Consider me thy friend, dear, ever.
J. Wilkes Booth.

"This is not the hour that we part," she protested. "We'll enjoy many hours together before my family sets sail. And I will return, John, but until then we can write, and perhaps you can visit us in Madrid."

"It won't be the same."

"No, but it will have to do." She rested her hand on his shoulder. "Dearest John, this is not farewell. This is not an ending. We've not yet performed our final act together."

Unexpectedly, he allowed a small smile. "The very thought of you, the senator's—no, the minister to Spain's daughter, treading the boards—"

Lucy laughed weakly. "Oh, my poor dear mother. She would never recover from it."

Behind her, Parker cleared his throat.

"My parents are waiting." Lucy kissed John on the cheek, swift and chaste. "I'll see you soon."

"Take this," he said, handing her the envelope.

"Don't you want it?"

"I'd rather you kept it. Take it to Spain and read it over whenever you miss me."

"Very well." She took the envelope and pressed it to her heart. "You may be sure I'll read it over every day."

John nodded and opened the door, but he spoke not a word as Lucy and Parker left the room and he closed the door behind them.

John was not mistaken—everything had changed.

On the night of Monday, March 6, Lucy was among the Washington elite who attended the Inauguration Ball at the Patent Office, and she arrived to find it beautifully transformed for the occasion. The marble hall appropriated for dancing was about two hundred and eighty feet long and about a quarter that in width, with blue-and-white marble floors, an elaborately frescoed ceiling, and walls tastefully appointed with emblems, banners, and devices among which the Stars and Stripes and flags of various army corps were prominently featured. At the north end of the room, sofas and chairs furnished in blue and gold were arranged on a dais for the comfort of the president and his family. A fine brass band occupied a gallery at the east end, ready to provide music for the promenade, while in the center on the south side, a string ensemble would furnish music for the dance.

Although Lucy had arrived with her parents and Lizzie, John was understood to be her escort, and he met her upon her arrival and claimed the first dance. The music was excellent, the gentlemen handsome and gallant, the ladies dazzling in their finery, and John was perfectly charming and attentive. Lucy had not forgotten the scandal at the New Year's dance at the National Hotel, however, and she made sure to dance with other gentlemen and to encourage John to dance with other ladies. She danced a quadrille with John Hay, who spent most of the evening attending to their mutual friend Kate Chase Sprague, whose delicate condition obliged her to sit out the dancing. Lucy also enjoyed a lancers with Robert Lincoln, who looked dashing in the splendid dress uniform of an army captain.

Soon after Robert escorted her from the dance floor, John appeared at her side and claimed her for the waltz, although they had danced the schottische together not long before. "You seemed to enjoy whirling about with Hay and young Lincoln," he said close to her ear.

"I did, thank you."

"A little too much, one might say."

Lucy laughed. "Only if one were being perfectly ridiculous."

"*I* say it."

She had assumed he was only teasing before, but the strain in his voice betrayed him. "Mr. Hay and Captain Lincoln are my friends, nothing more and nothing less."

"I wonder how many new friends you'll make among the caballeros of Spain."

She was painfully conscious of the curious glances his raised voice drew from the couples nearest them. "John, do stop. Jealousy does not become you."

"If you don't like my jealousy, don't provoke it."

"I've done nothing to deserve such censure," she said tightly. "If you cannot speak to me politely as a gentleman ought, I'll thank you to say nothing at all."

He said nothing more for the rest of the waltz, but as soon as the song ended he escorted her from the floor, bowed curtly, and departed. Angry and embarrassed, she found Lizzie and her father in the crowd and joined them in watching her mother take the floor for a quadrille with Chief Justice Chase. John did not attempt to claim another dance with her, nor was she sorry he did not.

The next morning, a bouquet of flowers and a note of apology were delivered to her suite, and although the rest of the family looked askance at the peace offering, her heart softened. John would not have become so jealous and upset if she had not so recently announced that she was going abroad. So she forgave him, but afterward, their brief conversations were polite and tentative, until Lucy began to dread crossing his path at the National.

Thus, soon after the Senate confirmed their father's appointment, when an invitation came for Lucy and Lizzie to visit family friends in New York City, Lucy was happy to accept, especially after their mother noted that the trip would offer an excellent opportunity to purchase new wardrobes for their journey to Spain. The sisters passed a delightful fortnight in Manhattan, shopping, dining out, attending balls and receptions, and occasionally remembering to study their Spanish. Lucy and John exchanged a few letters while they were apart, and once John even rode the train from Washington to visit her. He stayed at his brother Edwin's residence in the city, and one evening John escorted her and Lizzie to see his brother portray Hamlet at the Winter Garden, the one hundredth and final performance in an extraordinary, unprecedented series he had begun the previous November. Edwin's performance was truly magnificent, astonishingly sublime, and the evening had passed so pleasantly that upon the sisters' return to Washington, Lucy—with Lizzie as chaperone—agreed to accompany John to see Max Maretzek's Italian opera company perform Bellini's *La Sonnambula* at Ford's Theatre.

But it was no mere performance; it was an enchantment.

When the chorus sang to Miss Kellogg in the role of Amina, "*In Elvezia non v'ha rosa fresca e cara al par d'Amina*," John bent close and murmured his own paraphrased translation—"In Washington there is no flower sweeter, dearer, than Lucy." When Amina's betrothed, Elvino, appeared and implored, *"Perdona, o mia diletta!"* John took her hand, kissed it, and echoed sorrowfully, "Forgive me, my beloved." As Elvino, Amina, and the chorus joined their voices in the achingly beautiful, soaring phrase, *"Prendi: l'anel ti dono che un di receva all ara,"* he kissed the ring she had given him and whispered, "Here, receive this ring that the beloved spirit who smiled upon our love wore at the altar."

John did love her with boundless devotion, Lucy realized. His strange, erratic behavior was not a sign of his unworthiness or a lack of affection but of the other conflict within his heart—his mysterious but essential duty to his country and his love for Virginia and her people. And then, after months of trying to win her parents' blessing to marry her, instead they intended to take her across the sea. Of course he was mercurial and jealous. How strange indeed it would be if he were not!

Throughout the turmoil and separation of their months together, her heart had remained constant. Lucy loved John dearly. The end of the war was surely close at hand. His service to his country would be fulfilled. Virginia would be restored to the Union, her people fed and comforted, all that had been destroyed rebuilt. Then, relieved of the great burdens of war, the good man that John was would emerge, and her parents would at last see him as she did. They loved her and wanted her to be happy, and when they finally realized that she would never know true joy unless she was united in marriage to her true love, they would give their blessing.

Enthralled by the music and caught up in her own passion, she sat spellbound as the final curtain fell and thunderous applause filled the theatre. Belatedly Lucy joined in, overjoyed to be seated beside her darling John, to have her uncertainty at last resolved.

When the carriage left them at the National Hotel, Lizzie kindly walked a few paces ahead to allow Lucy and John a precious few moments of intimate conversation.

Lucy spoke first, and she said all that needed to be said between them.

"I will return from Spain in a year," she told him. By then, she prayed, the war would be over, her parents' blessing earned and received. "At that time, if you still love me as you do today, I will marry you, John."

Heedless of the curious eyes upon them, John took her in his arms and kissed her.

CHAPTER FOUR

MARY

1864–1865

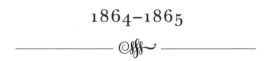

Away, and mock the time with fairest show.
False face must hide what the false heart doth know.
—William Shakespeare, *Macbeth*, Act 1, Scene 7

Only the most desperate pecuniary circumstances would have compelled Mary to rent out the Surratt Tavern and Inn in Prince George's County in southern Maryland and move to the Yankee capital, but by the autumn of 1864, she resigned herself to the harsh, bitter truth that she had no other choice.

It seemed that all her life misfortune and cruelty had pursued her from one unhappy home to another. When she was still quite young, she had become unwelcome in her childhood home after abandoning her mother's Episcopalian faith to convert to Roman Catholicism. As soon as she had come of age, her mother's smoldering resentment had compelled her to flee into marriage. Though John Surratt had been ten years her elder and had fathered an illegitimate son with another woman, the prospect of future happiness he had dangled before her had been preferable to remaining another night beneath her mother's roof, so she had seized it, and gratefully.

In the four years that had followed, Mary had borne John three children, but he had despised her Catholic faith so intensely that it had taken many heated arguments and many tears on her part before he had consented to have Isaac, John Junior, and Anna baptized. By then the Church had become her only consolation for a marriage that had turned into a bitter misery. Mary had learned too late that her husband was prone to violent, drunken tirades, but when she had appealed for help, broken and afraid, everyone had looked the other way, ignoring her bruised and swollen face as if they believed it had been more important to spare her from embarrassment than from injury.

Resigned to her fate, strengthened by prayer, Mary had devoted herself to protecting her two young sons and daughter from their father's violence, sheltering them within the safest, most comfortable home it had been within her power to create. She had been married eleven years when even that was taken from her. In 1851, a disgruntled slave had set fire to their house, and although the family had escaped with their lives, their home had been utterly destroyed. Later, as she, her husband, and the children had raked through the ashes searching for any possessions they could salvage, Mary's heart had burned with resentment as she imagined Northern abolitionists celebrating the news of her family's ruin. From the safety of their stone mansions in far-off Boston and New York, those self-righteous Yankees incited colored folk to violence with their pamphlets and their preaching, utterly indifferent to the suffering that innocent Southern women and children would endure as a result.

Mary firmly believed that Northerners ought not to condemn what they did not understand. Slavery had existed since antiquity, and it could not offend God or He would not have established so many rules governing it in the Holy Bible. Mary's family and John's had been slave owners going back generations, just like most of their neighbors. Although she heard occasional tales of slaves treated roughly on farms elsewhere, her kinfolk had always been responsible stewards of their property, whether slave, livestock, hammer, or plow. It seemed to Mary that good, decent, God-fearing white citizens were more likely to suffer at the hands of their slaves than the other way around. Reports of arson and murder at the hands of vengeful slaves sped from farm to town all too frequently, sending ripples of fear and anger through entire counties. The Surratts themselves had barely escaped being burned alive, and their family physician had suffered the worst loss imaginable when a fourteen-year-old housemaid had poisoned his three children with arsenic. If the darkies could wreak this much violence on innocent white families while enslaved, what horrors would they inflict if, as the Yankees demanded, they were set free? And what would happen to the economy of the South, which depended upon their labor? The people of the North were determined to destroy the Southern way of life, and Mary—and every true Southerner of her acquaintance—hated them for it.

In the aftermath of the fire, Mary had found a measure of peace and security when she and the children had moved in with a cousin's family while her husband worked out of state as a contractor for the Orange and Alexandria Railroad. As thankful as she had been for the respite from her husband's dreadful presence, she had always known it would not last. After two years, her cousin's family had put them out, and to keep a roof over her children's heads, Mary had suffered the indignity of moving her little brood into abandoned slaves' quarters on the land where the ruins of their burned house stood.

In the meantime, John had decided to become a tavern keeper. Over Mary's objections, he had purchased land at an important cross-roads in Prince George's County, twelve miles south of Washington City, and the construction of a tavern and adjacent inn had swiftly commenced.

"I won't live at a tavern," Mary had told him fiercely. "A den of drinking and gambling and sin is no place to raise children."

For her defiance, she had earned a derisive laugh and a blow across the face that had sent her reeling.

When the building had finally been completed in the summer of 1853, Mary had summoned up her courage, dug in her heels, and declared that John could live there alone if he insisted, but she and the children would not. At first he had tried to remove her by force, because that had always been his most efficacious method of accomplishing anything, but when that had failed, he had sold the farm, slave quarters and all, leaving her no choice but to join him in the crossroads village that soon became known as Surrattsville.

The enterprise had left John deeply in debt, and although the inn and tavern had proven successful and John had been named town postmaster, his constant drinking and gambling kept the family teetering on the brink of bankruptcy. Determined to protect her children from the worst of their father's excesses, and with charitable assistance from the Church, Mary had managed to send Isaac, John Junior, and little Anna away to school. As the years passed, Mary had quietly assumed her dissipated husband's duties as postmaster rather than lose his income, and she had been obliged to sell off livestock, slaves, and parcels of good farmland to satisfy creditors and pay his gambling debts.

After John Surratt Sr. finally dropped dead from a sudden apoplexy in August 1862, Mary had barely escaped bankruptcy, but hardship had taught her to be clever and capable, and she had managed to wrestle his estate through probate, consolidating the debt, securing new mortgages, and retaining ownership of her home in Surrattsville as well as a four-story town house they rented out in Washington City. But with the onset of war, burdened with the strain and fear and constant danger of being a Confederate sympathizer in a Union state, running the tavern and farm became too much for her—especially as the Surratt Inn and Tavern had become an important post on Confederate spy and smuggling routes. Anna, now twenty-one, was a great help and support, but nineteen-year-old John Junior, a Confederate courier, was often away on business for the Cause. Her eldest son, Isaac, had joined the Confederate army shortly before his father's death, and he was somewhere in the Deep South serving with the Thirty-Third Texas Cavalry, unable to assist his mother except in a higher sense, by fighting the Yankees. As much as Mary loathed to admit it, she and Anna could not manage the business on their own.

Marrying again was absolutely out of the question. Though she had been only thirty-nine when John died—and was still quite pretty judging by the compliments to her deep blue eyes, shining brown hair, and pretty, firm, well-shaped mouth that some of the bolder tavern guests tossed her way now and then—Mary was not about to risk losing the little she had left on the slim chance that she might choose a better husband in middle age than she had as a girl of seventeen. While it was true that she had learned a great deal about men in the interim, what she had learned about husbands was that she was better off without one.

By late summer of 1864, Mary had decided that the most prudent course—perhaps her only course—was to find a tenant to manage the tavern and property in Surrattsville, to move her family to the town house at 541 H Street in Washington, and to supplement her income by taking in boarders. But she had another reason to leave Prince George's County, one even more compelling than keeping a roof over her family's heads and bread in their bellies.

One week after his father's death, Junior had succeeded him as postmaster of Surrattsville, a federal appointment that required him to swear an oath of loyalty to the Union. He had so sworn—as countless numbers of Marylanders had before him, submitting to the meaningless, degrading, but necessary ritual to avoid prison or to acquire a job—but he had not abandoned his work as a courier for the Confederacy. As postmaster he could smuggle important dispatches from Confederate agents in the North through Union lines to Richmond and the Confederate armies entrenched around it in greater volume and more reliably than ever.

Unfortunately, although Junior had taken every precaution, his frequent travels had raised suspicions, and on November 17, 1863, Union authorities arrested him just south of the Union pickets with dozens of letters addressed to Confederate officials in his saddlebags. After a few days of absolute terror on Mary's part, a carefully placed bribe had secured his release from prison, but immediately thereafter he had been sacked as postmaster on the grounds of disloyalty.

Junior's exemption from the draft vanished with his title, and since the Surratts could not afford to hire a substitute to serve in his place, it was essential for him to find another federal position before he was forced into the Yankee army. "Such work is easier to find in the capital," Mary reminded him when he recoiled at the thought of surrounding themselves with so many Yankees, "and Washington City is full of Confederate sympathizers. It is, at heart, a Southern city."

What she did not admit was that, ever mindful of the federal agents watching Junior and the army recruiters scouring the villages and farms for every last potential enlistee, she was determined to whisk her brave, daring son out of range of their scrutiny. And since his arrest had not discouraged him from working as a Confederate courier, perhaps, Mary hoped, he could serve the Cause even better from the heart of the Yankee capital.

She had set her course, but she could not lease the Surrattsville property to just anyone, not after devoting so much time, effort, and personal risk to establishing the crossroads tavern as a reliable Confederate courier post and safe house for spies. Fortuitously, an ideal candidate came along by early autumn. John Lloyd was a former Washington police officer and a bricklayer by trade, but it was his experience running a tavern and running the blockade that suited Mary's needs perfectly. The five hundred dollars he would pay in annual rent for the tavern, the farm, and the numerous outbuildings would relieve some of Mary's pecuniary worries, but equally important, since he sympathized with the Southern cause, the Surratt Tavern would remain a crucial station on the routes the Signal Corps and Secret Service followed through southern Maryland.

The four-story, gray brick town house in Washington City had been one of John Sr.'s better investments, although when he had purchased it in 1853, Mary never could have imagined that she would one day assume the role of a widowed landlady there. It was built in the Early Republic style, spacious and comfortable, with a modest entrance for servants and deliveries on the ground level leading to a dining room facing the street and a kitchen to the rear. A wooden staircase along the front of the house led to the formal entrance for tenants and guests on the second floor, which opened into a hallway that ran the length of the building and ended at the interior stairs. The hallway passed two doorways on the left, the first belonging to a pleasant sitting room with a fireplace and two large windows overlooking the street, and the second to a spacious rear bedroom with a small piazza. Mary and Anna planned to share that room, although they knew they might need to change accommodations depending upon the tenants they acquired. Two more bedrooms, one large and one smaller but with a parlor, comprised the third floor, and above that was a small attic with two bedrooms and a small sitting room, somewhat cramped, though the uncomfortable sense of confinement was relieved by gabled dormers that let in sunlight and air. The boardinghouse was ideally suited in a respectable neighborhood convenient to businesses, churches, and numerous public buildings, and despite the blow to her pride, her sense that widowhood had sent her tumbling down in the world, Mary was profoundly thankful that she had managed to hold on to the house through the long, tense, arduous struggle with John Sr.'s creditors. It very well could prove to be her family's salvation.

In early September, Anna moved into the town house and began advertising for boarders, while Mary stayed behind to help Mr. Lloyd settle in and to reassure herself that the Surratt Tavern would not go under within a fortnight of her departure. Junior traveled between the two towns as well as to points farther south, helping his sister unpack and meeting potential boarders in Washington, supervising the harvest in Surrattsville, and smuggling important dispatches through the lines wherever duty beckoned him.

"You will be pleased to know that I have welcomed our first tenant," Anna wrote to Mary in early October. "Honora Fitzpatrick, or Nora, as she charmingly begged me to call her, is a young lady of nineteen years, quite shy, and unkind people might call her plain although I will not. She comes from a devout Catholic family, like ours, and I am certain Nora and I shall become fast friends."

A few weeks later, Junior informed her that on the first day of November, a second tenant had moved in—Louis Weichmann, Junior's longtime friend and former schoolmate, a cheerful young man with a round face and rosy cheeks, carefully combed hair, and a small, neatly trimmed mustache. Although he was presently employed as a clerk in the Department of War under the Commissary General of Prisoners and proudly served in the War Department Rifles, he had confided to Mary that his most earnest desire was to enter the seminary and become a priest.

The harvest in Surrattsville lasted well into November, and instructing Mr. Lloyd in the proper management of the tavern took much longer than Mary had expected, so it was not until the first day of December that she finally joined Anna in Washington City, accompanied by another new boarder, her eighteen-year-old niece, Olivia Jenkins.

Although it was the capital of the Union, Washington was geographically if not politically of the South, bordered by Maryland to the north and east on the other side of the Chesapeake Bay, and by Virginia to the west and south, with only the Potomac separating them. She might have felt at home there if not for the Union encampments filling every park and public square with rows and rows of white tents, and if not for all the free colored folk strolling about boldly without showing proper deference. Slavery had thrived in the city until the Yankee president abolished it in April 1862, or Mary could have brought her favorite maid and cook with her from Surrattsville. As it was, she would have to throw away money she could scarcely afford hiring help instead.

By the end of her first week, Mary had hired a suitable colored housemaid, who soon had the boardinghouse well scrubbed and organized. She had also welcomed four new tenants: Eliza Holohan, the sister of one of Mary's dearest friends; her husband, John; and their two young children. Before the war, Mr. Holohan had worked as a stonecutter in Baltimore, but the war had created new professions, and he now worked as a bounty broker, disbursing cash bonuses to entice suitable men into enlisting in the Union Army.

When Mary could spare time from running the household, she explored her new neighborhood, searching out the best markets, hiring a reputable laundress, and finding a church. She felt most at home at St. Patrick's Church on Tenth Street between F and G Streets, which was led by Reverend Jacob Ambrose Walter, a young priest in his middle thirties, fair-haired, bespectacled, and wise for his years, or so it seemed to Mary. He too was a Marylander, a native of Baltimore, and when she introduced herself one morning after Mass, she was compelled to ask, "Father, would you please pray for my eldest son, Isaac, who is off fighting in the war?"

"Of course, Mrs. Surratt," he said, so kindly and with such warmth that for the first time she felt welcome in the capital. It was a measure of Father Walter's compassion that he did not ask which side her son fought for, even though he knew she hailed from southern Maryland.

It was through Father Walter that the boardinghouse acquired another resident, a nine-year-old girl from Alexandria named Apollonia Dean. She was a student at the Visitation School, a preparatory academy for young ladies affiliated with the parish, and she soon proved to be a sweet and respectful girl, though often wistful and homesick for her family in Virginia, ever more so as the holidays approached.

On the morning of Christmas Eve, as Mary and Anna washed the dishes after serving their boarders, Junior came down to the kitchen for a late breakfast alone. "You'll never guess who I ran into when I was out walking with Weichmann last night," he greeted them, pulling up a chair at the small kitchen table.

"Santa Claus?" Anna inquired as she poured her brother a cup of coffee.

"No, sis," he said, grinning up at her, warming Mary's heart. It was not merely a mother's vanity to say that Junior had always been a handsome boy, and he had grown into an even more handsome man. Although he was quite tall, his smooth, fair skin and fine, light brown hair made him seem younger than he was, an asset in his clandestine activities. He had deep-set, thoughtful eyes, a long, elegant nose, and an intellectual brow that Mary loved to kiss when he sat still long enough to endure it.

"Go on, tell us," Mary urged, using a dish towel to protect her hands as she removed his breakfast plate from the oven, where she had been keeping it warm.

"I met our old neighbor from Charles County, Dr. Mudd."

"My goodness, how very nice," said Mary, setting his plate on the table before him and pulling up a chair at his right hand. "How is Dr. Mudd? What brings him to Washington City?"

"As to your first question, the doctor looked well, if a bit harried. As to your second, like the rest of the teeming masses out last night, he was Christmas shopping. He mentioned wanting to find a cooking stove for his wife." With a sidelong grin for his sister, he added, "You'll never guess who he was with—and no, it was not a jolly old elf from the North Pole."

"General Lee," said Anna promptly.

"Wouldn't that have been a fine surprise? No, he was accompanied by none other than John Wilkes Booth."

Anna let out a squeal and sat down in the third and last chair. "The actor?"

"No, the dentist. Yes, dear sister, the actor."

Anna squealed again, covering her mouth with her fingers and drumming her heels against the chair rail.

"Anna, please. Do contain yourself." Sighing, Mary turned her attention back to Junior. "How astonishing. How is Dr. Mudd acquainted with Mr. Booth?"

"Apparently Mr. Booth hopes to buy some land in Charles County.

He made an offer on Dr. Mudd's farm, but when the doctor said it wasn't for sale, I gather he agreed to help Mr. Booth find another property instead."

"John Wilkes Booth is going to become a farmer?" asked Anna, dismayed. "Surely he doesn't mean to give up the stage. He's too magnificent an actor to quit."

"When you say magnificent, I suspect you mean pretty." Junior laughed when Anna swatted him with the dish towel. "Booth was a perfectly amiable fellow. He invited us all back to his rooms at the National Hotel for drinks. Weichmann was keen to go, but Dr. Mudd was disinclined—he had friends waiting for him elsewhere, or so he said—but when I accepted the invitation, Dr. Mudd decided to join us after all."

"I wish I had been invited too," lamented Anna.

Mary gave her a sidelong frown. Over her dead body would her pretty, naïve daughter go for drinks in a hotel room with four gentlemen, even if they were gentlemen in the best sense of the word and one was her brother.

"I have to say . . ." After a moment's hesitation, Junior leaned forward to rest his forearms on the table, and Mary and Anna instinctively drew closer. "I believe Mr. Booth is sympathetic to our cause. That chance meeting on the street was not entirely by chance. While Booth was pouring drinks and chatting with Weismann, Dr. Mudd pulled me into the hall, apologized, and confessed that Booth has been badgering him to introduce us for quite some time. When our paths crossed on Seventh Street, they were actually on their way here."

"Here?" exclaimed Anna. "Oh, how delightful it would have been if he had come!"

Mary felt more wary than delighted. "Did Dr. Mudd say why Mr. Booth wanted to make your acquaintance?"

"He didn't, but he warned me that he suspects Booth might be a secret agent for the Union." Junior shook his head. "That was not at all my impression. Booth couldn't speak freely, not with Weichmann there in his War Department Rifles uniform, but he said enough. He told me that he had gotten lost while searching Charles County for a suitable farm to purchase and that he had ridden several miles out of his way. As he spoke, he took an envelope from his pocket, sketched a map of his route, and asked me to help him identify the roads he had traveled and landmarks he had passed along the way. He spoke of Virginia as his beloved country, and he boasted that he can travel freely because his name and his trunk of costumes serve better than any passport."

"What do you suppose this means?" Mary lowered her voice and spared a glance for the doorway. "Has he heard rumors that you work for the Confederate underground? Does he wish to join it?"

"I don't know," Junior replied, "but I'm sure I'll see Mr. Booth again, and I doubt very much that his interest in the Maryland country-side has anything to do with farming."

The next morning Mary prepared a special Christmas Day break-fast for her lodgers, but even as the enticing aromas of fried sausages and roasted apples and fresh cornbread filled the boardinghouse, her thoughts turned to the poor Confederate soldiers shivering in their tents and entrenchments, missing home desperately, their stomachs growling, their ears aching for the music of the festive season and the laughter of loved ones. Tears filled her eyes as she imagined the brave men in butternut and gray making a feast of small rations of hardtack and salt pork, washing the dry mouthfuls down with ersatz coffee boiled up from chicory and toasted rye.

Mary found consolation in the beauty of Mass, in the wonder that unfolded anew with every retelling of the birth of the Christ Child in the Gospel of Luke, but the love and hope and peace that filled her heart as she sat among the worshippers at St. Patrick's Church vanished later that night, when news raced through the city that General Sherman had captured Savannah.

"What will become of our beloved country?" she lamented to Junior as they mulled over the dreadful news alone in the kitchen while their lodgers made merry in the sitting room overhead.

"We'll fight to the last man," he said, his voice low and tight, his ex-pression bleak. "But, Ma, the Confederacy can't go on as it has been and still win this war. General Lee must stun the Yankees with an enor-mous victory. Great Britain has to enter the war on our behalf. Some-thing must turn the tide or the Cause will be swept out to sea."

"But what could this something significant be?" Mary asked. "From what you've seen beyond the lines, our resources and morale are at their lowest ebb of the war. What can we possibly muster up now that we couldn't do before?"

"Better minds than mine are pondering that question even as we speak, even as the Yankees—" Junior glanced at the ceiling. "Even as they make merry and sing carols. But I swear to you, Ma, whatever Jeff Davis or General Lee need from me, I will give, whether it's my liberty, my blood, or my life."

Not your life, Mary almost blurted, but somehow she managed to hold back the shameful confession that there was only so much she was willing to sacrifice to the Cause.

On the penultimate day of the year, Junior was hired as a courier by the Adams Express Company, one of the most successful cargo and freight transport companies in the nation. Not only would his new job grant Junior greater freedom to travel unimpeded and provide an irrefutable alibi for his illegal activities, but as the majority of the company's business came from parcels shipped to soldiers in the field, their couriers were required to know the location of the Union troops down to the regiment and company.

Junior had every reason to celebrate his good fortune that frosty New Year's Eve, and so Mary made no complaint when he headed out for a night of carousing with friends. Too anxious to sleep, she lay awake in her bedroom saying the rosary and praying for the Blessed Mother to preserve him, body and soul, and was able to sleep only after she heard him return home very late. She did not rebuke him when he staggered down to breakfast the next morning, gray-faced and bleary-eyed, his haggard slump over a cup of coffee at the kitchen table painfully reminiscent of his father's.

Junior was too unwell to attend Mass, so Mary bundled up in her warmest wraps and set out for St. Patrick's Church with Anna, Louis Weichmann, and Nora Fitzpatrick. "Do you know," she told Junior afterward, as she prepared him tea and toast, for his stomach would tolerate nothing more substantial, "when I was leaving church, Mr. Brewster, one of the ushers, asked me if I planned to take Anna to shake hands with Mr. and Mrs. Lincoln at the White House reception tomorrow. Honestly, can you imagine? Anna and I, shaking hands with that Illinois ape and the dreadful creature who turned her back on her own Southern kin to marry an abolitionist?"

Junior's eyebrows rose, and for a moment a new alertness broke through his lethargy. "Could you attend, if you wished? Wouldn't you need an invitation?"

"Not at all. The Lincolns are so taken with the notion of equality that anyone may attend, and hundreds if not thousands do."

He peered at her, his eyes bloodshot and bleary. "Anyone can simply stand in line and get close enough to the president to shake his hand?"

"Indeed, if one is disposed to do so, and if one considers the dubious honor worth waiting in line several hours."

"Astonishing," said Junior, shaking his head, wincing from the pain the motion induced, and slumping back in his chair again. "These Yankees must think him invulnerable. They ought to watch out. The Fates always punish such hubris."

"Junior," she admonished him, crossing herself. "No pagan blasphemy under this roof, not even in jest."

He mumbled an apology, glanced at the tea and toast she had placed before him, and closed his eyes, his weak appetite apparently fled.

By early evening Junior had recovered from his indisposition enough to come to the table for supper with the family and several of the lodgers. Afterward, Olivia, Nora, and Louis joined the Surratts in the formal parlor to enjoy the warm fire and share an apple cake Mary had baked in honor of Anna's birthday. Mary had just finished clearing away the dishes and was settling back into her chair when the doorbell rang.

Junior left the parlor to answer. "Well, hello, Booth," they heard him say as he greeted the caller. "Happy New Year."

Anna gasped, and as the front door closed and footsteps approached, Anna, Olivia, and Nora straightened in their chairs and quickly smoothed their hair and skirts, mere moments before Junior led the most handsome man Mary had ever beheld into the parlor. "Ladies, Weichmann," said Junior, "please allow me to introduce you to a recent acquaintance of mine, Mr. John Wilkes Booth."

Mr. Booth smiled warmly as Junior made introductions. The celebrated actor's brown eyes, luminous and fringed with the longest lashes Mary had ever seen on a man, rested on each of them as he echoed their names and bowed politely, his full mouth curving in a smile beneath a half-moon mustache, his gaze curiously stirring. His wavy, black hair shone like ebony in the lamplight, and his features were as perfect as if they had been chiseled from marble by a master sculptor. "Happy New Year to you and yours," he added cordially when he had met everyone, his voice rich and musical.

Junior invited him to sit, and as Mr. Booth crossed the room, Mary could not help admiring his lithe, athletic grace. His splendid attire suited him well—fitted black twill trousers, a snowy white shirt, a fine black jacket with a velvet collar, an elegant silk cravat adorned with a diamond stickpin, and gleaming black boots with silver clasps.

"It's kind of you to welcome me into your home on this auspicious New Year's Day," Mr. Booth said, settling into his chair with a dancer's fluidity. "I have no family in the city, and I confess holidays can be rather lonely."

"You're welcome here, Mr. Booth," said Mary, finding her voice. "May I offer you some coffee or tea?"

"Oh, if only you had come earlier," lamented Anna. "You could have shared my birthday cake."

Mr. Booth turned to smile at her. "Is it your birthday, Miss Surratt?"

Spellbound, blushing extravagantly, Anna managed a nod.

"Then I am doubly glad to have come." Rising, he went to her side and kissed her hand. "Many happy returns of the day, Miss Surratt."

Anna beamed, but she looked as if she might faint and she only reluctantly released his hand when he returned to his chair.

So dazzling and unexpected was their illustrious guest's presence that afterward Mary could not clearly recall the conversation. They discussed the holidays, of course, and the recent cold snap, and after Anna summoned up her courage to ask when they might next enjoy seeing him perform upon the Washington stage, Mr. Booth entertained them with several amusing tales from behind the scenes at the theatre. Noting the piano in the corner, he asked who among them played, and when Anna admitted that she did, he charmingly implored her to grant them a song. Cheeks scarlet and eyes shining, Anna consented, and although her fingers trembled through the opening measures, by the end of the second refrain she played and sang with sweet confidence, and Mary felt immeasurable pride.

All too soon, Mr. Booth rose, bowed, and bade them good evening, but his enchantment lingered long after he departed, much to the amusement of Junior and Louis, who could not resist teasing the ladies for being so thoroughly wonderstruck by the famous thespian. "You acted much the same when you first met Booth," Junior said, grinning at Louis, and as his friend spluttered protests, the ladies enjoyed the last laugh.

"Why do you suppose Mr. Booth came to visit?" Mary asked her son after the others retired for the night.

He shrugged. "Perhaps it's just as he said. His family is far away and he didn't want to spend the holiday alone."

"But you became acquainted only recently. Surely someone as famous and admired as Mr. Booth has a great many better friends in the capital, any one of whom would have welcomed him into their homes."

"Why should he come here instead?" said Junior, anticipating her question. "I'm sure I'll find out soon. When I saw him to the door, he asked if we could meet tomorrow to discuss a subject of mutual interest."

Mary's heart thumped. "What subject is that?"

"I don't know, but he said to come alone."

The men had arranged to meet at noon, but not at the boarding-house, nor at the National Hotel, where Mr. Booth resided whenever he was in the city. Instead Mr. Booth asked Junior to meet him at a tavern near Grover's Theatre, a popular watering hole among actors and managers. Mary and Junior surmised that Mr. Booth had deliberately chosen a place he visited often so that his presence, even with a stranger, would be noted and disregarded as nothing out of the ordinary.

After Junior departed, Mary kept busy to make the time pass more swiftly and to stave off apprehension, but the minutes, and then hours, dragged by. The clock struck three, and Mary and Anna served tea to their lodgers in the parlor, and still Junior had not come home. Nearly frantic with curiosity, Mary did her housework, said the rosary, watched from the windows, and waited.

Junior arrived home just in time for dinner, but although Mary thrilled to see a new eager determination lighting up her son's face, she held back her questions for another nearly unendurable hour until the meal was finished, the dishes were cleared away, and the lodgers had gone their separate ways. Only then did Junior take her by the elbow and lead her off to the quietest corner of the ground floor, a storeroom in the kitchen where only they, Anna, and the occasional servant ever had reason to go.

"What did Mr. Booth want?" Mary whispered eagerly, holding the lamp while Junior took one last look up and down the hall before closing the door behind them.

In the flickering light, his face appeared as unfamiliar as a stranger's, wild with excitement and somehow immeasurably solemn. "Do you remember how we spoke at Christmas of how some drastic measure must be taken if the Confederacy is to seize control of this war?"

"Yes," said Mary, breathless, pressing a hand to her heart. "Of course I remember."

"Mr. Booth has a plan for this very thing, a cunning, daring plan. It cannot fail—it *shall not* fail—and I have pledged to help him."

As John confided to her all he and Mr. Booth had discussed, Mary set the lantern on the floor, groped for a stool, and sank down heavily upon it, growing more astonished with every word her son uttered.

Even as President Lincoln celebrated the New Year in the White House by basking in the adoration of thousands of Yankee visitors, thousands of Confederate soldiers languished in Yankee prisons. Their numbers had swelled ever since prisoner exchanges had ceased in the summer of 1863, brought to an abrupt halt by Mr. Lincoln's General Order No. 252, which demanded that the Confederacy treat colored men in Yankee uniforms as they would white Union soldiers, trading them equally, soldier for soldier, for white Confederate troops. It was ridiculous, unconscionable, and yet Lincoln wrote the false equivalency into law and Grant upheld it.

If those valiant Confederate prisoners could be freed, the armies of the South would be replenished, invigorated, infused with new, indomitable strength. The tide of the war would turn, the demoralized armies of the North would retreat to their own country, and the South would triumph at last.

"Mr. Booth cannot possibly think to free our soldiers from prison by use of force," Mary interrupted, bewildered. "Not when they can scarcely hold Petersburg and Richmond. If we had twenty regiments of Mosby's Raiders, perhaps, but—"

"I assure you Mr. Booth does not conceive of a massive prison break."

"But surely he sees the folly in resuming the prisoner exchanges. If Jefferson Davis would acquiesce to the requirement that a colored Yankee be treated as the equal of a white Confederate—a notion so absurd, so unnatural—" The very idea so upset Mary that she was obliged to pause and take a breath. "In that case, the Yankee armies would be replenished too, giving us no advantage whatsoever."

"My dear mother, I said our prisoners would be freed, not exchanged."

"What on earth would compel the Yankees to free Confederate prisoners if they receive none of their own in return?"

"They *will* receive a prisoner in return, but only one."

"What? A single prisoner?"

Junior smiled. "The Yankees would empty their prisons of every last Confederate soldier from the highest general to the lowliest private in exchange for their commander in chief."

It was common knowledge that Mr. Lincoln often fled the heat, stench, and frenzy of the city for his summer residence on the grounds of the Soldiers' Home, an asylum established as a place for wounded Yankee veterans to convalesce. It was about two miles north of the city, a cool, wooded, secluded haven on a hilltop, far enough away from the Capitol and the White House to act as a restful retreat, but near enough for Mr. Lincoln to travel back and forth as required. It was well known too that he often traveled along the isolated country roads alone, without a guard, much to the consternation of his wife and his staff. A small group of determined men on swift horses could overtake the presidential carriage, render him unconscious with chloroform, and carry him off across the Potomac, through southern Maryland and Virginia, and into Richmond.

"The United States government would pay any ransom to have their president and commander in chief restored to them," declared Junior, forgetting in his excitement the need to whisper. "They would release every Confederate soldier within a day. The Confederate army could be restored almost to full strength within a fortnight."

Mary's thoughts raced as she envisioned the plan unfolding, her excitement rising even as a doubt tempered it—the long-suffering soldiers surely would not be recovered enough to take up arms and march to battle within a fortnight. She was unsure, too, how often Mr. Lincoln visited his favorite summer retreat in midwinter. Then it came to her, another profoundly important factor Mr. Booth and Junior had overlooked. "Why squander the most valuable hostage we could ever possess on having our soldiers freed so they may fight again?" she asked, her voice shaking with excitement. "Why prolong the war when we could end it?"

"End it?"

"Yes, my dear son, end it." She placed her hands on his shoulders and met his gaze firmly. "Mr. Davis could submit any terms he wished, and the Yankee government would agree to everything—an end to the fighting, the establishment of a permanent border between North and South, their acknowledgment before the world that we are an independent sovereign nation. That course would save thousands of lives, countless thousands. It would save the Confederacy itself!"

Slowly he nodded. "Yes. Yes, it could." He placed his right hand over hers, where it rested on his shoulder. "This would end the war, swiftly and decisively."

"It will not be easy to capture Mr. Lincoln, even if he does often travel alone."

"It certainly will not," he agreed. "So you understand, Ma, why I must consent to join the plot, even at the risk of my life. Mr. Booth needs me."

The next day, Junior went out after breakfast to meet with Mr. Booth again, and when he returned later that morning, he took Mary aside and told her that Mr. Booth had advised him to take certain legal actions to protect the family's assets from seizure should he be accused of treason. "It's only a precaution," he told her. "I don't intend to be caught."

He explained that he had signed a quitclaim deed transferring his portion of the Surratt estate to her, including parcels of land, livestock, farm equipment, furniture, and a few mortgages owed to the family. "I also relinquished all claims to property I now own or will own in the future."

"This seems quite drastic," said Mary, unsettled, "and final."

"If you like, you can transfer everything back to me after the war is won." Junior took her hand. "Ma, it's better to plan for the worst and discover that it was unnecessary than to have the family's assets seized by the Yankees. If, God forbid, I'm caught and charged with treason, the government won't be able to take the boardinghouse and the tavern and throw you and Anna out on the streets. I'll rest easier if I know that you'll be safe."

In the weeks that followed, the plan came together swiftly, with Mr. Booth and Junior at the center. Other courageous, trustworthy men had already pledged themselves to Mr. Booth, but it was necessary to recruit more, although as a security precaution, Mr. Booth kept the parties separate and did not reveal their identities to one another.

Money was needed as much as men. They would have to buy swift horses to speed their captive out of Washington, and to acquire rowboats and hire oarsmen to carry him across the river. They needed weapons to command his submission, ropes to bind him. Time was a resource even more precious than money or men. Junior devoted himself so completely to Mr. Booth's mission that he soon lost his job with the Adams Express Company, although he told none of the boardinghouse tenants rather than lose the excuse for his frequent travel. This, and all that he and his fellow conspirators did, was with a heightened sense of urgency that they must act soon, before the Union armies ground the Confederate forces into the blood-soaked soil of the South, the government at Richmond fell, and all their elaborate preparations went for nothing.

Mr. Booth visited the boardinghouse often, unwittingly sending the ladies of the household into a flurry of snatching off aprons, inspecting themselves in mirrors, tucking away loose strands of hair, and smoothing their gowns. Mary suspected that, although Olivia had remained sensible, Anna and Nora had fallen at least partly in love with the famous actor, for they begged her to escort them to see him portray Romeo in the benefit for Miss Avonia Jones at Grover's Theatre, and afterward they purchased photographs of him and displayed them throughout the house. Mary did nothing to encourage their farfetched hopes. Junior was alternately amused and exasperated by the young ladies' sighs and silliness, but Louis, who had long admired Anna, became increasingly annoyed by Mr. Booth's frequent visits. Other lodgers too had remarked how very interesting it was that their boardinghouse was so often visited by a famous actor, and some looked askance when, if Junior happened to be traveling on behalf of the mission, Mr. Booth asked to speak with Mary instead—urgently, at length, and alone.

Mary was not insensible to Mr. Booth's charms, and it was true that in their brief acquaintance she had become quite fond of him, but not with the starry-eyed infatuation of the younger women. In the course of Mr. Booth's frequent visits, they had spent much time in conversation, and they discovered that in matters of politics, they were true kindred spirits. They both despised Lincoln and the Republican Party, they considered Northern abolitionists to be the true instigators of the war, and they both lamented the end of slavery and the slow demise of the Southern way of life they both cherished. They denounced the injustices inflicted upon the citizens of their native state since the beginning of the hostilities—the federal occupation of Baltimore; the arrest of the mayor, police marshal, and other prominent citizens soon thereafter; the reprehensible incarceration of Southern sympathizers within the Maryland state legislature right before the scheduled vote on succession. They both agreed that Maryland surely would have left the Union if not for the outrageous and illegal actions of Mr. Lincoln's proxies, for which he alone should and must be held responsible.

Sometimes Mr. Booth spoke of his family, of his beloved mother, whom he seemed to revere as an angel of mercy and compassion despite her Union sympathies, and of a favorite sister, Asia, who had married a comedian and was raising his sweet young nieces and nephews in humble, genteel poverty in Philadelphia. Once or twice Mr. Booth alluded to a sweetheart, but Mary did not press him on that subject, reluctant to learn anything that maternal duty would oblige her to share with Anna. At any rate, Mary preferred their lively discussion of the war and politics and serving the Cause. It pleased her and flattered her pride that Mr. Booth sought her counsel on important aspects of the developing mission, and that he trusted her implicitly, as much as he trusted Junior.

She was less certain about some of the other men Mr. Booth seemed to trust. Strangers called at the boardinghouse at odd hours, some elegantly dressed, others wearing what she was certain were disguises. It would have been unwise for her to know their true names and occupations, so she asked no questions when Junior and Mr. Booth came in quietly late at night and spoke in hushed voices in the ground-floor storage room, or when men with their hats pulled low and scarves covering most of their faces knocked on the front door and gruffly asked to see Mr. Surratt. She would merely nod, show them to the parlor, and go and fetch her son, resisting the temptation to listen from the hallway. What she did not know, as Junior occasionally reminded her, she could not be forced to confess.

She understood that the nature of their clandestine activities sometimes required Junior to mix with unsavory characters, but she was careful to shield Anna from them, as she had struggled to protect her from her father's alcoholic rages and dissipation—but now, as then, she often failed. In early February, much to her chagrin, she was obliged to leave Washington for a few days to visit her estranged, ailing mother at her home in Prince George's County. Upon her return, she was astonished to discover exactly the sort of undesirable creature she wanted kept away from her daughter making himself at home in the back room of the attic.

She soon learned that in her absence, Junior had invited the man to board with them. George Atzerodt was a Prussian immigrant of about thirty years, filthy and consumptive. His spine curved so that he stooped when he stood and he walked with his head tilted to the side, and there was a greedy, complacent gleam in his eye that she found unsettling. It offended Mary to see Anna, Olivia, Nora, and Eliza chatting pleasantly with him in the parlor, struggling to pronounce his German surname correctly, and failing that, dubbing him "Port Tobacco" after the town from which he hailed.

"I don't want that sort living beneath our roof," she told Junior flatly.

"He's one of Booth's men," Junior reminded her. "He's been running the blockade since the early months of the war, and we'll need him to transport our captive across the river."

Fuming, Mary let the subject drop, but a few days later while cleaning Mr. Atzerodt's room, she discovered several bottles of liquor concealed beneath his bed, with more empty bottles scattered around the floor. A white-hot fury seized her, flooding her with hateful memories of her late and unlamented husband. She demanded that Junior evict

Mr. Atzerodt immediately, though her son insisted that due to his important role in Mr. Booth's plan, they would have to endure his frequent visits.

Mary's displeasure did not go unnoticed, especially by those who shared it. "Why does John bring such men as Atzerodt and Herold into the house?" Louis asked her one afternoon as she swept the sitting room so fiercely that straws snapped off the broom. "Why does he even associate with them?"

"John wants to make use of them for his dirty work," she said irritably, adopting the name Louis used. Only Mary, Anna, and Isaac called him Junior, as his father once had.

Louis's brow furrowed. "What sort of dirty work?"

Silently Mary berated herself for speaking without thinking. "Oh, John wants them to take care of his horses boarding at Howard's Stables on G Street," she replied airily, and to her relief, Louis nodded and went about his own business. In recent days his questions had taken on the quality of prying, and she resolved to be more circumspect.

Thankfully, the next of Mr. Booth's associates to request room and board with them was a lovely dark-eyed young woman, charming and intelligent and ostensibly demure. She also provoked Louis's curiosity, but of an entirely different kind. When she arrived on an icy February day wearing a veil down to her chin and a stylish fur-trimmed coat that emphasized her exquisite figure, Louis was the first to volunteer to fetch her trunk from the carriage and haul it upstairs to her room, scarcely pausing to pull on his coat to ward off the frigid wind before racing to complete the errand.

The young woman introduced herself to him as Kate Thompson, come to Washington to seek a preferment for her brother, but in truth she was Sarah Antoinette Slater, a French national residing in North Carolina and an accomplished agent with the Confederate Secret Service. She had learned of the Surratt boardinghouse through a mutual acquaintance, Augustus Howell, a Marylander they had known before the war and a Confederate Army veteran turned blockade-runner and smuggler.

Miss Slater and Mr. Howell, Mr. Atzerodt and Mr. Herold, as well as another man who had introduced himself as Lewis Payne but later confided to Mary that this was one of several aliases—and of course, Junior and herself—comprised the conspirators Mary knew, all of whom had pledged themselves to Mr. Booth and his daring mission. Whoever else he might have recruited Mary did not know—nor should she, for their sake and her own.

In late February, Junior returned to the boardinghouse from a late-night meeting with Mr. Booth shivering from the lingering chill of late winter and looking deeply unsettled. Although the hour was late and their lodgers had retired to their separate rooms, Junior nonetheless insisted that they descend to the ground-floor storage room before he told her what was amiss. Lighting a lamp, she handed it to him without a word and followed him below, where he shut the door, inhaled deeply, and said, "Booth has changed the plan."

She studied his expression, steeling herself. "And the change displeases you."

"Yes, it certainly does, and I told him so, though he seems not to care." He shook his head, his jaw set, his eyes narrowing. "The success of his scheme has always depended upon Lincoln traveling alone on an isolated road out in the countryside, but now—"

"Please, Junior," she said, placing a hand on his forearm. "Be calm and tell me plainly."

"Booth says a change to the plan is necessary because Lincoln no longer travels to the Soldiers' Home as frequently as he once did." When Mary began to speak, Junior anticipated her question. "He studies the president's movements meticulously and I have no reason to doubt him. Lincoln might resume his regular trips to the country when the weather improves, but we can't delay until summer. All could be lost in the meantime."

"Do you mean—" Mary hardly knew what to say. "The plan is aborted?"

"I could almost wish it were. As you know—as everyone knows—the president is very fond of the theatre. One of his favorite actors, Edwin Forrest, is engaged for several performances at Ford's Theatre, a place Booth knows well. If Lincoln attends one of Forrest's shows, which he is very likely to do, Booth believes we could snatch him from the presidential box, fling him over the back of a horse, and whisk him off to Richmond."

Mary stared at him, dumbfounded. "But Mr. Lincoln never attends the theatre alone. He always shares the box with at least a few companions, not to mention his bodyguard. How does Mr. Booth expect to subdue him when he's surrounded by friends?"

Junior shook his head. "Perhaps he intends to strike when the president's accompanied by no one but his wife."

"He shouldn't discount Mrs. Lincoln. Her shriek of alarm would bring at least a dozen men in all haste." Mary clasped her hands together at her waist, steadying herself. "But let's say that Mr. Booth and his party are able to subdue Mr. Lincoln with the aid of chloroform. How would they wrestle him out of the presidential box, down the stairs, and outside the theatre to the horses without being apprehended? They can't fold him in half and stuff him in a sack."

"We told Booth all this, Ma. It made no impression on him."

"We?"

"I and two other men you haven't met."

Mary knew better than to ask their names. "And you all told Mr. Booth firmly that you think his new scheme is doomed to fail?"

"We did. We tried. We also pointed out to him that to do as he wishes, we'd essentially have to throw out all the preparations we've made so far and start over. He insisted we were mistaken, that only the site of the abduction would change, and everything else would remain the same. To prove his point, he led us off to Ford's Theatre, took us on a tour of the exterior, and argued that the structure of the building, the exits, the alleys, were perfectly suited for a quick escape."

"An escape while carrying an unconscious, very conspicuous, very well-known man who stretches more than six feet in height?"

"Ma, I like Booth. I admire him, and I wholeheartedly approve of his intentions. But this new scheme—" Junior sank down on the stool and buried his face in his hands. "It's ridiculous. It's a farce. It would never work."

"I can't disagree with you." With her son's revelation, all Mary's hopes seemed to have been swept from her grasp by a capricious winter wind— the end of the war, the capitulation of the North, Isaac's safe return home, if he were still among the living. "What are you going to do?"

"I'm going to wait and hope he changes his mind. In the meantime, I'm going to keep doing my bit for the Confederacy as I have since the beginning—carrying dispatches, smuggling necessities, observing the placement and movement of Yankee troops and seeing that the details get to General Lee."

"And if Mr. Booth sets a date to put his new scheme in motion?"

"In that case you'll have to inform him that I'm off on a courier mission for Jeff Davis, because if Booth insists on putting this disaster in motion, I intend to be as far from Ford's Theatre as my horse can carry me."

As February drew to a close, Mary could hardly bear to leave the boardinghouse as the preparations for Mr. Lincoln's inauguration spread through the capital like the pervasive stench from the ubiquitous military hospitals. The Stars and Stripes hung from every flagpole; shop windows were transformed into a tangle of red, white, and blue ribbons; balconies fairly dripped with bunting; and offensive slogans blared from every wall big enough to post a sign upon. Offended, Mary drew the curtains and refused to look at the newspaper, but Louis, thinking himself useful, read aloud excerpts as she went about her chores.

"Listen to this," he exclaimed, after subjecting her to lengthy descriptions of the order of the parade and of the elaborate menu for the inauguration ball. "The editors of the *Louisville Journal*, speaking of Lee's army, boast, 'We have reason to say that the rebels are expecting very soon to startle the whole country and astonish the world. No matter what our reason may be, it is a good one.' What do you suppose they mean? Have the rebels developed some new weapon? Is this merely a bluff?"

"I assure you, it is no bluff," snapped Mary, her head throbbing, her patience spent. "Very soon something will happen to prevent Old Abe from swearing his presidential oath again, and soon thereafter General Lee will take action that will startle the whole world."

Louis gaped at her. "Mrs. Surratt, what do you mean?"

Mary felt the blood drain from her face. She clasped a hand to her forehead and looked about the sitting room, distressed. "I—" She took a deep, shaky breath. What had she done? "I don't know what I'm saying. Forgive me. I let my fears get the better of me. The threats on the president's life, this endless war, and Isaac—you know I haven't heard from Isaac in more than two years—"

"Oh, my dear Mrs. Surratt." Louis shoved the paper aside, rose from his chair, and strode across the room to take her hand in both of his. "Forgive me. Here I am prattling along, insensitive and unfeeling, entirely forgetting that your son may be— I'll say no more of it. I've upset you enough. Pray, forgive me."

She extracted her hand from Louis's grasp, managed a tremulous smile, and fled the room. Let him think her overcome by womanly distress and delicacy of nerves. Far better he believe that than suspect the truth.

When March 4 dawned, gray and sodden, Mr. Lincoln was still at liberty, and he was still about to embark upon his second term, and it seemed that nothing could prevent it. Late that morning, Mr. Herold and Mr. Atzerodt called for Junior and sat with him in the formal parlor, speaking in hushed voices and falling silent at every creak of a floorboard signaling a lodger's approach. It was nearly eleven o'clock when Mr. Booth arrived, but he stayed only long enough to offer Mary a polite greeting before the men departed for the Capitol to witness Mr. Lincoln's oath and hear his address. A lady of Mr. Booth's acquaintance had given him a ticket granting admission to the Capitol rotunda, but Junior and the others would be obliged to stand on the grounds, which surely had been churned into a field of mud courtesy of the previous night's heavy rainfall and the trampling of many feet. "If one of us carried a pistol . . ." Mary overheard Mr. Herold say as the door swung shut behind them. She shivered, wondering who else might have heard him.

Junior returned home in time for dinner, visibly weary, and with little to contribute to the conversation around the table. His reticence passed unnoticed, as the other lodgers who had joined the throng outside the East Portico had plenty to say about the shaft of light that had broken through the clouds to illuminate Mr. Lincoln's haggard but kindly face, about the profound beauty of his speech, about the thunderous applause he had received, the roars of approval, the tears shed, the hats flung into the air, this and that and every other thing. Mary thought Junior might give her his own, more cynical, review of the spectacle when they found a moment alone, but all he did was shake his head and say that Mr. Lincoln was a fool to walk about so openly when so many people despised him. "We never caught up with Booth afterward," he added. "We lost him in the crowd. He said he expected to come so close to the president that he might snatch a button off his coat. Perhaps he'll bring you one as a trophy."

"I'll display it proudly on the mantel," she said dryly.

She longed for the dreaded day to speed to an end, but before it was quite over, a knock sounded on the ground-level door, a soft rapping that she and Junior might have missed except they had sought solace in the relative quiet of the kitchen, away from their happy lodgers.

Mr. Booth stood before them, as handsome as ever, though he was dressed for the muddy streets and not for the theatre. "May I commiserate with you?" he inquired, holding up a bottle of port.

Mary rarely indulged, having learned to associate the sensation of tipsiness with her husband's revolting drunkenness, but she knew from her years working at the tavern that the bottle Mr. Booth carried was a very fine vintage indeed. The day had been so wretched that it demanded something stronger than tea.

Somewhat abashed to receive such an illustrious guest in her humble kitchen, Mary tentatively suggested that they go upstairs to the formal parlor, but Mr. Booth shook his head and said wearily that if he had wanted to drink with their lodgers he would have called at the formal entrance as usual. So Mary took the small port glasses from the cupboard while Junior offered Mr. Booth a chair at the kitchen table, and soon they were seated together with wine in their glasses and woe in their hearts.

After a long, brooding moment, Mr. Booth raised his glass in a toast. "Today, many of our neighbors celebrated a beginning, but nothing lasts forever. Let us drink to the end of Mr. Lincoln's second term in office, and to anything and anyone that will speed that day."

"Hear, hear," said Junior, and they all drank. Then Junior raised his glass again. "To General Robert E. Lee, the greatest military mind of our century."

They all drank again.

"To Jefferson Davis," Mary said, because if she did not speak up for him, no one else would. "And to Mrs. Davis."

They drank. Mary's head buzzed pleasantly, and she did not protest when Mr. Booth refilled their glasses.

"I was so close to him tonight," Mr. Booth said mournfully. "So close. I stood in the rotunda, and I had worked my way through the crowd until I reached the double line of police standing to create a clear path for Lincoln to pass from the Senate chamber to the east door to the portico. The dignitaries were supposed to proceed according to rank, but the press of the crowd banished all protocol. Then Lincoln passed by me, and in the chaos, I was able to push my way through the line until I joined the procession only a few feet behind the president."

"Goodness," exclaimed Mary.

"I doubt he ever knew I was there," said Mr. Booth. "A police officer seized my arm, but I pressed onward, hoping to escape his grasp but only pulling him from the line. He shouted for help, and some fellow officers came to his aid, and they detained me just long enough for the doors to swing shut, cutting me off from Lincoln."

Junior leaned forward, intrigued. "What would you have done if you'd been able to reach him?"

"I don't know." Mr. Booth took a deep drink. "Improvised a performance beyond anything ever before witnessed on the stage, I suppose."

"Were you arrested?" asked Mary.

"No. I got into a bit of a shouting match with the officers, but they eventually shoved me behind the lines and ordered me away. I lost myself in the crowd and took the place to which my ticket entitled me." He patted his breast pocket absently, and for a fleeting moment his expression turned ineffably sad. "I'll say this much for Old Abe: He certainly knows how to deliver a speech."

Junior shook his head and muttered something caustic under his breath, but Mary conceded, "You're right, from what I hear, but I for one am enormously thankful that I've never been obliged to sit through one of his speeches." She drank, savoring the rich flavor of the wine, knowing she mustn't have too much. "I pray I never will."

They sat and talked quietly awhile more, and when bottle and glasses alike were empty, Mr. Booth sighed and said, "I must bid you both good night."

"Don't go, Booth," said Junior. "Stay the night."

"Yes, do stay," said Mary, her words slurring just a bit. "This is a boardinghouse, after all. We have plenty of beds."

"You're very kind, but an acquaintance is expecting me at half past ten, and if I leave now, I should still make it." He planted his palms on the table and pushed himself to his feet, but his natural grace failed him for a moment, and as he kept his hands on the table to steady himself, his gaze fell on a silver ring he wore on the smallest finger of his right hand.

Junior studied him, brow furrowing. "Are you all right, Booth?"

Mr. Booth closed his eyes, raised his right hand to his lips, and kissed the ring. "Two nights hence," he declared, his voice ringing with irony, "I will be escorting a lovely young lady to President Lincoln's inauguration ball—that is, if the young lady will still consent to speak to me."

Mary felt a pang of regret for Anna, who would have given anything to attend a ball with the handsome actor. "The young lady would have to have a heart of stone to resist your charms, Mr. Booth," she said. "Whatever you did, or neglected to do, I'm sure you'll find the right words to soothe her temper."

"Temper? Oh, this lady is too good, too kindhearted, to ever suffer from an ill temper." He straightened, rubbed his neck, and managed a rueful smile. "Her only objection to me is that I am an actor. My only objection to her is that she is an abolitionist."

"Your young lady is a Yankee abolitionist," said Junior, incredulous, "and her only objection to you is your profession?"

"She might object to my politics as well, if I were not obliged to dissemble for the sake of my mission, my livelihood, and I daresay my very life, here in the Yankee capital."

"There's no shame in that," said Mary stoutly. "We've all been obliged to play the part of loyal Unionists for our own protection."

"This young lady is very clever, with rare understanding. I know I could make her see the justice of our great Cause in time—" Mr. Booth paused. "But of course, time is something I do not have in abundance. And that being so, I must bid you good night."

Mary and Junior exchanged a quick look as they rose to accompany Mr. Booth to the door. They bade him farewell as he stepped out onto H Street, where the sounds of merrymaking could still be heard in the distance until Mary closed the door against them.

The jubilant visitors who had flooded Washington City to celebrate Mr. Lincoln's second inauguration departed soon afterward, but the city remained full of strangers of an entirely different sort. Confederate soldiers were abandoning General Lee's army in greater numbers than at any point in the war, and while most of the deserters presumably went home, others crossed the lines and surrendered to Yankee pickets.

Some gaunt, unkempt former rebels straggled into Washington on foot, the tatters of their gray or butternut uniforms hanging from their emaciated frames, but most arrived around four o'clock every afternoon on the "deserters' transport," unloading on railway platforms one or two hundred at a time. One newspaper reporter warned that they could represent a devious invasion by the enemy—experienced soldiers stealthily gathering, lulling the citizens into pity and complacency, awaiting the order to strike at the vulnerable Yankee capital from within. Junior, who continued to observe the troops in the field on his courier routes, told Mary that the truth was far simpler and more troubling. The Confederate soldiers were starving, and they seemed to have concluded that an army that could not feed its soldiers could not withstand its enemies much longer. They were hungry and tired and sick of war, and they did not want to die needlessly with the end so evidently near, especially as the arrival of spring always heralded a renewed intensity to the fighting. Junior had overheard many resentful troops decrying the futility of doggedly pursuing what they called a "rich man's war but a poor man's fight."

Time was running out, if it was not already too late. Mr. Booth's bold plan might yet overturn what was increasingly appearing to be an inevitable Union victory, but Mary was certain that every postponement weakened the will of the conspirators and rendered their mission less likely to succeed.

Junior assured her that Mr. Booth had nearly completed his meticulous preparations and was studying Mr. Lincoln's movements scrupulously, awaiting the ideal moment to strike. "Lincoln changes his schedule on a whim, or so it seems," said Junior. "Booth might have to make a decision only hours ahead of time, if an opportunity suddenly appears. Believe me, Ma, none of us have grown bored or disinterested from waiting."

The men who called for Junior at the boardinghouse certainly seemed as determined and committed as ever, and the frequency of their visits had steadily increased with time—though perhaps at the cost of discretion. On March 14, when the afternoon breezes were so mild that Mary was able to open all the windows to let in the fresh air, Louis tracked her down in the kitchen to say that he mistrusted one of their newest boarders, a certain Mr. Payne. "Curiosity compelled me to go upstairs to his room in the attic," Louis confided, frowning worriedly, "but when I knocked and he invited me to enter, I discovered John and Payne sitting on the bed, playing with bowie knives."

"In the house?" said Mary, feigning dismay. "You're right; that will never do. I hope they were careful not to cut the quilts and pillows."

"It's not just the knives, Mrs. Surratt. Beside them on the bed I spotted two revolvers and four sets of new spurs."

"You needn't think anything of it. Junior often rides out into the country on various matters of business, and also to check in to see how our tenant is managing the tavern. The roads are hazardous, and he must carry these weapons with him for protection."

Louis appeared somewhat mollified, and yet he shook his head. "I tell you, don't trust this fellow Payne. He claims to be a Baptist minister, but he resembles that other man who came to us last February calling himself Mr. Wood—in fact, I have heard some of the ladies address him by that name."

Mary hid a frown and resolved to speak to Mr. Payne about his carelessness. "I don't recall this Mr. Wood, but perhaps they bear a striking resemblance to each other, and the ladies have simply confused the two men."

"I also overheard him tell John that he had been arrested in Baltimore for beating a young colored housemaid, but he managed to secure his release by swearing an oath of allegiance to the Union."

"I don't know anything about that," said Mary shortly, "but if the Baltimore authorities are satisfied, why shouldn't we be?"

The next morning, Junior took her aside and told her that Mr. Booth had arranged for the conspirators to meet at Ford's Theatre that evening to study the arrangement of the building, to examine the presidential box, and to plan the abduction. "Booth knows the owner well, as he's performed there many times," Junior said. "Mr. Ford owed him a favor, so he allowed Booth to engage the two boxes usually reserved for the president and his party whenever they attend performances there."

"That sounds ideal." So desperate was Mary for decisive action that she was prepared to jettison all her perfectly logical reservations about Mr. Booth's revised plan just to see the matter begun. "If you asked to see the state box at any other time, you would provoke suspicions, but if Mr. Booth has tickets—"

"We will have every reason to be there."

Later, at supper, Louis inquired if Junior wished to accompany him to a performance of *The Magic Flute* at Grover's Theatre that evening. "President and Mrs. Lincoln will be attending," he added, "so you may be sure we'll be in good company."

"I wish I could," replied Junior, "but I'm already engaged for the evening. Booth has invited me and Payne to see *The Tragedy of Jane Shore* at Ford's."

Louis made a face. "Come with me instead. Mozart is far superior to Nicholas Rowe."

"Very true, but the seats Booth has arranged are better than anything you or I could get at Grover's Theatre tonight." To prove it, Junior reached into his breast pocket and withdrew the tickets. "We'll be watching the performance from Mr. Lincoln's own box."

"Looking forward to it," mumbled Mr. Payne through a mouthful of boiled turnips.

"Those are ten-dollar seats," exclaimed Louis, peering across the table enviously. "How on earth did Booth manage to secure—" He frowned. "Never mind. No doubt he charmed the box-office clerk."

"Actually, it was the owner," said Junior, smiling, "and it was in payment of a debt."

Suddenly Louis brightened. "I see four tickets there. Could you spare one for an old friend?"

He extended a hand, but Junior held the tickets out of his reach. "I'm sorry, Lou, but Booth specifically instructed me to invite two charming young ladies to accompany us. Anna, sister? Would you grant me the pleasure of your company?"

"No," Anna replied, startled, but after a frantic glance to her mother, she added, more calmly, "I mean, thank you very much, but I would prefer to see *The Magic Flute*."

Junior smiled. "What perfect luck. Lou, you will have the honor of escorting my sister to see Mozart at Grover's, while Payne and I will escort . . ." He made a show of looking around the table, where at the moment only two young, unmarried ladies sat, smiling expectantly. "Dare we hope that you are not engaged for the evening, Miss Fitzpatrick and Miss Dean? Would you have any interest in sitting in the presidential box?"

"Oh, yes, indeed," exclaimed Nora, while Apollonia nodded eagerly, eyes shining.

Mary muffled a sigh of relief. The young ladies would be too entranced by the performance and their luxurious seats to notice their escorts studying the arrangement of the box, whereas Louis would find their intense scrutiny strange, at the very least. As Anna smiled across the table at Louis, Mary silently congratulated her for her quick thinking, for diverting Louis's attention and taking the sting out of Junior's rejection—and saving the conspirators' plans from ruin.

Soon thereafter, the young people dressed for the theatre and went out, leaving Mary in blessed solitude to pray, to write letters, and to study her ledgers and bemoan the state of her finances. The boarding-house did not bring in as much money as she had expected, and at the tavern, Mr. Lloyd was always demanding one expensive repair or another. For his work as a Confederate courier, which he did out of conviction rather than the expectation of riches, Junior received barely enough to cover his expenses. It was an unfortunate inconvenience that his commitment to serving the Cause rendered him unable to seek additional work.

If they could just hold on until the end of the war, Mary thought, and then she pushed her ledgers aside and bowed her head in prayer once more.

Later that night, Junior and Mr. Payne escorted Nora and Apollonia safely home, but after the two young ladies chimed their thanks and bade them all good night, glowing with happiness, Junior told Mary that Mr. Booth had called a meeting at a private dining room at Gautier's Restaurant at Twelfth Street and Pennsylvania Avenue. "We may be there quite late," he said. "We have much to discuss, and time is of the essence."

A thrill of anticipation raced through her. "I want to hear everything. I'll wait up for you."

"No, Ma. Go to bed. I might not be back until morning." He

quickly kissed her cheek and hurried off to join Mr. Payne, who waited outside.

Exhausted, Mary waited up until Anna returned safely home with Louis before she retired for the night. Twice she woke with a start, thinking she heard Junior come in, but the first time it was only a delivery wagon passing and second a shutter banging in the wind. At dawn she rose, washed and dressed, and went down to the kitchen to start breakfast, but the coffee was not quite ready when Junior came in through the ground-floor entrance, haggard, smelling of cigar smoke, and red-eyed from lack of sleep, his frown telling her at a glance that the meeting had not gone well.

She pulled out a chair and urged him to sit, and soon placed a steaming cup of hot coffee on the table before him. "For the first few hours we did nothing but eat, drink, smoke, and play cards," he began wearily. "We were seven in number, including two men I'd never met. Booth held off until the last of the waiters departed at half past one, and then we got to the real purpose of the meeting, going over the plan." He took a deep drink of coffee and looked up at his mother, grim. "I couldn't believe it, but there were some among us who were hearing for the first time that Booth intends to capture Lincoln at the theatre."

Astonished, Mary sank into the chair across from her son. "Why didn't he mention it before? How could he expect them to prepare properly if they didn't know the plan?"

He shook his head. "He didn't say, and I couldn't ask, but, Ma, the news was not well received."

"I would imagine not."

"We went over the mission, again and again, changing this detail, and then that one, with men raising objections and Booth calmly reasoning them away, but one of the fellows—you don't know him—became angrier and more obstinate as the hours went by. He declared that he had agreed to take Lincoln in the countryside, not in a crowded theatre, and he didn't see how the new scheme could possibly succeed."

"You and I have said much the same."

"Yes, but not in front of Booth and all the men who have pledged to help him. This fellow complained about the delays, and the expenses, and then he pointed out that prisoner exchanges had resumed in January, and so why should we risk our lives and liberty to force the Yankees to release the Confederate prisoners when it was already happening?"

"Doesn't he understand that we could ransom the president for so much more?" protested Mary. "A simple resumption of one-for-one prisoner exchanges will not save the Confederacy."

"I tried to explain that, but this fellow was too far gone in his anger to listen. But he did accomplish what I thought was the impossible—he got Booth to agree to keep to the original plan, to abduct the president as he travels to the Soldiers' Home rather than from the theatre."

"Oh my," Mary gasped, wondering why her son did not seem more pleased. "But—that's very good news, isn't it?"

"It would be, except that this fellow, having won the battle, decided to press his advantage. He stood up, looked around the table, and declared, 'Gentlemen, if this is not accomplished this week I forever withdraw from it.'"

"I see." Mary inhaled deeply and pressed a hand to her heart. "Very well. How essential is this argumentative fellow? Can you manage without him?"

"We may have to."

Junior slept well into the afternoon, and when he came down to the kitchen and asked for something to eat, she was reminded so intensely of his four-year-old self, rubbing his eyes sleepily as he padded across the floor, flinging his arms around her waist and smiling up at her, that her breath caught in her throat and she had to close her eyes tightly against tears. Junior would always be her darling little cherub, no matter how tall he grew, no matter how daring he became. She believed passionately in the Cause, but she did not want to lose her youngest boy to it, as she had almost certainly lost her eldest.

Perhaps it would not be such a terrible thing for Mr. Booth's plan to fall apart before he could set it in motion.

The boardinghouse was quiet for the rest of the day, strangely hushed rather than peaceful, with no mysterious visitors, no clandestine meetings in the kitchen storeroom, no urgent commands to report for meetings that lasted throughout the night. Over supper, Junior unexpectedly asked Louis if his office employed couriers, and if he was aware of any vacancies. Somewhat startled, Louis affirmed that they did indeed, and messengers as well, but he was not aware if they were hiring. "Would you like me to inquire?" he asked, and when Junior said that he might as well, if he didn't mind, Mary felt her spirits rising as she imagined her son safely and gainfully employed in a secure department of the government, even if it was not her government.

That night Mary slept better than she had in months, and in the morning she woke feeling refreshed and almost hopeful. At her last confession, Father Walter had encouraged her to practice prayerful resignation when life's course did not go as she pleased. Perhaps she was finally learning what that meant.

Then, just after she had finished cleaning the dining room and kitchen after serving lunch and had retired to her bedroom to lie down with her feet up, she heard a loud knock on the front door, and a moment later, Mr. Booth speaking urgently. Then came the sound of rapid footfalls on the stairs, and then voices, low and urgent, in Junior's room, followed by the sound of two pairs of boots on the steps, descending.

One pair halted outside her door; someone knocked, but the door swung open before she could reply. "Ma," said Junior, striding into the room. "It's happening. It's happening now. I have to gather the others."

"What is it?" Mary quickly sat up. "*What* is happening?"

"The abduction. Booth's plan." Junior sat down on the bed beside her and clasped her hand. "He just learned from a theatre friend that Mr. Lincoln plans to attend a benefit performance for patients at the Campbell Hospital, not far from the Soldiers' Home."

"When?"

"Today. This afternoon. Professional companies put on shows in a theatre at the hospital every Friday as an act of charity, but Lincoln has never before attended a performance there." A strange excitement lit up Junior's face. "The way to Campbell Hospital follows almost the same route as to the Soldiers' Home, so the original plan can be carried out almost to the letter." He released her hand and bolted to his feet. "I have to alert the others. We're meeting here at two o'clock for our final assignments, and then we'll be off. I don't know when I'll be able to contact you or when I might be able to return."

Her heart plummeting, she scrambled to her feet. "Don't forget to say goodbye to your sister." She felt tears gathering but tried to steady her voice. "What can I do to help? Let me pack some food for you, at least."

"I've had a rucksack packed with my gear for months, but food— that would be the very thing. Thank you, Ma." With one last hasty peck on her cheek, he darted from the room.

Mary smoothed loose strands of hair away from her face, straightened her clothes, and went downstairs to the kitchen, where she searched the pantry for suitable provisions for a rough journey on horseback. She had assembled enough, probably too much for Junior to carry, by the time Anna joined her in the kitchen, trembling and silent, her face streaked with tears, her lips pressed together as if to hold back sobs.

Junior burst into the kitchen soon thereafter, dressed for the road. He embraced them both and murmured words of reassurance and farewell. Just before two o'clock, Mr. Payne hurried downstairs with his kit, tugged the brim of his hat to Mary and Anna, and followed Junior outside, where they waited beneath the staircase for the others.

Pressing her face close to the narrow gap between door and frame, Mary signaled for Anna to remain silent while she strained to hear Mr. Booth issue the orders. Mr. Herold would take the carriage already loaded with weapons, ropes, and tools to the rendezvous point along the road to Surrattsville. The rest of the party would take up positions on horseback in a remote area along Seventh Street, and when the president's carriage passed on its return from Campbell Hospital, they would surround it, force it to a halt, and subdue the driver. Junior would take over the reins and, with the others riding alongside and the president trapped inside, he would drive the carriage across the Benning Bridge over the Anacostia River. Heading into southern Maryland, they would meet up with Mr. Herold, move the president to Mr. Herold's carriage, and speed off to the lower Potomac. After stopping for fresh horses at a small village just beyond Surrattsville, they would wind their way through rural Charles County to a farm near Nanjemoy, where Mr. Booth had arranged to leave their horses and carriage. From there they would cross to Virginia by boat, and have Mr. Lincoln securely confined within Confederate borders within a few hours of his abduction.

The men dispersed. Mary's last glimpse of her beloved son was the swirl of the hem of his coat above his boots as he ran off to the stable to mount his horse.

They had planned every detail with great precision, Mary told herself, slowly easing back from the door. Every man knew his part. The conspirators would descend upon the carriage so swiftly, so unexpectedly, that Mr. Lincoln and his driver would be overpowered almost before they realized they were under attack.

"Ma?"

Startled from her reverie, Mary turned to discover Anna standing before her, hands clenched, eyes brimming with tears, chin quivering.

"Oh, my dear girl," Mary murmured, holding her arms out to her daughter. With a sob, Anna collapsed into her embrace, and they clung to each other, trembling from fear, too afraid for Junior to feel any thrill of excitement that the mission so long in the planning was at last under way.

"When will we see him again?" Anna asked when they had recovered from their initial shock enough to dry their eyes and compose themselves.

"I don't know." Mary managed a smile. "I'm sure Junior will find a way to get a message to us from Richmond. When the papers announce that the president has disappeared, we'll know that the capture was successful."

Anna inhaled deeply, nodded, and returned a tremulous smile. "I'm very proud of him."

"So am I." Kissing her daughter briskly on both cheeks, Mary forced herself to resume her housework, and she encouraged Anna to keep up appearances by carrying on as she would on any ordinary day.

But as soon as Anna left her, Mary's mask of proud confidence crumbled. She fought back tears as she prepared the evening meal, set the dining room table, arranged the platters in the center, and rang the dinner bell. Then, as she heard the lodgers descending, she slipped outside through the ground-floor entry and up the exterior staircase, and after waiting a suitable interval she let herself into the formal sitting room, now empty, and sank into a chair, trembling with apprehension.

"Mrs. Surratt?"

She jumped at the sound of Louis's voice coming from the hallway behind her. "Yes, what is it?" she said shakily, raising her handkerchief to her face.

"My dear Mrs. Surratt, are you weeping?"

"I'm indisposed. Please leave me be."

"But, Mrs. Surratt, something is quite wrong. When I came home from work, I found our room in disarray, and when I went looking for John, I was told that he and Payne rode off earlier this afternoon with five other men. What is happening?"

"John has gone away," Mary choked out, pressing the handkerchief to her lips. "Please, Louis, go down to dinner."

Bolting from her chair, she fled past him and off to her room, where she shut the door behind her and fell back against it, weeping as if her heart had torn in two.

Eventually Mary took to bed and drifted off to sleep, too exhausted to weep anymore. She thought she was dreaming when she woke with a start to the sound of the front door slamming and the familiar tread of boots on the floorboards. "Junior?" she murmured, sitting up in bed as the man whose footfalls sounded like her son's climbed the stairs two at a time.

She heard another door burst open and slam shut, and then the sound of Junior's voice, muffled through the walls but unmistakably his. Astonished, anxious, overjoyed, she rose from the bed, straining her ears to listen. Junior was upset, that much was obvious, and when another voice rumbled a reply, she recognized the speaker as Louis. The creaking of the floorboards told her that her son paced in agitation, and she clutched her hands to her heart when she made out some of his words—something about his prospects being gone, his hopes blighted. As she stepped into the hallway, she thought she heard him beg Louis to get him a clerkship, but that couldn't be right—and then she heard the front door open again, and in strode Mr. Payne in his fine long gray coat, armed with a pistol and jittery with agitation. He raced past Mary as if he did not see her, took the stairs two at a time, and burst into the room Junior shared with Louis. When the door closed behind him she heard two pairs of boots pacing, three voices murmuring in consternation—although what Junior and Mr. Payne felt free to say in front of Louis, Mary could only imagine. Drawn by the noise, Anna emerged from the room she shared with Nora and peered down the stairwell at her mother, bewildered, but just as her mouth formed a question, the front door opened again and Mr. Booth entered carrying a whip, his face as pale as bone china, his expression preternaturally calm.

"Good evening, Mrs. Surratt," he said as he strode past Mary, nodding politely. As he climbed the stairs, he glanced up and spotted Anna. "Miss Surratt."

While Anna stared at him in wordless disbelief, Mary nodded in reply, but by then he had disappeared into the room with the other men. Anna flew down the stairs to Mary's side, but Mary had only time enough to put her arm around her daughter before the bedchamber door burst open and Mr. Booth, Junior, and Mr. Payne emerged, climbed the stairs to Mr. Payne's room, and shut the door behind them. Junior spared the women a glance over his shoulder as he went, and his stark, grim, frightened expression froze Mary to the marrow.

Taking Anna's hand, Mary led her to the sitting room, where they waited and listened, but the men had remembered caution and their voices never rose above a faint murmur. Thirty minutes passed before the door to Mr. Payne's room opened again. The pounding of boots on the stairs compelled Mary and Anna from their chairs just as Mr. Booth led Junior and Mr. Payne down the hall, past the parlor doorway toward the front door.

Mary hurried over and managed to catch her son's arm just as he was about to leave. "Junior, what happened?"

"Mr. Lincoln's carriage never appeared," he said, his voice brittle with anger and frustration. "He never went to Campbell Hospital. It was all for nothing."

He turned to go, but she held fast to his sleeve. "Where are you going? What are you going to do?"

"I'll be back in a few hours," he promised, kissing her swiftly on the cheek, throwing a look of apology to his sister. And then he was gone again, leaving Mary with her hand on the doorknob, her mind reeling, her heart racing with elation and terror. Junior was unharmed and restored to her sooner than she had ever expected, but the mission had failed utterly. What did that mean for her son, for his companions, for all of them? Why had Junior followed Mr. Booth from the house, and what would they do now, with all their grand plans lying in ruins at their feet?

Mary and Anna agreed that they could not possibly sleep until Junior was safely home again, and so they sat up in the dining room, drinking tea and gazing out the front windows while the rest of the household slumbered. At last, shortly before eleven o'clock, the door quietly eased open and Junior came in, alone, weary but unharmed.

They ran to embrace him, and when he assured them that he was perfectly fine, though exhausted and ravenous, they all but pushed him into a chair and dashed about preparing him a quick supper. He wolfed down bread and cheese and cold ham, and only after he paused to take a deep drink of water did Anna tentatively ask him what had happened on the road to Campbell Hospital.

"We rode out in pairs," said Junior between bites. "I stayed with two others nearer the city alongside the road to watch for the carriage, while Booth and the rest went on ahead to wait for us at a restaurant near Seventh and Boundary out in the countryside near the hospital."

Mary nodded, although she did not know the place.

"We were supposed to alert the others as soon as we spotted the carriage, but although we waited and waited, it never showed. About the time we figured the performance was half over and Lincoln would not be coming, we split up and made our separate ways to the restaurant. Because we were so long delayed, Booth had ridden alone back to the city. All of us but Herold were waiting at the restaurant by the time he returned."

"With what news?" asked Mary.

Junior scowled. "The president had spent the afternoon at a ceremony at the National Hotel, making a speech and presenting a captured battle flag to the governor of Indiana or something of that sort. He had never intended to go Campbell Hospital today, and why Booth's theatre friends were so certain he would, I have no idea."

Mary and Anna exchanged a look. "Well, all you lost was half a day," Mary consoled him. "There's no harm done, and perhaps it was good practice for the next time Mr. Lincoln goes to the Soldiers' Home."

Anna nodded, but Junior set down his fork and fixed his mother with a bleak stare. "No, that's not all we lost. Don't you see? We were lying in wait for the president for hours, and that in and of itself is a crime, some might say treason, even though we never caught so much as a glimpse of him. I can't even guess how many witnesses saw us together on the road and at the restaurant today. We're all complicit now, and it would do us no good whatsoever to quit. No matter what we do, we'll all be held accountable for anything that might come of Booth's plot in the days to come."

Anna gasped, and Mary pressed a hand to her heart, dizzy. "Mr. Booth did that on purpose," she said, disbelieving. "That fellow who threatened to quit—he can't quit now."

Junior picked up his fork and resumed eating. "Nor can I. You've got to give Booth credit. He has us where he wants us. None of us dares betray him or turn coward now."

Mary sat in dumbfounded silence, absorbing the revelation. Perhaps Mr. Booth had the conspirators in the palm of his hand, but even if he closed his fist, Junior could yet slip through his fingers. If he quit the conspiracy, he could flee the country, and then, though he might be condemned for the crimes of his former comrades, he would not suffer their punishment.

But Mary and Anna would suffer, for they would surely never see him again.

"I'll have to do the same to Weichmann," Junior said reluctantly. "He's seen too much, living here with us. Booth and I will have to create evidence placing him in the center of our plans, as insurance against any inclination he might have to betray us."

"But Louis is your friend," protested Anna. "You were boys together."

"We're not boys anymore, and he's a Yankee."

"Your brother is right, Anna," said Mary. "I don't think Louis will betray us, but we need to have some leverage over him, just in case."

"Don't worry about Weichmann, sister," said Junior. "He'll be all right, as long as he doesn't turn against me, and I don't think he will. Even so, I'd be a fool not to take precautions."

Anna nodded, eyes downcast. "Where is Mr. Payne?" she asked. "You left together, but returned alone."

"He said he was going on to Baltimore."

"And what of Mr. Herold?" Mary asked.

Junior swallowed, hard, and reached for his water glass. "You mean he didn't return here?"

"I don't think so," said Mary. "We didn't hear him come in, at least."

Junior blanched. "I'll check his room."

"No, I'll go." Anna rose. "You finish your supper."

She darted away and returned moments later to report that Mr. Herold had not answered her knock upon his door.

"He's likely still waiting for us on the road to Surrattsville," Junior said, pushing his plate away. "He'll figure it out eventually and come back here."

"With a carriage full of weapons and tools," said Mary, dismayed.

Junior shook his head and muttered that he hoped the man would have better sense than that, but he was clearly unsettled, and he stood by the window looking out upon the street while Mary and Anna cleared away his dishes and tidied the dining room and kitchen. Herold had still not returned by the time exhaustion compelled them upstairs to bed.

When Mary came down to the kitchen the next morning, she smelled coffee and discovered Junior dressed for the road and making a hasty breakfast. "Herold never came home last night," he said, a thick slice of toast in one hand and a cup of coffee in the other. "Atzerodt and I are going out to look for him."

Before nightfall, Junior returned through the ground-floor entrance, smelling of horses and sweat, with Mr. Herold trailing after him. Mary immediately bustled about fetching them food and drink, and after Mr. Herold wearily dragged himself off to wash up, Junior explained that he and Mr. Atzerodt had found Mr. Herold in southern Maryland making his way back to Washington, wondering what had become of the other six men and hoping to run into them along the way. When they had failed to appear the previous night, he had taken a room at an inn, and before setting out that morning, he had tried to persuade the innkeeper to store the weapons for him until he could return, but the man refused.

"I didn't want to bring the guns back to Washington in case the Yankee guards stopped us on the bridge," said Junior, "so I suggested that we leave them with Lloyd at the tavern. He's loyal to the Cause, and I thought he would be agreeable."

"And you know all the best hiding places there," said Mary.

He grinned wickedly. "Better than you do, I'll bet." His grin faded as swiftly as it had appeared. "When we arrived in Surrattsville, who should we run into but Atzerodt's brother, who just happens to be a detective for the state provost marshal, passing through on the hunt for Yankee deserters."

"Oh, dear me," exclaimed Mary. "Did he see the rifles?"

"Thankfully, no. We had left them in the carriage, wanting to talk to Lloyd before bringing them into the tavern. Atzerodt could hardly ignore his own brother, so they sat down and had a drink together, while Herold and I had one at the bar. Eventually the detective left, and Lloyd agreed to let us hide the weapons and other things in the tavern, but it was obvious he wasn't happy about it."

"If everything is well concealed and he keeps his mouth shut, he has nothing to worry about," said Mary, a trifle sharply.

Heaving a weary sigh, Junior rose from the table. "Everything will be safe and secure until we need it, which I think will be soon. And now, if you'll excuse me, I want to wash up and rest before supper. Booth is performing at Ford's tonight, and he got tickets for me, Weichmann, Herold, Atzerodt, and Holohan."

"You're going to the theatre?" exclaimed Mary. "After all that's happened, Mr. Booth is going to perform?"

"*Especially* after all that's happened, we have to carry on as always. We can't raise suspicions now." On his way to the staircase, Junior paused to kiss her cheek. "That goes for you and Anna too. This must be an ordinary day, like yesterday was and tomorrow will be."

For Mary, carrying on as always meant that she was obliged to resolve certain unpleasant financial and legal matters that had plagued the family too long. A former neighbor from Prince George's County who had purchased land from Mary's father more than two decades before had never paid the entire amount owed. As for creditors, there were too many bills and not enough money to go around. Mary knew she had no choice but to write to her debtor and creditors, travel to Surrattsville to meet with them, and settle the fraught matters once and for all.

She needed Junior to drive her, but his duties in service to the Confederacy delayed her trip. Miss Sarah Slater was en route to Washington from New York, and on the morning of March 25, Junior was to pick her up at the train station and take her to Surrattsville, where Mr. Howell would meet them and escort Miss Slater to Richmond. Mary eagerly agreed to travel with the clandestine party, pleased to think that her maternal presence could help deceive any Yankee guards they might encounter along the way.

The carriage sped them southeast from the capital, leaving behind the public squares thick with soldiers' tents and the makeshift hospitals that gave the city the appearance of one vast military encampment for the pale green hills, budding trees, and freshly tilled fields of the countryside. Mary expected Miss Slater to say nothing of her errand, so she was surprised and flattered when the beautiful young secret agent confided that she had come from Montreal and carried letters from General Edwin Lee, a cousin of General Robert E. Lee, to Confederate Secretary of State Judah Benjamin in Richmond. "Do you know what the letters say?" asked Mary, intrigued.

"Oh, yes," replied Miss Slater, nodding and offering a small, mysterious smile. She said nothing more.

Before long they arrived in Surrattsville, but Junior told them to wait in the carriage until he had taken a look around the tavern. He soon returned, his expression grim. "Howell has been arrested," he said in an undertone. "Federal detectives seized him at the tavern last night on suspicion of rebel activities."

Mary gasped, but Miss Slater merely nodded thoughtfully. "I must continue on to Richmond, and I cannot travel without an escort."

"Certainly not. I'll escort you."

"Junior—" Mary began, but a look from her son silenced her. He returned to the tavern to make discreet inquires, and when he returned twenty minutes later, he brought with him a trusted neighbor, a staunch Confederate who had agreed to take Junior and Miss Slater to the next stop on the route and to return the rented team and carriage to Howard's Stables on time the next day, the better to avoid raising suspicions. When Junior asked Mary if she would be willing to take the public stagecoach back to the capital after completing her business, she readily agreed, proud to do her bit without complaint, though it was a very small sacrifice compared to all that Junior, Miss Slater, and poor Mr. Howell gave to the Cause.

Mary arrived home late that afternoon, and the next morning, as Louis was leaving for church, she asked him to stop by the National Hotel and tell Mr. Booth she needed to see him at once. Louis delivered the message, but Mr. Booth did not come by until later that day, and he was greatly displeased when she told him that Junior had escorted Miss Slater to Richmond in Mr. Howell's place and might not return for a week or more. "I need him here," he snapped, glowering. "We all must be in place and ready when the opportunity we have so long awaited presents itself."

"Miss Slater's work is essential," said Mary, taken aback. "My son could not simply abandon her in Surrattsville. At any rate, Mr. Lincoln is not even in Washington. I read in the papers that he and his wife and a party of companions departed yesterday for General Grant's headquarters at City Point in Virginia. The mission cannot possibly be undertaken without him, so John will miss nothing."

"Lincoln may return at any time, and your son may miss everything."

"I'm truly very sorry, Mr. Booth," she said, bristling, "but there was nothing to be done. Miss Slater required an escort, and there was no one else."

Mr. Booth nodded, but he was obviously not appeased. "Tell him to come see me the moment he returns."

Mary agreed, and as Mr. Booth strode out the front door, she turned away with a sigh to discover Louis watching her silently from the top of the stairs. "Goodness," she said, pressing a hand to her heart, wondering how much he had overheard. "You startled me."

He studied her for a moment, expressionless. "My apologies, Mrs. Surratt." Inclining his head politely, he withdrew to his room.

Unsettled, Mary felt a sudden wave of relief that Junior had contrived evidence against Louis, just in case.

She prayed they would never need to use it.

On the last day of March, a knock sounded upon the front door, and Mary answered to discover two police detectives on the landing.

"Are you the proprietress of this boardinghouse?" the first asked.

"I am," she said, offering him a polite nod.

"And you are the mother of John Hamilton Surratt?"

"I am that too."

"May we speak with your son, madam?" the second asked gruffly.

"I'm sorry, but he isn't home."

"Where is he?" asked the first.

"He's off supervising the spring planting at our farm in Maryland."

"When will he return?"

"Soon, I hope." She sighed forlornly. "His sister and I do miss him terribly while he's away."

"Mrs. Surratt," the second detective said, his voice sharp with exasperation and annoyance, "you can desist with the sighs and sad looks. We know about your son's previous arrest, and we know he's fallen back into his rebel ways."

"How could you possibly *know* something that isn't true?"

"So you mean to say that if we rode out to your family farm in Surrattsville, right now, we would find John Surratt there, toiling in the fields?"

"Whether *you* could find him, I couldn't possibly know, but he is there."

Frowning, the first detective handed her his card. "Tell your son to call on me as soon as he returns."

Heart pounding, Mary took the card. The detectives exchanged significant glances when they observed how her hand trembled.

Neither Junior nor Mr. Lincoln had returned to Washington City by the afternoon of April 3, when Mary, Anna, and several other ladies of the household, sewing and chatting in the sunny formal sitting room, had their conversation drowned out by the cacophony of passing artillery. They paused, shook their heads, and sighed in amusement or exasperation as they waited for the noise to fade. They had grown accustomed to such disruptions, for the Yankees seized any opportunity to loudly celebrate a victory, no matter how insignificant. When the sound did not diminish, but instead swelled with the addition of whistles and shouts and cheers, the ladies exchanged looks of bewilderment, and Anna and Nora darted to the window.

"What's going on out there?" asked Mary, suddenly afraid to see for herself. The celebration signified dreadful news for the Confederacy, but how bad, she dared not guess.

After one long look Anna turned away from the window, stricken, but Nora leaned forward eagerly, bracing her arms on the sill. "The artillery is a salute to celebrate a new military victory, I assume, but as for the shouts and whistles—" Nora's eyes widened and her mouth fell open as she took in the scene. "Oh, my. People are rushing from their houses and shops and are filling the streets, and they're tossing their hats in the air and waving handkerchiefs and—oh my goodness, they're embracing and kissing and crying for joy!"

Anna inhaled deeply and squared her shoulders before returning to the window. "Excuse me, sir," she called to someone on the sidewalk below. "What's going on? What's the news?"

"Petersburg and Richmond have fallen," a man shouted in reply, his voice nearly lost in the din. "General Grant's army has taken the Confederate capital!"

Nora shrieked with delight and flung her arms around Anna, who stood frozen in her embrace, pale and wide-eyed. "Praise be to God," said Eliza, setting her sewing aside and hurrying to the window. The other ladies quickly joined them, laughing and crying and embracing, all save Mary, who sat silent and still in her chair, though inside, unseen, she moaned in anguish and tore her hair.

Richmond had fallen. The Yankees had taken the city. And Junior—Mary could scarcely breathe. Junior must have been taken too.

"Come on," Nora cried, releasing Anna, tears streaming down her face, her expression rapturous as she beckoned the ladies to follow her outside. "We can't stay indoors at such a time. Come along!"

Delirious with joy, the ladies did not notice that two of their number stayed behind as they hurried off to join the celebration. When the door slammed shut behind them, the reverberations jolted Anna from her paralysis. With a heart-wrenching sob, she ran to Mary, sank down beside her chair, and buried her face in her arms upon her mother's lap.

Later, all Mary remembered of that long, dreadful, disquieting afternoon was the harshness of the light, the grating quality of the music, the jittery chattering of fireworks, the bone-shaking thunder of distant cannon. Elsewhere, she knew, down the street or around the corner, other Washington households had plunged into mourning too, but they could not seek out one another for comfort, not that day, when to grieve was to commit treason. Mary sought comfort in her rosary and tried to resign herself to God's will, although she was too heartsick and bewildered to make any sense of it.

It was nearly twilight before the ladies and some of the gentlemen—James Holohan and Louis, their resident Unionists—returned for the dinner Mary and Anna had kept warm for them. "You should've joined us in celebration rather than staying behind to cook for us," protested Eliza.

Mary could not bring herself to lie and say she was sorry to have missed the revelry. "Isn't a good, hot meal more suitable for a celebration?" she said, keeping her voice steady.

Unwittingly hurtful, the ladies described the jubilant celebration Mary and Anna had missed—how they had linked arms as they had joined the impromptu parade of citizens filling the streets of the Union capital, how their hearts had overflowed with joy to see their happiness reflected in the faces of the people they passed, clerks and shopkeepers and housemaids and waiters whose businesses had declared a holiday so that all might join in the rejoicing. Residents had draped patriotic banners and bunting from their windows, and bands had gathered on street corners and parks to play spirited marches and merry jigs.

Crowds had massed outside the homes and offices of illustrious men of government and had demanded they appear and make speeches. Secretary of War Stanton was one of those who consented, and according to Eliza and Nora, in his remarks he had thanked God, President Lincoln, and all the generals and all their troops. He had asked Providence to teach them to be humble in the midst of triumph, virtuous in their hour of victory, and to help the Union secure the foundation of their country, blood-soaked though it had become, so that the nation would endure forever.

When Vice President Andrew Johnson had emerged from the War Department to address the people, however, he had adopted a far less conciliatory tone. The high cost of the war in lives and treasure demanded vengeance against those who had started it, he had said grimly, and as for those Southern firebrand instigators, "I would arrest them, I would try them, I would convict them, I would hang them." He would grant mercy to the masses, he had added, but wanted "halters for the leaders." He had spoken with grave sincerity and sobriety, Nora said, not shouting, not angry, but deadly serious.

258 · JENNIFER CHIAVERINI

It was Secretary Stanton who had ordered the eight-hundred-gun salute that had shaken the city, three hundred booms for the fall of Petersburg, five hundred for Richmond.

"Yes," murmured Mary. "We heard them."

They had heard, but had not understood the significance, and it tore Mary's heart to know.

After supper, as night descended on the victorious capital, Mary remained below, saying the rosary and praying for Junior, fighting back tears. Depleted of prayers, she found herself drawn to the window, and gazing outside, she glimpsed in the flickering gaslight bands of young men merry and boisterous with drink, their arms flung over one another's shoulders as they staggered along, singing and proclaiming the glory of President Lincoln, General Grant, and the Union Army.

One solitary figure caught her eye as it trudged across the street, moving to the left and then to the right to avoid the passing clusters of drunken revelers, but always, it seemed, on a course toward the boardinghouse. The stride was familiar but the young man wore his hat pulled down low and it was too dark to distinguish his features or his clothing—but then he was at the doorstep and crossing the threshold and then he was there, standing in her kitchen, his disgruntled frown giving way to astonishment as she flung her arms around him and cried out his name and wept upon his shoulder.

"Ma?" Junior said, wrapping his arms around her. "What the devil is going on?"

"You're alive," she choked out. "Praise God, you're alive and safe and home again!"

"Of course I am. Why wouldn't I be?" He patted her on the back, alarmed. "Ma, please, calm yourself. What's the matter? Have there been riots in the city?"

She laughed shakily, a shrill note of madness in the sound. "Only of the most cruelly joyful kind."

"What is it, then? What's Grant gone and done now? I assume all this fuss is for some little hill he's taken or stream forded, anything to hearten the ignorant masses."

She pulled back and studied his face, his dear, beloved face. "You don't know? Richmond has fallen."

He stared at her, uncomprehending.

"Junior," she said, "did you hear me? Richmond has fallen. General Grant has taken the city."

"But that's impossible. I was just there. I left not two days ago. The city was holding fast."

"I tell you, it's true. That's the reason for this merciless, unrelenting celebration." The tears she had struggled to hold back throughout that long, terrible day began to slip down her cheeks. "You must know what this means. The Confederate government is either captured or in flight. It is only a matter of time before the remnants are swept up and forced to concede defeat, and the war will end, in failure and in degradation!"

"No." Junior set his jaw and turned away. "No."

"Junior," she cried as he took the stairs two at a time. She hurried after him, up to the third-floor bedroom he shared with Louis, and burst in to find her son standing in the middle of the room, chest heaving, confronting his friend, who looked up at him in astonishment and alarm from his seat on the bed.

"It can't be true," Junior was saying. "It can't be."

"But it is, John," Louis replied, earnest. "I was at the War Department earlier today and I know this is no mere rumor. Richmond has been taken. Jefferson Davis and his entire cabinet evacuated the city this morning by train and the defending troops retreated. The rebels set fire to tobacco warehouses, stores of liquor, and railroad bridges as they fled, and a significant portion of the city is engulfed in flames."

"But I've just come from Richmond and the government was still seated," Junior shot back, shaking with anger. "I saw Jeff Davis and Judah Benjamin and they said Richmond would never be surrendered!"

Utterly bewildered, Louis fumbled for a reply, but Mary leapt forward and seized her son by the arm. "No, Junior," she murmured. "Silence. Calm yourself."

He turned to her with a jerk, a wild light in his eyes, but she discerned no recognition there. Then, swiftly, he grew calm. He staggered backward, and it was all Mary could do to keep him on his feet. "He's had too much to drink," she said to Louis, who stared at them both, dumbfounded. "He's gone quite mad from it—his father always did—but it will pass. He won't remember a word of this in the morning and you must try to forget it too, or he couldn't bear the shame."

Louis nodded. At that moment Anna came racing up the stairs, and with her help Mary was able to stagger downstairs with Junior and put him into her own bed.

"I can't believe it," he said, his voice strangely flat. "Richmond, fallen. It can't be."

"It is," Mary said shortly, struggling to remove his boots. "Now, you aren't really drunk, just upset, but no more than I or your sister. Compose yourself and let's figure out what to do."

Junior needed but a few moments to collect his scattered thoughts, steel himself, and sit up on the edge of the bed. Anna hurried off to make tea, and by the time she returned with the tray, Mary and Junior had agreed that they need not abandon all hope quite yet. Jefferson Davis and his cabinet were in flight, but perhaps they intended to retreat into the Deep South or Texas and reorganize the government out of reach of the Yankee armies. General Lee still controlled his forces in Virginia, as General Johnston did in North Carolina. If those valiant men had not yet given up the fight, neither should the Surratts.

It was certain, however, that Junior could not remain in Washington, for the two detectives would surely come looking for him again. While in Richmond, Junior had received a new assignment that obliged him to travel to Montreal, carrying dispatches to General Edwin G. Lee and escorting Miss Slater, who had traveled with him to Washington on the Leonardtown stage and had taken a room at the Metropolitan Hotel. The fall of Richmond made carrying out their orders all the more urgent.

After a brief, intense debate, Mary and Junior agreed that he should take no chances but should leave the boardinghouse and check into the Metropolitan Hotel for the night. In the morning, he and Miss Slater would depart on the first train to New York, and from there arrange transport to Montreal.

Mary grieved to part from her son again so soon, but she knew it was for the best. Surely it would be a relief in the days to come to know that he was safely out of Yankee reach in Canada.

One day of wretched news followed another. Mary could hardly endure her lodgers' cheerful amazement when reports came to Washington that President Lincoln had entered Richmond early on the morning of April 4, while flames of the fires the fleeing Confederates had set to destroy precious stores of cotton, tobacco, and liquor still flickered among the ruins. A group of colored workmen had recognized the president from a distance as he approached and—according to the fawning Yankee reporter—they had shouted, "Glory, hallelujah," and had fallen to their knees to kiss his feet.

"Please don't kneel to me," an embarrassed President Lincoln had urged them, or so the stories told. "You must kneel only to God and thank Him for your freedom."

Escorted through the streets by a squadron of Yankee cavalry, Mr. Lincoln had continued on to the Confederate Executive Mansion, where he had explored the offices strewn with documents and records and had sat at Jefferson Davis's desk, taking a glass of water as refreshment while his officers shared a bottle of whiskey they had found in the cellar. Later he had gone on a carriage tour to see "what was left of Richmond," and rode out to Broad Street to visit an encampment of colored soldiers, and from thence to inspect the abandoned and ransacked Capitol Building. Gazing up at the statue of the revered Virginian George Washington in Capitol Square, Mr. Lincoln was said to have remarked, "Washington is looking at me and pointing to Jeff Davis."

When Mary considered how meticulously Junior, Mr. Booth, and the others had conspired to get Mr. Lincoln to Richmond, only to read of him making witty remarks as he went about on a sightseeing tour amid smoldering ruins and suffering, demoralized citizens, she felt hysterical laughter bubbling up within her chest, but she managed to contain it.

That same evening, Secretary of State William Seward ordered all the public buildings in Washington to be illuminated by thousands of candles to celebrate the Yankee triumph. Once again Mary's tenants ventured out into the streets to witness the city glowing with rockets, fireworks, and dazzling lights. The streets were full of people and music, laughter and rejoicing. Sick with misery, revolted by the jubilation in the aftermath of so much death and destruction, Mary shut her curtains tight to block even the tiniest gleam of the brilliant spectacle, too upset to care what any malicious Yankee neighbor might make of her darkened windows, her silent house.

The commencement of Holy Week offered Mary no respite from

despondency. On the morning of April 9, she dragged herself wearily from bed, prepared a simple breakfast for the household in keeping with the solemnity of Palm Sunday, and attended Mass at St. Patrick's Church with Anna. There she prayed fervently, as Christ the Lord had prayed in the Garden of Gethsemane, that her Father in heaven might let that bitter cup pass from her, if it were possible—and to help her accept His will, whatever came next.

Later that evening, even as President Lincoln and his party were returning by steamship from General Grant's headquarters at City Point, rumors abounded that the Union Army had cut off General Lee's retreat and had surrounded the Army of Northern Virginia. Yet again exultant citizens filled the streets of the capital, celebrating and seeking out news, while fireworks crackled and bonfires burned luridly on every street corner.

Mary tossed and turned all night, haunted by the horrid rumors, by memories of the raucous celebrations blaspheming the Holy Day. The next morning at daybreak, a five-hundred-gun salute jolted her awake, shaking her bed and rattling the windows. She heard Anna and Apollonia shriek in terror, and then sleepy cheers from elsewhere in the boardinghouse, and then her own involuntary moan of dread. Steeling herself, she climbed out of bed and methodically washed and dressed, her heart heavy. Surely the artillery salute meant that General Lee and his valiant Army of Northern Virginia had suffered another terrible defeat.

She went downstairs to the kitchen to start breakfast, and she was nearly finished when Anna joined her, clad in a plain black dress despite the balmy spring weather, her face pale and wan above the white lace collar. If Anna stepped outside, she would easily be mistaken for any of the thousands of young war widows who had haunted the streets of the Yankee capital for four long, grim years.

"What was the reason for that cannon salvo?" Anna asked, her voice dull with resignation as she opened the cupboard and took out dishes to set the table. "Does it mean that the war is over?"

"I don't know," Mary said, but at that moment, a loud thunderclap boomed and a heavy rain began to pelt the dusty streets, drowning out any words she might have offered of comfort or consolation. She suspected she knew why the Yankees had fired yet another cannon salute so early that morning, but she could not bring herself to say it. Until she knew for certain, she could hope.

All too soon, the morning papers delivered the wretched news she had feared and expected since Richmond fell. The previous day, in a solemn ceremony at Appomattox Court House in Virginia, Confederate general Robert E. Lee had surrendered to Union general Ulysses S. Grant.

CHAPTER FIVE

JOHN

1865

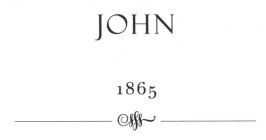

Come not between the dragon and his wrath.
—William Shakespeare,
King Lear, Act 1, Scene 1

He lay on the bed staring up at the ceiling, fully dressed but for his coat, which he had draped neatly over the back of a chair to prevent it from wrinkling. He could not have said what time he had returned to his room at the National Hotel after wandering the streets the previous night, alone amid the vast crowds, spellbound and plunged into despondency by the grand illumination that had commenced after sundown. Thousands of candles, gas jets, lamps, and lanterns had lit up Washington City, creating a scene awe inspiring in its extent and magnitude. All this to mark the defeat of his beloved country.

Virginia, he thought. My beloved Virginia.

From the streets and sidewalks, it seemed as if the very stars had been broken free from the firmament and had descended gently upon the government buildings, hotels, theatres, and offices like a celestial snowfall, glowing and warm. From a distance, from the camps of Union soldiers encircling the city, it must have appeared as if the capital were burning. As Richmond had burned.

A sharp knock sounded on the door. "Booth? Are you in?"

John did not move, except to raise his eyebrows in mild surprise. Michael O'Laughlen had been his friend since they were children, working up mischief in the streets of Baltimore together. Although O'Laughlen was an ardent Confederate, after the failed abduction in mid-March, he had wanted desperately to be released from his pledge to help John take Lincoln. The previous morning, John had gone to Baltimore in hopes of persuading his longtime friend not to abandon the mission, but O'Laughlen, regarding him with shock and horror, had adamantly insisted that he could take no part in it. After the fall of Richmond, after Lee's surrender, he had assumed that the plot had been scrapped, and he had tried to convince John that it was too late, that no good could come of it. They had parted angrily.

Another knock. "Booth, let me in. Let's talk."

John might have unlocked the door and allowed him to enter, except his friend's tone betrayed his intentions. O'Laughlen had not come to tell John that he had changed his mind but to try to convince John to change his.

The very idea that John could, that he might want to, was absurd.

Two nights before the illumination, O'Laughlen had been safe and comfortable at home when Payne and Herold had accompanied John to the White House, where they had stood among the thousands of jubilant Yankees that had assembled on the grounds to hear Lincoln make his victory speech. John had expected a certain amount of grandiose crowing in the speech, interlaced with the sort of folksy, frontier humor the president was known to favor, so he had been surprised when Lincoln had spoken instead of the policies he thought the government ought to adopt toward the vanquished South. Riveted, John had stared intently as the president had addressed critics of the new Louisiana state constitution. "It is also unsatisfactory to some that the elective franchise is not given to the colored man," Mr. Lincoln had said from his place at a center window above the front entrance of the Executive Mansion. "I would myself prefer that it were now conferred on the very intelligent, and on those who serve our cause as soldiers."

John had stared at him, thunderstruck. "That means nigger citizenship," he had fumed to his companions. "That is the last speech he will ever make. Now, by God, I'll put him through."

Payne had carried a pistol, and John had urged him to shoot the president right then and there, but Payne had refused.

"Booth?" O'Laughlen called, knocking again. "Wake up. Let me in, or come down and breakfast with me."

John flung an arm over his eyes and muffled a sigh. He had forgiven his old friend, but that did not mean he wished to speak to him.

Three more loud knocks sounded on the door. "All right, Johnny. If you're entertaining a fair frail one, I promise to avert my eyes, and I won't try to charm her away from you."

That earned O'Laughlen a sardonic smile. John would never bring a lady friend to the National and risk turning a corner on the way to or from his room and running into Lucy. Absently he kissed the silver ring he wore on the smallest finger of his right hand, her Christmas gift to him. Sweet, darling Lucy. By late June she would be half a world away—unless he should follow her to Spain. And why should he not go abroad now that his country lay in ruins? What remained to hold him here? Why should he linger to watch the Yankees grind what remained of the Confederacy into dust underfoot?

"Suit yourself, then," grumbled O'Laughlen, and a moment later, John heard his footsteps receding down the corridor.

Sighing, he crossed one ankle over the other, folded his hands beneath his head, and studied the pattern of fine lines and shadows on the ceiling. Just when he decided that if he had a pencil and sketchbook he might be able to reproduce the shifting patterns from memory, another knock on the door interrupted his study. "Mr. Booth?" It was the day clerk, tentative and concerned. "Are you unwell, Mr. Booth?"

If he has a key and dares let himself in, John mused, he takes his life into his own hands, for in this temper I might gut him before I realize I'm holding the knife.

Fortunately for them both, John's dagger—the handle of horn, the blade engraved with the words "Liberty" and "America"—was out of reach in his top bureau drawer with the derringer, and the clerk soon made himself safer yet by sighing and walking away from the door. John wondered why O'Laughlen thought John would answer a clerk's knock when he wouldn't open the door to his oldest friend, but he could almost admire him for trying.

Instinctively, his gaze traveled to the door, but instead fell upon a sheet of creamy ivory paper on the table beside his bed. A pen lay on the floor beneath it, and suddenly John vaguely recollected writing to his mother very late the night before. What the devil had he wanted to say to her at that hour? He hoped he had not castigated her for turning her back on the South, on Maryland, on the once-verdant and prosperous land that had given her and his father a home after they fled their native country in shame. In truth, he was thankful that she and Rosalie were safe in Edwin's luxurious home in New York, Asia in that dullard Clarke's Philadelphia mansion. Though he regretted their misplaced loyalties to the Union, it would have been unbearable to see the women he loved suffer in this terrible war as the flower of Southern womanhood had suffered.

But what, then, had he written? Bemused, he reached for the letter and held it up to a thin shaft of sunlight peeking through the curtains.

April 14, 2 A.M.

Dearest Mother:

I know you expect a letter from me, and am sure you will hardly forgive me. But indeed I have nothing to write about. Everything is dull; that is, has been till last night.

Everything was bright and splendid. More so in my eyes if it had been a display in a nobler cause.

But so goes the world. Might makes right. I only drop you these few lines to let you know I am well, and to say I have not heard from you. Had one from Rose. With best love to you all,

I am your affectionate son ever.

John

It was not much of a letter. His dear mother deserved better, but if he waited until he had a more eloquent missive to send, she might never hear from him again. He decided to post it.

Soon thereafter, John realized with some surprise that he was famished, and if he did not descend before the dining room closed, he would have to walk out and find breakfast elsewhere. Swinging his legs over the side of the bed, he rose and stretched, tucked in his shirt and smoothed his trousers, and slipped into his coat—purchased in New York City, perfectly tailored, excellent fabric, one of his favorite garments. Inspecting himself in the looking glass, he ran a comb through his hair, smoothed his mustache, and concluded that he looked well enough.

He tucked his mother's letter into his breast pocket and left the room, locking the door carefully behind him. He went down to breakfast, but only after pausing at the top of the staircase to make sure O'Laughlen was not stubbornly encamped in the lobby. In the dining room, he hoped to see Lucy seated with her family—or better yet, with only her sister or alone—but he was apparently the last to come down for breakfast, and the Hales, dutiful early risers, were nowhere to be seen. A handful of gentlemen were scattered among various tables, and one lady sat alone by the window. When his gaze lingered upon her, she inclined her head, gestured to the empty seat across the table from her, and raised her eyebrows in inquiry. It was then that he recognized her—Mrs. Carrie Bean, a young widow with three small children, the daughter of a prosperous merchant, pretty and charming and the sort of undemanding company he could tolerate that morning.

They chatted pleasantly as they breakfasted, discussing news of mutual acquaintances, the previous night's illumination, and the magnificent welcome that had been accorded to General Grant earlier that same morning, when he, his wife, and numerous staff officers had arrived in Washington aboard the steamer *Mollie Martin*. John nodded politely as Mrs. Bean described the scene at the wharf, how it had seemed that every gun and cannon had burst forth with a thunderous salute to the victorious general, and the bells on every ship and in every steeple had pealed a glorious and grateful welcome. A large Stars and Stripes had flown proudly from a tall flagpole on the dock, unfurled to its full length and breadth above the sparkling river.

"I missed it," John said evenly, sipping his coffee and quietly seething. He had not known that the general in chief had come to the capital. He wondered if the slight, bloodthirsty, deceptively stoic fellow felt any shame in knowing that the Virginian who had surrendered to him at Appomattox was vastly his superior in every way one could measure a man.

Mrs. Bean shook her head, bemused. "It seems to me that the ink had scarcely dried on the surrender documents before General Grant was steaming up the James away from City Point. Did you hear that as soon as he had settled his wife and son in at the Willard Hotel, he hastened over to the War Department to urge Secretary Stanton to cease drafting and recruiting?"

"Did he indeed?"

"General Grant also advised Secretary Stanton to stop purchasing arms and supplies and to reduce the numbers of officers and civil servants on the government payroll—to cut expenses, I suppose."

"It seems to me that Grant is demobilizing the army before the war is entirely over."

"I must agree. One shouldn't forget that Mosby's Raiders and General Johnston's army are still at war, and Mr. Davis has not yet surrendered either." She shuddered prettily. "How curious it is. All along I've thought that no man wanted the war to be over more than President Lincoln did, but now I believe General Grant surpasses even him."

"Perhaps he's eager to return to his father's tannery," John offered. "Or perhaps he wants to make another go at that farm in Missouri, which rumor has it he ran into the ground. He's lucky that the war came along and he stumbled into gainful employment in time to escape bankruptcy and ruin."

"Oh, Mr. Booth," Mrs. Bean said mirthfully, scandalized. "You mustn't speak of the great hero of the Union in this way."

"I'm certain the general does not care one spent cigar what opinion I might have of him."

"Speaking of postwar careers," she said, regarding him speculatively, "when do you think you might return to the stage? I did so enjoy your portrayal of the evil Duke Pescara at Ford's Theatre last month."

"Return to the stage?" echoed John, feigning astonishment. "My good woman, I assure you, I never left it."

He was playing a role even then—that of the complacent Washington gentleman, content to sip coffee and engage in inane chatter while the world burned.

After breakfast, John parted from Mrs. Bean with a courteous bow and went to the front desk to post his letter to his mother, an act that reminded him he ought to collect his own mail, which due to his peripatetic existence he arranged to be sent to him in care of Ford's Theatre.

Entering the lobby, he found Harry Ford—manager, brother of the owner—debating the surrender at Appomattox with Tom Raybold, one of the ticket agents. At the sight of John, Ford gestured dramatically. "Now, *here* comes a man who does not like General Lee."

"Let it be, Ford," Raybold said, disappearing into a back office to fetch John's mail.

"I'm sure I like Lee as much as you do," said John easily. "I just don't like that he gave up. He received a sword for the defense of Virginia at the Capitol in Richmond, and rather than surrender, he should have died upon it."

Ford looked taken aback. "General Lee is a brilliant commander, and I guess he knew what was best. If he judged the cause to be hopeless and decided he ought not to squander any more young lives for it, who are we to question him?"

"Who indeed?" asked John, just as Raybold returned and handed him a rosewater-scented envelope. " 'Why, man, he doth bestride the narrow world/Like a colossus, and we petty men/Walk under his huge legs, and peep about/To find ourselves dishonorable graves.' "

"We will have a colossus or two at the theatre tonight," said Raybold, smiling. "We were expecting a mostly empty house tonight on account of Good Friday, but now that's all changed."

John nodded absently, opening the letter and smiling as he recognized the signature of the besotted fair frail one who had sent it. "How so?"

"President Lincoln is going to be here tonight with General Grant," said Ford, and then, grinning wickedly, he added, "They've got General Lee here as a prisoner."

John looked up, shocked. "What's that you say?"

"It's true. He's coming to the performance too. We're going to put him in the opposite box."

"Never," John exclaimed. "Lee would never let himself be used in that way, to be paraded around as Romans did their captives. Does Lincoln think himself a Caesar, deserving of a triumph in the forum?"

"Ford, don't goad him so," said Raybold, offering John an apologetic shake of the head. "It's not true—well, it *is* true that the president and the general will be here, but Lee hasn't been taken prisoner, not as far as I know."

"That's a poor jest," said John sharply, glaring at Ford. "I don't believe a word of it."

"It's not all in jest," Ford protested. "About half past ten this morning, a messenger from the Executive Mansion called on behalf of Mrs. Lincoln to reserve the State Box."

"Check the house plan," said Raybold, indicating the ticket counter with a jerk of his head. Frowning, John went behind the desk and studied the map of the theatre—and his heart thudded when he saw crosses marked through boxes seven and eight, which by the removal of a partition formed the larger State Box. Nearby, a note in pencil listed the president, the general, and their wives. "Well done, Ford," he said, careful to keep his voice steady. "That's quite a coup, if you're right. I would've thought Lincoln would be at Grover's tonight, to see that patriotic spectacle Hess is putting on to commemorate the fall of Fort Sumter."

Ford waved a hand dismissively. "Someone will take young Master Tad to see that, no doubt, but President and Mrs. Lincoln want to see Miss Keene perform one last time before her engagement here ends."

"And they've invited General and Mrs. Grant to join them. You're certain."

"I am, and better yet, the good news came early enough for me to announce it in our ad in the *Evening Star*." With every word, Ford's voice rose in excitement. "We'll sell out the theatre. It wouldn't matter what we put on the stage. The people will snatch up every last ticket at any price to see the president and his victorious general in the state box, even if they've seen *Our American Cousin* half a dozen times already."

"How fortunate for Miss Keene," said John, mustering all his skill as a thespian to disguise his sudden elation. "This is her benefit night, is it not?"

"It is." Ford beamed with happiness and the anticipation of lucre, his earlier glee in taunting John forgotten. "If I had an extra ticket I would give you one, Booth, but I expect to sell them all."

"I understand completely, and in any case, I wouldn't want to deny Miss Keene one cent of her benefit." Smiling, John seated himself and made a show of reading his letter, but his thoughts churned, his gaze focused somewhere beyond the page. "Yet I wouldn't want to miss such a historic occasion. Perhaps I'll come by and watch from backstage."

John strode away from the theatre, the letter shoved into his breast pocket, barely able to hear the cacophony of the streets over the sudden roaring in his ears. Lincoln and Grant, sharing a box at Ford's Theatre. The opportunity he had so long awaited and prepared for was imminent. He would never have a more perfect chance to take them both.

But he must be sure.

He strode off to the Willard Hotel, where he engaged the front-desk clerk in friendly banter and, with the vague promise of theatre tickets, managed to pry out of him that General Grant was out, and that he had not requested a carriage to take him to the theatre that evening, or anywhere else. "Mrs. Grant is having lunch in the dining room," the clerk said helpfully. "Perhaps the general will join her."

Smiling, John thanked him and strolled on to the dining room, where he spotted the short, plump little matron seated at the best table with her young son and another lady with a child. With a wink, the maître d'hôtel agreed to seat John nearby, where he ordered soup and pretended to eat it, watching the general's wife steadily and straining his ears to catch the ladies' conversation. Although Mrs. Grant did refer proudly to her husband several times, as best as John could determine, she said nothing of the theatre, an invitation from the Lincolns, or any plans for the day.

John departed soon after the ladies and their children and made his way to Pumphrey's Stable at Sixth and C Streets, where he reserved a horse, explaining that he would come by for it in the late afternoon. He crossed the street to the National Hotel, and after glancing about for Lucy as he crossed the lobby and climbed the stairs, he went to his room and retrieved his field glasses, wrapped carefully in paper and stored in the bottom drawer of the bureau. He quickly left the hotel again, ignoring a few attempts by acquaintances to engage him in conversation.

With the field glasses tucked under his arm, John strode up Sixth Street to the Surratt boardinghouse. Mrs. Surratt answered his knock and welcomed him into the sitting room, a melancholy twist to her mouth, her brow furrowed in worry. She was a handsome woman in her early forties, matronly, but with only a trace of lines around her eyes and mouth and a few threads of gray in her dark-brown hair. Even so, she seemed to have aged a year since the fall of Richmond.

When he asked to speak with her son, Mrs. Surratt shook her head. "He isn't here. Earlier today I received a letter from him postmarked from Montreal, and as far as I know, he's still there."

Silently, John cursed his luck. "You don't know when he might return?"

"I only wish I did." She peered up at him, frowning. "Mr. Booth, you look quite pale. Are you unwell?"

"If I am pale, it is from excitement." Glancing about to be sure they would not be overheard, he said, "The plan goes off tonight."

For a long moment she stared at him, dumbfounded. "You cannot mean it."

"I do, madam."

"But Mr. Booth—" She clasped a hand to her forehead, glanced toward the front door, then shook her head and let her hand fall by her side again. "Why? What could you possibly hope to accomplish? The Confederacy is finished. The war is over."

"The war is not yet over, madam, not while Davis still has his liberty and Johnston an army." Disappointed by her reaction, he smiled to inspirit her, exuding confidence. "Now is the perfect moment to strike, when they aren't expecting an assault on the president."

"Forgive me, Mr. Booth, but they aren't expecting it because it would be pointless. If you managed to abduct the president, where would you take him now that Richmond has fallen? Who would negotiate the terms of his release with the Confederate government in flight? Why risk your lives to have all our prisoners freed so they may invigorate our armies, when they'll be released soon anyway and they have no army to return to?"

"Lee surrendered, but we have four other generals in the field commanding nearly ninety-one thousand troops. Even if we had but a single regiment remaining, I would still act. Virginia must be avenged."

"Virginia must be rebuilt, her people fed, her families reunited," said Mrs. Surratt, agitated. "The same is true of all the South."

"Mrs. Surratt," he said, adopting his most reasonable tone, "that is precisely what I mean. The Yankees have lain waste to our country. Our cities lie in ruins. Our farmers' fields are spoiled and fallow. Our roads and railways are torn up and impassible. A generation of our young men lie in unmarked graves beneath the blood-soaked soil of a hundred battlefields. The Yankees must bear the burden of restoring what they have destroyed. The Radical Republicans in Congress are determined to punish before they provide. We must secure any advantage we can before the real negotiations begin—whether they're debating how to fund reconstruction, or how soon Confederate soldiers may be allowed to return to their families."

"I suppose you make a fair point," said Mrs. Surratt uncertainly. "But Junior isn't here and I have no idea where to send a letter or telegram."

"Perhaps you can help me instead. Are any of your servants planning to go to the tavern soon?"

"I intend to go there myself this afternoon, on a matter of business."

"Very good, very good." He held out the package. "Would you carry this to Mr. Lloyd and ask him to keep it for me?"

Even as she accepted the package and weighed it in her hands, her expression revealed that she could not guess what it contained, so thick was the brown paper wrapping. "I suppose there would be no harm in that."

"Would you also please tell him to retrieve the weapons and gear from their hiding places and have them ready for me?"

Mrs. Surratt nodded, but she had begun to tremble, rattling the brown paper wrapping. "Of course, Mr. Booth." She quickly set the package on the nearest table. "I can certainly pass along your message, since I'm going to the tavern anyway."

At that moment, the front door opened, and they both turned to see Weichmann enter. "Good afternoon," he greeted them, smiling. "We were given a half day off on account of Good Friday."

"What a stroke of good luck," John replied affably, and then, before Weichmann could draw him into a conversation about his own plans for the afternoon, he bade them both farewell and quickly departed.

Mrs. Surratt would not fail him, despite her obvious reluctance, John thought as he strode down Sixth Street. It was unfortunate that

Surratt was away, but they had sufficient numbers without him, and John would gather the others for one last summit to announce that the moment had come and to give them their final orders. He left messages at his comrades' hotels and boardinghouses, instructing them to meet at the Herndon House at eight o'clock, and at the last stop on his rounds, an idea suddenly took hold of him and he asked the clerk for several sheets of stationery and pen and ink. He retired to the bar, ordered a whiskey and water, and, needing only a moment of contemplation, for he knew well what he wanted to say, he swiftly wrote a letter justifying all he intended to do that night.

His glass was empty before he reached the end. "For a long time I have devoted my energies, my time and money to the accomplishment of a certain end," he concluded. "I have been disappointed. Heartsick and disappointed, I turn from the path which I have been following into a bolder and more perilous one. Many will blame me for what I am about to do, but posterity, I am sure, will justify me." He signed his name with a flourish, and then, feeling obliged to give credit where it was due, he added the names of Lewis Powell, David Herold, and George Atzerodt, praising them as men who loved their country better than gold or life.

He sealed the letter and slipped it into his pocket, and then, noting the time, he hurried on to Pumphrey's Stable to claim the horse he had reserved earlier that day. To his consternation, the sorrel he preferred was gone, taken by another customer. "Not to worry, Mr. Booth," the hostler assured him. "I've got an even better horse for you, well suited for an expert rider such as yourself."

The hostler disappeared into the stables and returned leading a graceful bay mare, about fourteen hands high, with a white star on her forehead, a black mane, and a long black tail. "She looks quite lively," said John, looking her over, feeling her withers, her flanks.

"She's a spirited one, all right, but swift and sure, for an experienced horseman. I wouldn't offer her to a novice."

"Very well, then. She'll do nicely. I'll take a tie line as well."

"Oh, no, Mr. Booth. I wouldn't recommend that. She don't like to be tied, and she's likely to break loose if you try it. She'll stand if you have someone hold the reins for you."

John frowned, thinking of the inconvenience this might cause him later, but he had not seen any horse there he liked better, so he thanked the hostler for the warning, mounted, and rode off up Sixth Street toward Ford's Theatre. By the time he reached Baptist Alley, he was satisfied that he had made the right choice. The mare was swift and responsive as he rehearsed his escape, racing down from E Street, pausing, then riding out the other side toward F Street. He walked the mare for a moment, studied his surroundings, considered, then repeated the exercise. Twice more he rode at full speed, coming to a stop behind Ford's Theatre, until he was confident that the mare would perform well at the critical moment. "Well done, my girl," he said, patting her on the neck. She tossed her mane and nickered as if she understood the praise and the important role she had been awarded, an understudy snatched from the chorus and promoted to leading lady.

"Say, Booth," a man called. "Training that mare for the races? Or for an escape from some besotted lady's enraged husband?"

Whirling about, John spied James Maddox, the property man, standing outside the back door to Ford's with Ned Spangler and William Ferguson, two stagehands. "The latter, of course," said John, smiling. "Can't be too careful."

"She's mighty fast," Spangler remarked. "Will she stand long enough for you to come have a whiskey with us?"

"Not this afternoon. I have pleurisy in my side, and a drink won't help it any." Then John reconsidered. He had worked up quite a thirst, and he did not know when he might see his friends again after that night. "Maybe I'll take a glass of ale," he said, dismounting. It was a simple matter to find a boy who agreed to hold the mare for the promise of a penny afterward, and so John slung his arms around the other men's shoulders and went off with them to the Greenback Saloon next door.

One drink did not quench John's thirst, so he had another, then parted from his friends with assurances that he would see them backstage later that night. With a rising sense of urgency, he paid the urchin, mounted the mare, and hurried off to Grover's Theatre.

He had reason to believe manager Charles Hess would not be entirely happy to see him. On Thursday, after he had returned from his unsuccessful trip to Baltimore to speak with O'Laughlen but before the capital had been lit up for the illumination, he had burst into the manager's office, agitated and near despair, interrupting a script reading to urge Hess to invite Lincoln and his Cabinet secretaries to attend the commemoration of the fall of Fort Sumter the following evening. Though Hess had been displeased by the intrusion, he had acknowledged that he had intended to invite the president, his wife, and whatever companions they chose to attend the performance as honored guests. Although Hess had assured John that he would not forget to inquire, John had lingered until he had seen Hess dispatch a messenger to the Executive Mansion with the invitation in hand—but John had departed before a reply came rather than risk raising suspicions. He had to be sure the Lincolns planned to go to Ford's Theatre and not Grover's, or all would be lost.

Hess greeted him warily, still annoyed from the disruption the previous day. "Mrs. Lincoln declined the invitation on behalf of herself and the president," he replied to John's question, "but Master Tad Lincoln will attend, with an escort."

"Not his father, though. You're certain."

"Quite certain." Hess gestured ruefully toward the *Evening Star* spread open on his desk. "The Lincolns and the Grants will be at Ford's—and that bodes well for Miss Keene, so for her sake I won't begrudge Ford the ticket sales."

John smiled. "I'm sure you'll have a full house as well."

"I'm counting on it," Hess said. "I spent a fortune on these theatricals."

John wished him good luck and departed, but just as he prepared to mount his horse, the sound of hundreds of pairs of worn boots pounding in rhythm caught his attention. He turned to discover columns of captured Confederate troops marching down Pennsylvania Avenue. Transfixed by their haunted eyes, resisting the sudden urge to salute, he watched as the gaunt, haggard figures in tattered uniforms of butternut and gray approached, more than four hundred by his rough calculation. To his astonishment, the citizens they passed did not mock them, but instead offered them sympathetic glances or pretended not to notice them rather than add to their disgrace. A few men clad in Union blue even called out encouraging remarks, assuring the broken, weary men that the war would soon be over and they would return to their mothers, sisters, wives, and sweethearts awaiting them back home.

John felt a surge of indignation—perhaps that was not what those gallant men wanted, even in their exhaustion; perhaps they wanted to escape so that they could fight another day—but the sentiment was quickly replaced by a rush of horror and fury when he realized that the Confederate prisoners were being guarded by colored soldiers. It was, it had to be, a deliberate insult, a mocking reminder of what lay in store for the Southern gentility now that the natural order had been overturned.

And then even fury was usurped by a stronger emotion—the shock of recognition when his gaze lit upon a familiar face. These twenty-two score men were from General Richard Ewell's corps, he overheard a man in the crowd say, captured on the retreat to Appomattox at Sailor's Creek, and among them were the Richmond Grays. He spotted John Pitt, who had given him a cap to complete his makeshift uniform as they rode the train to Charles Town to defend Harpers Ferry from an attack by John Brown's abolitionist partisans. Near him marched their former captain, Wyatt Elliot, now attired in the uniform of a lieutenant colonel. As the bedraggled columns passed, John's gaze fell upon one familiar face after another, soldiers he had called comrades during his brief stint with the Richmond Grays, others he had known as civilians in Richmond, brave defenders of Virginia who had abandoned shops and farms and businesses to take up arms beneath the Confederate banner.

There they were, his once-proud friends and acquaintances, reduced to marching in a shameful parade through the enemy capital.

"Booth," someone called to him, but not from within the columns of vanquished men steadily disappearing around the corner. Turning his head, he glimpsed John Mathews, an actor with the Ford's Theatre stock company, working his way toward him through the crowd of gawkers that had gathered to watch the prisoners pass. They had once been quite good friends, but when John had approached him about joining the plot against Lincoln, Mathews had recoiled in horror and had firmly refused, earning John's enmity. John was briefly tempted to pretend he had not seen him and ride swiftly away, but as that might be the last time they ever spoke, he lingered.

"Did you see the rebels pass?" Mathews asked as he halted before him. "Poor fellows. That was a veritable funeral procession."

Sympathy was the last sentiment John had expected to hear pass his erstwhile friend's lips, and something in his chest wrenched. "I no longer have a country," he lamented, sick at heart, steadying himself on the mare's strong flank. "This is the end of constitutional liberty in America."

"Booth, what are you saying?" Concerned, Mathews drew closer, studying him. "You're as pale as a ghost. How much have you had to drink today?"

Not nearly enough, John thought. "I'm all right."

"You don't look all right. What's wrong?"

"It's nothing, but"—John inhaled deeply—"would you do me a favor?"

"Why, certainly, Johnny. What is it?"

"I may leave town tonight, and I have a letter here which I desire to be published in the *National Intelligencer.*" John reached into his breast pocket and withdrew the apologia he had written only a few hours before. It was a hasty sketch compared to the lengthier document he had entrusted to Asia, although she did not know the nature of the document he had asked her to lock up in her safe. Still, hastily composed or not, he meant every word, and he would have the world know it. "Please attend to it for me, unless I see you before ten o'clock tomorrow. In that case I'll see to it myself."

"All right, Johnny." Mathews tucked the letter into the pocket of his frock coat. "If it will help you."

John thanked him and mounted the mare, who, perhaps sensing her rider's feelings, seemed impatient to be off. The grim parade had moved on, and carriages and riders were beginning to pass freely again. "Goodbye, Mathews."

Mathews nodded, but his gaze had fixed on something moving along the avenue behind John. "There goes the great man," he said, shaking his head. "They won't be happy to hear about this at Ford's."

"Hear about what?"

Mathews gestured, and John turned the mare and spied a two-seated top-carriage heavily laden with trunks and carpetbags moving by, so overfull that a Union officer sat up beside the driver instead of inside with the other passengers. "That's General Grant, and from the look of things, he's leaving town. John and Harry were expecting him in the State Box with President Lincoln tonight."

John stared after the carriage as it receded down the avenue toward the Baltimore and Ohio Railroad station. "You're certain that was Grant?"

"Of course. Doesn't everyone know him by sight?"

Without a word of farewell, John turned the mare, walked her into the clear, and kicked her into a gallop. He easily caught up to the carriage and peered into it as he passed, immediately recognizing Mrs. Grant and her young son from the Willard earlier that day, but not the other lady seated across from them. He rode twenty yards ahead, wheeled the mare about, and returned at the same swift pace, passing closely on General Grant's side and studying him so intensely that it appeared to him that the so-called Hero of Appomattox instinctively drew back.

Breathing heavily, exultant, John slowed the mare to a walk as the carriage continued on its way to the train station. He felt a thrill of triumph to have made the great general flinch, for it was unmistakably Grant, and he was unmistakably leaving Washington. John was not sure whether he ought to feel relieved or disappointed. He was sorry that he would not have the chance to kill Grant as well as Lincoln, but Grant was an experienced military man, and probably carried a sidearm. Grant's absence no doubt improved John's chances of success a thousandfold.

Grant was leaving town. John knew where Lincoln would be that night, for Hess and Mathews had confirmed it. Seward was confined to bed, recovering from life-threatening injuries he had received in a terrible carriage accident nine days before. That left Johnson. Atzerodt was supposed to be keeping abreast of the vice president's whereabouts, but with the hour steadily approaching, John could not leave anything to chance. He rode to Johnson's hotel, the Kirkwood House at Twelfth Street and Pennsylvania Avenue, paid a boy to hold the mare, and entered the lobby. Glancing about, he did not see Atzerodt, but he dared hope that meant the German had either hidden himself remarkably well or that Johnson was out and Atzerodt was stealthily following him through the city.

Catching his breath, he smoothed back his hair, assumed an affable smile, and approached the front desk, but this clerk was not so easily charmed as the fellow at the Willard, for he refused to confirm whether Johnson was in or out, or even whether he had taken a room there at all, though it was common knowledge. He only reluctantly granted John's request for a blank card and a pencil, and then he stood nearby looking decidedly put out while John dashed off a few quick lines. "Don't wish to disturb you," he wrote. "Are you at home? J. Wilkes Booth." He waited until the clerk placed the card in Johnson's box before bowing sardonically and quitting the hotel.

John had not eaten since his late breakfast with Mrs. Bean, and the whiskey and ale were not sitting well in his empty stomach, so he rode back to Ford's Theatre and stabled the mare in the place Maddox had found for him in Baptist Alley, about sixty yards from the back door of the theatre. It was really a modified shed that Spangler had fixed up to store a buggy, but John rented it from a widow lady for five dollars a month and he let theatre friends use it in exchange for keeping an eye on it in his absence.

It was a short walk to the National Hotel, and as John made his way south down Sixth Street, he thought of Lucy and his pace quickened. He wished he had thought to invite her to dine with him that evening, but the day had been so strange and swiftly changing, his thoughts so full of the impending mission, that he had hardly thought of her since morning.

He did not glimpse Lucy or any of her family as he entered the hotel, but other guests were mingling in the lobby and the parlor, and several couples and families were heading down the hallway to the dining room. Hurrying upstairs, he unlocked his room, filled the basin with cool water from the pitcher the maid had left, and swiftly washed and dressed, his heart racing with hope and anticipation. The moment he had crossed the threshold of the hotel where he and Lucy had passed so many pleasant hours together, he had been seized by an urgent hope and apprehension, an intense desire to see her that must be satisfied.

He did not know whether he would ever see Lucy again after that night. He had dallied with other women, but Lucy—lovely, sweet, unspoiled, warmhearted Lucy—was the only one he truly loved. It pained him to imagine the life he might have enjoyed had not the Fates decreed otherwise—the adoration of an affectionate wife, the counsel of her distinguished father, ingress into the highest levels of society, the prosperity and respect that would follow. In recent days he had considered following Lucy to Spain, but in the immediate aftermath of his mission, he knew he would be needed in the South, to rally the demoralized people, to inspirit them with confidence and hope. After Confederate independence was established, he might be able to spare the time to go abroad, but he could not be sure Lucy would welcome him. She would not approve of what he must do that night—he had no doubt she would consider his actions abhorrent—but perhaps, in time, when she saw from afar what good had come of his brave deed, her heart would soften and she would love him again. Only time would tell, but that night he wished to leave her with one last, fond, affectionate memory of him, so in the years to come she would never doubt that he had loved her.

Impeccably groomed and dressed in a plain dark suit, John checked his pockets for the derringer and the knife and the other things he typically carried on his person. Once satisfied that all was in order, he descended to the lobby, looked around in vain for the Hales, and strolled down the corridor to the dining room, hoping to discover the family just sitting down, and with one extra chair at their table. Passing the parlor, he glanced inside and was delighted to see Lucy seated with her parents, her sister, and a lady he did not know. His heart warmed to see his sweetheart smiling at some jest her sister had made, her dark hair shining in the lamplight, her blue eyes bright with intelligence and humor. Her elegant black silk gown made a pleasing contrast with the red velvet of her chair—and she must have felt his gaze upon her, for at that moment she glanced up, saw him lingering in the doorway, and smiled radiantly.

Her family followed her line of sight, and it pained him to see their expressions turned guarded, even indignant, in Mrs. Hale's case. Nevertheless, he fixed his smile in place, crossed the room, bowed politely, and was introduced to their companion, a Mrs. Temple, no one that he knew or needed to know. He lingered so long that Mr. Hale was obliged to invite him to dine with them, an obligation Lucy encouraged with numerous pointed looks. John graciously accepted.

"Where have you been all day?" Lucy murmured as he escorted her to the dining room, following a discreet distance behind the rest of their party.

"Oh, running here and there, to Grover's Theatre to take care of business and to Ford's to watch the rehearsal for *Our American Cousin.*" Her face fell slightly, and he hastened to add, "I was simply tying up loose ends. I didn't accept any new engagements. They implored me to, they even offered me some rather enviable roles, but I declined. Frankly, my oil interests won't allow me the time."

Her smile returned. It occurred to him then that soon he would no longer need to conceal that his oil speculations had ended in massive failure, that he was living on borrowed money and gifts from sympathetic friends. That awareness flooded him with an enormous sense of relief. How he would support her, if she would still have him after tonight, he did not know, but that was a concern for another day.

Dinner was a pleasant affair, with Lucy on his right hand and the extraordinarily talkative Mrs. Temple on his left. Gentle, affectionate smiles were his reward when he looked in one direction, inane chatter and silly questions whenever he was obliged to turn toward the other.

"Mrs. Hale and I have been talking about going to Ford's Theatre tonight to see Miss Keene perform in *Our American Cousin,*" Mrs. Temple said, glancing to Mrs. Hale, who inclined her head in confirmation.

"Mr. Booth observed the rehearsal earlier today," said Lucy, smiling. "Perhaps he would share his professional opinion."

John's throat constricted, and he raised his napkin to his mouth as he fought to chew and swallow. "Miss Keene was marvelous as ever," he said hoarsely, pausing to sip water, "but comedy depends as much upon the mood of the audience as the skill of the performers. Tonight the theatre is likely to be half empty on account of Good Friday, so the play is sure to drag, through no fault of the incomparable Miss Keene."

"I would rather expect the audience to be excellent," remarked Mrs. Hale. "The president, General Grant, and their wives are expected, or so it was announced in the papers."

"The papers are wrong," said John. "General Grant and wife have left the city. I myself passed their carriage as they were heading for the train station earlier today."

"Oh, indeed?" Mrs. Temple pouted across the table at Mrs. Hale. "And I had so been looking forward to it."

"Perhaps we should go to the theatre tomorrow night instead," suggested Mrs. Hale. "I'm sure we will find an enjoyable program, if not at Ford's than elsewhere. We can see Miss Keene the next time she returns to Washington."

Brightening, Mrs. Temple agreed that Mrs. Hale's plan suited her very well. "How fortunate we are that Mr. Booth was here to spare us a disappointing evening," she added, smiling up at him, fluttering her eyelashes in girlish admiration.

"It was my great pleasure, madam," he said, and as Lucy looked on proudly, he felt a pang of love and regret so intense that it was all he could do not to seize her hand, kneel before her, and beg for her understanding.

Perhaps it was not absurd to hope that one day he could make her understand.

When the supper ended, John escorted Lucy to the foot of the grand staircase in the foyer, and then he bade her, her family, and Mrs. Temple good evening. He waited for Lucy to move out of sight down the second floor corridor before he mopped his brow with a handkerchief and went to the front desk, where the evening clerk, Henry Merrick, was checking in a young man dressed in the uniform of a private with the 189th New York Infantry.

"Hand me a piece of paper, would you, Henry?" he asked the clerk.

"Sure, Mr. Booth." Frowning, the clerk brought out both paper and pencil. "You feeling all right?"

"You look very pale," said the young private. "If you don't mind my saying so, sir."

"I don't mind," said John shortly. His head spun.

"Why don't you have a seat back here at the desk?" offered Henry.

Nodding, John seated himself and began writing at a furious pace. He had so much to say and so little time to say it. He wrote and wrote, and then signed his name, and then for the life of him he could not remember the date. Looking up from the page, he found Henry and the private watching him, concerned.

"Is it 1864 or 1865?" he asked.

The clerk and the private exchanged a look. "Don't you know what year it is?" queried Henry.

Eighteen sixty-five. Yes, that was it. Quickly John scrawled the date, rose from the chair, folded the paper, and dropped it into the mailbox. "Are you going out tonight?" he asked the young soldier cheerfully, feeling suddenly refreshed and restored to himself, as if the words had been a sickness he had purged from his body through the pencil.

"I haven't made any plans yet," the soldier replied, as if the question surprised him, "aside from washing up and finding a good meal."

"You ought to go to Ford's Theatre," said John emphatically. "There's going to be some splendid acting tonight."

Striding briskly down Pennsylvania Avenue and turning north on Ninth Street, John reached the Herndon House and rapped on Powell's door a few minutes before eight o'clock. Powell and Herold were already waiting, and Atzerodt scurried in just as the bells of St. Patrick's Church fell silent after chiming the hour.

"It's no use trying to abduct Lincoln," John told them flatly. "He's proved impossible to catch. We have to kill him, and we have to kill those who would succeed him. I'll take the old fox myself."

His words met with silence. Powell and Herold nodded, but Atzerodt only stared.

He turned to Powell. "You take Seward." Unflinching, Powell nodded again. An army veteran who had lost two brothers to the war, he wanted to avenge the wrongs done to the South as much as John did. He would not fail.

"Here's something." Herold spoke up. "All day long, doctors are calling at Seward's home on account of his injuries. I used to work as a pharmacy clerk, and I'm sure Powell would be admitted to the house if he claimed to be delivering medicines from Seward's doctor."

"I'll do that," said Powell.

Booth turned to Atzerodt. "You take Johnson." When the German winced, he added, "Nothing could be easier than reaching that dirty tailor from Tennessee." He beckoned to Herold. "Show him the letter."

Herold leapt up from his chair, took a folded paper from his coat pocket, and held it out to Atzerodt, who reluctantly accepted it. "It's a document meant for Johnson," Herold explained. "I got it off a printer. You can get close to Johnson by pretending to deliver it."

Atzerodt regarded the letter in his hand with revulsion, and then quickly set it on the arm of his chair as if it had scorched his fingers. "I went into this thing to capture, not to kill," he said quietly, his gaze falling to the floor. "I will not do it."

"Then you're a fool," snapped John. "It is death for every man who backs out. It's too late for that anyway. Don't you see? You're in this as deep as the rest of us. If we hang, you hang."

"*Nein, nein,*" Atzerodt moaned, shaking his head. "I did not come for that. I am not willing to murder a person."

"Boy," said John, low and menacing, drawing closer to the quavering man. "Boy." He slapped his hand heavily on Atzerodt's chest, pushing him back a step. "What is to become of you?" Suddenly John swung and struck him, sending him sprawling to the floor. "You must kill Johnson! Do it or I'll blow your brains out!"

Gasping, wide-eyed, Atzerodt scrambled to his feet and backed away.

"What will become of you?" John said again, disgusted. "Young Herold has more courage than you. *He* will kill Johnson, and you, Atzerodt, will help."

Gulping air, tears in his eyes, Atzerodt nodded, eyes downcast, defeated.

"Get your horses," John ordered, in a voice that would allow no dissent.

Anticipation drove out anger as John walked down G Street alone. Atzerodt would be all right with Herold there to mind him. He had no concerns at all about Powell, who would do his duty. Turning north onto Sixth Street, he arrived at the Surratt boardinghouse as the bells of St. Patrick's Church struck nine.

Anna answered his knock, and, blushing prettily despite her obvious distress, she showed him into the sitting room and invited him to wait for her mother, whose step he soon heard on the stairs leading up from the kitchen and dining room on the ground floor.

"Mr. Booth," she greeted him with some surprise, as Anna left them to confer alone. "I thought you would be at Ford's by now. Dare I hope that you've changed your mind?"

The question did not merit a reply. "Did you see Lloyd?"

"Yes," she said, with a sigh of resignation. "I gave him the package. He said he would remove the various items from their hiding places and move them to his room, to have them convenient for any parties that might call tonight."

"Very good."

"Mr. Booth—" She hesitated and seated herself in the chair nearest him. "In his recent speeches Mr. Lincoln has spoken of forgiveness and reconciliation. I think he is inclined to be merciful to the South. Mr. Johnson, however—" She shook her head, her lips pursed together in worry and distaste. "He speaks of punishment, and of vengeance. If you remove Mr. Lincoln from the presidential chair, you allow an even worse villain to take it."

"Oh, you needn't worry about that. Johnson will be taken care of."

She peered at him quizzically, but she knew better than to ask questions. "Well, then, that leaves Mr. Seward to lead, though not officially, and I don't imagine he would be much better than Johnson."

"We'll see to Mr. Seward too." Smiling, John rose. "And now, madam, I must bid you good night and goodbye."

She inclined her head in farewell, and escorted him to the door, but just as he stepped outside and put on his hat, she gave a little start. "Oh, Mr. Booth. I just remembered. When Mr. Weichmann and I were traveling to Surrattsville, we passed some Yankee pickets just off the road. I asked one of the soldiers if they would be out there all night, and he told me no, they were being pulled in after eight o'clock."

"Thank you, Mrs. Surratt," he said, pleased. "It's good to know that."

"Good evening, Mr. Booth, and good luck to you," she said quietly, and closed the door.

It was about half past nine o'clock when John rode down Baptist Alley again and brought the lively mare to a stop at the back door to Ford's Theatre. Dismounting, he peered through the open doorway, through which the faint sounds of the audience's laughter drifted. "Spangler," he called softly, but although he glimpsed figures moving in the shadows, no one replied. "Spangler," he called again, projecting his voice. "Ned, come here."

Spangler neither answered nor appeared, which probably meant he was working the far side of the stage. Just then John saw a stagehand passing nearby. "You there," he said. "It's John Wilkes Booth. Tell Ned Spangler I need him right away."

The stagehand nodded and hurried off, and soon Spangler appeared in the doorway. "What is it, Booth?" he asked, joining him in the alley. "What do you need?"

When Spangler was close enough, John tossed him the reins. "Hold my horse for a few minutes, would you? Don't let go or tie her. She'll run off."

"Say, Booth," Spangler protested as John headed for the back door. "I can't stay out here. I'm working the show."

"I won't be long," John called over his shoulder as he entered the theatre, quickening his pace.

As he walked along the back passageway, he listened to the dialogue, noting the act and scene. It was not yet his time. He knew the play well, knew the moment when a particularly amusing line would provoke uproarious laughter from the audience—enough, he hoped, to mask the sound of the derringer firing. Powell, Herold, and Atzerodt ought to be taking their places soon.

He paced in the lobby, walking in and out, chatting with the doorman, asking the time. Restless, he checked the progress of the play again and wandered outside the theatre and next door to the Star Saloon, where he ordered whiskey and water. He rehearsed the plan in his mind as he drank, checked the time, and returned to the theatre, where he paced some more until a particular line of dialogue caught his ear and sent an electric jolt of anticipation running through him.

Stealing quietly into the theatre, he surveyed the house, not entirely sold out as Ford had boastfully predicted, yet satisfactorily full at that, especially for Good Friday. A handful of actors, all of whom he knew, performed on a stage set as the interior of a drawing room in an English country house, with double doors at the center. John glanced upward, stage left, and his heart thudded when he spied the president seated with his wife and a younger couple in the State Box, which was adorned with four large Stars and Stripes—two standing on either side of the box and two more gracefully draped over the balustrade—with luxurious gold and ivory draperies hanging above. A portrait of George Washington was affixed to the center of the railing, beneath a tall staff bearing the blue standard of the Treasury Guards. Although Lincoln had viewed performances from those same seats many times before, John had never seen the State Box so impressively decorated.

While the audience smiled and laughed at the clever exchanges between the players, John eyed the distance from the proscenium, where the president sat, to the stage floor, and judged it to be roughly twelve feet—a substantial drop, to be sure, but he was athletic and fit, and on several occasions in performances past he had leapt from similar heights to the same stage. Fortunately, the orchestra chairs were empty, as he had known they would be, for the musicians had departed at the end of the second intermission and were not meant to return until the final scenes. The set was clear of furniture there, and soon the other players would exit and only Harry Hawk would remain onstage to utter the most amusing line of the entire play.

The way would be clear. The moment was almost upon him.

A few minutes after ten o'clock, in the second scene of the third act, John climbed the steps to the dress circle, and once upstairs, he strolled along the rear wall toward the State Box on the south side of the theatre. Along the way he passed two acquaintances, but so intent was he on his destination that he did not return their nods. Then, roughly six feet from the outer door to the box, he encountered two army officers whose seats were arranged so that they nearly blocked the aisle. With a pointed glare and an impatient gesture, John indicated that he must be allowed to pass, so with some scowls and sharp looks, they shifted their chairs to make room.

As he made his way toward the box, John glimpsed the president's messenger sitting in a chair outside the door. The blood pounded in his ears, but his hands were steady as he approached the stocky valet, who glanced up at him and nodded in recognition—he was John Wilkes Booth, as recognizable in a theatre as any thespian in the world—and raised his eyebrows in inquiry.

"You crave affection, you do," he heard Harry Hawk declare from the stage in the role of Asa, the Vermont bumpkin who was wrongly thought to have inherited enormous riches. "Now I've no fortune, but I'm biling over with affections, which I'm ready to pour out to all of you, like apple sass over roast pork."

The audience laughed. John dug into his pockets, took a small stack of calling cards from his pocket, and selected one that bore a name he knew would impress the man impeding his progress. His face a mask of genial confidence, John held his breath as the messenger studied the card. If he did not conclude that John had come to see the president on that man's behalf, all would be lost.

"Mr. Trenchard," said Helen Muzzy in a huff, portraying the haughty, avaricious Englishwoman Mrs. Mountchessington, "you will please recollect you are addressing my daughter, and in my presence."

"Yes," Harry Hawk replied, "I'm offering her my heart and hand just as she wants them, with nothing in 'em!"

Another ripple of laughter went up from the audience. Glancing at the stage, smiling faintly, the valet gestured for John to proceed. Nodding graciously, John made to open the door—but it stuck. Heart thudding, he pressed his knee against it, forced it loose, passed through the doorway, and closed the door silently behind him.

He knew the empty corridor well. He had prepared it for this moment, carving a niche into the wall by the door, hiding a pine board nearby. Quietly, he wedged one end of the plank against the door and the other into the crevice he had made, bracing the entryway so firmly that no one would be able to enter without breaking down the door.

Two small doors were on the wall to his left, the nearest with a small peephole he himself had made, the other, astonishingly, left ajar. Both doors, neither of which were ever locked, offered views of the president seated in a large rocking chair, the nearest of the box's four occupants to the place where John stood. Mrs. Lincoln sat beside him, the young lady in a chair to her right, her escort on a sofa beside and slightly behind her. All four had their backs to the doors, their attention riveted by the action onstage. The younger gentleman was clad in military dress, but John could not see if he carried a sidearm. His presence was regrettable, but there was nothing to be done for it now. John drew his dagger with his left hand and stepped silently forward.

Mrs. Lincoln leaned close to her husband, smiling, and murmured something to him. He smiled back and made a quiet reply that seemed to please her.

"I am aware, Mr. Trenchard," declared the lady onstage, "you are not used to the manners of good society, and that, alone, will excuse the impertinence of which you have been guilty."

John drew closer and slowly drew the derringer from his pocket with his right hand, knowing the actress was at that moment storming off stage right.

"Don't know the manners of good society, eh?" said the Vermonter. "Wal, I guess I know enough to turn you inside out, old gal—you sock-dologizing old man-trap!"

The audience burst into shouts of laughter.

Inhaling deeply, John strode into the box, leveled his pistol at the back of President Lincoln's head, and fired.

There was a loud bang and a sharp burst of acrid smoke. The officer bolted from his chair and rushed toward him, a look of wild alarm in his eyes, but he halted at the sight of John's knife. Instinctively John dropped the derringer, switched the knife to his right hand, and lunged at the officer, slashing his arm and sending him staggering backward. Heart pounding, he strode through the chairs to the balustrade, placed one hand on the railing, and leapt over it. The air rushed past his ears as he dropped twelve feet and landed on the stage, crouching to absorb the blow, spurs clanging.

He rose steady and sure, the blood surging through his veins.

He faced the audience, squared his shoulders, and raised his dagger overhead. "*Sic semper tyrannis*," he proclaimed, and then, as the audience murmured and stared and a woman screamed, he turned and fled.

He raced toward the back of the stage and into the wings, past dumbstruck actors and stagehands paralyzed with shock, down a darkened passageway to the back door. Flinging it open, he dashed into the alley, seized the reins from the hand of the boy holding the mare—Spangler was gone—and the mare spooked and tried to pull away, but John threw himself over her back and into the saddle and brought her under control. Turning her about, he glimpsed Joseph Stewart bursting out the door and racing after him, shouting his name, reaching for the reins—

His fingertips barely brushed them; his fist closed on empty air.

John spurred the mare into a gallop and fled for the Navy Yard Bridge.

CHAPTER SIX

ENSEMBLE

1865

And pity, like a naked newborn babe,
Striding the blast, or heaven's cherubim, horsed
Upon the sightless couriers of the air,
Shall blow the horrid deed in every eye,
That tears shall drown the wind.
>   —William Shakespeare,
>   *Macbeth*, Act 1, Scene 7

Lucy had already accepted John Hay's invitation to join him and Robert Lincoln at the White House to study Spanish that evening, so she was relieved when, after the subject came up at supper, John did not ask if she intended to accompany her mother and Mrs. Temple to the theatre. She had not told John that ever since her father had been confirmed as Minister to Spain, she and John Hay had met occasionally to study, or that Robert joined them whenever he was in the city. Lucy would prefer to tell John the truth, but she knew it would only provoke his jealousy.

John Hay called for her at half past eight o'clock, and they conversed in Spanish as they walked down Pennsylvania Avenue to the White House, she haltingly and laughing at her mistakes, John Hay fluently but generous with encouragement and praise she did not entirely merit. Robert Lincoln welcomed them in the Red Room, where books and notes, as well as tea and cakes, were arranged on a lovely antique table his mother had purchased during her infamous refurbishments. Diligent students, they devoted an hour to memorizing vocabulary and conjugating verbs before turning to the more pleasant exercise of conversation.

"*España no está lejos de Francia*," John Hay said to Lucy, smiling as she poured him another cup of tea.

She paused, thinking, and set down the teapot. "Spain is not something of France."

"*Lejos de*," prompted Robert. "Come now, Lucy. You knew it a half hour ago."

"Far from," she declared, suddenly remembering. "Oh, yes, that's it. Spain is not far from France."

"You're right, and so am I," said John Hay. "You could come and visit me in Paris."

Lucy smiled fondly. "I think I should like that very much. And you could visit me in Madrid."

At the inaugural ball, John Hay had confided to her that he intended to submit his resignation now that President Lincoln had been safely reelected. Although he loved and respected the president, his duties had become overwhelming and exhausting, for he and John Nicolay were not only secretaries, but also gatekeepers, companions, emissaries, and surrogate sons, living and working in the Executive Mansion, with very little time for any other life of their own.

When John Hay had first accepted the position on Mr. Lincoln's staff, he had regarded the new president with condescension and a cocksure college man's intellectual superiority, but over time, he had entirely revised his opinion. Soon after John and Lucy met, he had told her that he believed that God himself had put Mr. Lincoln in the White House. In the summer months before the election when it seemed unlikely that the president would win a second term, John had declared that if the snobbish elites of Washington and New York could not recognize Mr. Lincoln's genius, it was because they knew "no more of him than an owl does of a comet, blazing into its blinking eyes." Lucy knew he was devoted to the president, and that it pained him to leave the president's service, which he had vowed not to do until Mr. Lincoln had found a satisfactory replacement. But recently he had been appointed secretary of legation of the United States in Paris, and he would likely sail for France in June.

They were all parting company, she thought wistfully. The end of the war, imminent and inevitable, would bring peace and reunion, but also changes—some welcome, some less so.

"You must come and visit me too," she said, turning to Robert.

"I'd like that very much," he said, "but after my commission in the army is finished, it's back to Harvard Law for me."

"Harvard Law *and* the cozy parlor of a certain Miss Harlan," teased John Hay, and Robert grinned back.

It was about eleven o'clock when they decided to close their books for the night. "I shall dream in Spanish tonight," Lucy predicted as her friends saw her to her carriage, where an army lieutenant stood at attention, waiting to escort her home.

"*Buenas noches,*" John Hay called to her through the window as the carriage pulled away. She waved and smiled as John said something to Robert that made him throw back his head and laugh. It was good to spend time with friends who shared her thankfulness and joy that the Union had emerged victorious from the dreadful war, that the fractured nation would soon be made whole. Their optimistic company provided a respite from John Wilkes's erratic flashes of temper, his dire predictions about restoration, his endless lamentations about his beloved Virginia—although of course she would not tell him that.

The streets were busier than she expected for so late on a Good Friday evening. Men strode rapidly along the sidewalks, while others clustered outside hotels and telegraph offices as if waiting for news. Perhaps Mr. Davis had been captured, she thought, her hopes rising, or perhaps General Johnston had at last surrendered. When the carriage halted in front of the National Hotel, she accepted the lieutenant's hand, swiftly alighted, and hurried inside, breathless from excitement and eager for news.

She found the lobby teeming with people, ladies and gentlemen in all manner of dress, some recently come from the theatre, others who had evidently returned downstairs after retiring for the evening. After her expectation of glad tidings, she needed a moment to realize that their expressions were frightened, anxious, and angry, and her heart plummeted.

"Lucy," Lizzie cried, hurrying toward her, tears in her eyes. "Oh, Lucy, you're safe."

"Of course I am." Lucy spotted her parents making their way through the crowd toward them, their expressions stricken. "What has happened? What's going on?"

Lizzie put her arm around her shoulders, but before she could speak, a man behind her turned and bellowed, "The president was shot at Ford's Theatre tonight, and they say a guest of this hotel is the murderer. The detectives are tearing his room apart right now."

Lucy could not breathe. "Lizzie?" she managed to say, clutching her sister's arm.

"The president is dead," a woman shrieked. Lucy whirled about to find two gentlemen easing a white-faced matron into the chair by the window where Lucy had so often met John. "Shot in the State Box. It was John Wilkes Booth. The actor. I saw him. We all saw him. Oh, God help us! God preserve us!"

"John?" Lucy whispered as her vision went gray and her head rang and spun and all went dark.

Hours before dawn, Mary woke to an insistent rapping upon her door. "Mrs. Surratt?" It was Louis Weichmann, his voice strangely shrill. "Mrs. Surratt? Do wake up."

"What is it?" she replied groggily.

"Detectives have come looking for your son and Mr. Booth."

Her heart thudded. "They aren't here."

"I told them so, but they want to search the house."

"For God's sake." Inhaling deeply, Mary sat up. "Let them come in."

He had done it, she thought wildly as she threw back the covers and climbed out of bed. Mr. Booth had captured President Lincoln—and he and his comrades must have escaped the city with their prisoner, or the detectives would not be searching for him.

But how had they known to come to her boardinghouse?

She made a quick toilette and dressed, her head turning this way and that as she traced the detectives' movement by the sounds seeping through the walls and floorboards—boots tramping through the halls and on the staircases, furniture scraping across floors, voices from the direction of Louis's bedchamber, then the Holohan family's rooms. Mary checked her hair in the looking glass, fixed her expression into a serene mask, and went to the formal sitting room, but she had not had time to seat herself before she heard boots on the stairs again. Looking down the hall from the doorway, she saw four grim-faced men in uniform descend, and as they halted at the foot of the stairs, conferring in low voices and throwing occasional glances her way, she recognized two of them as the detectives who had come to the house in February seeking Junior.

Louis had followed the four men downstairs, his face pale and drawn in shock, and he edged around them and hurried into the parlor to Mary. "What do you think, Mrs. Surratt?" he asked, his voice shaking. "President Lincoln has been murdered by John Wilkes Booth, and the Secretary of State has been assassinated!"

Mary felt all the blood drain from her face as she stared at him, dumbfounded. Her mouth formed a question, but no sound emerged.

One of the detectives who had come to the house before broke away from the others and approached her, while two others climbed the stairs again and another headed below. "Mrs. Surratt, I am Detective Clarvoe," he said, fixing her with a level gaze. "I want to ask you a couple of questions, and be particular how you answer them, for a great deal depends on them. When did you last see John Wilkes Booth?"

"I—I saw him at two o'clock in the afternoon, yesterday." It seemed the safest reply.

"When did you last see your son John, and where is he now?"

She clasped her hands together at her waist to still their trembling. "I have not seen him for two weeks. I believe he is in Canada."

"Why would you think so?"

"I— Because I received a letter from him on the fourteenth, and it had been postmarked on the twelfth from Montreal."

His eyes narrowed as he studied her. "May I see this letter?"

She nodded. "Certainly. It's in my bedchamber." She dared hope that they would not follow her there. Dazed, she went to her room, shut the door, and found Junior's last letter in the top drawer of her wardrobe. It said nothing of Mr. Booth's plans, nothing of abduction or murder, but what it did say was enough to condemn Junior as a Confederate courier and spy.

Swiftly Mary concealed the letter beneath a loose floorboard along the wall, and then she sat down on the edge of her bed, struggling to compose herself. She stood, made the bed, and sat down again, taking deep breaths to still her racing heart.

Then she rose again and returned to the sitting room, where another detective had joined Detective Clarvoe. "I couldn't find the letter."

The two detectives exchanged skeptical looks. "Are you sure you don't know where John Surratt is tonight?" the second one asked.

Their arrogance made her anger flare. "I didn't know five minutes ago and I still don't know now. In these troubled times, a great many mothers have no idea where their sons are." She drew herself up to her full height and looked from one man to the other. "What is all this about? Why have you come here in the middle of the night, rousing us from our beds, disturbing me and my lodgers with your questions and searches?"

"You know why we're here, madam," said Detective Clarvoe.

"I certainly do not, sir."

Frowning, he bent his head to speak in the other detective's ear, and then, ordering Mary to stay in the parlor, they resumed the search. Soon Anna darted into the room, tearful and trembling, her dress hastily buttoned, her hair loose down her back. "Ma, what is happening?" she asked, flying into her embrace.

Gently, holding her close, Mary kissed her brow and murmured the little she knew, that the president and secretary of state had been assassinated, that Mr. Booth stood accused of one murder and Junior of the other. "That's impossible, impossible," said Anna faintly, sinking into a chair. "Junior is in Canada."

"Yes, and thank God for that." Mary fell silent as another detective appeared in the doorway and gave them a long, speculative glare before turning back down the hall. A moment later, Mary heard the door to her own bedchamber open, followed by the sounds of rummaging, of moving furniture aside.

It seemed an age before the four detectives, having found neither Mr. Booth nor Junior nor anything incriminating within the boardinghouse, departed with a stern warning for Mary to tell them immediately if Junior returned. She made no answer, but locked the door behind them and returned to the parlor, heart pounding, head spinning.

"Oh, Ma," exclaimed Anna, her breath coming in quick, short gasps of hysteria. "Just think of it—that dreadful Mr. Booth having been at this house before the assassination! I'm afraid that it will bring suspicion upon us!"

Mary knew it already had. "Anna, come what will," she said, with all the reassuring calm she could summon up, "I am resigned. I think John Wilkes Booth was an instrument in the hands of the Almighty to punish this proud and licentious people."

A sudden movement from the corner of her eye startled her, and she turned to discover Louis Weichmann standing in the doorway, staring at her in dismay.

After Lucy had been revived with smelling salts and escorted upstairs, her father bearing nearly all her weight on his strong arm, her mother had undressed her while she stood staring into space—distressed, insensible, disbelieving—and had put her to bed with a glass of brandy.

"They must be wrong," she had said when Lizzie had put out the lamp, had lain down beside her, and had beckoned her to snuggle up close for comfort. "I just came from the Executive Mansion. Nothing was amiss there. No one said a word about an assassination. Robert was happy—"

Oh, God help him. Robert, her poor, dear friend, how he must be suffering, if the rumors were true. God grant that they were not.

"Sleep, Lucy," Lizzie had said soothingly. "We'll know more in the morning."

The brandy had sent her head spinning, and she had been too exhausted to argue, so with her sister's arm around her she had fallen into the restless sleep of the brokenhearted.

Morning came, gray and somber, and Lucy woke to the sound of a steady downpour to find herself alone. Just before half past seven, a distant church bell began to toll, and then another joined it, and another, until all the bells in Washington resounded with the terrible pealing. At once Lucy understood the dire news they proclaimed.

The president was dead.

She lay in bed, listening to the bells, paralyzed by grief and worry. Then a sob escaped from her throat, and she rolled over onto her side, squeezing her eyes shut, weeping. She covered her ears with clenched fists, but nothing would block out the mournful sound.

Distantly she heard the door open, and swift footsteps, and then her mother was sitting on the bed beside her, stroking her hair, kissing her brow, murmuring soothingly, urging her to calm herself.

"John could not have done this terrible thing," said Lucy, anguished. "He could not have done it."

"Calm yourself, my darling," said her mother tenderly, but Lucy heard the confirmation of her worst fears in all that her mother did not say.

Asia lay in bed with her fingers interlaced over her amply rounded abdomen, eyes closed, murmuring perfunctory replies to Clarke, who liked to tell her his plans for the day while he shaved and dressed. Distantly she thought she heard the nurse bustling about the nursery with little Dottie, Edwin, and Adrienne, her "little trotters," as she affectionately called them.

This pregnancy—five months under way, she was certain, although by the look of things she seemed much further along—had been more difficult than the others. She had scarcely been able to keep down a morsel of food in the first three months, and although the fourth month had brought some relief from headache and nausea, for the past fortnight she had been alarmed to find occasional spotting of blood in her undergarments. Her physician ordered bed rest and attended her regularly, and Clarke had hired extra help around the house so that she could have lain about all day if it would not have driven her utterly mad. She endured it as much as she could to appease Clarke, who was endearingly concerned for her health, and for her unborn child, whose steady growth and strong activity assured her of its vigor.

"I thought I might take the children walking in the park today," Asia said, just as the maid brought in her tray and the newspapers. Clarke insisted that she take her breakfast in bed, the one restriction upon her activities that she actually enjoyed.

Clarke frowned as he ran the razor along his jawline. "Do you think that's wise?"

"I think the fresh spring air would do us all good."

"Well, perhaps you should, then, if Nurse goes with you."

Asia sipped her tea and picked up the newspaper. "I wouldn't dream of going without—"

She fell abruptly silent. Her gaze had fallen upon the largest headline, and her brother's name leapt out at her, and she dropped the teacup and screamed. She was still screaming when Clarke came running and grasped her by the shoulders, asking her over and over what was wrong until he saw the headlines and then he knew.

Newsboys shouting the horrifying headlines up and down East Nineteenth Street had summoned Mary Ann to the windows. She had stood frozen in horror, listening to the treble voices calling out her precious son's name, accusing him of murdering the president.

"It cannot be true," she had murmured aloud, first to herself and then to Rosalie, who had eventually persuaded her to come away from the window, away from stares of gawkers gathering on the sidewalks below, gazing up at her and pointing. *There is the mother of the man who killed the president*, Mary Ann imagined them saying to one another, and she felt so desperately ill that she was obliged to dash for the water closet. Rosalie quickly followed and knelt beside her, holding her hair and stroking her back gently.

Thank goodness Rosalie was there, Mary Ann thought afterward as she sat on the sofa brooding over the cup of tea her eldest daughter had prepared for her. Edwin was in Boston, performing to packed houses and rave reviews at the Boston Museum. June was in Cincinnati for a lengthy engagement at Wood's Theatre. Joseph . . . she did not know where Joseph was, it had been so long since he had written from San Francisco, but suddenly she missed her youngest, most sensitive, and often troubled child so desperately that her arms ached to hold him.

"Is Edwin coming home?" she asked Rosalie.

"I don't know," came her daughter's soft reply. "He hasn't sent a telegram."

"Asia," Mary Ann said, her heart leaping. "Oh, dear me, I hope she was not alone when she heard this dreadful news, not in her delicate condition."

"I'm sure she's fine. She has Clarke and the children."

"Still, we should go to her. We should all be together at this dreadful time." Mary Ann set the teacup aside, rose, and began pacing and wringing her hands. "It is wrong for us always to be so scattered. Why must we live so far apart?"

The doorbell rang then, and she and Rosalie froze, staring at each other. The maid came in and announced Thomas Bailey Aldrich and wife, friends of Edwin's, a kindhearted, generous couple. There was little else to do but to allow them to enter, and call for tea, and tell them that Edwin was not at home. The Aldriches promised not to stay long; they had come only to offer their condolences and help, if there was anything they could do. Mary Ann thanked them, tears filling her eyes. She doubted very much that the Booth family would meet with much kindness elsewhere in the days ahead, in the years to come.

Just as the Aldriches rose to depart, another newsboy outside the window bellowed the horrid news that John Wilkes Booth had killed President Lincoln. "Oh, God," Mary Ann moaned, "if this be true, let him disappear into the South, let him not be hanged! Spare him, spare us, spare the name that dreadful disgrace!"

"My poor, dear Mrs. Booth," exclaimed Mrs. Aldrich, putting her arms around Mary Ann, who trembled from the effort of holding back her sobs. "I'm sure he hasn't done it. The authorities must have made a dreadful mistake. I'm sure your son is innocent."

Mary Ann thanked her, wishing with all her heart that she could be as sure. John Wilkes had made no secret of his hatred of the president and the Union, nor of his deep and abiding affection for the South. He had always been a good boy, optimistic and joyful, boundlessly enthusiastic, but somehow, the events of the war had twisted all that was good in him. His adamant and vocal defense of the Confederacy had led to many a furious argument between John Wilkes and his elder brothers, and to Mary Ann's distress, John Wilkes and Edwin had become estranged. She had hoped that the end of the war would eventually lead to their reconciliation, but now—

The doorbell rang again, and the maid announced members of the Century Club, more friends of Edwin come to express their sympathy and offer their assistance.

"They act as if John Wilkes is dead," said Rosalie flatly after they departed.

He might as well be, Mary Ann thought, but could not bring herself to say.

She wondered where he was, if he had committed suicide in Washington City as one newspaper claimed, if he had fled to Canada as another insisted, or if he was escaping into the Deep South or Texas, which was what Mary Ann and Rosalie agreed was most likely. Was it wrong, she wondered, to hope that he was unharmed, that he would elude capture and escape overseas? She did not care if it was wrong. Who would condemn a mother for hoping and praying for her son to live, regardless of his wrongdoing?

The morning post brought two letters, one of such importance that the other was immediately forgotten. Mary Ann's heart nearly stopped when she beheld the Washington postmark, and her hands trembled so violently as she held the page that she could scarcely make out John Wilkes's handwriting.

"April fourteen, two a.m.," she read aloud, her throat constricting around her voice. "Dearest Mother: I know you expect a letter from me, and am sure you will hardly forgive me. But indeed I have nothing to write about. Everything is dull; that is, has been till last night."

The letter slipped from her fingers and fell lightly upon the floor.

After the detectives had finally left the Surratt boardinghouse a few hours before dawn, Mary had urged Anna back to bed, but she had found it impossible to sleep herself. Instead she had lain upon the bedcovers fully dressed, every nerve strained, expecting at any moment to hear fists pounding upon the door, detectives demanding entry.

When the bells of St. Patrick's had begun to toll at about half past seven, joining the funereal pealing of what must have been every bell in Washington City, Mary had dragged herself from bed, splashed water on her face, and set herself to the task of preparing breakfast. She had known then that President Lincoln was dead.

Anna joined her soon thereafter, looking wan and exhausted, and they worked in silence, setting the table, brewing coffee, preparing the meal, though the smell of food turned Mary's stomach.

She had not realized that Louis Weichmann and James Holohan had gone out until she heard the front door open and close overhead, and soon thereafter, the sound of their boots descending the stairs, their voices low and hushed, the rustle of newsprint as they settled in at the dining-room table. Of course they had gone out to get the papers. Everyone in Washington would be desperate for news.

An open doorway connected the kitchen and dining room, so as Mary and Anna worked, they could not avoid overhearing the two men read aloud to each other the most sensational headlines and stunning paragraphs. President Lincoln had died at 7:22 a.m. that morning, they learned, but Secretary Seward yet lived and his physicians believed he had sufficient vitality to recover from his wounds. His son Frederick, however, had been even more seriously injured in defending his father, and his condition was considered extremely precarious.

"Weichmann, listen to this," Mary overheard Holohan say. "'From all the facts obtained this morning it seems perfectly evident the murder was committed by John Wilkes Booth. He, in company with another man, passed over the Eastern Branch Bridge before half past eleven o'clock. His companion gave his name as Smith but undoubtedly his name is Surratt, from Prince George's County, Maryland.'"

Anna pressed a hand to her mouth, muffling a sob.

"Don't worry," Mary ordered in a whisper. "You know that isn't true. Junior is in Montreal. Whoever Mr. Booth's companion may be, he cannot be your brother."

Anna nodded and resumed slicing a loaf of bread, her hands shaking so badly that the slices were of erratic, widely varying thicknesses. Mary took the knife from her and nodded to a chair to indicate that she should sit.

"Nonsense," replied Louis. "Surratt was in Montreal on the twelfth. He could not have returned to the capital so quickly."

"You're referring to his letter," said Holohan, lowering his voice. "The one Mrs. Surratt could not produce."

"She may have misplaced it, but I know it exists. I saw the postmark on the envelope myself when it first arrived."

Mary went cold. What else had Louis observed? Too much, she knew, far too much, and without understanding half of it.

She heard more footsteps on the stairs as the others came down to breakfast, and, gesturing for Anna to help her, she quickly began carrying platters and bowls into the dining room and setting food on the table, nodding in reply to her lodgers' tentative greetings. As they all took their seats and Louis, the aspiring priest, led them in the blessing, it occurred to Mary that perhaps she ought to apologize for the disruption of their sleep. Then anger and indignation flared, and she decided that if anyone owed the household an apology, it was the detectives— but she did not expect anything so courteous from them.

The mood was anxious and somber as they ate, although Louis, apparently insensible to the tension, continued to read aloud from the paper, as was his habit.

"Goodness. Andrew Johnson was sworn in as president this morning in the parlor of the Kirkwood House," he said, seeming startled, as if he had forgotten that the country would need a new president. " 'He says he has no enemies to punish except rebels, and asks the support, in this crisis, of all men who love the country without distinction of party or creed. He does not desire to be considered a politician, but wishes only to give all his energies to the impartial discharge of his weighty duties.' "

"Good luck to him," said Holohan, dubious.

"Ah!" Louis exclaimed. "This may interest you Marylanders. 'The Excitement in Baltimore: The feeling here at the horrible crime which has deprived the country of its revered President is too deep for utterance. Sorrow profound and rage intense pervade all loyal hearts. All kindly feeling toward rebels and rebel sympathizers has, as it were, been obliterated, and one intense feeling of detestation and abhorrence for all connected with the rebellion takes its place.' "

Mary felt a chill. If that were truly the sentiment in Baltimore, Confederate sympathizers would be even more despised in Washington City and elsewhere across the North.

Louis fell blessedly silent for a few moments, but then he cleared his throat and peered at Mary. "You will be happy to know, I think, Mrs. Surratt, that they provide here a very detailed description of Booth's fellow fugitive, and he in no way resembles your son John."

"That is because the man could not possibly be my son," she said shortly, passing the bread basket to the center of the table. "Junior is in Canada on a courier assignment for the Adams Express Company."

Louis studied her curiously for a moment, then deliberately folded the newspaper and set it on the sideboard. "Mrs. Surratt, everyone," he said, "I want you to know that after breakfast I am going directly to police headquarters to tell them all that I know about this terrible crime, although I admit that I do not, at this moment, clearly understand what it is precisely that I do know."

Mary gave him a thin smile. "Perhaps you should wait until you've figured that out before you waste the detectives' time with idle rambling."

Louis frowned. "I tell you this not to threaten or boast, but to make you aware—" He looked around the table. "To make *all* of you aware, that there will likely be a more thorough investigation of this house if—"

"Stop talking," Anna snapped, setting down her fork with a clatter. "Just stop talking. I cannot bear the sound of your voice another moment."

Silence descended over the table. Louis gave Anna one long, wordless look that she either did not see or willfully ignored. She took up her fork again and resumed eating. After a moment, Louis pushed back his chair, rose stiffly, and strode from the room without looking back. They all heard him climb the stairs to the second floor, and after a few minutes of tense quiet broken only by the sounds of cutlery upon china, they heard him leave the boardinghouse.

Lucy stayed in bed until well after noon—dozing, brooding, praying, going over every detail of her last encounter with John. He had been so pleasant at supper last night—had it only been last night?—chatting cordially with her parents, indulging the loquacious Mrs. Temple without so much as a flicker of an eyebrow in annoyance. How could he have been a perfect gentleman at table, kissed her hand, bade them all good night, and then dashed off to murder the president? It made absolutely no sense. He was a fine actor, to be sure, but only a madman could have enjoyed a delightful meal with his sweetheart and her family and then gone off and coldly committed the most atrocious of crimes.

She knew John as well as she knew anyone, and she knew he was no madman.

Her father was out, she knew not where, and her mother and sister were conversing in hushed voices in the sitting room. Suddenly inspired, she threw back the covers, rose from bed, washed, and dressed, growing more determined with every moment. She loved John, and she knew he was innocent. He probably *had* been at Ford's Theatre, and why not—he knew nearly everyone in the cast and the crew and likely wanted to show his support for Miss Keene's benefit. Someone had glimpsed him or someone resembling him near the State Box, and someone had misunderstood and shrieked his name, and the rumors had spread and the crowd had turned ugly, violent—of course under such circumstances he had considered it necessary to flee for his life. He had, no doubt, found refuge somewhere in the capital, and was waiting for the uproar to subside so he could make his way through the city and report to the authorities. What if at that very moment he were pacing in a tiny room somewhere, peering out the windows and praying that his devoted Lucy would plead his case to her father, rendering it safe for him to emerge from hiding and clear his name?

Emboldened, Lucy quit her bedchamber and briskly crossed the room to the window where her mother and sister sat, their grave expressions turning surprised as she approached. "I know John is innocent," she declared, but the scene outside the window abruptly silenced her. The sidewalks were nearly empty of people, and those few whom Lucy did see moved about as if in a daze, their heads lowered, bands of black crepe around the gentlemen's arms, ladies clinging to their escorts as if they grieved too deeply to walk unassisted. Flags that had waved proudly in victory the day before had been lowered to half staff. The brass bands that had played stirring martial tunes from dawn until well after twilight had fallen silent. Government offices and shops that only days before had been illuminated by the light of thousands of candles and gas jets were darkened and closed, and every doorway, every window, every storefront up and down the street as far as she could see had been draped in the black crepe of mourning.

"Lucy, come away from the window," her mother urged, rising and taking her hand.

"No," said Lucy, slipping her hand free. "I will be heard. I know John, and I know that he is innocent. Where is Papa? I must speak with him. He must appeal on John's behalf to—to whomever is leading this investigation."

"Your father is out," her mother said in steady, measured tones meant to calm her. "He attended Mr. Johnson's swearing in ceremony at the Kirkwood House this morning, and he only briefly returned before setting out again."

"Where is he now?"

Her mother hesitated, and then, exchanging a glance with Lizzie, she said, "He's downstairs in the salon."

"I will go to him."

"Lucy, wait." Her mother caught her by the arm. "You cannot interrupt him. He's busy assisting with the preparations for a meeting of citizens of Illinois. They have much to discuss, much to arrange regarding Mr. Lincoln's funeral."

The word hit Lucy like a fist to the heart. Of course there would be a funeral, and terrible mourning to follow for months, years, throughout the land. Oh, poor Robert. Her courage faltered, and she turned away from the door. "When will Papa be back?"

"I don't know," her mother replied. "Why don't you sit and wait with us?"

"Do you want something to eat?" asked Lizzie. "You haven't had a bite since supper."

Lucy's stomach rebelled at the thought of food. "I'm not hungry," she said. "I'll just sit and—" She glanced about and spied the disorderly pile of newspapers. "I'll read while I wait for Papa."

She snatched up the *Evening Star* and carried it to an armchair farthest from the window. "Perhaps you shouldn't," said Lizzie, but Lucy sat down and fixed her gaze on the page. She nearly flung the paper aside when she glimpsed one horrifying report after another, lurid descriptions of her John firing a pistol at the back of Mr. Lincoln's head, of his slashing a young major called Rathbone with a knife, of John leaping from the State Box to the stage, brandishing the dagger, and shouting out the dramatic line from Shakespeare's *Julius Caesar*, from the state motto of his beloved Virginia.

Her heart plummeted. Those words, those dreadful words. How like John in his rages they sounded—how exactly, shockingly like him.

Then her gaze fell upon another bold headline, and her throat constricted until she could not draw breath.

THE MISTRESS OF BOOTH ATTEMPTS TO COMMIT SUICIDE.

Ella Turner, mistress of John Wilkes Booth, at No. 62 Ohio Avenue, attempted to commit suicide this morning by taking chloroform. About 11 o'clock, some of the inmates of the house entered Ella's room and found her lying upon the bed apparently asleep. Efforts to rouse her proving fruitless, several physicians were called in, when it was discovered that she had taken chloroform. The proper remedies were immediately applied, when Ella soon revived and asked for Booth's picture, which she had concealed under the pillow of her bed, at the same time remarking to the physicians that she did not thank them for saving her life. The house, No. 62 Ohio Avenue, is kept by Ella Turner's sister.

"The mistress of Booth," Lucy murmured, and the newspaper fell to her lap.

John had a mistress, apparently of longstanding ties, a prostitute rendered so distraught by his death that she sought to take her own life. And Lucy had never known, nor even suspected.

Who was this strange, vile, monstrous John Wilkes Booth emerging from the horrid tales in the paper?

On Saturday evening, a full twenty-four hours after her brother had shot President Abraham Lincoln, Asia lay awake in her darkened bedchamber, agonizing over her brother's terrible act while Clarke snored quietly beside her. If only she had known, if only she could have prevented him, if only she had warned the president—but for all her beloved brother's tirades and invective, she never would have imagined him capable of murder.

And yet, when she wasn't praying for her brother's soul and wondering frantically where he was, her mind ceaselessly churned over conversations they had shared over the course of their intertwined lives, sifting his words for clues, for the telling phrase that should have warned her of his intentions.

Then, suddenly, she remembered the packet.

Wilkes had last come to see her in the second week of February. Clarke had been away—in Washington, she remembered with a jolt, performing in *Everybody's Friend* at Ford's Theatre before an audience that had included the president and Mrs. Lincoln and General and Mrs. Grant. Wilkes had stayed only two nights in Philadelphia before departing for New York to visit their mother and Rosalie, and late in the evening of the second day, he had suddenly said, "Let me show you the cypher."

"No, Wilkes," she had immediately replied, knowing he must mean a code he used in his smuggling activities for the rebels. "I shall not consent to any knowledge of that kind."

"But I might need to communicate with you about my financial affairs, and I don't want to let everyone know what I'm worth."

"No, Wilkes. I'm sorry, but I must refuse, and you must never ask me again."

He had frowned but had nodded acquiescence. Rising, he had left the room and had returned moments later with a thick, sealed packet with her own name written on the outside. "Lock this in your safe for me," he had instructed. "I may come back for it, but if anything should happen to me, open the packet—alone—and send the letters as directed. The money and papers, give to their owners."

She had accepted the packet, not liking such talk but not finding it unusual either, considering the tumultuous times they lived in and the inherent dangers on road, rail, and sea he was exposed to as a traveling actor. "I'll do as you ask," she had promised, studying the envelope, "but I would prefer that you keep yourself safe."

"I would too," he had said, smiling. "Let me see you lock up the packet."

"Now?"

"Yes, dear sister, now."

So she had led him to the safe, and with Wilkes's help she had unfastened the heavy wooden door, then had unbarred the inner door of iron and had placed the packet within the safe. Afterward she had carefully secured both doors behind them and had returned the key to its hiding place. "Satisfied?" she had asked Wilkes, smiling indulgently at his curious insistence, and he had declared himself thoroughly so.

Recalling that night, Asia felt a strange prickling on the back of her neck and down her spine. She climbed awkwardly from bed, threw on her dressing gown, and made her way to the safe, and before long, among Clarke's papers and documents, she found the packet Wilkes had entrusted to her.

She seated herself behind Clarke's desk and held the packet in her lap, tracing her name with a fingertip, tears welling up when she realized that these could be the last words she would ever know from her beloved brother. Then she cleared her throat, blinked the tears away, and carefully opened the envelope.

Inside she discovered a thinner envelope addressed to a man whose life would be destroyed if his name were linked to her brother's, so she set that aside and quickly leafed through the rest—a smaller envelope addressed to their mother in her brother's familiar hand, another for her brother's friend and fellow actor Sam Chester, some federal and city bonds, and several documents regarding his oil wells.

The creak of a floorboard gave her a start, and she held perfectly still and silent until she decided it was only the sound of the house settling or someone upstairs turning over in bed. Quickly she returned all but the first letter to the packet and back into the safe, and then she carried the incriminating envelope to the kitchen, set fire to it, and scattered the ashes as an extra measure of caution.

Relieved for that man's sake yet deeply troubled for her family, she left the kitchen to return to bed, but when she reached the foot of the staircase, she discovered Clarke standing at the top.

"Why are you wandering the house at night?" he asked, descending the stairs. "You ought to be sleeping."

"I was hungry."

He halted on the step above her. "Then you should have woken me. I would have brought you something."

"I wanted to let you sleep."

"Next time, wake me."

He offered her his arm, and she took it, and she allowed him to lead her to their room.

"Clarke," she ventured as they returned to bed, "I would like to telegraph my mother and Rosalie and have them join us here."

"I think the less we associate with the Booths, the better."

I am a Booth, she was tempted to declare, but instead she said, "Edwin is traveling, and I don't like to think of them alone and unprotected. They will not be recognized here, but in New York, coming in and out of Edwin's house, they will be known to all. It would be a great relief to me to have them near and safe."

She clasped her hands over her belly again, and the gesture seemed to remind him of her delicate condition. "Very well," he grumbled. "I'll send a telegram in the morning."

She thanked him quietly and closed her eyes and silently prayed for her brother, for the Lincoln family, for her own, until she fell asleep.

When Mary Ann received Clarke's telegram requesting that she come to Philadelphia, she in turn telegraphed Edwin at his hotel in Boston to inform him of her plans. To her chagrin, he neither replied nor returned to his Manhattan residence before she and Rosalie departed by train for Philadelphia, clad in mourning black with dark veils concealing their faces.

"This is unnecessary," Rosalie murmured as they stowed their luggage and took their seats. "We are not Edwin or John or June. No one knows us."

It was true that their faces were not as well known as those of the actors in the family, but Mary Ann feared that the shame and anger and horror that seared her heart and scoured her veins was so tangible that any stranger would know with a single glance that she must be the mother of the most hated man in America. She had grieved for her husband every day since he had passed, but now—she could almost be relieved that Junius had died before he witnessed how his beloved son had made a mockery of his highest principles, that all life was sacred.

They arrived in Philadelphia on the afternoon of Easter Sunday. Clarke greeted them somewhat reservedly, but Asia was so glad to see them that her tearful gratitude wrenched Mary Ann's heart. Asia looked to be in good health, though wan and red-eyed from worry, and Clarke complained that she was not getting as much rest as the doctor ordered.

"You mustn't think that just because you've had three good pregnancies you needn't pay as much attention to your health this time around," Mary Ann scolded her as she helped her back upstairs and into bed, and for a moment it was bliss to be nothing more than an ordinary woman of three score and two years, fussing about her daughter and her unborn grandchild.

"You're quite enormous," said Rosalie, in her usual voice, barely above a whisper. "Do you suppose you might be carrying twins?"

Asia laughed bleakly. "I hope not. I prefer for my little trotters to come along one at a time."

She had received a letter from Edwin that morning, she told them as Mary Ann and Rosalie seated themselves at her bedside. "He wrote that he had remained in Boston on the advice of friends who thought that, since the people of that city have been so good to him, he ought not to leave until they understood that he had no part in Wilkes's terrible deed. I expect that by now he is on his way to New York."

"I suppose he sent a similar letter to us there," said Mary Ann, "but unfortunately we will not see it, or him, until we return."

"He said something else that deeply troubled me." Asia reached into the drawer of the bedside table and took out two envelopes, withdrew a sheet of paper from one, and unfolded it. " 'Think no more of him as your brother; he is dead to us now, as he soon must be to all the world.' " She paused and pressed a hand to her lips, composing herself. " 'But imagine the boy you loved to be in that better part of his spirit, in another world.' "

Mary Ann found Edwin's attempt to comfort his sister appalling. "He writes as though his brother is truly dead."

"Perhaps he expects that he soon will be," said Rosalie, barely audible.

"I love Wilkes and I cannot think of him as no longer my brother," said Asia. "The doom that fell on him was not wrought from a maniac brain nor a wicked heart, not from an irreligious soul nor a degraded nature. He would have died to save the people of the South, and when Richmond fell and Mr. Lincoln made his triumphant entry into the smoldering ruins of the city, it reignited the fire of patriotism—for *his* country, as he thinks of it—a zeal that consumed him."

"Country," Mary Ann murmured, remembering her vision in the flames when her precious John Wilkes was no more than a baby nursing at her breast, perfect and beautiful. Her gaze met Asia's, and she knew Asia was thinking of it too. Then Mary Ann caught herself. "Let us not join in the multitudes that have condemned John Wilkes without a trial, without allowing him to speak in his own defense. We don't know that our boy has done this terrible thing."

"If he has not," whispered Rosalie, "then where is he?"

They fell into a mournful silence, broken when Asia took a letter from the second envelope and said that she had heard from June too. He had just finished performing a farewell benefit of *The Merchant of Venice* at Wood's Theatre when the news of the assassination had reached him backstage. He had fled to his hotel and had barricaded the door, terrified that a mob would descend upon him and tear him to pieces.

His fear was not without merit, Mary Ann knew. Even Edwin, beloved as he was to theatergoers around the world, had received threatening letters in the post. In cities both North and South, foolhardy men who had publicly expressed satisfaction at the president's death had been set upon by angry, vengeful crowds and killed.

"As soon as June feels it is safe to travel," Asia said, putting both letters away, "he is coming here."

"Clarke won't mind?" Mary Ann ventured.

Asia smiled thinly. "Clarke has nothing to say about it."

Mary Ann regarded her with surprise, taken aback by the sharp edge to her voice. She knew Clarke and John Wilkes did not get along, and that Asia usually sided with her brother, but until that moment Mary Ann had never suspected any ill feeling between Asia and Clarke.

But Asia looked tired and hollow-eyed, so rather than worry her with unwanted queries, Mary Ann urged her to lie down and rest. Rosalie offered to sit up with her, while Mary Ann quietly left the room to seek out her grandchildren. By early evening some color had returned to Asia's cheeks, and she insisted upon coming down for supper, declaring that she knew her own strength and she would not be a prisoner of her doctor's vigilance.

Supper was a subdued affair, with the only bright moments springing from the sweet, innocent remarks of the three dear little lambs who knew nothing of their uncle's dreadful crime. For the children's sake the adults avoided mentioning the late tragedy, but as soon as the nurse whisked the youngsters off, they began comparing rumors overheard and stories read. John Wilkes had been sighted in cities throughout the eastern states and as far away as Canada and California, but the most credible reports stated that hundreds of federal agents were scouring Washington City for evidence and searching the Maryland countryside for John Wilkes and a companion believed to be responsible for the attack on Secretary Seward.

When Mary Ann imagined her darling boy fleeing on horseback through the wilderness with vengeful men and snarling dogs in swift pursuit, her heart pained her until she almost thought she could feel it fracturing into jagged splinters beneath her breast.

"The last time I saw Wilkes—" Asia took a deep breath, sipped water, and started again. "In February, when he last visited, he entrusted a packet to me in case something should happen to him. He said it contained papers and money, and letters he wanted me to deliver."

"Something certainly has happened to him," said Clarke bitterly. "Why did you not mention these papers before?"

Mary Ann frowned, disliking his tone, but Asia merely regarded him calmly. "In all the distress and confusion, I have only just remembered it."

Clarke announced that he would inspect the packet immediately, and without offering Asia assistance from her chair, he strode off to his study. Rosalie helped her sister to her feet, and Mary Ann followed behind as they went to join Clarke at the safe.

As they drew closer, Mary Ann observed that Asia's name was written on the envelope in John Wilkes's familiar scrawl and that the seal had been broken, but in his haste Clarke seemed not to notice. Mary Ann winced at his carelessness as he shook the contents out upon his desk and spread them out with a broad sweep of his hand. They discovered federal bonds worth $3,000 and city bonds worth another $1,000; a deed to Wilkes's Pennsylvania oil property, signed over to June; and two smaller envelopes, one addressed to Wilkes's longtime friend and fellow actor Samuel Knapp Chester, and the other to Mary Ann.

Clarke handed Mary Ann the second envelope and regarded her expectantly, which she understood to mean that she was to read the letter aloud. She opened it, took out a sheet of paper, steadied herself with a deep breath, and complied.

Dearest Beloved Mother,

Heaven knows how dearly I love you. And may our kind Father in Heaven (if only for the sake of my love) watch over, comfort & protect you, in my absence. May he soften the blow of my departure, granting you peace and happiness for many, many years to come. God ever bless you.

I have always endeavored to be a good and dutiful son, and even now would wish to die sooner than give you pain. But dearest Mother, though I owe you all, there is another duty, a noble duty for the sake of liberty and humanity due to my country—For four years I have lived (I may say) a slave in the north (a favored slave its true, but no less hateful to me on that account). Not daring to express my thoughts or sentiments, even in my own home, constantly hearing every principle, dear to my heart, denounced as treasonable, and knowing the vile and savage acts committed on my countrymen, their wives & helpless children, that I have cursed my wilful idleness, and begun to deem myself a coward and to despise my own existence. For four years I have borne it mostly for your dear sake, and for you alone, have I also struggled to fight off this desire to be gone, but it seems that uncontrollable fate, moving me for its ends, takes me from you, dear Mother, to do what work I can for a poor oppressed downtrodden people. May that same fate cause me to do that work well. I care not for the censure of the north, so I have your forgiveness, and I feel I may hope it, even though you differ with me in opinion.

I may, by the grace of God, live through this war dear Mother, if so, the rest of my life shall be more devoted to you, than has been my former. For I know it will take a long lifetime of tenderness and care, to atone for the pang this parting will give you. But I cannot longer resist the inclination to go and share the sufferings of my brave countrymen, holding an unequal strife (for every right human & divine) against the most ruthless enemy, the world has ever known. You can answer for me dearest Mother (although none of you think with me) that I have not a single selfish motive to spur me on to this, nothing save the sacred duty, I feel I owe the cause I love, the cause of the South. The cause of liberty & justice. So should I meet the worst, dear Mother, in struggling for such holy rights, I can say

"God's will be done" and bless him in my heart for not permitting me to outlive our dear bought freedom. And for keeping me from being longer a hidden lie among my country's foes.

Darling Mother I can not write you, you will understand the deep regret, the forsaking your dear side, will make me suffer, for you have been the best, the noblest, an example for all mothers. God bless you, as I shall ever pray him to do. And should the last <u>bolt</u> strike your son, dear Mother, bear it patiently and think at the best life is but short, and <u>not at all times happy</u>. My Brothers & Sisters (Heaven protect them) will add my love and duty to their own, and watch you with care and kindness, till we meet again. And if <u>that happiness</u> does not come to us on earth, then may, O may it be with God. So then dearest, <u>dearest</u> Mother, <u>forgive</u> and pray for me. I feel that I am right in the justness of my cause, and that we shall, <u>ere long</u>, meet again. Heaven grant it. Bless you, bless you. Your loving son will never cease to hope and pray for such a joy.

Come weal or woe, with never ending love and devotion you will find me ever your affectionate son

John.

Mary Ann's voice was so choked with sobs she could hardly finish the letter. Oh, her poor, dear, misguided, darling boy. She could not have been the best, the noblest of mothers to have raised him to believe that it could ever be right to shoot a man in the back of the head while he sat with his wife watching a play. What would his beloved late father, who had cherished all life, have thought of such a deed?

"Wilkes says nothing of planning to hurt the president," said Asia, stroking her belly absently, a faint light of hope appearing in her eyes. "He says he wants to go and share the sufferings of his brave country-men. That suggests only that he intended to join the Confederacy, or at the very least, to move to the South."

"So he felt in February," murmured Rosalie, "when he gave you that letter, before Richmond fell, before General Lee surrendered."

Reluctantly, Mary Ann added, "He also wrote here that he wanted to do what work he could for a poor, oppressed, downtrodden people. Perhaps, last Friday night, he believed he was doing precisely that."

Asia pressed her lips together and shook her head, her eyes shining with unshed tears. Mary Ann set the letter aside and embraced her, and as soon as she did, Clarke snatched up the page. "This letter exonerates us," he declared, visibly relieved. "Don't you see? He says here, 'even though you differ with me in opinion.' And here, 'although none of you think with me'—none of you." Grasping the letter firmly in his left hand, he slapped it with the back of his right. "He says too that he couldn't express his true feelings even in his own home. That proves he knew no one else in the family shared his opinions, and that none of us could have known about his desire to kill the president or would have condoned it."

"It doesn't exonerate us," said Asia. "It only condemns Wilkes."

"What of the other letter?" asked Mary Ann. "Should we deliver it to Sam Chester?"

Throwing her a look of thinly veiled exasperation that she would even suggest such a thing, Clarke tucked Mary Ann's letter under his arm, tore open the second envelope, and withdrew several pages. He unfolded them and read in silence while Mary Ann and her daughters stood watching him, exchanging uneasy glances. "There is nothing in this Confederate screed that will help us," he said. "He talks about a plan to make a prisoner of the man to whom the world owes so much misery—he means Mr. Lincoln—and about how he loved the Union once, but believes the South to be in the right. He goes on at length to defend the rebels, and to make a rather poor argument for slavery. He ends by calling himself—" Clarke turned to the last page. "He signs the letter, 'A Confederate, at present doing his duty upon his own responsibility.' And he crossed out 'at present.'"

"Burn it," said Asia, reaching for the letter, which her husband quickly pulled out of her reach. "Put it on the fire."

"That would be imprudent, I think," said Clarke, returning it to its envelope. "But the letter to you, Mrs. Booth, that may yet save us. If the world learns what he wrote there—"

"The world must never know." Mary Ann held out her hand. "That was intended as a private letter to me, and I would like it back now, if you please."

Clarke shook his head and tucked both letters into his breast pocket. "I can't do that. You might burn the only evidence I have to prove that I had no part in John's scheme."

"It is mine," said Mary Ann sharply. "I would thank you to return it."

"Can't do that," he said again, gathering up the other papers and bonds and returning them to the envelope inscribed with Asia's name. Clasping it tightly to his side, he bowed curtly and left the room, leaving them to watch and fear and wonder what he intended.

The furious pounding on the front door Mary had dreaded and prepared for since the detectives left the boardinghouse in the early morning hours of Holy Saturday came nearly three days later at eleven o'clock on the night of Monday, April 17.

It had been a long, fraught, exhausting day, but Anna, Nora, and Olivia had declared themselves too anxious to sleep, so Mary prepared a pot of tea and cut slices of a lemon cake left over from Easter supper. She had just finished pouring and had settled into her favorite armchair in the parlor when they heard a loud, insistent knock upon the front door. Perplexed, Mary went to answer, wondering if it was William Wallace Kirby, her good friend's husband and the brother-in-law of Eliza Holohan. The Holohans had left the boardinghouse the previous day—Mary and Anna had discovered the family packing up and moving out when they returned from Easter Mass at St. Patrick's—but the family had inadvertently left a box of their belongings behind, and Mr. Kirby had promised to fetch it for them. He had said that he might call that day or the next, although she would not have expected him so late.

The visitor pounded again just as Mary reached the front door, so loud and demanding that she hesitated to open it. "Is that you, Mr. Kirby?" she called.

"No, madam," a man replied gruffly, "but open the door at once, if this is Mrs. Surratt's house."

Steeling herself, Mary fumbled with the latch, opened the door, and discovered six officers standing on the staircase, grim-faced and steely-eyed.

"Are you Mrs. Surratt?" said the one nearest the door.

"I am."

"The widow of John H. Surratt Sr. and mother of John H. Surratt Jr.?"

She nodded, heart pounding, hand trembling on the doorknob.

"I am Major Henry Smith." He gestured to the two officers immediately behind him. "Detective Devore, Captain Wermerskirch. May we come in?"

She nodded again and stepped back to allow all six men to enter. She led them down the hallway and into the parlor, startling the young ladies, who abruptly fell silent. While the other men dispersed throughout the house, Major Smith regarded the ladies solemnly. "We're here to bring you to General Augur's office for interrogation," he said. "You'll be treated kindly as long as you're in my charge."

The younger ladies gasped, terrified. "And who is General Augur?" asked Mary coolly.

"Commander of the Department of Washington." Major Smith glanced over his shoulder at the sound of approaching footsteps, and he nodded to an officer escorting the newly hired colored servant, Susan, and her fiancé, Dan, into the room and ordered them to sit. The servants never sat in the formal parlor, and they glanced uneasily at Mary, who nodded her approval as they edged toward two unoccupied chairs.

"Are there any other lodgers unaccounted for?" asked Major Smith.

"Our tenant Louis Weichmann is out for the evening, I know not where," Mary replied. "My son is traveling in Canada on business."

Detective Devore entered in time to hear the last, and Mary bristled to see the two men exchange significant glances. "We're here to arrest you all," Detective Devore said with practiced nonchalance, perhaps unaware that his companion had already informed them, perhaps knowing but taking pleasure in their distress.

As the officers continued to search the house, Mary fought to remain calm, but Anna and the other young ladies became more upset the longer they sat and whispered frantically to one another. "Oh, Mother," Anna suddenly exclaimed. "Think of being taken down there for such a crime!"

"Anna, calm yourself," Mary warned, mindful of the young detective called Clarvoe standing in the doorway, taking notes on everything he heard and saw. She went to her daughter, embraced her, and murmured, "Don't carry on so, darling. You're already worn out with anxiety. You'll make yourself ill."

She continued to murmur soothingly into her ear, and soon Anna grew less agitated, though she still trembled and sighed.

Major Smith instructed Detective Devore to arrange for a carriage to take the ladies to headquarters for questioning. "Given the foul weather tonight," he added to Mary, "you might want warmer wraps for the ride, something to keep the rain off."

Mary inclined her head in thanks, but as she went to go fetch shawls and hats for them all, Major Smith ordered her to stop. "Remember, this house is under suspicion," he said, joining her at the foot of the stairs. "Wherever you go, I must accompany you."

She inclined her head again, and while Detective Clarvoe guarded the young ladies to see that, as he put it, no papers were destroyed and no secretive communication passed between them, Mary went from one bedroom to another gathering wraps and sturdier shoes, for good measure. Then she joined the others in the parlor, waiting and listening while the officers meticulously searched every room in the house from kitchen to attic, making observations and collecting evidence. Mary knew from the thickness of the packets three of the officers carried that they had found some items of interest, but she knew not what they had taken or from which rooms.

Then a young policeman called Dempsey bolted into the parlor carrying a framed picture that Louis Weichmann had given Anna for her birthday, a small colored lithograph titled *Morning Noon and Night*. Lieutenant Dempsey turned over the frame and showed it to Major Smith, and Anna gasped and went sickly pale as the officers removed something hidden behind the lithograph. Mary went cold as she recognized one of the photos of John Wilkes Booth Anna and Nora had arranged throughout the house. She had told Anna to destroy them all, and Anna promised that she had.

"May I kneel and pray?" Mary asked Major Smith shakily.

He considered for a moment. "Go ahead, but don't leave this room."

As Mary got up from her chair to kneel on the floor, she froze at the sound of boots on the outside staircase. Major Smith gestured sharply and two officers crept down the hallway toward the door with their pistols drawn. Through the open doorway Mary heard a knock, heard the door quickly swinging open, and men's voices, low and demanding, and the door banging shut. The women exchanged apprehensive glances as the interrogation went on, until Major Smith suddenly appeared in the parlor doorway.

"Mrs. Surratt," he ordered. "Come here."

She rose and followed him into the hallway, where she discovered a tall, strapping man with a pickax on his shoulder standing in front of the closed door. He wore a dark gray coat, dark pants soiled with mud up to the knees, and a strange skullcap fashioned out of what appeared to be a shirtsleeve.

Mary muffled a gasp. The man was Mr. Powell, or Mr. Payne, as he was better known to her tenants.

Major Smith beckoned her closer, and she reluctantly obeyed. "Do you know this man," Major Smith demanded, "and did you hire him to come and dig a gutter for you?"

Raising her right hand, she said, "Before God, sir, I do not know this man, and have never seen him, and I did not hire him to dig a gutter for me."

"Lewis Payne," said the major, "you are under arrest."

A slight smile played on Mr. Payne's face, but he did not so much as glance at Mary as Lieutenant Dempsey escorted her back to the parlor.

Soon thereafter, the carriage arrived and the ladies were shown aboard, some quietly sobbing, others murmuring prayers as they were driven to police headquarters. Mary was immediately taken in for questioning—and such bewildering questions they were, coming at such a pace and from so many directions that she felt as if she were surrounded by a flock of wild, panicking birds, scraping her with their wings and beaks and talons as she struggled in vain to fend them off. Colonel Henry Wells asked her repeatedly about Junior, and about Mr. Booth, and Mr. Atzerodt, and three men who the colonel seemed to believe had called at the boardinghouse late Saturday night although Mary had no idea whom he meant, and bizarrely, about how long it would take to cross the Potomac or travel to Fredericksburg and Richmond. Eventually she realized that someone must have informed on her, but the details had become garbled and jumbled and misunderstood. She tried to answer as simply and as honestly as she could without harming Junior, but the questions were so convoluted and confusing and the colonel so harshly insistent that Mary was seized by the dreadful fear that she was doing her son and herself more harm than good.

The interrogation finally ended at three o'clock, rendering Mary exhausted, afraid, and despondent. Eventually she was escorted to another room, where the other women were being held while they awaited their turns to be questioned by other members of Colonel Wells's staff. The young ladies were tearful and frightened, and Anna nearly hysterical, and it was all Mary could do to calm and comfort them.

Fighting to keep her own terror constrained, Mary was struck by sharp, unexpected misgivings that she had ever welcomed Mr. Booth into her parlor. It was his fault she and the young ladies were suffering and afraid, that Junior was in grave danger. After Richmond had fallen, she had tried to persuade Mr. Booth that it was futile to persist in his plan to abduct Mr. Lincoln. What on earth had possessed him to resort to such drastic, irrevocable measures instead? What had compelled him to murder? What good had he thought could possibly come of it?

As the hours passed, Mary felt a small flame of anger and indignation flare up deep within her. She and Junior had agreed to abduction, not assassination, but now they were mired up to their necks in Mr. Booth's crime, and if she were not very, very careful, she might find herself unable to extricate them from it. She would never deliberately betray Mr. Booth, but neither would she sacrifice herself or her children to save him.

They were held at headquarters throughout the long, harrowing night, and early the next morning, they were put into a carriage and driven to the Carroll Annex at the Old Capitol Prison. There three officers read the charges against them as Mary stood stoically, squeezing Anna's hand tightly, and the younger women wept and pleaded. The officers brusquely queried them—names, ages, addresses, occupations—and filled out forms, and led them off to separate rooms on the second floor.

"May my daughter and I stay together?" Mary asked as Anna was pulled from her side.

"No," came the officer's curt reply as he took Anna by the elbow, put her into a room, and shut the door.

"How long will we be held here?" Mary demanded shakily as he seized her by the upper arm and put her into the room next door.

"Indefinitely," he said, and slammed the door shut and turned the key.

On Tuesday evening after supper, while Asia rested in bed upstairs and the nurse tidied the children's rooms, Mary Ann was in the parlor reading fairy tales to the youngsters when she heard footsteps in the hall and glanced up to discover Clarke putting on his coat and striding to the door. He did not pause to bid them farewell, and as he passed she glimpsed two envelopes jutting out of his pocket.

"Clarke, wait," she called, scooping up baby Adrienne, settling toddler Edwin more securely on the sofa, and giving Dottie's head one quick pat before she hurried after her son-in-law. "Where are you going?"

He paused with his hand on the door. "I'm going out to meet a friend."

"What friend?" Shifting the baby to her shoulder, she freed one hand and gestured to his pocket. "Is that my letter? Where are you taking it?"

Heaving a sigh, he turned away from the door to face her squarely. "I'm meeting my friend John Stockton, an editor at the *Philadelphia Inquirer*. He's going to introduce me to William Millward, the United States marshal for the eastern district of Pennsylvania. I'm going to submit these letters to him to prove our innocence."

"You mustn't," she exclaimed. "No one is questioning our innocence. You'll only stir up trouble and make things worse for John Wilkes!"

"Things are already as bad for him as they could possibly be," he retorted. "Even so, I'd sacrifice him a thousand times before I'd let the rest of us go down with him. This letter proves that he knew none of us sympathized with the rebels, that he couldn't trust us with his plot. It must be made public before it's too late."

"That letter is mine," Mary Ann said tightly. "You mustn't take it from this house or show it to anyone. I forbid it."

He gave her one long, wordless, incredulous look before he tore the door open and strode from the house, carrying the incriminating papers beyond her reach.

Furious, Asia flung the quilt aside, climbed unsteadily from the divan, and made her way downstairs to send Clarke's valet running after her husband, knowing even as she did that Clarke was unlikely to heed her demands.

"I'm sorry I couldn't prevent him from going out," her mother apologized, patting little Adrienne and kissing her brow soothingly, though she seemed more in need of comfort than the babe in her arms. "I tried to reason with him, but he wouldn't listen."

"You're not to blame," said Asia. "You couldn't have restrained him. Let's hope he comes to his senses before the marshal sees him."

Her anger smoldered as the evening passed, and she spent the time alternately pacing and resting with her feet up. She watched the door, composing diatribes in her mind she intended to hurl at Clarke the moment he crossed the threshold. How could he have done this? Was he so frightened for himself that he would tie the hangman's noose for Wilkes to prove his loyalty to the Union?

The valet returned an hour later, abashed, to report that he had found Mr. Clarke at Mr. Stockton's office, and Mr. Clarke had ordered him to go home. "Did Mr. Clarke say when he might return?" Asia queried.

"He didn't, ma'am."

"Was any other gentleman with them?"

"Only Mr. Stockton's secretary, ma'am."

Then there was still a chance Mr. Stockton would advise Clarke not to take Wilkes's letters to the marshal. She dismissed the valet and re-signed herself to an anxious vigil.

The children had long been asleep and even her mother had re-tired for the night by the time Clarke finally crept in. "What did you do?" Asia demanded, rising awkwardly from her chair, crossing into the foyer and turning up the gaslight.

He jumped at the sound of her voice. "Asia. You should be resting."

"How could I rest after what you told my mother? I ask again, what did you do?"

He sighed heavily and shrugged out of his coat. "I gave the letters to Stockton. He read them and agreed I should take them to the mar-shal. You'll be pleased to know that Marshal Millward decreed that it would be improper to publish John's letter to your mother, because de-spite everything else your brother wrote, his affectionate words for her would create undue and false sympathy for him."

"Oh, thank God," said Asia, placing a hand upon her heart, faint with relief. "May I have the letters, please, to return to my mother?"

"I left them with Stockton for safekeeping."

Asia fixed him with a level glare. "You left them with a newspaper editor for safekeeping?"

"I did, and what of it?"

"A newspaper editor, Clarke!"

"I know what Stockton does for a living. What of it? He heard Millward's order to suppress your mother's letter. He won't disobey."

"And what of the second letter, the one you called a Confederate screed?"

For a moment Clarke looked taken aback. "I assumed Millward's prohibition applied to both."

"Why should it? The marshal objected to publishing my mother's letter because he thought it would provoke sympathy for Wilkes. He would have no objection to publishing a letter that would do the opposite."

Clarke ran a hand over his jaw. "I'll call on Stockton in the morning and take the letters back."

"You should call on him now."

"Asia, it's late. I'm sure he's retired for the night and that's what I intend to do myself."

She pleaded with him at least to send word, but he refused to wake one of the servants to carry a message that he insisted was not urgent. Asia prayed he was right.

In the morning, she resolved to be patient with Clarke, to put him in a good mood so that he would be willing to call on Mr. Stockton immediately after breakfast. And so while he shaved, she sat up in bed and replied cheerfully when he told her about his plans for the day, holding back a rebuke when he mentioned accounts to review and scripts to read but said nothing of visiting his editor friend.

Clarke was nearly finished when the maid brought in Asia's breakfast tray with the newspaper neatly folded next to her plate. She sipped tea, and finding that her appetite had returned, she nibbled at a piece of buttered toast while she unfolded the paper and scanned the front page. The news was almost too horrid to bear. The man accused of assaulting Secretary Seward had been arrested at a Washington boardinghouse, and theatre owner John Ford, a loyal friend of the Booth family since the era of Junius Brutus Booth Senior, had been confined to the Old Capitol Prison, along with his two brothers. Wilkes's childhood friend

Samuel Arnold had been arrested at home and was expected to turn state's evidence against him. Wilkes and several accomplices were believed to be in St. Mary's County, heavily armed and struggling to find a way through the Union pickets across the Potomac. The city councils of Baltimore were offering a ten-thousand-dollar reward for Wilkes's arrest, in part because "The feeling here against Booth is greatly intensified by the fact that he is a Baltimorean and our loyal people are anxious that one who so dishonored the fair name of Baltimore should meet with speedy justice."

"How now," Asia murmured to herself, disgusted. "Rebellious Baltimore is suddenly rife with Unionists."

There was some good news amid the bad. "Clarke," she said, raising her voice, "General Sherman has captured Raleigh. General Johnston has surrendered."

"Well, thank God for that," he called from the washbasin, drying his clean-shaven face with a towel. "It was only a matter of time."

Nodding, she finished her breakfast and turned the page, glancing at the headlines, unable to bear the lengthy descriptions of Mr. Lincoln's funeral and the arrangements to carry his remains to Springfield by a special railcar, skimming past financial news and announcements of club meetings and amusements and—

And then her glance fell upon her brother's name again and she went as cold as death.

"Letter of John Wilkes Booth," the first bold headline on the fourth page screamed. "Proof that He Meditated His Crime Months Ago. Confesses that He Was Engaged in a Plot to Capture and Carry Off the President. His Excuses for the Contemplated Act. His Participation in the Execution of John Brown. A SECESSION RHAPSODY."

It was not the letter Wilkes had written to Mother, but the second, more condemning document, transformed into a column and a half of rambling, vitriolic apologia for all the world to see.

"Clarke!" she shrilled, scrambling backward until her shoulders pressed against the headboard, staring in terror at the paper as if it were a venomous insect. "Clarke!"

In a moment he was at her side. "What is it? Is something wrong with the baby?"

Unable to speak, she gestured frantically to the paper. He bent over it, and as he read, his face went slack with confusion, then red with fury. "That bastard." Suddenly he lunged and with one swipe of his arm sent the newspaper flying off the bed and onto the floor. Cursing under his breath, he threw on his clothes and strode from the room. She called him back, but he did not reply.

When Asia had composed herself, she rose, washed, and dressed, and went downstairs to confirm that Clarke had quit the house—to see Mr. Stockton, she assumed, although what good that would do now, she could not say. She hoped Clarke would not kill him.

She sought out her mother, and when she found her in the parlor staring into space, tears in her eyes, seeming scarcely aware of baby Adrienne on her lap or little Dottie and Edwin playing at her feet, she knew her mother had seen the newspaper too.

Overcome with shock and trepidation, Asia, Rosalie, and their mother said little to one another while they waited for Clarke to return home, afraid to go to the windows, dreading a pounding on the door. When a knock did come, Asia boldly answered it herself, only to discover June on the doorstep, haggard, red-eyed, unshaven, his luggage set haphazardly at his feet as if he had dropped it. "Can it be true?" he asked hoarsely. "Has John killed the president?"

"Come inside and see Mother," Asia said, taking his arm and guiding him across the threshold. Mother and Rosalie had come to the foyer, summoned by the sound of his voice, and with Adrienne on her grandmother's hip and the other children toddling alongside, they embraced one another, their tears falling freely, their fears easing even though nothing about their dire circumstances had changed except that they were together.

Clarke's arrival interrupted the reunion, and though he greeted his brother-in-law courteously, his gaze was wary. "At such a time, yet another Booth taking refuge in my house might stir up talk," he said, managing a smile, though no one believed he spoke in jest.

"I'm no fugitive," said June. "I'm willing to report my whereabouts to any authority you choose."

"As it happens, I'm acquainted with a United States marshal."

June gestured sharply to the door. "Lead on, then."

"June, no," their mother protested, clutching his arm. "You've only just arrived."

June kissed her cheek. "I'm sure it won't take long."

Clarke helped him bring in his luggage, and then the two men set out. Asia instructed the staff to prepare a room for her brother and sent word to the cook to set an extra place for lunch, but their preparations were still under way when Clarke and June returned. "Marshal Millward was out," Clarke explained. "We'll call again tomorrow."

But early the next morning, a knock sounded upon the front door while the family was at breakfast. It was the marshal, accompanied by a large complement of officers. He asked to meet June, and as Clarke introduced them, the other officers strode past them into the house.

They searched every room, leaving no door unopened, no closet unexamined. Asia overheard some of the officers talking, and she was astonished and yet not to discover that they were searching for Wilkes, that they had expected to find him taking his ease there, attended by his devoted sister in a comfortable mansion in the North while legions of soldiers and detectives frantically searched for him in the South. The unexpected presence of his mother and eldest sister only strengthened their certainty.

"It's dangerous to have your family here," Clarke said to Asia in a rare moment alone. "They've brought suspicion down upon us."

"The publication of Wilkes's manifesto brought suspicion down on us," retorted Asia, incredulous, "and that is your doing."

"Your mother and sister should return home. Your brother should go with them."

Her heart plummeting, Asia rested her hands on her belly and took a deep breath. "Please, Clarke. For the love you bear me and our children, for the love you bear Edwin, please don't send my family away."

"I'm not casting them out," he retorted, "but for their sake and for ours, it would be better if they returned to New York."

Asia refused to ask them to leave, so Clarke spoke to them, and to Asia's dismay, they agreed that they would be safer beneath Edwin's roof, where they might share in the protection of his powerful friends.

Her mother and sister immediately began packing their trunks—June had not yet had time to unpack his luggage—but the wary officers ordered them to halt and summoned Marshal Millward. When Asia explained that her family intended to leave for New York on the evening train, the marshal considered this, then shook his head. "Mrs. Booth and Miss Booth may go, but Junius Booth will remain here, in case we need to question him."

Asia protested, but when Marshal Millward implied that if she did not relent, no one would be allowed to leave the house, she swallowed her bitter retorts and went to break the troubling news to her family. June accepted his detention stoically, but their mother worried about traveling without an escort until they assured her they would telegraph Edwin to meet her at the station in New York. Nodding acquiescence, she and Rosalie resumed packing while an officer observed them closely to make sure they took no documents or letters with them. Their luggage would be thoroughly examined again before they left for the train station, the marshal informed them. They did not complain, accepting the indignity rather than jeopardize their freedom to travel.

In the meantime, the search of the house continued. The officers questioned everyone in the household except the children. They collected papers, letters, playbills, scripts, maps, and mementos, sealed them in bags, and took them away. They ordered Clarke to open the safe, and they carefully scrutinized every sheet of paper within it.

They found the envelope Wilkes had entrusted to Asia, empty now, but with her name still inscribed upon it. "May I keep that?" Asia asked from the doorway, one hand resting upon her abdomen, the other supporting her lower back. They showed no deference to her distress or to her delicate condition, but tucked the precious relic of her brother into a bag and carried it off.

When the search finished, the officers departed, but armed guards took up positions around the house, entirely surrounding it.

If the assassin John Wilkes Booth sought refuge there, they would have their man.

On Saturday morning one week after President Lincoln died, Lucy sat in her family's sitting room looking out the window upon Pennsylvania Avenue, one newspaper lying open on her lap, others stacked on the table at her right hand. She had scarcely left the suite since that terrible night, taking her meals on a tray rather than creating a spectacle in the dining room, swathing herself in a heavy black veil when she went on her daily walk with her mother and sister. In a city full of mourners, their somber attire attracted little notice, granting Lucy the momentary relief of anonymity.

Earlier that week, the Hales had joined the nearly thirty thousand shocked and grieving citizens who had paid their last respects to President Lincoln as he had lain in state in the East Room of the White House, watched over by an honor guard of a dozen officers, including two generals. Commencing at half past nine o'clock in the morning and lasting well into the evening, the slow, solemn procession had filed past the president's casket, richly ornamented in silver and resting upon a black catafalque beneath a black canopy. The Hales had not attended the small, private funeral service that had taken place the following day, but they had observed the funeral procession that had carried the president's remains to the Capitol, where thousands more had paid their respects as he had lain in state in the rotunda all the next day. On April 21—only one day prior—a nine-car funeral train bedecked with bunting, crepe, and a portrait of Mr. Lincoln on the engine set out from Washington on a seventeen-hundred-mile journey west to Springfield, carrying the remains of the president and his young son Willie, who had died of typhoid fever at the White House more than three years before. The train was scheduled to stop at twelve cities along the circuitous route, and tens of thousands were expected to meet it, to mourn and to bid farewell to their fallen leader.

Lucy went numb with horror when she thought of the vast, immeasurable grief that one man, the man she loved, had inflicted upon an entire nation.

She wondered where he was. Although her parents urged her to ignore news and rumors, a strange compulsion forced her to try to trace his path from Washington, but the reports of sightings were so scattered and contradictory that it was no use. She suspected John was trying to make his way to Mexico, where the Austrian-born Emperor Maximilian had promised sanctuary and large bounties to fugitive Confederates, but it was difficult to imagine him starting a new life in a foreign country when he had made himself irredeemably despised in his homeland.

It was difficult to imagine that he would even complete the journey safely. Lucy doubted he would ever find more than a temporary refuge in his beloved Virginia, or in any other Southern state, for that matter. If John were in a place where he could read the newspapers, he would probably be shocked to discover what enormous outrage and worry his terrible act had provoked in the South, at least according to the Southern press, as reprinted in the Washington papers. The *Richmond Whig* declared, "The heaviest blow which has ever fallen upon the people of the south has descended," noting that Mr. Lincoln had toured the smoldering city in the aftermath of the Confederate evacuation and had not been accosted, proof that citizens of the erstwhile Southern capital had not wished any harm to befall him. Surely many ardent Confederates had cheered the announcement of Mr. Lincoln's death, but most people seemed appalled and dismayed, and many suggested that shooting an unarmed man in the back of the head while he watched a play was an act of profound cowardice. That sentiment, Lucy knew, would offend John most of all.

Even if rebel sympathizers were helping John in his flight, he would know no rest until he surrendered or was captured. Eventually a loyal Unionist would spot him, or an erstwhile rebel would be tempted by the promise of reward to betray him. Two days before, Secretary of War Edwin Stanton had issued a proclamation offering a fifty-thousand-dollar reward for John's capture, as well as twenty-five thousand apiece for his accomplices David Herold and John Surratt. Other bounties would be awarded for information that led to the arrest of any of the conspirators. But Secretary Stanton promised punishment as well. Anyone found to be harboring or concealing the fugitives would be considered an accomplice and would be subject to a trial by military commission.

Eventually, if it had not happened already, her once-adored John would find himself without friends. Even his own brother Edwin had inadvertently denounced him before the public when Henry Jarrett, the manager of the Boston Theatre, divulged to the press a private letter Edwin had sent him in the aftermath of the assassination. "The news of the morning has made me wretched indeed," Edwin had written, "not only because I have received the unhappy tidings of the suspicions of a brother's crime, but because a good man and a most justly honored and patriotic ruler has fallen in an hour of national joy by the hand of an assassin. The memory of the thousands who have fallen on the field in our country's defense during this struggle cannot be forgotten by me even in this, the most distressing day of my life. While mourning in common with all other loyal hearts the death of the President, I am oppressed by a private woe not to be expressed in words." Mr. Jarrett declared that his purpose in disclosing the letter was to prove Edwin Booth's steadfast loyalty to the Union and his absolute innocence of complicity in the crime, but when Lucy imagined John's reaction to the letter, her heart broke for him anew.

With a sigh, she returned her attention to the *New York Tribune* spread open on her lap, her gaze falling upon a column titled "A Chapter of Recent History," which promised news of Virginia rebels, Secretary Seward's condition, and the conspirators' plot. Yes, Lucy thought grimly, she ought to study that last report, so she could better understand how she had missed the signs of her beloved John's abhorrent intentions.

She scanned the column for the most pertinent piece, her brow furrowing when she read that unspecified evidence proved that there were ten conspirators involved in the plot, and that they had met in Memphis to draw lots to select the one who would kill the president—which seemed terribly farfetched to her, contradicting nearly everything else already confirmed about the plot—

But she froze, unable to blink or draw breath, when she read, "The unhappy lady—the daughter of a New-England Senator—to whom Booth was affianced, is plunged into profoundest grief, but with womanly fidelity, is slow to believe him guilty of this appalling crime, and asks, with touching pathos, for evidence of his innocence."

She trembled violently, unable to tear her gaze away. She heard a low moan of anguish that rose in pitch and intensity, and only when her mother and sister came running and seized her by the shoulders and shook her did she realize the tormented wail came from her own throat.

Her sister brought her water. Her mother pried the paper from her grasp and found the article that had so distressed her. They urged her to lie down, but anger and distress filled her with a strange surge of energy and she paced the room instead. Who would have divulged her secrets to the press? Not her family. Someone on the hotel staff? Someone in her father's employ? Some vindictive, spiteful, gossipy creature listening at doors?

Her father was summoned, and after he read the article, his gaze turned stony and furious, and yet when he placed his hand on Lucy's, his voice was gentle. "The article does not mention you by name," he said. "A handful of people who have seen you together may identify you as that unhappy lady, but this brief paragraph is buried on the fifth page, and hardly anyone will see it."

"But it will provoke curiosity and spark gossip," said Lucy shakily. "You know how these things happen. That brief paragraph will be reprinted in papers all across the North, and the South too perhaps, and before long some enterprising reporter hungry for notoriety will nose about until he has a name to print. 'The daughter of a New England senator'—it will be an easy mystery to solve."

"Lucy, I'm so sorry," said Lizzie, wringing her hands. "Papa, Mama, I meant to spare you distress, but—"

"What is it, Lizzie, dear?" asked Mama.

Without a word, Lizzie hurried off to the bedchamber she and Lucy shared and returned moments later with a newspaper folded open to the second page. "This is yesterday's *Springfield Republican*," she said tremulously, handing the paper to her mother and indicating an article near the top.

As their mother read, their father came and peered over her shoulder. "Well, there it is," he said flatly.

Steeling herself, Lucy held out her hand, and after a moment's hesitation, her mother gave her the paper. Familiar names leapt off the page: "It is stated and not yet authoritatively contradicted, though we are confident it ought to be, that J. Wilkes Booth was to have been married soon to a daughter of John P. Hale of New Hampshire. Aside from his recent heinous crime Booth wasn't the kind of man that any young lady of character would have noticed, much less married."

Her father strode over to the table beside Lucy's chair, leafed through the stack of newspapers she had not yet read, and took out one. He scanned each page, and Lucy's heart plummeted when he scowled and shook his head. " 'It cannot be denied,'" he read aloud, " 'we are afraid, that John Wilkes Booth, the assassin, was engaged to be married to a daughter of Senator Hale. He has been very much of a beau among the ladies of the National Hotel at Washington the past winter.' "

"It was not enough to report this ugly gossip once, that they had to do it again the next day?" said her mother, incredulous.

"We'll publicly disavow this," her father declared. "I'll compel the *Springfield Republican* to print a retraction. I'll contact my friends in the press and have them denounce this claim as lies and slander."

"How can we hope that anyone will believe it?" Lucy asked. "John and I have been seen together by too many. We've dined here at the hotel, we attended the theatre, and I cannot forget my shameful behavior at that New Year's Dance—"

Her father took her by the shoulders and held her at arm's length. "We will deny it," he said emphatically, holding her gaze. "If we say it clearly enough and often enough, people will accept that."

She shook her head, distressed. "It isn't right." It was a lie. She not only knew John, she loved him.

After all he had done, to her great remorse, she still loved him.

"It is right, and it is necessary," said her mother. Turning to her husband, she added, "Tell her what else happened."

"What?" she asked when their father hesitated. "What else has happened?"

Their father inhaled deeply. "The other day, two Confederate officers were being escorted through the streets from the train station to the office of the provost marshal, where I happened to be on business, and some fool shouted that they were Booth and this Surratt fellow. Never mind that Booth's face ought to be recognizable to all and sundry by now and that neither he nor Surratt served in the rebel army. The shout was taken up by others—'Booth! Booth!'—and a mob quickly formed and threatened to tear the men to pieces. The guards barely got their prisoners to the provost marshal's office in time, and a general and I were obliged to go out and convince the crowd that neither man was the president's assassin. If we had been unable to persuade them—" He shook his head. "I think they would have broken down the door and killed them both."

"Oh, how dreadful," said Lucy faintly, sinking into a chair.

Her father stooped beside her and reached for her hand. "So you see, dear Lucy, why it is dangerous for you to be associated with that man. Your friendship will not redeem him in the eyes of the public, but it can and will endanger you."

"And Papa too," said Lizzie, pale with dread. "And all of us."

Blinking away tears, Lucy looked from one beloved, stricken face to another, overwhelmed with remorse for the pain she had unwittingly inflicted upon them. She felt ashamed too, and unworthy of their steadfast love, for not one of them had confronted her with the report's most damaging revelation—that she and John were affianced, that she had become engaged to him without her parents' blessing or even their knowledge.

For a fleeting moment, her remorse and shame expanded to embrace John too, as she imagined him reading in the papers that she had denied knowing him; she imagined his bewilderment, his sorrow—but then she remembered his suicidal prostitute mistress, and she felt the tender region of her heart reserved for only him slowly ossifying.

"We shall do as you say," she said steadily, though every word tore at her soul. "It is no lie. I never truly knew John Wilkes Booth."

The Old Capitol Prison had once been a boardinghouse, significantly larger than Mary's on H Street, but the Yankee government had purchased it in the early months of the war to hold criminals and political prisoners when the other prisons became overfilled with captured Confederates. When it too had become dangerously overcrowded a little more than a year into the war, the Carroll Annex had been constructed to hold female criminals, Confederate spies both male and female, and Yankee deserters. It had been designed to accommodate one thousand prisoners, but by the time Mary, Anna, Nora, and Olivia were locked up inside, it contained more than twenty-seven hundred.

Each cell in the Carroll Annex housed two women, and to Mary's great relief, after a few days of anguish and calling out to each other through the walls, she and Anna were permitted to share a cell. Anna's fragile, desperate state alarmed Mary, for although her daughter had always had a nervous temperament, under the strain of incarceration and questioning she had become so anxious and fearful that Mary worried she might have a breakdown if she were not released soon.

Mary summoned up reserves of courage and fortitude for her daughter's sake, determined to make the best of their situation until the detectives finally concluded that Junior had not attempted to murder Secretary Seward or anyone else, and that he had been hundreds of miles from Ford's Theatre on the night of the assassination. "It's only a matter of time until the truth comes out and we will be released," she assured Anna, but with each passing day her words lost more of their power to comfort.

It did not help that their living conditions were utterly deplorable. Their cell had two barred windows that looked out upon the prison yard, where the inmates were permitted to take their daily exercise, but since they let in very little light and air, they did little to relieve the stifling darkness. Beneath the windows stood several barrels the warden had provided for their use, one to hold food, a second to store their few personal belongings, and a third to contain their own waste—hence the barrel's position by the window, though there was insufficient breeze to carry away the stench. The walls, floors, and even the ceiling were covered in dirt, soot, mildew, and grease, with spiderwebs in every corner dangling insect carcasses. Long ago, perhaps when the building had first opened, two of the walls had been papered in a large floral pattern, but the damp air had spoiled the adhesive, and the paper bulged away from the walls in some places and hung in grimy, tattered strips from others. Mary and Anna were each assigned to an iron bed with a straw mattress and were issued a pillow, sheets, and a coarse brown blanket, but although the sheets, though worn, appeared clean, the pillowcases were bloodstained, and the mattresses and blankets were infested with vermin.

It was impossible to keep themselves clean, and Mary lived in terror that Anna would contract dysentery or typhoid.

They heard the other inmates during the day, coughing, weeping, shouting complaints to the guards and encouragement to one another through the walls and through the narrow crack beneath the doors. At night, Mary's fitful sleep was repeatedly broken by harrowing shrieks of women caught in the throes of nightmare, by the scurrying of rats, and by Anna's sobs. The only time they saw their fellow prisoners was during daily exercise, when they could walk about the flat, barren yard, their faces turned up to the sun, inhaling deeply of air that did not reek of waste and filth and unwashed bodies. The guards permitted them to talk as long as they did not shout, so it was in the yard that they acquired news of the prison and the world outside. They gossiped about other prisoners, what crimes they had allegedly committed, who had broken down during interrogations, who languished in a sickbed, who had been released.

Mary and Anna learned that Olivia was one of these fortunate few, for she had been released after spending only a night or two in prison. Nora too had been released, but she had enjoyed only a few days of freedom before she had been arrested again and returned to her cell, without a word of explanation ever given. Her wealthy father regularly brought her large hampers of food, clean clothes, and comfortable blankets, but Nora suspected the guards kept at least half of what he delivered. Even so, Nora smuggled food from her precious stores as well as scraps of newspaper to Mary and Anna whenever they found themselves in the yard together. Though Nora was three years younger than Anna, she bore the rigors and deprivations of their horrid circumstances much better than Anna did, and Mary was glad to see Anna's melancholy lift, albeit fleetingly, whenever she was reunited with her friend.

Mary, Anna, and Nora were interrogated, sometimes several times a day, until they were thoroughly exhausted and felt as if their brains had been put through the mangle. The officers demanded information about Junior, Mr. Booth, Mr. Payne, and other men they had never heard of, queried them about papers and letters discovered in the boardinghouse, showed them cartes de visite uncovered during the search of their rooms, pictures of Confederate generals emblazoned with the Confederate flag and bold slogans. "You do know that this is what the assassin John Wilkes Booth shouted after he murdered the president, do you not?" one officer snarled as she showed Mary a card emblazoned with the inscription *Sic Semper Tyrannis*.

"I did not know that, sir," she replied. "I had never seen that card before you showed it to me."

Although they were questioned separately, Mary and Anna were able to converse freely in their cell and with Nora in the yard. Mary urged them to be evasive, to answer simply, to avoid getting caught in a trap of lies, to protect themselves and one another. The younger women nodded solemnly in reply, their expressions bleak, their courage faltering.

Mary prayed they could hold out until time and truth exonerated them.

· · ·

The arrival of Abraham Lincoln's funeral train in Philadelphia was announced by the firing of cannon and a salvo of minute guns, which startled Asia as she sat on the sofa trying to coax little Adrienne into a nap. Only later did she learn that a soldier had been accidentally killed in the exercise, and she wondered bitterly if her brother would be blamed for his death too.

Clarke, who had voted twice for Mr. Lincoln and deeply mourned his passing, attended the memorial services, with a pair of detectives following conspicuously after him. Later, at supper, he told Asia and June how thousands of mournful citizens had lined the streets to honor the martyred president as his funeral cortege had made its slow and solemn journey from the train station to Independence Hall. "Every flag along the route was at half staff and heavily draped," Clarke reflected, his comedian's malleable face sculpted into lines of grief. "Every house and storefront along the way was quiet and swathed in black. The dismal tolling of the bells, the mournful dirges of the bands— every face was wet with tears, from the youngest children weeping for Father Abraham to the most hardened veteran grieving for his fallen commander in chief."

Asia and June exchanged a long look across the table, a silent agreement to let Clarke talk uninterrupted. Crisis and tragedy had transformed her husband, Asia thought, or perhaps they had revealed the man he always had been, with weaknesses of character she had not allowed herself to see. Sleepy, the boy from Baltimore who had walked her to school, would have realized that his long narration of the nation's grief would upset his listeners, the elder siblings of the villain responsible for it. This new Clarke was someone else, someone she scarcely recognized.

Clarke had waited in line for three hours before he had entered Independence Hall, and many of the other roughly thirty thousand mourners had waited even longer. The president's casket had been placed on an oblong platform covered in black cloth in the center of the hall, opposite the old Independence bell. The same Stars and Stripes that had covered the casket during the funeral procession had been folded back over the foot and covered in wreaths of brilliantly colored flowers. "The lid of the casket been removed far enough so that we could view his head and shoulders," said Clarke, pausing to clear his throat, his eyes shining with tears. "He seemed to be in perfect repose, as if he were peacefully sleeping. And I say that if any man earned eternal peace, it is Mr. Lincoln, although it should not have come so soon— no, not on the eve of his greatest victory. He should have been granted enough time here on Earth to see peace restored to a reunited nation. That should have been his just reward."

Asia made no reply, not a look, not a sound.

A few days later, citing suspicious comments discovered in letters June had written to Wilkes, a special agent with the Fourth District of Philadelphia appeared at their door with an order from the War Department for June's arrest.

Asia was horrified, but June seemed only dumbfounded. "Do you know what letter this order refers to?" he asked. The agent curtly replied that he was not there to answer questions, but to interview June and convey him to Washington. Then, with a pitying glance for Asia, he said that although his orders were to take June away in irons, he would allow June to walk out unencumbered. June thanked him, and in a state of considerable agitation, he gathered a few belongings, kissed Asia, and departed on foot, the special agent at his side.

Frantic, Asia sent a servant running to the theatre to alert Clarke, and by calling in a few favors he was able to learn that June was being held at the Station House on Thirteenth and Brandywine Streets. That evening, he would be taken by carriage to the depot, where he and the special agent who had arrested him would depart on the eleven o'clock train for the capital. Clarke demanded to see his brother-in-law, but his request was denied. All the authorities would reveal was that a letter had been received at Ford's Theatre, in his handwriting and signed "June," advising Wilkes to abandon "the oil business," because it was unlikely to be profitable now that Richmond had been captured and General Lee had surrendered. The "oil business," according to another man implicated in the plot, was a code phrase the conspirators had used for the scheme to capture Lincoln.

"Wilkes received all his mail at Ford's Theatre because he traveled so much," protested Asia to a guard standing outside her front door, in vain hope that he would pass on the information. "Wilkes truly was involved in the oil business. One of your fellow officers carried away the deeds to his properties when the house was searched!"

The guard gave Asia only one impassive glance in reply.

Soon thereafter, Clarke was arrested. "On what grounds?" he demanded as the officers placed him in handcuffs, an indignity they had spared June. He was told that President Johnson had personally ordered his arrest upon learning that the assassin John Wilkes Booth had left his incriminating letters at Clarke's home in his safe. Shocked, Clarke struggled to speak as the officer led him from the house, and for a moment Asia's heart was in her throat, for she expected him to declare that Wilkes had left the papers with her, not him. "Telegraph your mother and tell her to come to you," he called over his shoulder instead, and Asia's eyes filled with tears as she promised him she would, her heart warming to him as it had not since the first months of their marriage.

The guards posted around her house forbade Asia to leave, but she was permitted to send a servant to telegraph her mother. He had not yet returned from the errand when a carriage and pair pulled up in front of the house and a young officer emerged and knocked upon the door. "Are you Mrs. Clarke?" he inquired when she answered. He looked to be no more than one and twenty years.

"I am."

"Madam, you are under arrest by order of the War Department. You may pack one small satchel with necessary items, and then I am to escort you at once to Washington."

"Are you mad?" Asia exclaimed, gesturing to her ample midsection. "My doctor says I am not even supposed to be out of bed! And who would watch my three young children if I were to go? You?"

The young officer looked discomfited. "I'm sorry, madam, but I'm under strict orders."

"I must assume that the person who issued those orders has no idea that I am with child," she snapped. "Is that not possible? Should you not inquire before hauling me away?"

A flush had risen in the young man's cheeks. "I'll—I'll have to consult my superiors," he stammered. "In the meantime, you should not attempt to leave the premises."

"Leaving the premises is precisely the last thing I want to do," she said, and closed the door in his face.

Within an hour, the young officer returned and informed her that she need not accompany him to Washington if she could procure a statement from her doctor confirming that she was unable to travel. Her longtime physician, who had seen her through her previous pregnancies and had tended the family through many an illness, could only with great difficulty be persuaded to come to examine her, presumably wanting nothing to do with a household under such suspicion and shame. But he did confirm the state of her health, and upon receipt of his telegram in Washington, she was informed that she had been placed under house arrest instead. Guards surrounded the residence, and a detective was assigned to accompany her constantly within the house, following her from room to room, observing her even when she simply sat and played with her children.

Her mail was carefully examined before she received it, and she had no way to determine if anything had been withheld from her. Newspapers were allowed, and she studied them thoroughly for news of her brothers and husband. June's arrest was described in abundant if not entirely accurate detail, and although there were reports of many sightings of Wilkes all over the known world, none of them was plausible, save a brief piece describing a bulletin from the War Department. St. Mary's, Prince George's, and Charles Counties in Maryland had been well known for their hostility to the government throughout the war, Secretary Stanton declared, and Wilkes had certainly fled in that direction, and if he escaped it would be due to assistance from rebel accomplices in the region. In addition, reports from informants rendered it "nearly certain that Booth's horse fell with him on Friday night and, it is believed, caused a fracture in one of his legs."

Asia felt a stab of pain to imagine Wilkes suffering so. She wished he would surrender, but the whole country had become so frenzied with rage that she could not imagine how he could approach his pursuers without hazarding his own death, even if he lay down his weapons and waved a white flag. His circumstances seemed utterly hopeless, and yet she prayed for his deliverance.

On the morning of April 26, Asia lay on a sofa in the parlor, eyes closed, willing the hours to fly past. Her mother had received her telegram and had replied to say that she would come as soon as Edwin could arrange an escort. Asia expected her that afternoon, and she prayed the trains would run on time.

A knock sounded on the door, startling her, but before she could rise, the maid hurried past and answered. Asia felt too lightheaded to sit up, so she was still reclining when Thomas Hemphill, Clarke's and Edwin's business partner at the Walnut Street Theatre, entered the room, pale and haggard. He could not meet her gaze or even greet her, and his gait was so unsteady that he was obliged to grasp the edge of a table to stay on his feet.

She knew at once what he could not bring himself to tell her. "Is it over?" she asked quietly.

"Yes, madam," he choked out.

"Taken?"

"Yes."

She steeled herself. "Dead?"

"Yes, madam."

She could not draw breath. She rolled over on her side and lay with her face against the wall, her heart pounding slowly, but with such great force that she thought it would burst from her breast. Silently she prayed, thanking God that it was over, hoping against hope that her beloved brother had not suffered.

Wilkes was gone. Her childhood companion, the confidant of her youth, the beautiful man by which she measured all others, was gone. The brightest star in her sky had flared once, blindingly bright, and had gone dark.

Mary Ann agreed that it would be unwise for Edwin to escort her to Philadelphia. Although his influential friends had interceded on his behalf so that he was not forced to join June and Clarke in the Old Capitol Prison, he had voluntarily placed himself under house arrest, not only to avoid provoking suspicions that he intended to flee the country, but for his own safety. Every day he received letters condemning him for his brother's crime, threats that he would be murdered, his home burned. "Revolvers are already loaded to shoot you down," wrote one fiend, signing his name as Outraged Humanity. "You are a traitor to this government. Herein you have fair warning. We hate the name of Booth."

"You cannot travel to Philadelphia alone," said Edwin tiredly. He had resigned himself to accepting the hatred of the people. He understood that they were compelled to pour out their vitriol upon someone, and John was beyond their reach. Edwin had confided to Mary Ann that he believed he would never again be able to take to the stage. His brilliant career was over.

"I will escort you, Mrs. Booth," offered Launt Thompson, the celebrated sculptor and Edwin's loyal friend. He and Mr. Aldrich had hardly left Edwin alone for a moment since he had returned to New York.

Edwin thanked him sincerely, and Mary Ann swiftly packed a bag, and after swathing herself in a heavy black veil, she embraced Edwin and Rosalie and set out on Mr. Thompson's arm. He stowed her luggage in the carriage, helped her aboard, and settled himself in the seat facing her, and soon they were off, heading toward the Hudson River and the ferry. A train leaving from Jersey City would have them in Philadelphia before nightfall.

As they drove through Manhattan, over the sounds of the horses' hooves Mary Ann heard what sounded like scores of newsboys hawking extra editions, their voices shrill with excitement. "What are they shouting about?" Mary Ann wondered aloud.

"Heaven knows." Mr. Thompson leaned over to shut the windows and close the curtains. "With so many of them yelling at once, it's difficult to make out, isn't it?"

At last they reached the ferry dock. Mr. Thompson urged her to wait in the carriage while he attended to her luggage, and when he returned to help her descend, he hurried her down the pier, aboard the ship, and into a seat in a secluded corner of the deck so quickly that she hardly had time to catch her breath. "If you'll excuse me for a moment, madam," he said, and darted off. She watched, bemused, as he left the ship, ran down the pier, vanished inside a news shop, and returned with a newspaper folded beneath his arm, mere moments before the ferry set out.

He said very little as they crossed the water, and he did not glance at his paper even once. An intense sensation of dread stole over her, but she willed herself to remain calm, determined to extend this last little time before the unknown blow fell.

The crossing completed, they collected her luggage, disembarked, walked to the railroad platform, and boarded the train. There Mr. Thompson regarded her solemnly and gave her the newspaper. "You will need all your courage now," he said. "The paper in your hand will tell what, unhappily, we must all wish to hear."

Over the sudden roaring in her ears, she became aware of the passengers all around them, talking in varying shades of excitement, anger, gladness, and shock about the assassin John Wilkes Booth. She shut out the clamor of voices and unfolded the paper and read of how only yesterday her darling boy had taken shelter for the night in a tobacco barn on a farm in Virginia, how Union officers had surrounded him and had demanded that he come out, how his companion had obeyed but he had not, how the officers had set the barn ablaze, how John had emerged rather than burn, how a zealous officer had shot him through the neck, how he had fallen where he stood.

How he had died in the early morning hours, calling for her.

She was thankful for the heavy veil that hid her anguish from the world.

For five days Mary, Anna, and Nora had endured especially grueling interrogations, questions that twisted and turned back upon themselves so that Mary found herself dizzier, more bewildered, the more she tried to hold her ground. She loathed the officers who tormented her, despised them for how they treated Anna, humiliating the poor girl by laying out on the table before her items they had found beneath her bed—sketches of Mr. Booth costumed as Shakespeare's Romeo, illustrations of her initials and his intertwined within wreaths of rosebuds, pages upon which she had written "Elizabeth Susanna Booth" over and over again in her finest hand, and of course, the photograph of Mr. Booth she had been unable to bring herself to discard. Mary was grimly satisfied when she learned that Anna's profound embarrassment had rendered her even more reluctant to speak to the officers than before, not that she had much to tell them. Mary had been careful to divulge as little as possible to her tenderhearted, innocent girl.

On a Wednesday afternoon, more than a week after her arrest, Mary was again brought into the interrogation room, where she was startled to discover the warden himself awaiting her. "Be seated," he instructed her, and by recently acquired habit, she promptly obeyed. "Perhaps you have already heard the news out of Virginia this morning."

Mary shrugged and offered him a plaintive frown. "I'm afraid that I have not. We are so cut off from the outside world in here."

"Last night John Wilkes Booth was found, and when he refused to surrender, he was shot. He died early this morning."

"I see." Mary was careful to keep her face impassive, though she felt an intense pang of grief and loss. "Forgive the question, sir, but what has this to do with me?"

His eyebrows rose. "I understand that you and Mr. Booth were great friends, and your daughter too was very fond of him."

Mary managed a small, wry smile. "As innocent girls sometimes can be of handsome actors they scarcely know."

"Indeed." The warden put his head to one side and regarded her curiously. "Mrs. Surratt, I had been told that you are cold and unwomanly stoic, but I had not believed it until now. I expected you to show more sorrow or regret regarding Booth's death."

She hesitated. When Mr. Booth decided to kill the president, he surely had known that it might cost him his life. If he had to die, it was a mercy that he had escaped the hangman's noose. She could not imagine any worse death than hanging—except to burn as Saint Joan of Arc had done. Of course, she could not tell the warden that—

"Mrs. Surratt?" the warden prompted.

Startled, she quickly composed herself and held his gaze steadily. "Sir, my only regret regarding Mr. Booth's death is that he died before he could exonerate my son. Then you would be obliged to admit my son's innocence and release me and my daughter."

The warden gazed back at her in genuine surprise. "Madam, I hardly know what to say. You seem utterly unaware of the serious nature of the allegations against you."

"What do you mean?" she asked, the barest tremor in her voice.

"I'm astounded that you did not know," he said. "You are not being held on account of your son's crimes, but for your own."

H e cannot be dead."
Lucy's voice sounded dull and lifeless in her own ears. The assertion had become mechanical by repetition, and yet they were the only words she could speak.

"Oh, Lucy," said Lizzie, anxious, stroking her hair, kissing her brow. "Perhaps it's for the best."

Lucy pressed a handkerchief to her lips to muffle a sob. Lizzie meant well, but it was not, could not be for the best. As devastated as she had been to learn that her beloved John was a murderer, the thought that he was lost to her forever staggered her.

They sat on the sofa in their suite at the National Hotel, Lucy reclining in her sister's arms, newspapers scattered on the floor around them. Several of the papers, Lucy knew, had printed the assertions of a correspondent identified only as "one competent to give a correct statement" denying that she and John had been engaged, insisting that there was no foundation to any such claims, and requesting that, in justice to Senator Hale and his family, the editors would give the denial the same publicity they had given to the falsehoods. Two days before, the *Daily National Republican* had responded in even stronger terms, insisting that not only were the allegations without the slightest shred of truth, but that "Booth attempted to force his attentions upon MISS HALE; but she always manifested a decided aversion to the handsome villain." Only the *Springfield Republican*, the first paper to identify Lucy by name, had resisted the pressure to repudiate their original story. "The story that has gained such wide circulation that Booth was engaged to be married to Senator Hale's daughter is formally denied here," their Washington correspondent noted archly. "I hear there is positive evidence, however, of its truth; but this evidence is in private letters, which cannot be used."

Lucy had to give them grudging respect for their defiance, although it infuriated her father.

How many times in how many papers had she insisted through those anonymous proxies that she had not loved John, that she had not agreed to marry him? Even Peter had denied Jesus only three times. She had denied John a thousandfold more, and now he was dead.

"He cannot be dead," she whispered. Lizzie made no reply except to draw her closer.

Later that afternoon, she overheard her parents talking while they thought she slept, overcome by the medicinal brandy they insisted she drink to help her endure the shock. Among the personal effects taken from John's corpse was his pocket diary from 1864, in which were discovered the photographs of five women: four actresses and Lucy. "I've received assurances from the War Department that Lucy's name will be omitted from the official reports," she heard her father say. "They will do all they can to make sure the public never learns that he carried Lucy's picture."

John had carried her picture, Lucy thought distantly, a rekindled flame of love and longing warming her heart. And four more of four other women, she thought next, and the small, fragile light extinguished. When she saw John again, she would confront him about the photographs. Why did he carry the portraits of four actresses if he intended to marry Lucy? For that matter, why did he have a prostitute mistress? He had much to explain, not the least of which was whether he had ever truly loved her, or if he had only used her to get closer to President Lincoln.

When next she saw him, she would demand answers.

That evening, as they ate supper in their suite, too weary of curious stares to subject themselves to more in the dining room, her parents talked quietly of her father's appointment as the minister to Spain, which the new president intended to uphold.

Lucy sat in silence, touching her fork to her food now and then but tasting nothing. "I invited John to visit us in Madrid," she interrupted suddenly, her voice soft and slow. It seemed as if her words would take a very long time to cross the table to reach her family.

Her parents exchanged a look. "John Hay?"

She thought for a moment, remembering. "Oh, yes. I invited him too, and Robert Lincoln. But I meant John Booth."

Lizzie watched her, stricken, while her parents exchanged looks of profound dismay. "Lucy, darling," her father said, reaching across the table to take her hand, "Booth is dead. He died this morning. You know that."

"He cannot be dead," she said, puzzled. She picked up her fork again and took a bite of pheasant. It tasted of nothing.

Early the next morning, her father shook her awake, told her to dress and veil herself and to fetch her shawl, and then, while her mother and sister slept, he quietly led her from the suite and outside to a waiting carriage. He did not say where they were going, but she decided it did not matter, so she did not ask. Despite her disinterest, she was mildly surprised when they arrived at the Washington Navy Yard, although upon reflection, her father's longstanding ties with the navy made their destination no more unusual than any other. Two naval officers met the carriage, and they exchanged a few quiet words with her father before escorting them down the wharf and aboard a dinghy flying the Stars and Stripes. The sun had risen, but the wind was steady and cold as they crossed the water to a ship anchored in the Eastern Branch. She shivered and drew her shawl tightly about her head and shoulders.

"We're almost there," her father said, the first words he had spoken to her since they had boarded the carriage. She nodded, her trepidation steadily rising as they approached the ship—the *Montauk*, she read on the bow. It was no easy matter to climb aboard on her trembling, unsteady legs, but the naval officers assisted her, and her father offered her his arm once they stood on the deck.

"This way, Senator," said one of the officers. He turned on his heel and strode off, and Lucy was propelled forward on her father's arm as he followed after. She saw several guards stationed at equidistant points around what seemed to be a carpenter's bench, upon which lay an oblong form, its nature indistinct beneath a heavy brown horse blanket.

"Papa, no," Lucy murmured when they were no more than two paces away, but her father relentlessly guided her forward. Her breath came in soft, shallow gasps as they halted at one end of the bench, and she clung to her father's arm as the officer folded the blanket down to expose the head of a man—no, of a corpse, with silky dark hair, alabaster skin taking on a grayish cast, and a full, sensuous mouth drawn back in a rictus of pain.

Lucy shrieked and flung herself upon her dearest John, sobbing, pressing her ear to his chest, desperately searching for a heartbeat, but there was no sound but her own cries, and he was cold, so very cold and still and silent.

"Lucy, darling." Her father grunted from effort as he tore her away from her beloved and gripped her shoulders tightly. "He is gone. John Wilkes Booth is dead. Do you see his lifeless body? Do you understand?"

"Papa, stop," she choked out. "This is cruel."

"This is necessary," he replied, a tremor in his voice. "My darling girl, he is dead. You must accept that."

"I can't."

"You must. You will." His grip on her shoulders tightened. "He never cared for you. You were nothing to him but a means to an end. He must be dead to you as he is to the rest of the world. You must sever all ties with him in your heart and mind and memory."

Her father's words resonated with truth, and the sharpness of John's betrayal cut through her grief. "Oh, Papa." She threw herself into his embrace, weeping, her legs giving out beneath her.

He held her tightly, kissing her brow and promising her over and over again that she would be all right, that she was not alone, that she was loved, that she would always be loved.

In the evenings, as a reward for good behavior, the female inmates were permitted to socialize in a large room on the second floor. Mary had made one good friend among the prisoners, Nora's cellmate, a woman in her mid-thirties named Virginia Lomax. Handsome and self-possessed, Virginia was an alleged Confederate spy who had been arrested as a suspect in the assassination conspiracy, although privately she had confided to Mary that she had not been involved, but only wished she had been.

For Anna's sake, Mary never missed a social hour, and the last Sunday evening in April found her near the window chatting quietly with Virginia while Anna played a memory game with Nora and several other younger ladies in the center of the room. Pale and peaked, Anna was smiling wanly at something Nora had said and was just about to take her turn in the game when suddenly they heard racing footsteps and several soldiers burst into the room.

Instinctively, the women recoiled from the door, some seizing the hand of a friend, others uttering quick shrieks of alarm before fear silenced them. "Mrs. Mary Surratt," the officer in front bellowed. "Step forward."

Steeling herself, emboldened by Virginia's reassuring touch on her shoulder, Mary emerged from the crowd. "I am Mrs. Surratt."

"Gather your personal effects and put on your cloak and bonnet," he ordered. "You're being transferred to the Arsenal Penitentiary immediately."

A chorus of gasps went up from the room. Mary's heart thudded, but she slammed her mask of serenity in place and nodded to the officer. Turning, she embraced a horror-stricken Virginia, kissed her cheek, and murmured, "Please look after Anna."

As Virginia mutely nodded, Mary heard quick, light footsteps, and suddenly Anna's arms were around her. "No," Anna cried, clinging to her with all her strength. "Don't go! Don't leave me here alone!"

"Anna, my darling," she said, low and steady, glancing over her daughter's head to the stern-faced guards quickly approaching, "you're going to have to be very brave."

"Mama, oh, Mama!"

The guards seized Anna and demanded that she release her grasp, but Anna refused, sobbing hysterically, tightening her embrace until Mary almost could not draw breath. Before long the guards wrenched Anna away, and while two of them held the frantic girl by the arms and shoulders, thrashing and wailing, another propelled Mary to her cell, where she collected her shawl, bonnet, and Bible, then followed him back down the hall past the room where she heard her daughter desperately weeping. A few of the inmates emerged to bid her farewell in passing, tears in their eyes, sympathy in their touch. "Pray for me," she asked each woman, hugging her Bible to her chest. "Pray for me."

The guard who rode with Mary in the carriage closed the windows and drew the curtains to deny her a glimpse of the world outside, but she could imagine the route, and she dreaded every turn of the wheels that brought her closer to her foreboding destination. The Arsenal Penitentiary lay about two miles south of the Capitol on the northern tip of the Greenleaf Peninsula, the Washington Channel of the Potomac River on its western side, the Anacostia River curving along the south and east. Numbly, she cooperated mechanically as she was processed and escorted to a private cell on the third floor, Number 200. "You're among friends," the guard told her nastily as he unlocked the door, shoved it open, and waved her into the small, dark, cramped room.

"Who?" Mary asked, bewildered. The cell reeked of urine and terror.

"Seven of your fellow conspirators are locked up here too, all those who yet live and have been captured." He jerked his head in the direction they had come. "Payne and Atzerodt are down the hall, Herold's on the third floor." Grinning, he gestured above and behind himself, the direction so vague he could have meant anywhere in the building. "Arnold, O'Laughlen, Mudd, and Spangler are here too, but you won't see them, nor will you speak to them."

As the door clanged shut and the key turned in the lock, Mary sank down heavily upon the musty bed, tears springing to her eyes—of despair and loneliness, yes, but also of overwhelming relief. They did not have Junior—at least, they did not have him at the Arsenal.

A pounding on the door woke her early the next morning, groggy, her face damp as if she had wept in her sleep. Hastily she tried to clean her face with the edge of the bedsheet, tried to finger-comb her hair and braid it without the benefit of brush or looking glass, and smoothed the plain muslin dress she had been issued at the Carroll Annex. She was fed a scant breakfast alone in her cell, and afterward, guards took her to a small room where a stone-faced colonel informed her that she had been accused of conspiring to assassinate President Abraham Lincoln. He read aloud a statement that made her dizzy and sick as it informed her that she and a man called Dr. Mudd had been indicted for sheltering the conspirators and helping to plan the killing. President Johnson had decreed that the eight accused individuals would be tried not in a civilian court but before a military commission.

"I don't understand," Mary said shakily. "I don't understand what this means."

"You murdered President Lincoln," said the officer, while the guards looked on impassively. "You were involved in the attempted assassination of Secretary Seward, and you intended to assassinate other officers of the federal government at Washington City in wartime. That makes you subject to the jurisdiction of and lawfully triable before a military commission."

"But I wasn't," Mary protested. "I didn't. I never intended a murder."

His eyebrows rose as he leaned toward her. "Then what did you intend, Mrs. Surratt?"

Suddenly she remembered Junior, and she pressed her lips together and shook her head, blinking away her tears. She would give them nothing, she resolved, silently vehement. They had her, but they would not get her boy.

·   ·   ·

A prisoner in her own home, Asia mourned her beloved brother alone, unwilling to burden her young children with her grief. They would not remember their uncle Wilkes, which would perhaps prove to be a mercy in the years to come. She resolved to shield them as long as she could from the knowledge of how and why he had died, and she dreaded the day the truth would come out—in a jeering taunt from a bully at school, in a headline on the anniversary of Mr. Lincoln's death.

It was a torment to be denied Wilkes's remains so they might give him a proper funeral. Of all the family only Edwin and their mother were in a position to appeal to the government, and their mother had been too distraught to address them, and Edwin had firmly resolved not to. He seemed to think that whatever ignominious disposal Wilkes received was better than he deserved.

If Edwin should have a sudden change of heart, it would come too late. No one in the government had informed the family what had become of Wilkes's remains, so they relied upon the newspapers for information, but they presented two contradictory stories. The first, drawing upon the observations of witnesses gathered along the riverbank near the *Montauk*, stated that a large covered object resembling a coffin had been transferred from the ironclad to a steam tug, which had then headed down the Potomac. Soon thereafter the crowd watching from the shore had observed a large rowboat cast off from the tug and meander out into deeper waters, where the mysterious object had been dumped into the river. "Last night, the 27th of April, a small row boat received the carcass of the murderer," reported the *New York World*, among many others. "Two men were in it; they carried the body out into the darkness, and out of that darkness, it will never return. In the darkness, like his great crime, may it remain forever, impalpable, invisible, nondescript, condemned to that worse than damnation, annihilation."

Most of the papers Asia saw ran that story, but a scant few told another tale: "The navy-yard in Washington was yesterday closed against visitors, by order of the Department," a minority report began. "The body of Booth was quietly conveyed, last evening, to an ignominious burial place. The head and heart were removed prior to its burial."

Asia wept when she read the last—it was unnecessary to desecrate Wilkes's corpse, despite the severity of his crime—but she could not say whether one interment was preferable to the other, only that it would be better for his loved ones to know. The uncertainty was agonizing, infuriating, and Asia worried for her mother, knowing how she had found comfort through the years visiting the graves of her other lost children. In its righteous rage, the vindictive government would needlessly deny an innocent, grieving mother that small measure of comfort.

As the weeks passed, whenever she read about the trial of the eight conspirators—and it was covered in meticulous detail in the papers, every day—Asia could almost be grateful that Wilkes had perished rather than be subjected to the fresh horror of that public spectacle. Her mother pleaded with her not to follow the grim saga for the sake of her health, but Asia knew several of the defendants, those boyhood friends who had been pulled into the plot out of love and loyalty to Wilkes, and it was better to know what they suffered than to wonder and to imagine much worse. To her immeasurable relief, June and Clarke had not been implicated in the conspiracy, but her anger and indignation rose day by day when they were neither charged with a crime nor released. How much longer would her brother and husband languish in prison before the authorities realized they were innocent and let them go? Were they being held out of spite, as scapegoats for Wilkes, who was beyond the reach of their justice?

Scattered among the accounts of the trial proceedings were sensational, malicious stories of Wilkes, of the entire Booth family, tales spread by false friends as well as distant acquaintances who pretended to intimate knowledge of the Booths they had never had. The old stories of their father's eccentricities were retold, embellished with new exaggerations. One newspaper dredged up an old interview with the late Adelaide Delannoy and presented it to a public that had mostly forgotten her. Asia was astonished to read about herself too, that upon hearing the news of her brother's death, "Mrs. J. S. Clarke had gone mad, and was at present confined at the Asylum at West Philadelphia." Former neighbors harboring grudges or craving momentary fame turned ordinary childhood mischief into foreboding portents of future evil. The trench Wilkes and Asia had dug at The Farm in search of Indian relics was transformed into an underground cache of arms and ammunition. Silly Halloween pranks became the most egregious theft and vandalism. Everywhere, it seemed, except in Wilkes's beloved South, the papers teemed with the most preposterous adventures, peculiarities, and ill deeds of the vile Booth family.

If any friends and neighbors sympathized with them, they did so in silence. Few wrote, and none dared come to their door. One exception was Asia's longtime friend Jean Armstrong, ever faithful, who sent many comforting letters from Baltimore, and to her alone Asia poured out her grief, her misery, her loneliness. Then, after so many longtime friends had failed her, Asia received a letter from the actress Effie Germon, who had shared a stage with Wilkes years before. "Although a perfect stranger to you, I take the liberty of offering my sympathy and aid to you in your great sorrow and sickness," she wrote. "If my mother or myself can be of the slightest use to you in any way in this world we should be only too happy."

The unexpected kindness caught Asia entirely off guard, and she burst into such heart-wrenching sobs that the children's nurse came running to see who had been murdered or arrested this time. In the midst of her ceaseless, bitter anguish, Miss Germon's letter was a token of rare and unexpected friendliness in a world that despised Asia for her brother's crimes, and it was almost enough to revive her belief in human goodness.

In Washington the trial dragged on, witnesses were called, evidence presented. On May 27, without notice, explanation, or apology, Clarke was suddenly and unexpectedly released from prison, without ever being charged with any crime. Asia was elated when she received his telegram, and she and the servants and even the children prepared a wonderful homecoming for him, but her joy turned to shock when he crossed the threshold, haggard and hollow-eyed, sick and malnourished, aged beyond his years. She saw him straight to bed, and it was some days before he was restored enough to join the family at table or to play with the children. Whenever Asia thought of June, who had been sent to prison before Clarke and languished there still, she thought she would go mad from worry. She did not know how she could bear to live in her native country any longer, how she could possibly raise her children there. What hope had they of finding happiness in a nation where their uncle was the most hated, most notorious citizen in its history?

As soon as Edwin received word that Clarke had been set free, her brother, selfless in his despair, wrote to his old friend and longtime business partner urging him to dissolve all partnership with him. "My dear friend, you must not be bound in any way to one whose name and fame are irremediably clouded," he wrote in a subsequent letter, after Clarke flatly rejected the first. "You must sever all connection with me, theatrically and for ever now."

Asia respected Edwin for generously offering Clarke the chance to renounce their friendship at a time when he had all the world against him and needed every loyal friend he could name. But Clarke adamantly refused to repudiate him, and Asia was certain that she had never loved her husband more than when he wrote to her brother firmly insisting that he never mention it again.

"I am more grateful than words can express," she told Clarke fervently one evening as they retired for the night, blinking back tears as she settled her cumbersome body into bed. "I'll need a lifetime to express my thanks for your loyalty to my brother."

Standing at her bedside, Clarke gave her a faint, misshapen smile. "I won't require a lifetime," he said, his voice oddly pitched. "It can all be managed quickly and soon."

"What—" Suddenly uneasy, Asia propped herself up with a pillow. "What is it you do require, then?"

"I would like you to consent to a divorce."

She stared at him. "You can't mean that."

"I do. Your own brother urged me to sever ties with anyone with the name of Booth."

"He meant business ties, not matrimonial," she said sharply, "and I doubt he would have been so generous if he had known what you intended for me. In any case, my name is Clarke now."

"Divorcing you would be my only salvation."

"Clarke, I am soon to be delivered of your fourth child!"

"I'm aware of my obligations. I'll continue to provide for you and the children."

"No," she declared. "I will not consent to a divorce. You are speaking from emotion, not reason, and I won't endure it. You will not put me aside."

He watched her bleakly as her tears began to fall. "You condemn me to ruin if you refuse."

"I condemn myself to ruin if I consent."

He frowned, inhaled deeply, and shook his head. "I'll sleep in my study." He turned to go, but before he left the room he said to her over his shoulder, "This discussion is not finished."

"It is," she insisted. "It most certainly is."

But he had already shut the door behind him. She seemed to hear an echo of Wilkes's voice in the reverberations, a warning whisper that she was no more than a professional stepping-stone to Clarke, that her name was her dowry. Now Clarke reviled the very name upon which he had built his entire career, all his fame, his worldly success.

Shaking uncontrollably, she wrapped her arms around the child in her womb and rocked gently back and forth. She would never consent. She would not allow him in a moment of despair to doom her and the children to a miserable existence of poverty and shame.

It was her name he despised, not her. She had to believe that.

" 'My name, dear saint, is hateful to myself,' " she murmured to the empty room, " 'because it is an enemy to thee.' "

But the name of Booth was not hateful to her. Her brother had tarnished it, but it had been a good, proud, even revered name before Wilkes's strange fits of passion consumed him. It would be a grave sin if she allowed the world to forget her father's greatness because of her brother's crime.

Years before—a lifetime ago—she and Wilkes had resolved to write their father's biography, a token of the profound love and reverence with which they had regarded him in life, and had hoped to honor him in death. More recently, before Dottie was born, Asia had taken up the manuscript again, and after much tedious research, she had nearly completed it when the demands of motherhood had forced her to set it aside.

She knew then, as the sound of her husband's footsteps receded down the hallway, that she must complete the great work of writing the story of her revered father's life. In those dark days when so many tongues were free to calumniate her family, a faithful history of the renowned tragedian Junius Brutus Booth would confute the aspersions of unscrupulous men.

Asia would redeem the name of Booth in the eyes of the world, and in so doing, she would banish any thought her husband might have of divorcing her. She was innocent of any crime, and Clarke could not sentence her and the children to ignominy and destitution so that he could emerge from the shadow of Wilkes's crime unencumbered.

Clarke had evidently mistaken her for Edwin. She would never allow him to cut her loose to save himself.

The courtroom was established in a large hall on the second floor of the Arsenal Penitentiary, and when Mary was led inside with the seven men known to the world as her co-conspirators, she was struck by the smell of raw pine and fresh paint. The walls had been recently painted to impress the dignitaries of the government and the military who would attend at least a portion of the hearings, and new furniture had been swiftly constructed to accommodate the twelve members of the tribunal, the eight defendants, and the multitude of lawyers, clerks, stenographers, newspapermen, and spectators who were expected to fill the room for the duration of the trial.

The black iron bars on the windows stood out starkly against the fresh whitewash, reinforcing the bleak truth that Mary was trapped, at the mercy of men who despised her. She lowered her gaze, reluctant to sear the bars upon her mind's eye, and yet she would rather stare at them directly than wear a stifling hood as did the seven men. Instead of a thick hood she wore a heavy black veil, which she had donned willingly, trusting that it would offer her some protection from the curious stares of the many strangers filling the courtroom. The men wore manacles too, another encumbrance she had been exempted from on account of her sex, and when the guards showed them where to sit in the prisoners' dock, their chairs alternating with seats for the guards, Mary was startled when she was instead escorted to a place at the defense attorneys' table adjacent to the dock. A few weeks before, she would have dared to hope that in additional deference to womanhood, all the charges against her would summarily be dismissed, but the Arsenal had driven all hope and daring out of her. She felt broken down, humbled, fearful, despondent, and only the knowledge that Junior yet eluded capture kept her from breaking down entirely.

The prisoners' dock sat on a raised platform at the western end of the room, while the judge advocate and the military commission sat on both sides of a long table along the northern wall. In the center of the room facing the commissioners stood the witness stand, and beside that, a smaller table for the court reporter. Three other tables, two for clerks and one for evidence, were arranged nearby, a second long table for the press stood in the southeastern quarter, and chairs for spectators filled all the available space along the walls.

As the court was called to order, Mary resolved to keep her composure, fearful that her uncontrollable trembling and weeping would be interpreted as signs of guilt. Lightheaded from worry and lack of sleep, she found the proceedings confusing and difficult to follow—eight defendants prosecuted simultaneously, multiple lawyers querying and raising objections, witnesses offering testimony relevant to one defendant or several but not others—hours and hours of it, until her head spun. In desperation she resorted to silently reciting the rosary rather than paying close attention to the testimony, which her lawyers had strongly urged her to do.

She was devastated when the prosecution called Louis Weichmann, and when he began hesitantly answering their questions, she took no comfort in his obvious reluctance to label her a conspirator. He asserted that he had ever found her to be a pious, kind, and caring lady whom he regarded with affection. But he went on to say that she and Junior had fallen under the power of Mr. Booth's allure, and that they both had been more involved with the terrible plot than he had realized until it was too late. In condemning detail, he described her numerous meetings with Mr. Booth in the boardinghouse and her frequent trips to and from Surrattsville in the weeks leading up to the assassination, making the prosecutors smile in satisfaction and Mary's heart plummet.

Next John Lloyd took the stand, and he had much to say about Junior, Mr. Herold, Mr. Atzerodt, and the guns and ammunition they had concealed within the Surratt Tavern. The courtroom fell silent with expectation when he told the court he had met Mary on the road between the capital and Surrattsville on April 11, and again at the tavern on the afternoon of Good Friday, and how on the latter visit she had given him a package wrapped in brown paper—field glasses, he had discovered when curiosity compelled him to unwrap it—and had told him to have the hidden items ready, for they would be retrieved that night. He insisted that Mary had never mentioned a plot against the president, nor had she mentioned who would come to collect the weapons and supplies, but she could tell from the expressions on the commissioners' faces that they did not doubt that she knew who would claim them and why.

The next day Louis Weichmann returned to the stand for cross-examination, but although Mary's lawyer tried to cast suspicion upon him, the testimony only made Mary appear more complicit in the plot. Other witnesses followed, and, sweltering beneath the heavy veil, Mary's thoughts began to drift. She knew that to an outsider, Louis Weich-mann and John Lloyd seemed at least as guilty as she, but one of the lawyers had warned her that according to the law, a witness who testi-fied for the prosecution could not be charged in the conspiracy. It was a curious legal code, protecting the men at her expense, for they could admit wrongdoing to implicate her without fear of punishment for themselves.

On and on it went, day after day, one witness after another. Mary steadfastly maintained her innocence, but it seemed that the entire court, from the judges to the clerks and certainly the entire table of re-porters, believed her to be guilty. Then the lead attorney for Mary's de-fense began absenting himself from the court, and she could not shut her ears to the whispers that he had abandoned her because he had become convinced of her guilt.

Every day Mary felt weaker and more broken. Lacking the strength to sit properly, she rested her head on her hand, clutching a handker-chief, blotting perspiration from her brow and sighing. Whenever she made the slow journey from her cell to the courtroom and back, she was obliged to lean heavily upon her guard's arm until, trembling, she was permitted to sink into a chair.

As spring turned to summer, the temperature in the stifling court-room soared and the number of spectators swelled until they spilled out into the aisles and doorways and halls. Mary noticed more women among the crowds; some murmured encouragement and assured her of their prayers, others hissed invective, all peered at her with eager curiosity as if she were an exotic creature in a menagerie. Eventually one of the judges limited the number of curious onlookers allowed into the building, a measure Mary welcomed and considered long overdue.

The prosecutors continued to pound away at her, and at the other

seven defendants, and at Junior in absentia. Her well-meaning but inex-
perienced attorneys seemed vastly overwhelmed by the sheer volume of
evidence the government had assembled, and Mary knew that her reticence did not help them—but as long as it did not harm Junior or
Anna, she could endure the accusations, the angry glares, even the rid-
icule.

Then came a few days of blessed relief when the prosecutors turned
their attention to the other defendants. Mary still had to suffer through
the long, tedious hours in the sweltering courtroom, but at least she
was spared listening to slanderous remarks about her character and
outrageous misinterpretations of her actions in the weeks leading up to
Mr. Lincoln's assassination.

And then, on May 25, just when Mary thought she could bear it no
longer, the prosecution rested its case.

After receiving final instructions from President Johnson and the
Department of State, Lucy's father checked out of the National
Hotel and escorted his family back to New Hampshire. Lucy found herself overwhelmingly relieved to depart the capital, and she would consider it a blessing if she never returned.

For weeks Lucy, Lizzie, and their mother studied Spanish and
packed their trunks for the voyage while their father worked from his
study at home and instructed the capable manager he had hired to
tend to his affairs in Dover while he was abroad. Gradually, Lucy found
her grief and confusion ebbing as she became more involved in the
family's preparations, and from time to time she even felt faint curiosity and stirrings of anticipation. Lizzie was her constant companion—
affectionate, gentle, understanding, patient—and as the days passed,
Lucy began to see the tumultuous events of the previous seven months
as her family did. Her love for John, which had once burned so brightly,
faded into embers, obscured by bewilderment, pity, and regret.

She hoped someday she could forgive him for what he had done.

On the eve of their departure, the family traveled to Boston, where
the next day they boarded the steamer *Africa* and settled into their
stateroom. Soon thereafter, the ship set out for Liverpool, from whence
it would depart for Madrid.

Standing at the railing, her mother on her right side and Lizzie on her left, her shawl drawn about her head and shoulders and her skirt whipping in the ocean winds, Lucy gazed at the New England shore as it receded into the mists behind the ship.

When she could see land no more, she inhaled deeply and turned away from the railing. She linked her arms through her mother's and her sister's and strolled off with them down the deck, ready to embrace the new life that awaited her, across the ocean and in all the years to come.

On the day the defense of the conspirators began, one of Mary's lawyers announced to the court that the attorneys had agreed to begin with the testimony on her behalf. Mary wondered uneasily if it would have been better to have her case presented last or somewhere in the middle, so that the testimony about her good character would be fresh in the judges' memories when they withdrew to deliberate. But no one had consulted her, and she had no choice but to resign herself to the lawyers' decision.

The first witnesses they presented were priests, called to the stand to testify to her devout Christian character. Inexplicably, her lawyers had chosen priests who hardly knew her, and so they could say very little about her piety and nothing at all about her political beliefs. Next they called Eliza Holohan, who firmly stated that Mary disliked Mr. Atzerodt and he was not welcome in her home, but any good her assertions did was undermined by her acknowledgment that Mr. Booth visited the boardinghouse often, and that if Junior was not home, he would ask for Mary. Nora Fitzpatrick followed Eliza, but if anything, she was even less helpful. She said that she knew nothing about the photograph of Mr. Booth concealed behind the lithograph *Morning, Noon, and Night*, although she had often seen a portrait of Mr. Booth displayed on the mantelpiece of Mary's bedroom.

Mary listened with increasing trepidation as her lawyer questioned a number of Surrattsville neighbors and police officers in an attempt to discredit John Lloyd and cast suspicion on him, but the defense witnesses did not testify as expected and only made her seem more deeply involved in the plot. George Calvert and John Nothey were called to the stand, and they confirmed that Mary had legitimate business with them to account for her numerous trips to Surrattsville, but Mary could not imagine how that small verification of her claims could possibly undo the damage the other witnesses had inflicted.

In the days that followed, her lawyers produced other witnesses to speak in her defense—the Confederate spy and blockade-runner Augustus Howell to discredit Louis Weichmann's testimony, Mary's brother John Jenkins to vouch for her character—but very little went in her favor. Every day, Mary's hopes and fortitude diminished as her own attorneys inadvertently strengthened the prosecution's case. From time to time, the other defense attorneys called to the stand witnesses in support of their own clients, but whenever Mary's lawyers presented their case, they seemed caught off guard by their own witnesses' testimony. Instead of exonerating Mary, their sworn assertions cast doubt upon her real reasons for going to Surrattsville on the day of the assassination.

And then they called Anna to the stand.

Mary caught only a glimpse of her daughter as she was escorted into the courtroom and up to the witness stand, and soon even that was denied her. One of the guards quickly shifted to stand in front of her, ordered to block her from Anna's view to prevent them from communicating through secret signals. As far as Mary could tell, Anna had not spotted her at all.

They had not seen each other in more than a month, but despite her heavy black veil Mary could not mistake her precious child's dreadful condition—she was thin and pallid, her eyes hollow and shadowed, her once glossy hair dull and limp. Mary pressed her lips together to hold back a sob, squeezing her eyes shut against tears. Anna had nothing to do with any conspiracy, and she never should have been forced to endure such terrible treatment.

Mr. Aiken, one of Mary's lawyers, began questioning Anna, and it was evident to Mary that she had thought carefully about what she might be asked and had rehearsed her answers. She replied clearly and concisely when Mr. Aiken queried her about Louis Weichmann and those among the conspirators who had visited the boardinghouse. She was quite successful, Mary thought, in drawing suspicion down upon Weichmann, whom Anna strongly suggested was the real conspirator within the household. Her mother had made it clear to Mr. Atzerodt that he was not welcome in the house, Anna affirmed, but they had treated him with politeness, as they did every visitor. It was Mr. Weichmann that Mr. Atzerodt came to see when he called at the boarding-house, and it was Mr. Weichmann who had brought Mr. Payne to the house the first time. Yes, Anna had met Mr. Booth, but he never stayed long when he visited.

Mr. Aiken questioned Anna about Junior's acquaintance with Mr. Booth, and then, after digressing into a few questions about Junior's education, he abruptly changed course. "Miss Surratt," he said, "did you at your mother's house, at any time or any occasion, ever hear a word breathed about any plot, or plan, or conspiracy in existence to assassinate the president of the United States?"

"No, sir," replied Anna.

"Did you ever hear it discussed by any member of the family to capture the president of the United States?"

"No, sir," she said, a tremor in her voice. "Where is Mama?"

Mr. Aiken hesitated for the barest of moments. "What year did your brother leave college?"

"In 1861 or 1862, the year my father died." Anna's voice had become shrill, panicky. "Where is Mama?"

A stir went through the courtroom. Mary craned her neck, but the little she could see told her only that Anna glanced repeatedly toward the prisoners' dock, and there was a faint, quick sound as if she nervously tapped her foot. Mr. Aiken continued to question her, but Anna asked for her mother after every reply, increasingly frantic. Before long one of the judges interrupted the questioning and told Anna that she was dismissed. "Where is Mama?" she demanded as she stood, looking wildly about the courtroom as an officer hurried to the witness stand.

"You will see your mama soon," Mr. Aiken replied soothingly as the officer led her into the adjacent anteroom. Anna departed so willingly that Mary knew she assumed she was being escorted to her mother, and her heart ached as she imagined her nervous, distraught child's reaction when she realized she had been deceived.

"No cross-examination?" a man inquired. Mary could not discern who had spoken, for her gaze was riveted on the door through which Anna had departed. Oh, her poor darling. What she would not give to hold her, to comfort her.

"No," answered one of the judges. "It would have been cruel. The girl has a greater load of sorrow upon her than she can bear."

At that, the composure Mary had desperately held in place from the first day of the trial shattered, and she broke down in tears.

Later, as she was escorted back to her cell, she was told that when Anna had entered the anteroom, one of the officers had told her about the scheme to conceal Mary from her view, and Anna had immediately fainted. Cold water had been splashed in her face to revive her, and when she had come to, she had become hysterical, tearing frantically at her hair and clothing until a doctor sedated her.

Alone in her cell, Mary wept until she collapsed onto her cot and slept from sheer exhaustion. The next morning, her lawyers informed her that Anna had been released from prison the night before. "Was that her reward for enduring such torment in the courtroom?" Mary demanded, but she dried her eyes and composed herself when Mr. Aiken said that Anna would be permitted to visit her that day—for poor Anna's sake, not her own.

Thenceforth, as the trial continued, Anna was allowed to sit near her in the courtroom, although they were not allowed to speak or to touch. Thus it was from her lawyers and not Anna that Mary learned that the government had seized the boardinghouse, and since Anna had no money, she was living with sympathetic friends elsewhere in the city.

Although at first Anna's presence heartened Mary, the emotional strain of the dismal proceedings and the weeks spent in the sweltering, malodorous courtroom relentlessly eroded her strength, and the rest of the trial passed in a sickening blur. New witnesses appeared, old witnesses returned to the stand, but every statement anyone made on her behalf diminished her credibility and made her seem guiltier than before. On June 13, her lawyers rested her defense, and soon thereafter, the other lawyers finished presenting their clients' cases.

On June 19, Mary's long-absent lead attorney suddenly resurfaced, just in time for closing arguments. He did not appear in court himself, but instead submitted a lengthy document to one of her other lawyers to present to the court. His summation took hours to read and was devoted almost entirely to insisting that the tribunal was unconstitutional and therefore the entire trial was illegal, an argument that had been overruled and dismissed early in the trial. He mentioned Mary only very briefly, in the last few sentences, but even there he neglected to argue for her innocence.

As the hours passed and the summation unfolded, Mary had listened with steadily increasing horror, stunned, bewildered, dismayed, hopeless. " 'As far, gentlemen, as I am concerned,' " her lawyer read, his tone conveying that he had reached the end, " 'her case is now in your hands.' "

That could not be all, Mary thought, her head spinning. Hours and hours spent upon nothing in her defense. That could not be all.

A wave of nausea seized her, and she took violently ill. As gasps of alarm rose from those seated nearest her, two guards swiftly appeared and escorted her from the courtroom. After that, in consideration of Mary's health, Anna was allowed to remain with her in her cell during the day.

Two days later, Mr. Aiken made his own closing argument on Mary's behalf, and he argued determinedly for acquittal on the grounds of reasonable doubt, the standard of the civil court, where her case should have been tried. He argued that all the evidence presented against her was tenuous and circumstantial. He attempted to shift the blame to Junior, which nearly caused Mary to faint from terror, and he emphasized her devotion to her children, her piety, and her womanly virtues.

It was a fair argument, but Mary despaired of its power to erase from the judges' memories all that had been said against her throughout the trial, said and repeated and emphasized over and over, often by those brought forward to testify on her behalf.

In the week that followed, the other defendants' attorneys presented their closing arguments, but Mary did not hear them. Her spirit shattered, her health failing, she was too ill to attend the final days of the trial.

On June 28, the trial concluded and the twelve commissioners withdrew to deliberate in complete isolation. In two days they reached a verdict for each of the eight defendants, but President Johnson was ill and unable to review the court's decision. The verdict would remain sealed until he could attend to it.

Thus it was not until the afternoon of July 6 that two generals, commanders of the prison, came to Mary's cell and gravely informed her that she had been found guilty, and the next day, she would be hanged by the neck until dead.

On the morning of July 7, Mary Ann heard newsboys shouting up and down Nineteenth Street before she went down to breakfast, and although she could not discern their words at such a distance, the shrill excitement in their treble voices told her the commission in Washington City had reached its verdict.

Apprehension slowed her pace as she descended the stairs and walked down the hallway to the dining room where her children waited. Rosalie, seated in her customary place, murmured a soft greeting when she entered, and Mary Ann paused behind her chair to rest her hand on her shoulder and kiss her brow.

"Good morning, Mother," said Joseph, rising from his chair on the other side of the table, home at last from California. He had set out from San Francisco aboard the *Moses Taylor* on April 13 and had learned about the assassination while crossing the Isthmus of Panama. Alerted to his travels by the ship's crew and suspicious of the timing, the authorities had arrested him at the dock upon his arrival in New York. Major General John A. Dix had subjected him to a grueling interrogation, but after concluding that Joseph knew nothing about his brother's plot, the general had released him. Joseph had come immediately to Edwin's house and there he had remained.

June was at the table too, painfully gaunt and hollow-eyed from his weeks in prison. He had been released on June 22 and had immediately gone to Asia's home in Philadelphia, where Mary Ann, Rosalie, and Edwin had met him. The pained look June gave her as she kissed him good morning told her that he wished he could spare her all the troubles and grief the day was sure to bring.

At that moment Edwin came in from the street, newspapers tucked under his arm. "*Times, Herald,* or *Tribune?*" he asked Mary Ann, a melancholy tinge to his voice, as he came around to kiss her cheek and pull out her chair.

She did not suppose it mattered. "The *Tribune,* I think," she said, sitting down and bracing herself, her appetite long since fled.

Edwin handed her the paper, distributed others to his siblings, and settled into his own chair at the head of the table. The cook brought in their breakfasts, but except to murmur their thanks, only June, still ravenous from his ordeal, dug into the fragrant, steaming platters set before them. The others studied the printed pages, the bold headlines announcing the sentences of John's fellow conspirators, the dire fates that might have been his own.

THE ASSASSINATION. ALL THE PRISONERS FOUND GUILTY, proclaimed the top headline on the front page of the *Tribune*. PAYNE, HARROLD, ATZERODT, AND MRS. SURRATT TO BE HANGED TODAY.

"Oh, dear me," Mary Ann exclaimed. "They're going to hang a woman. They cannot." Shocked, she looked down the table to Edwin, who looked back bleakly. "Can they?"

"They can, but surely they will not," Edwin replied. "President Johnson will pardon her. The American government has never executed a woman, and I can't imagine Mr. Johnson would want to go down in history as the first president to give such a horrendous order."

Shaken, Mary Ann returned her gaze to the page and learned that John's childhood friends Sam Arnold and Michael O'Laughlen would be imprisoned for life, along with Dr. Mudd. Edman Spangler, a stagehand at Ford's Theatre, had been sentenced to six years.

Mary Ann pressed a hand to her heart, shaken. Thank God the authorities had realized early on that Junius and Clarke had nothing to do with the plot, sparing them this horror.

"Mrs. Surratt begs for more time," noted another headline, and Mary Ann quickly scanned the column below until she found the story: "Payne was the first to whom the intelligence was communicated. It did not seem to take him by surprise, as doubtless he anticipated no other sentence, and had nerved himself accordingly. The other prisoners were naturally more or less affected. Mrs. Surratt, particularly, sank under the dread announcement, and pleaded for four days' additional time to prepare herself for death."

Surely they would give her more time than that, Mary Ann thought. Surely Edwin was right and President Johnson would commute her sentence, giving her many long years in prison, perhaps all the years remaining to her on Earth, to prepare for a natural death not hastened by vengeful man.

" 'We do not concur with those who deem it particularly revolting to hang a woman,' " Rosalie read aloud in a voice barely above a whisper. " 'It seems to us horrible that a woman should murder; but, if she does so, she should fare neither better nor worse than other murderers. Let there be no exclusive privileges, even at the gallows.' "

"An appalling perspective," said Edwin, his voice brittle with disgust. "What man would put a noose around a woman's neck?"

"One ordered to do so?" Joseph suggested.

June scowled. "What man would accept such an order?"

"A soldier would have to, wouldn't he?"

"There are a great many people," said Mary Ann, pushing the newspaper away and resting her head in her hands, "who wish with all their hearts and every breath in their bodies that our John would be among those sent to the gallows this day."

"Our John died horribly, in excruciating agony," Edwin retorted, his voice rising. "That will have to be enough for them."

June and Rosalie frowned at him, Joseph recoiled in shock, but Mary Ann nodded, her eyes filling with tears.

"I'm sorry, Mother," Edwin said quickly, but it was too late. Mary Ann covered her face with her hands and wept.

Was there anything she could have done to prevent this unspeakable tragedy? How had she missed the signs that her bright, beautiful boy had become a monster?

God had granted her that vision in the fire when John was an innocent babe nursing at her breast, but that could have meant anything—greatness or ignominy. She had always assumed it would be the former, but she had been so wrong, so terribly wrong.

When Anna returned to the prison in the midmorning, stricken and hysterical, Mary knew all hope was lost.

When the two officers had come to her cell the previous afternoon to announce the court's verdict and the sentence, she had plummeted into hysteria, collapsing to the floor, screaming and weeping uncontrollably. The officers had immediately summoned the prison doctor, who had administered wine and sedatives, calming her enough that she had been able to request to see her daughter, her two priests, and Mr. John Brophy, a former schoolmate of Junior's, now an instructor at St. Aloysius College. In recent weeks he had tried to assist her hapless legal team with her defense, and perhaps—God help her, God help him—he could find a way to spare her life even at that late hour.

The officers had agreed, but in the interim Mary and the three other condemned prisoners had been transferred to cells on the first floor overlooking the prison yard. Soon thereafter, Anna, the two priests, and Mr. Brophy were escorted to her. Tears streaming down her face, Anna assured her that her lawyers were employing every legal maneuver they could to arrange for a stay of execution to give them time to file an appeal.

Mary had thanked her, but as the night had passed and no word had come from her lawyers, she had grown ever more frantic, praying, weeping, crying out that she was innocent. Her companions had tried to comfort her, but to no avail.

Mary's lawyers had told Anna that they hoped a personal appeal from her would move President Johnson to commute her mother's sentence, and so at dawn, Anna had departed for the White House with one last embrace and promises to return soon, and with good news, God willing. Mr. Brophy too had rushed off to take statements from Mr. Payne affirming Mary's innocence to President Johnson. As she awaited their return, Mary had prayed fervently with the priests, dissolving into sobs anew when she had heard the sounds of sawing and hammering outside in the prison yard and realized that carpenters were building the scaffold.

With the sunrise the morning had turned unbearably warm, and the heat and the sounds of construction and of soldiers shouting orders back and forth and spectators arriving early to claim the best vantage points had struck Mary with the force of physical blows. At about half past eleven, Mary had jumped in alarm at a loud snap and thud. "What is it?" she had asked the priests shakily, wringing her hands, pacing the length of the small cell. "What is it?"

Father Walter had peered out the window and reluctantly told her that the soldiers were testing the gallows platform drops with weights. One had not been opening properly, so it would be tested and modified and tested again, over and over, until both drops opened promptly, evenly, and simultaneously. Horrorstruck, Mary had backed away from the windows, but the cell walls had restrained her before she had been able to go far enough to escape the dreadful noise.

The tests were still ongoing when Anna returned from the White House, sobbing, utterly wretched. "The president would not see me," she choked out. Wordlessly Mary embraced her, struggling to maintain her composure for her daughter's sake as her heartrending cries echoed through the prison corridors.

Soon thereafter, Mr. Brophy returned, his expression one of bleak despair as he told Mary that his efforts had been no more successful. "I've been told that the officials here expect President Johnson to grant you a reprieve," he said. "General Hancock has ordered cavalry to clear and to guard the roads from the White House to the penitentiary. If the president should do what we all hope and pray he will, the messenger will be able to bring the orders with all speed."

Mary nodded, but she despaired of any last-minute pardon being sped to the Arsenal to stay the executioner's hand. Shortly before dawn, the most malicious of her guards had told her that upon signing her death warrant, President Johnson had declared that Mary had "kept the nest that hatched the egg" of the conspiracy, and that she must be punished accordingly. She knew she could expect no mercy from him.

Summoning up her last reserves of courage, Mary issued Mr. Brophy instructions for Anna's care, the disposal of her estate, and other personal matters. She made her last confession to Father Wiggett and Father Walter—she had sins to confess, like anyone else—and again she professed her innocence of the crime for which she was soon to be executed.

By noon the searing, oppressive heat had soared to a temperature of nearly one hundred degrees, but Mary insisted upon wearing her heavy black dress, black bonnet, and black veil. Anna was escorted from the cell, sobbing, wailing, struggling against the guards, and Mary wept to part from her, no longer praying for herself, but for her precious daughter, her absent sons.

After Anna's cries of grief faded, Mary prepared herself, and Father Wiggett and Father Walter administered the Last Rites, the sacrament of the dying.

Soon thereafter, two officers came for her.

They led her from the cell and down the dank, dimly lit corridor, the two priests following after, murmuring prayers. Lightheaded, heart pounding, Mary heard other cell doors opening behind her, other footsteps heavy and slow, and she knew the three condemned men had joined the grim procession.

Her escort halted before the heavy wooden door to the prison yard. Narrow bands of bright light filtered in through the cracks all around it, and from the other side came the clamor of hundreds of voices. "God help me," Mary whispered, her heart pounding, her breath coming in shallow gasps. "God help me."

Shortly after one o'clock, the door swung open. Mary found herself blinded by the sun and overcome by a sudden wave of intense heat. Blinking, squinting, she hesitated on the threshold until the guard urged her forward, and then, aided by the bonnet and veil, her eyes adjusted and she spotted the gallows, fifty feet away along the northeast wall of the prison yard. The sheer size of the scaffold staggered her— twenty feet high, thirty across, with two large, hinged trapdoors cut into the platform and four armchairs arranged behind them. She glimpsed four soldiers positioned beside four large wooden beams supporting the drops, four nooses dangling empty from the crossbar high above, strange mounds of dark-red soil on the ground behind the scaffold, and over to one side, four pine coffins in a disorderly pile.

A hush fell over the crowd—so many people, hundreds of them. How could there be so many eager to witness this gruesome spectacle? Her legs trembled and buckled, and she would have fallen except one of her escorts held her up, and the other swiftly attended to her other side. Leaning heavily upon them, Mary approached the scaffold stairs—and from there she could see that the mounds of red earth surrounded four gaping, empty graves. Moaning, aghast, she went limp, and the soldiers had to carry her up the fifteen steps to the platform, where she was brought to the armchair on the far right.

Mr. Payne was led to the chair on Mary's left, and then came Mr. Herold, and then Mr. Atzerodt. Dazed, sickened, she fixed her gaze straight ahead, but when she saw the nooses swaying back in forth in the hot air before her, she grew so dizzy that she dropped her gaze to the platform, but that was no better, for the dark outline of the trapdoor stood out starkly against the wooden planks. The only way she would leave that platform was through that opening, she thought wildly.

She murmured prayers, swiftly, desperately. She would not have time to recite them all. Father Wiggett held a crucifix to her lips, and trembling, she kissed it.

The sunlight was so intense that General John Hartranft ordered soldiers to shield Mary and the three condemned men with umbrellas so that they would not faint. He read the charges and the sentences, his voice carrying across the hushed prison yard.

The hangman approached and halted before Mary. It seemed to her that he hesitated before he bound her hands and arms—painfully tight—but when he bent to tie her legs, her long black dress, billowing in the hot wind, seemed to confound him. After pondering a long moment, he quickly wrapped the cotton cords around her skirt, tightening it around her legs.

Her hands and fingers, once tingling, had grown numb. "My wrists are bound too tightly," Mary managed to gasp. "They hurt."

"They won't hurt long," a man retorted.

The hangman approached again, removed her veil and bonnet, and slipped the noose around her neck. As the rough fibers scraped the tender skin, an agitated murmur rose from the crowd. Suddenly a man standing among the spectators turned his back to the scaffold, threw his hands in the air, and shouted, "Gentlemen, I tell you this is murder. Can you stand and see it done?"

No one responded. The man's arms fell to his sides, and without another word he turned back to face the scaffold.

The hard knot of the noose pressed roughly against Mary's left ear. Without warning the hangman slid a white muslin hood over her head until all she could see was the weave of the cloth, illuminated from behind.

The priests and ministers intoned their final prayers. Mary heard some of them thank the soldiers and the general for their courteous behavior, but Father Walter's and Father Wiggett's voices were not among them. Instead, nearby, she heard Father Wiggett murmur, "We are right here with you, Mary."

"Shall I say anything?" she murmured back, heart beating so rapidly she feared it would burst.

"What would you like to say?"

"I wish to say to the people that I am innocent."

He sighed softly. "It would be useless to say that now."

"I am innocent," Mary said, forcing the last of her strength into her voice, "but God's holy will be done."

"The prisoners will stand and move forward," a deep voice commanded.

With great effort, Mary obeyed, inching forward, constrained by the long skirts bound around her legs. She heard the chairs scrape the platform as they were taken away.

"A little farther, Mrs. Surratt," someone said.

With a sob, Mary took a few more awkward steps forward. "Don't let me fall," she cried out as she nearly lost her balance, but no one answered.

"Gentlemen, take warning," she heard Mr. Atzerodt call to the crowd. "Goodbye, gentlemen who are before me. May we all meet in the other world."

Mary whispered the rosary, quickly, desperately. She heard footsteps on the platform, boots striking the stairs as an officer descended. Beneath the scaffold, a soldier retched.

Someone clapped three times. Mary fell into space, the wooden crossbeam groaned, and then all was dark and silent.

EPILOGUE

LUCY

1890

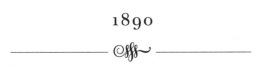

Out, out, brief candle!
Life's but a walking shadow, a poor player
That struts and frets his hour upon the stage
And then is heard no more:
—William Shakespeare,
Macbeth, Act 5, Scene 5

When Malcolm Elsie of the *Washington Evening Star* wrote to Lucy to inquire if she would permit him to interview her for a feature he was writing about the wives of prominent senators, her first instinct was to decline. Her husband had been involved in quite a few controversial matters during his tenure in the Senate, and she was reluctant to be thrust into the role of his apologist. Then she thought of all the advice her mother had given her through the years regarding the duties of a political wife, and she decided to consult William before sending her regrets.

As she had expected, William thought it was a wonderful idea. "What feature on Senate wives would be complete without a profile of Lucy Hale Chandler?" he asked, kissing her, scarcely able to contain his pride. "I can imagine the resounding cheer that will shake the editorial offices when they learn you've agreed to do it."

"You're a silly old dear," she teased him. "You're giving me too much credit. The honor of this request, such as it is, goes to you. Mr. Winchester said the feature will be about the wives of prominent senators, not about the *prominent wives* of senators. That makes all the difference."

Nevertheless, William's enthusiasm pleased her, and she smiled as she sat down with pen and paper to reply to Mr. Elsie that she would be delighted to meet with him.

As the appointed day approached, Lucy found herself at unexpected moments lost in thought about what sort of questions Mr. Elsie might ask. She supposed it would be only natural if he asked how she and William had met, but that was a fraught subject to discuss with a stranger, as William had been twenty-one and she but twelve years old when they first became acquainted. It had been love at first sight for William, or so he confessed to her many years later, but if he had known she was so young, he never would have written her those ardent letters and poems. He was aghast when her father had informed him of her age and had requested that he cease courting her, and he immediately complied, with apologies. Lucy had developed quite a crush on William because of those lovely missives, and when she had heard he had married a certain Miss Gilmore, the governor's daughter, she had been utterly heartbroken for a few days and then had quite forgotten him.

When her father was appointed Minister to Spain, Lucy had gladly gone to Madrid with her family, escaping scandal and heartbreak and the aftermath of war in her homeland. For five years she had dwelled abroad, forgetting her troubles amid the excitement and wonder of exploring a foreign land and culture, as well as in the delights of what seemed to be an endless array of state dinners and legation parties and dances. She had traveled extensively throughout Europe, adoring Italy, Switzerland, and France most of all, and in Paris she had reunited with her old friend John Hay and former beau Oliver Wendell Holmes Jr. Unwittingly, she had beguiled many European gentlemen who had courted her charmingly, extravagantly, but in the end had found themselves rejected and sent away, lovelorn.

It had been a wonderful, restorative, exhilarating time for Lucy, but a change in presidential administrations back home had meant many changes in government appointments. Lucy's father had found himself caught up in an ugly feud, which had culminated in Secretary of State Hamilton Fish requesting his resignation. In early August 1869, the family had left Madrid for Paris, where Lizzie and her husband had recently taken up residence, and from there Lucy and her parents had traveled on to Rome to spend the winter. In the spring of 1870 crowds of cheering citizens had welcomed them home to New Hampshire with a thunderous cannon salute and the glorious ringing of all the bells in Dover. Lucy's father had been pleased and deeply touched, but his health had been declining over the past year, and he did not resume his former public life. Lucy, twenty-eight, had resolved to devote the rest of her life to caring for her beloved father at home.

In 1871, he had suffered a stroke that had rendered him paralyzed on his right side, but with the tender ministrations of his wife and youngest daughter, he had recovered sufficiently to visit with friends, to read and write, to putter in his garden, to play backgammon with his wife, to go for carriage rides with Lucy, and even to travel to Washington City, where he had reunited with aging former colleagues and had reminisced about their days as young lions waging the antislavery crusade. But in July 1873, he had broken his right hip in a fall from his chair, and his ailing body had been unable to recover from the blow. He had died peacefully at home at nine o'clock on the evening of November 19, 1873, with his wife and daughters around him.

William, who by then had been a widower three years, had read the mournful announcement of Senator Hale's death in the papers. Astonished to discover that Miss Lucy Hale, the girl he had admired so many years before, was yet unmarried, he began writing to her, first to express his condolences for her loss, and later, as their correspondence continued, to express his love. They married on December 23, 1874, in Dover, at the home of Lucy's mother.

William had become a prominent lawyer, and he had previously served as solicitor and judge advocate general of the Navy Department and as the First Assistant Secretary of the Treasury, so when he decided to resume a career in politics, Lucy had dedicated herself to helping him achieve his ambitions. He entered the New Hampshire State House of Representatives in 1881, and was appointed Secretary of the Navy the following year. In 1886 he was elected to the United States Senate to fill a vacancy caused by the death of his predecessor, and in 1888, he had been elected to another term.

Lucy assumed that Mr. Elsie would have discovered the facts of her husband's storied career on his own, from numerous other sources, so she presumed he hoped to learn from her those interesting details only a wife would know—what Senator William Chandler was like at home as a devoted husband to her and a loving father to their five-year-old son.

On the appointed day, Lucy arranged for tea to be served in the parlor of their I Street residence, entrusted her son to his nanny, and distracted herself with letter writing as she awaited Mr. Elsie's arrival. He knocked on the front door promptly at three o'clock, as agreed, which earned him her approval, but when he was shown into the parlor, she was somewhat dismayed to discover that he was very young, perhaps only twenty-one, a slim dandy of a man, with short, neatly combed and oiled dark hair; a walrus mustache; a smart Derby hat; a high stand collar and four-in-hand tie; and a high-buttoned coat that opened to reveal a brocade waistcoat. She had expected someone older, more experienced, more familiar in the ways of Washington. As long as he wrote well and honestly, she decided, she could forgive him his youth and inexperience.

They passed swiftly through the usual perfunctory rituals of greetings, small talk, and the pouring of tea. Mr. Elsie had brought a briefcase, and from it he took a stack of assorted papers, blank sheets to write upon, and a pencil, which he arranged on the table before him.

He began with precisely the sort of questions she had expected him to disregard—where William had been educated, what his first political appointment had been, when he had first come to the Senate. Then he offered her a winning smile and said, "You've been a part of Washington society and politics since long before your marriage, haven't you, Mrs. Chandler? You first came to the capital when your father served in the Senate?"

"I suppose you could say I did," Lucy replied, "although I didn't reside here continuously. My father often lived here alone while my mother and sister and I remained at home in Dover. At other times, I was away at boarding school."

"I wondered—" He leafed through the stack of assorted papers, withdrew a newspaper clipping, and set it on top of the pile. "In all of your time in Washington, were you ever acquainted with a woman named Louise Worcester?"

Lucy quickly searched her memory, but she could not remember a senator, congressman, cabinet secretary, or military officer with that surname. "I don't believe so. Should I have been? Who is her husband?"

"I don't know that, or even whether she's married at all," said Mr. Elsie. "She claims to be the former confidante of John Wilkes Booth."

Lucy's heart thumped once, painfully hard, but she had been in Washington City long enough to learn the fine art of concealing her emotions. "Oh, Mr. Elsie," she scolded lightly. "You ought to be ashamed of yourself, coming to me on false pretenses."

"I am somewhat abashed," he admitted, but his grin told her that the feeling would not trouble him long.

"I do not know any Louise Worcester," she said evenly. "There is no feature on Senate wives forthcoming, is there, Mr. Elsie?"

"Not that I'm planning to write. I have another story in mind, a refutation of Miss Worcester's claims that John Wilkes Booth is alive."

Lucy froze, and for a moment she could not breathe.

Studying her, Mr. Elsie took the newspaper clipping from the top of the pile and held it out to her across the table. When she did not take it, he set it next to her plate, offering her an apologetic shrug for good measure. Involuntarily, her gaze drifted to the headline: J. WILKES BOOTH ALIVE. LOUISE WORCESTER, THE CONFIDANTE OF BOOTH, SAYS HE IS NOT DEAD—A VERY THIN YARN.

The subtitle was correct at any rate, she thought, and although such nonsense did not deserve her attention, she read on.

> **Chicago. April 21.**—The Times publishes a story from Birmingham, Ala., in which Louise Worcester, at one time the confidante of J. Wilkes Booth, the assassin of Abraham Lincoln, is credited with saying that Booth is not dead. She declares that in 1867, two years after Booth's supposed death, she received a letter without date or signature, but unmistakably in Booth's handwriting. This letter, she says, is still in existence. As to the probabilities

of the man shot by Boston Corbett being Wilkes Booth, she points out that the body was closely guarded and secretly buried without an opportunity having been given for identification by any of those intimately acquainted with him. She believes that the man killed was one of the conspirators and that Booth made good his escape, but that in the excited and clamorous condition of the public mind it was thought best by the authorities, if they knew of the deception, to allow it to pass unchallenged in order to allay the fever of excitement which the assassination aroused.

"How interesting," Lucy said ironically, fixing Mr. Elsie with a level gaze as she slid the clipping back to his side of the table. "A thirdhand account that even this reporter admits is unlikely to be true. This was not published in the *Evening Star.*"

"No, our editors have higher standards," he admitted. "They require verification. And that's what brings me to you."

She feigned puzzlement. "My family was acquainted with Mr. Booth in the last year of the war when we all resided at the National Hotel, but I'm afraid I have no idea how you might reach his family. Have you inquired with any of the local theatres? Surely they would be able to put you in touch with his brother Edwin, or perhaps you could interview him when he next comes to perform in the capital."

She had seen Edwin Booth perform on several occasions since the war ended, though he resembled John enough that seeing him pained her until she could lose herself in the drama and no longer regard him as John's brother but as the character he portrayed. Edwin Booth was simply the best actor of his generation, perhaps of any generation that had ever been, and to witness his extraordinary gifts, she was willing to endure a few minutes of agony. She was far from the only avid theatergoer who had rejoiced that his retirement from the stage, which he had publicly announced in the aftermath of the assassination, had lasted only six months.

Mr. Elsie smiled ruefully. "Edwin Booth will not speak to me. Nor will his younger brother, Joseph. His eldest brother, Junius, died in 1883, and their mother passed away five years ago."

"Have you considered writing to his sister Asia, Mrs. John Sleeper Clarke?" Lucy knew she was admitting to more knowledge than she wanted anyone to know she possessed. "I believe she and her family moved to England shortly after the war. She has written quite prolifically on her father and her brother Edwin. If anyone knows the family history, Mrs. Clarke would."

"Edwin and Joseph are John Wilkes Booth's only living siblings," said Mr. Elsie, leafing through his stack of papers again. "Mrs. Clarke died two years ago in Bournemouth, on the southern coast of England, although she was buried in the family plot at Green Mount Cemetery in Baltimore. I hear she extracted a deathbed promise from her husband to ship her remains across the ocean so she could be buried in her native land." He lowered his voice to a confidential stage whisper. "From what I hear, Mr. Clarke had made her final years so miserable that he truly owed her that much, at least."

Lucy ignored that bit of gossip. "The family plot—yes, of course. I read in your own newspaper that Mr. Booth's remains were interred there after they were returned to his family." The burial at sea had all been a ruse to discourage relic hunters from robbing the grave and to forestall Confederate sympathizers from turning his burial site into a shrine. Instead his corpse had been put into a gun box and buried on the grounds of the Arsenal Penitentiary. Years later, when the Arsenal was slated to be razed to make way for new construction, his remains— like those of his four conspirators hanged in the prison yard—had been unearthed and turned over to their families. "Surely the Booth family verified that the remains they were given were indeed those of their son and brother."

"They might have," he acknowledged, "but as I said, none of his survivors will speak with me. Even if they would, my editors require stronger verification than what they could provide."

"What do you mean? Who would know better than they?"

He shrugged. "Perhaps the Booth family were given a sealed box and were obliged to accept the authorities' word that it held John Wilkes's remains. Perhaps they were able to view the corpse, but after so many years it must have been decayed beyond recognition."

Lucy suppressed a shudder at the gruesome images his words evoked. "That all may be true, but to be frank, Mr. Elsie, this is no concern of mine. I have never met Edwin or Joseph Booth, and I cannot persuade them to speak with you—nor would I, if I could."

"Mrs. Chandler, I think you misunderstand me." Mr. Elsie leaned back in his chair and studied her expectantly. "I'm not seeking confirmation of John Wilkes Booth's death from his brothers. I'm seeking it from you."

For a moment she could neither speak nor breathe. "I don't understand."

He studied her for a moment, and then he leafed through his pile of papers again and withdrew another clipping. When he set it before her, she refused to give it even the smallest glance. "When the assassin's corpse was brought to Washington," he said, "witnesses reported seeing a young woman, heavily veiled, who had been escorted aboard to identify the remains. According to eyewitness accounts, she became distraught and flung herself upon the body, weeping, and had to be pulled away."

"Perhaps the young woman was his sister," said Lucy, her voice steady. "I recall hearing that they were very close."

He shook his head. "Mrs. Clarke was in Philadelphia under house arrest at the time, and she was delivered of twins a few months later. Her delicate condition would have been readily apparent at that time, and none of the witnesses mentioned it." He regarded her intently, as if waiting for a flicker of emotion to betray her. "Numerous sources claimed that you were engaged to John Wilkes Booth. Your father, with his strong ties to the navy, easily would have been able to get permission to take his heartbroken daughter aboard the *Montauk* to confirm that her secret fiancé was dead."

Lucy raised her eyebrows. "'Secret fiancé'?" She laughed shortly and shook her head. "Oh, Mr. Elsie. You should know better than to believe every salacious rumor that comes your way." She put her head to one side, feigning intense thought, then started as if struck by inspiration. "Oh! Perhaps the mysterious young woman was Louise Worcester, Mr. Booth's great confidante, so dear to him that he wrote to her from the afterlife. I suggest you get in touch with her if you decide to pursue this matter, because I cannot help you."

She rose from her chair, and decorum obliged him to stand as well. "Mrs. Chandler—"

"As I said, I cannot help you." She stepped away from the table and inclined her head in dismissal. "The butler will show you out. Good day, Mr. Elsie."

She turned and walked away, leaving him to stew in his own curiosity.

Let history decide what to make of the misguided, vengeful man who had killed a great and noble president. That was not the man she had known and loved. She had already said all she ever intended to say about the assassin John Wilkes Booth.

ACKNOWLEDGMENTS

Fates and Traitors: A Novel of John Wilkes Booth is a work of fiction inspired by history. Numerous events and people that appear in the historical record have been omitted from this book simply because it would have been impossible to include them all.

I offer my sincere thanks to Maria Massie, Maya Ziv, and Denise Roy for their contributions to *Fates and Traitors* and their ongoing support of my work. I'm grateful for the generous assistance of my first readers, Marty Chiaverini, Geraldine Neidenbach, and Heather Neidenbach, whose insightful comments and questions always prove invaluable. I also thank Nic Neidenbach, Marlene and Len Chiaverini, and other friends and family for their support and encouragement.

I am indebted to the Wisconsin Historical Society and their librarians and staff for maintaining the excellent archives on the University of Wisconsin campus in Madison that I rely upon for my research. The most significant sources for this book were:

Terry Alford, *Fortune's Fool: The Life of John Wilkes Booth* (New York: Oxford University Press, 2015).

Stephen M. Archer, *Junius Brutus Booth: Theatrical Prometheus* (Carbondale, IL: Southern Illinois University Press, 1992).

Arthur W. Bloom, *Edwin Booth: A Biography and Performance History* (Jefferson, NC: McFarland & Company, 2013).

John Wilkes Booth, *"Right or Wrong, God Judge Me": The Writings of John Wilkes Booth*, ed. John Rhodehamel and Louise Taper (Urbana, IL: University of Illinois Press, 1997).

Asia Booth Clarke, *Booth Memorials: Passages, Incidents and Anecdotes in the Life of Junius Brutus Booth (the Elder) by His Daughter* (New York: Henry L. Hinton, 1870).

———. *The Elder and the Younger Booth* (Boston: J. R. Osgood, 1882).

———. *John Wilkes Booth: A Sister's Memoir,* ed. Terry Alford (Jackson: University Press of Mississippi, 1996).

———. *Personal Recollections of the Elder Booth* (London: privately published, 1902).

———. *The Unlocked Book: A Memoir of John Wilkes Booth* (New York: G. P. Putnam's Sons, 1938).

Ernest B. Furgurson, *Freedom Rising: Washington in the Civil War* (New York: Knopf, 2004).

Edwina Booth Grossman, *Edwin Booth: Recollections by His Daughter, Edwina Booth Grossman, and Letters to Her and to His Friends* (New York: The Century Company, 1894).

Michael W. Kauffman, *American Brutus: John Wilkes Booth and the Lincoln Conspiracies* (New York: Random House, 2004).

Kate Clifford Larson, *The Assassin's Accomplice: Mary Surratt and the Plot to Kill Abraham Lincoln* (New York: Basic Books, 2008).

Virginia Lomax, *The Old Capitol and Its Inmates: By a Lady, Who Enjoyed the Hospitalities of the Government for a "Season"* (New York: E. J. Hale & Son, 1867).

Arthur F. Loux, *John Wilkes Booth: Day by Day* (Jefferson, NC: McFarland & Company, 2014).

Richmond Morcom, "They All Loved Lucy," *American Heritage* 21, no. 6, October 1970.

Richard H. Sewell, *John P. Hale and the Politics of Abolition* (Cambridge, MA: Harvard University Press, 1965).

Gene Smith, *American Gothic: The Story of America's Legendary Theatrical Family—Junius, Edwin, and John Wilkes Booth* (New York: Simon & Schuster, 1992).

Elizabeth Steger Trindal, *Mary Surratt: An American Tragedy* (Gretna, LA: Pelican Publishing, Inc., 1996).

Nora Titone, *My Thoughts Be Bloody: The Bitter Rivalry That Led to the Assassination of Abraham Lincoln* (New York: Free Press, 2010).

Louis J. Weichmann, *A True History of the Assassination of Abraham Lincoln and the Conspiracy of 1865*, ed. Floyd E. Risvold (New York: Alfred A. Knopf, 1975).

I also consulted several excellent online resources while researching and writing *Fates and Traitors*, including the archives of digitized historic newspapers at the Library of Congress (http://chroniclingamerica.loc.gov) and GenealogyBank.com; Dave Taylor's excellent blog, *BoothieBarn: Discovering the Conspiracy* (http://boothiebarn.com); and websites for the Surratt House Museum (http://www.surrattmuseum.org), the Ford's Theatre National Historic Site (http://www.nps.gov/foth/index.htm), and the Junius B. Booth Society (http://juniusbrutusbooth.org and https://www.facebook.com/SpiritsofTudorHall).

Most of all, I thank my husband, Martin Chiaverini, and our sons, Nicholas and Michael, for their enduring love and tireless support. I couldn't have written this book without you, and I love you beyond measure.

ABOUT THE AUTHOR

JENNIFER CHIAVERINI is the *New York Times* bestselling author of *Mrs. Lincoln's Dressmaker, The Spymistress, Mrs. Lincoln's Rival, Mrs. Grant and Madame Jule,* and *Christmas Bells,* as well as the Elm Creek Quilts series. A graduate of the University of Notre Dame and the University of Chicago, she lives in Madison, Wisconsin, with her husband and two sons.